Jimbo

"We dance with phantoms and with shadows play..." Jimbo is a very imaginative boy, and together with his brothers and sisters, they make up a lot of games around an old building on their father's property that they call The Empty House, their object of "dreadful delight." Then the Colonel hires a new governess. Miss Lake is much too level-headed to believe any of the children's stories about the Empty House. She knows that it's all nonsense. But in order to "knock the nonsense" out of young Jimbo's head, she makes up a story about the Inmate of the House, a very bad creature indeed. Instead of bringing Jimbo to his senses, the story fills him with a real sense of dread. He becomes convinced that something evil lurks within The Empty House. And, of course, he is right—for Fright itself lives within, ready to reach out and snatch young Jimbo into his clutches!

The Education of Uncle Paul

Paul Waters returns to England after having lived for the past twenty years in the Canadian wilderness. Unused to adult company, emotionally he feels little more than a boy inside. When he moves in with his widowed sister Margaret and her three children, he tries hard to keep this inner child hidden. But Nixie, Toby and Jonah figure him out right away, and introduce him to their imaginative games. These are no mere hide-and-seeks, but "aventures" that take them all to another realm, the land beyond the Crack, where all the lost and disgarded things can be found—a land of beauty and mystery. And it is here that Paul truly comes alive, finally coming to understand himself, and all that truly matters in life.

ALSO BY ALGERNON BLACKWOOD

NOVELS:
Jimbo: A Fantasy (1909)
The Education of Uncle Paul
  (1909)
The Human Chord (1910)
The Centaur (1911)
A Prisoner in Fairyland (1913)
The Extra Day (1916)
Julius Le Vallon: An Episode
  (1916)
The Wave: An Egyptian Aftermath
  (1916)
The Promise of Air (1918)
The Garden of Survival (1918)
The Bright Messenger (1921)

CHILDREN'S BOOKS:
Sambo and Snitch (1927)
Mr. Cupboard (1928)
Dudley and Gilderoy: A Nonsense
  (1929)
By Underground (1930)
The Parrot and the - Cat (1931)
The Italian Conjuror (1932)
Maria (of England) in the Rain
  (1933)
Sergeant Poppett and Policeman
  James (1934)
The Fruit Stoners (1934)
How the Circus Came to Tea
  (1936)
The Adventures of Dudley and
  Gilderoy (1941)

AUTOBIOGRAPHY:
Episodes Before Thirty (1923)

ORIGINAL SHORT STORY
COLLECTIONS:
The Empty House and Other Ghost
  Stories (1906)
The Listener and Other Stories
  (1907)
John Silence —
  Physician Extraordinary
  (1908)
The Lost Valley and Other Stories
  (1910)
Pan's Garden: A Volume
  of Nature Stories (1912)
Incredible Adventures (1914)
Ten Minute Stories (1914)
Day and Night Stories (1917)
The Wolves of God and Other Fey
  Stories, w/Wildred Wilson
  (1921)
Tongues of Fire and Other Sketches
  (1924)
Full Circle (1929) [single story]
Shocks (1935)
The Doll and One Other (1946)
The Mysterious House (1987)
  [single story]
The Magic Mirror: Lost
  Supernatural and Mystery
  Stories (1989)

PLAYS:
Karma: A Reincarnation Play,
  w/Violet Pearn (1918)
Through the Crack w/Violet Pearn
  (1925)

JIMBO

The EDUCATION of UNCLE PAUL

TWO COMPLETE NOVELS BY ALGERNON BLACKWOOD

STARK HOUSE

Stark House Press • Eureka California
www.StarkHousePress.com

JIMBO / THE EDUCATION OF UNCLE PAUL

Published by Stark House Press
2200 O Street
Eureka, CA 95501, USA
griffinskye@sbcglobal.net
www.starkhousepress.com

JIMBO: A FANTASY

Originally published in 1909 by Macmillan, London and New York; copyright
© 1909 by Algernon Blackwood

THE EDUCATION OF UNCLE PAUL

Originally published in 1909 by Macmillan, London, and in 1910 by Henry
Holt, New York; copyright © 1909 by Algernon Blackwood

A Very Wonderful Aventure

Copyright © 2007 by Mike Ashley

All rights reserved

ISBN: 1-933586-13-3

Text set in Figural and Dogma. Heads set in Epitaph and Giddyup.
Cover design and layout by Mark Shepard
Cover illustration by Cammy Shepard
Proofread by Joanne Applen

Publisher's Note: Rather than tamper with Blackwood's prose, we have kept in
all cases to the spelling from the original hardback editions. The publisher
would personally like to thank Mike Ashley for all his help in bringing these
Algernon Blackwood books back into print.

First Stark House Press Edition: January 2007

0 9 8 7 6 5 4 3 2 1

A VERY WONDERFUL AVENTURE

Mike Ashley

It's interesting how we categorise people. Even those who know the work of Algernon Blackwood may loosely refer to him as a writer of ghost stories, perhaps even less accurately as a writer of horror stories. Blackwood gained the epithet "the Ghost Man" when he used to read stories on the Radio during the Second World War in Britain, but he did not like that title. It's true he wrote and told ghost stories and those are the ones most frequently reprinted, but to restrict Blackwood purely to that oeuvre is a bit like remembering Sir Winston Churchill solely as a painter or Oscar Wilde as a poet.

I haven't categorised every one of Blackwood's stories, but I'd be surprised if much more than a quarter of them could be classified as ghost stories, even by the broadest definition. Most of his work is far more subtle or daring than that. Blackwood looked beyond the basic senses both outwardly into the world of Nature or Mother Earth and inwardly into the spirit and the psyche. His stories deal far more with how we interact with the vastnesses of the world about us, both physically and spiritually, than they do with apparitions or hauntings by the dead.

Blackwood needed a broad canvas on which to explore these spiritual travels and it was not long before his "short" stories grew longer. Both "The Willows" and "The Wendigo", generally regarded as his greatest works, are almost novellas, and certainly neither are ghost stories, yet they will often be shuffled in with the more traditional form. By the time Blackwood was writing the stories collected in *Pan's Garden* and *Incredible Adventures*, he needed works almost of novel length in order to explore his subject adequately. Stories such as "Sand", "The Temptation of the Clay", "A Descent Into Egypt" and "The Regeneration of Lord Ernie" are really mini-novels and require the reader to undertake a mystical journey in order to appreciate the spiritual scenery.

Yet not only do we tend to think of Blackwood as a writer of ghost stories we also tend to think of him as a writer of short fiction. Both fall far from the truth. It is time that we remembered that Blackwood was also a novelist and that he dealt with far broader subjects such as in the two books collected together here for the first time, *Jimbo* and *The Education of Uncle Paul*. They allow us to reassess Blackwood's outlook on the world in a way that his "ghost stories" never allowed us to, and where some of his other works, especially *The Centaur* and "A Descent Into Egypt", demand more of our imagination than we might be able to give.

Moreover these two novels show us a Blackwood we may not have seen before. They have sometimes loosely been called children's books, and at one level they would appeal to younger readers, but they were not planned as children's books. They are books which feature children and, more crucially, children's imagination which is less shackled and conditioned than that of adults. Blackwood held the view that children were more open to wild ideas than adults and as a consequence if the reader could perceive the world through a child's eyes it would become a more entrancing and wonderful place.

And as if that were not enough, these two books were amongst the earliest books that Blackwood wrote. However because they were not published until 1909, after his first three story collections had appeared, it is easy to think of them as later works. In fact they – or earlier versions – had been finished almost a decade earlier, soon after Blackwood had returned from ten years in Canada and the United States which he writes about in his autobiography *Episodes Before Thirty*. Knowing that, puts an entirely different perspective on these books and allows us to understand what they were about.

So let us briefly backtrack. Blackwood had a strict evangelical upbringing. Although he adored his father, his mind would not accept unconditionally a narrow interpretation of Christian doctrine. In his late teens his mind was unlocked when he stumbled across various Buddhist teachings, which were further enhanced by experiences at Edinburgh University in informal studies with a spiritualist family and a fellow Hindu student. His interests soon turned to the theosophical teachings of Helena Blavatsky and when Blackwood was sent to Canada in 1890 by a despairing father, he joined the Theosophical Society.

But Blackwood's experiences in Canada were dire. Everything in which he invested his money failed and Blackwood subsequently fled to the Muskoka Lakes living rough amongst the islands. Later in New York his experiences were not much better, swindled out of money by a close friend, sleeping rough in Central Park, and only steadily coming to terms with life, first as a journalist and then as a Private Secretary. He found New York a living hell and his only pleasures came when he could escape for a brief holiday to the woods or lakes. Even then, an attempt to join in with gold prospecting in the Rainy River area of Ontario proved a failure, though Blackwood enjoyed the experience.

Throughout these years Blackwood regarded himself as a failure to his family and the sense of guilt, aggravated by the fact that his father had died in the intervening years with no chance of reparation, stopped Blackwood from returning home. However, a visit from his half-sister, Lady Kintore, and her family, stirred in Blackwood a longing to return home, which he did in February 1899.

But the horrors of those years in New York and Canada remained with him. He found therapy in writing. He recalled in *Episodes Before Thirty*:

It had been my habit and delight to spend my evenings composing yarns on my typewriter, finding more pleasure in this than in any dinner engagement, theatre or concert. Why this suddenly began I cannot say, but I guess at a venture that the accumulated horror of the years in New York was seeking expression. […] *Jimbo* I had already written twice, several of the "John Silence" tales as well, and numerous other queer ghostly stories of one sort or another.

Clearly *Jimbo* was one of the works that allowed Blackwood's troubled mind to work through its agonies in his escape from the vicissitudes of the 1890s. I also believe that Blackwood began work on *The Education of Uncle Paul* at about the same time. Surviving papers reveal that in July 1900 Blackwood had submitted a manuscript entitled "The Children's Secret Society" to the publisher John Lane, but having not heard anything by October his sister, Ada, enquired after it only to discover it had been returned and presumably lost in the post. I know no more about the book, but I suspect this was an early version of *The Education of Uncle Paul*, as a crucial part of the book relates to the children's secret society into which Uncle Paul is eventually admitted. Blackwood had to rewrite the story all over again.

So both of these books were part of Blackwood's own therapeutic process to rid himself of the horrors of his recent past and to face life anew, and knowing that allows for a deeper appreciation of both books.

Without revealing too much, I shall say that *Jimbo* is the story of a boy who, following an accident, is in a coma and requires all the ministerings of his governess to help him recover. Most of the story takes place in Jimbo's psyche where his governess comes to him and gives him the spiritual guidance to help him escape, provided he has the strength and courage to do it. Jimbo's coma could almost equate to Blackwood's New York hell and the anguish of the separation from his family. In his coma, Jimbo believes he is trapped in "the Empty House", a place where he had been forbidden to go. During his Canadian and New York experiences, Blackwood had entered several forbidden territories. His father had been an ardent temperance man and yet Blackwood ran a hotel selling liquor. Blackwood also experimented with drugs and found himself sucked into an insurance scam.

Throughout his life Blackwood suffered from perpetual guilt, the fear that knowingly or unknowingly he had committed some sin for which he would be punished. This was a legacy of the harsh evangelical indoctrination of his parents and one that never left him, no matter what else he came to believe. Though it may have dimmed in later years (though a radio talk he later gave showed no signs that it had) this guilt must have been almost paralysing upon his return to England and *Jimbo* was one release valve. Towards the start of the story Jimbo recalls a rhyme about children who live in fright of dark tales told by their nursery-maid. One quatrain goes:

> We hear the voices in the wind
> Singing of freedom we may never find,
> Victims of fate so cruelly unkind,
>   We are unblest.

In four lines Blackwood sums up how he must have felt in New York: a victim of fate, unblessed, yearning for an escape back to the world of Nature. All of Blackwood's fears appear in the story as some symbolic horror, such as the fearsome Inmate of the House, which is symbolic of Fear and threatens to keep Jimbo trapped forever, and the many other "Bad Things" that hinder his recovery. As such the story is an allegorical fantasy, with Blackwood drawing upon the supernatural and mystical to bring his story to life.

I'm not sure how many times Blackwood revised *Jimbo*. He had clearly drafted two versions, initially called *A Flying Boy*, and may have revised it again as the story incorporates some of the teachings when he studied in the Hermetic Order of the Golden Dawn with W. B. Yeats and A. E. Waite, which he joined in October 1900.

If *Jimbo* was one form of therapeutic release, what then was *The Education of Uncle Paul*? Whilst *Jimbo* takes place in a child's mind and is clearly full of childhood images, *Uncle Paul* explores the adult anguish. The book is clearly autobiographical, with Blackwood portrayed as the eponymous Uncle Paul. It opens with Paul Rivers returning to England from having spent twenty years in Canada. Feeling isolated and remote Rivers fears that he may not be able to reconcile himself to family life again. The opening chapters, describing Rivers's reactions upon returning to England not only echo Blackwood's own but are fresh in his mind. Rivers plans to stay with his widowed sister, Margaret, and her children at their home in the south of England. It is there, while playing with the children, and particularly the young girl Nixie, that Blackwood is allowed to enter their imaginative games and see things in an entirely different way. He witnesses the winds come alive at dawn and later he travels with them "through the crack"* between yesterday and tomorrow, and enters the Land where all lost things go. Through his association with the children Uncle Paul's spirit is revived and his soul restored.

All of the children in the two books relate to people in Blackwood's life. Both Jimbo and Uncle Paul are clearly Blackwood himself. He had three sisters of which his favourite was his younger sister Ada. I am fairly sure

---

*The novel was adapted as a stage play by Violet Pearn under the title *Through the Crack* in 1920. The 1922 production allowed for the first professional stage work by a young Laurence Olivier.

that Ada is the Nixie of *Jimbo* and, indeed, *Jimbo* is dedicated to her (and dated, 1900). There may be some of Ada in the Nixie of *Uncle Paul*, but this is a much deeper, richer, more fey child. Blackwood recorded in a letter he wrote years later that the children in *Uncle Paul* were those of a cousin of his. These were the children of Arthur Hobart-Hampden whose mother was Blackwood's father's stepsister. The first half of Hobart-Hampden's surname is pronounced "Hubbard" and was the character who served as John Silence's Watson in several of the stories. Arthur and his wife Henrietta had four children, Arthur, Aileen, Lucy and Vere, just like the four in *Uncle Paul*. At the time that Blackwood first began work on *Uncle Paul* these children were very young and Vere was a babe-in-arms, just as the baby is described in chapter five. But Blackwood revised the story over time and the children took on different roles. By then Vere had become Jonah, Lucy was Toby and Aileen was Nixie. Vere, incidentally, went on to become the 9th Earl of Buckinghamshire, but he was a very Blackwoodian character since he had no interest in the nobility. He had spent many years as a gardener and park attendant for Southend Council.

Children delighted in Blackwood's company as he acted like one of them rather than as a responsible adult. With him they would go on wonderful adventures, exploring the marvels of nature, looking at the world through the eyes of insects, pretending they were sailing down a river (on some occasions they actually did) or building dams and creating lakes and waterfalls, learning how to camp out over night, light fires and make breakfast. I spoke to adults in their seventies and eighties who remembered their childhood adventures with Blackwood and these remained their most treasured memories.

The setting for the story is probably a composite of at least two locations. One would be the Hobart-Hampden's home in Sussex on the South Downs. At the start of *Uncle Paul* he talks about the "space and freedom" of the hills and moorlands, which is exactly how he described his cousin's farm in a letter to a friend. But more significantly I think the setting was originally modelled on Rempstone in Dorset, the home of his close friends Edwyn and Mary Bevan. The description of the house and estate is very similar to that of Rempstone, on the Isle of Purbeck. The Gwyle Wood, which is mentioned in the story, is part of the Rempstone estate. Gwyle or *gwyl* is a Celtic word for stream which has lingered on in the Dorset dialect and there still is a brook called the Gwyle on the Isle of Purbeck. I also believe that Mary Bevan, who was another distant cousin of Blackwood's whom he had known from childhood, is the character of Margaret in the novel. The Bevans feature strongly in the early years of Blackwood's return from America and accompanied him on several of his travels, including one of his trips down the Danube and his holiday on an island in the Baltic which inspired the John Silence story, "The Camp of the Dog". Indeed, as I concluded in my biography of Blackwood, I suspect that Edwyn Bevan was the basis for the character of John Silence.

So we may picture Blackwood having returned from America, struggling to reunite with his friends and family and with life in Britain and looking for opportunities to retreat, to recharge his spiritual batteries and purge himself of the terrors of the last decade. His strength comes partly from his younger sister, the original Nixie, but also from his friendship with the Bevans and with his cousin, Arthur and their children. He finds an outlet in his writing and the two major early works that he produces are the books you are about to read.

In later years children always referred to Blackwood as Uncle Paul, and Blackwood even wrote a book, *A Prisoner in Fairyland*, as the book "that Uncle Paul wrote". That book is referred to towards the end of *The Education of Uncle Paul*, but that's another story entirely.

Here, then, are two books of escape, wonder and salvation. They were the books that allowed Blackwood to close a difficult chapter of his days in America and begin a new life. They are the books that gave us Blackwood the author.

—Chatham, Kent
December 2006

JIMBO

By Algernon Blackwood

To A. S. B. (1900)

CHAPTER I
"RABBITS"

Jimbo's governess ought to have known better—but she didn't. If she had, Jimbo would never have met with the adventures that subsequently came to him. Thus, in a roundabout sort of way, the child ought to have been thankful to the governess; and perhaps, in a roundabout sort of way, he was. But that comes at the far end of the story, and is doubtful at best; and in the meanwhile the child had gone through his suffering, and the governess had in some measure expiated her fault; so that at this stage it is only necessary to note that the whole business began because the Empty House happened to be really an Empty House—not the one Jimbo's family lived in, but another of which more will be known in due course.

Jimbo's father was a retired Colonel, who had married late in life, and now lived all the year round in the country; and Jimbo was the youngest child but one. The Colonel, lean in body as he was sincere in mind, an excellent soldier but a poor diplomatist, loved dogs, horses, guns and riding-whips. He also really understood them. His neighbours, had they been asked, would have called him hardheaded, and so far as a soft-hearted man may deserve the title, he probably was. He rode two horses a day to hounds with the best of them, and the stiffer the country the better he liked it. Besides his guns, dogs and horses, he was also very fond of his children. It was his hobby that he understood them far better than his wife did, or than any one else did, for that matter. The proper evolution of their differing temperaments had no difficulties for him. The delicate problems of child-nature, which defy solution by nine parents out of ten, ceased to exist the moment he spread out his muscular hand in a favourite omnipotent gesture and uttered some extraordinarily foolish generality in that thunderous, good-natured voice of his. The difficulty for himself vanished when he ended up with the words, "Leave that to me, my dear; believe me, I know best!" But for all else concerned, and especially for the child under discussion, this was when the difficulty really began.

Since, however, the Colonel, after this chapter, mounts his best hunter and disappears over a high hedge into space so far as our story is concerned, any further delineation of his wholesome but very ordinary type is unnecessary.

One winter's evening, not very long after Christmas, the Colonel made a discovery. It alarmed him a little; for it suggested to his cocksure mind that he did not understand *all* his children as comprehensively as he imagined.

Between five o'clock tea and dinner—that magic hour when lessons were over and the big house was fall of shadows and mystery—there came a timid knock at the study door.

"Come in," growled the soldier in his deepest voice, and a little girl's face, wreathed in tumbling brown hair, poked itself hesitatingly through the opening.

The Colonel did not like being disturbed at this hour, and everybody in the house knew it; but the spell of Christmas holidays was still somehow in the air, and the customary order was not yet fully re-established. Moreover, when he saw who the intruder was, his growl modified itself into a sort of common sternness that yet was not cleverly enough simulated to deceive the really intuitive little person who now stood inside the room.

"Well, Nixie, child, what do you want now?"

" Please, father, will you—we wondered if—"

A chorus of whispers issued from the other side of the door:

"Go on, silly!"

"Out with it!"

"You promised you would, Nixie."

"...if you would come and play Rabbits with us?" came the words in a desperate rush, with laughter not far behind.

The big man with the fierce white moustaches glared over the top of his glasses at the intruders as if amazed beyond belief at the audacity of the request.

"Rabbits!" he exclaimed, as though the mere word ought to have caused an instant explosion. "Rabbits!"

"Oh, *please* do."

"Rabbits at this time of night!" he repeated. "I never heard of such a thing. Why, all good rabbits are asleep in their holes by now. And you ought to be in yours too by rights, I'm sure."

"We don't sleep in holes, father," said the owner of the brown hair, who was acting as leader.

"And there's still a nour before bedtime, *really*," added a voice in the rear.

The big man slowly put his glasses down and looked at his watch. He looked very savage, but of course it was all pretence, and the children knew it. "If he was *really* cross he'd pretend to be nice," they whispered to each other, with merciless perception.

"Well—" he began. But he who hesitates, with children, is lost. The door flung open wide, and the troop poured into the room in a medley of long black legs, flying hair and outstretched hands. They surrounded the table, swarmed upon his big knees, shut his stupid old book, tried on his glasses, kissed him, and fell to discussing the game breathlessly all at once, as though it had already begun.

This, of course, ended the battle, and the big man had to play the part of the Monster Rabbit in a wonderful game of his own invention. But when, at length, it was all over, and they were gathered panting round the fire of blazing logs in the hall, the Monster Rabbit—the only one with any breath at his commend—looked up and spoke.

"Where's Jimbo?" he asked.

"Upstairs."

"Why didn't he come and play too?"

"He didn't want to."

"Why ? What's he doing?"

Several answers were forthcoming.

"Nothing in p'tickler."

"Talking to the furniture when I last saw him."

"Just thinking, as usual, or staring in the fire."

None of the answers seemed to satisfy the Monster Rabbit, for when he kissed them a little later and said good-night, he gave orders, with a graver face, for Jimbo to be sent down to the study before he went to bed. Moreover, he called him " James," which was a sure sign of parental displeasure.

"James, why didn't you come and play with your brothers and sisters just now?" asked the Colonel, as a dreamy-eyed boy of about eight, with a mop of dark hair and a wistful expression, came slowly forward into the room.

"I was in the middle of making pictures."

"Where—what—making pictures?"

"In the fire."

"James," said the Colonel in a serious tone, "don't you know that you are getting too old now for that sort of thing ? If you dream so much, you'll fall asleep altogether some fine day, and never wake up again. Just think what that means!"

The child smiled faintly and moved up confidingly between his father's knees, staring into his eyes without the least sign of fear. But he said nothing in reply. His thoughts were far away, and it seemed as if the effort to bring them back into the study and to a consideration of his father's words was almost beyond his power.

"You must run about more," pursued the soldier, rubbing his big hands together briskly, "and join your brothers and sisters in their games. Lie about in the summer and dream a bit if you like, but now it's winter, you must be more active, and make your blood circulate healthily,—er—and all that sort of thing."

The words were kindly spoken, but the voice and manner rather deliberate. Jimbo began to look a little troubled, as his father watched him.

"Come now, little man," he said more gently, "what's the matter, eh?" He drew the boy close to him. "Tell me all about it, and what it is you're always thinking about so much."

Jimbo brought back his mind with a tremendous effort, and said, "I don't like the winter. It's so dark and full of horrid things. It's all ice and shadows, so—so I go away and think of what I like, and other places—"

"Nonsense!" interrupted his father briskly; "winter's a capital time for boys. What in the world d'ye mean, I wonder?"

He lifted the child on to his knee and stroked his hair, as though he were patting the flank of a horse. Jimbo took no notice of the interruption or of the caress, but went on saying what he had to say, though with eyes a little more clouded.

"Winter's like going into a long black tunnel, you see. It's downhill to

Christmas, of course, and then uphill all the way to the summer holidays. But the uphill part's so slow that—"

"Tut, tut!" laughed the Colonel in spite of himself; "you mustn't have such thoughts. Those are a baby's notions. They're silly, silly, silly."

"Do you *really* think so, father?" continued the boy, as if politeness demanded some recognition of his father's remarks, but otherwise anxious only to say what was in his mind. "You wouldn't think them silly if you really knew. But, of course, there's no one to tell you in the stable, so you *can't* know. You've never seen the funny big people rushing past you and laughing through their long hair when the wind blows so loud. I know several of them almost to speak to, but you hear only wind. And the other things with tiny legs that skate up and down the slippery moonbeams, without ever tumbling off—they aren't silly a bit, only they don't like dogs and noise. And I've seen the furniture"—he pronounced it furchinur—" dancing about in the day-nursery when it thought it was alone, and I've heard it talking at night. I know the big cupboard's voice quite well. It's just like a drum, only rougher..."

The Colonel shook his head and frowned severely, staring hard at his son. But though their eyes met, the boy hardly saw him. Far away at the other end of the dark Tunnel of the Months he saw the white summer sunshine lying over gardens full of nodding flowers. Butterflies were flitting across meadows yellow with buttercups, and he saw the fascinating rings upon the lawn where the Fairy People held their dances in the moonlight; he heard the wind call to him as it ran on along by the hedgerows, and saw the gentle pressure of its swift feet upon the standing hay; streams were murmuring under shady trees; birds were singing; and there were echoes of sweeter music still that he could not understand, but loved all the more perhaps on that account....

"Yes," announced the Colonel later that evening to his wife, spreading his hands out as he spoke. "Yes, my dear, I *have* made a discovery, and an alarming one. You know, I'm rarely at fault where the children are concerned—and I've noted all the symptoms with unusual care. James, my dear, is an imaginative boy."

He paused to note the effect of his words, but seeing none, continued:

"I regret to be obliged to say it, but it's a fact beyond dispute. His head is simply full of things, and he talked to me this evening about tunnels and slippery moonlight till I very nearly lost my temper altogether. Now, the boy will never make a man unless we take him in hand properly at once. We must get him a governess, or something, without delay. Just fancy, if he grew up into a poet or one of these—these—"

In his distress the soldier could only think of horse-terms, which did not seem quite the right language. He stuck altogether, and kept repeating the favourite gesture with his open hand, staring at his wife over his glasses as he did so.

But the mother never argued.

"He's still very young still," she observed

"Exactly what I say. Now that your eyes are opened to the actual state of affairs, I'm satisfied."

"We'll get a sensible nursery-governess at once," added the mother.

"A practical one?"

"Yes, dear."

"Hard-headed?"

"Yes."

"And well educated?"

"Yes."

"And—er—firm with children. She'll do for the lot, then."

"If possible."

"And a young woman who doesn't go in for poetry, and dreaming, and all that kind of flummery."

"Of course, dear."

"Capital. I felt sure you would agree with me," he went on. "It'd be no end of a pity if Jimbo grew up an ass. At present he hardly knows the difference between a roadster and a racer. He's going into the army, too," he added by way of climax, "and you know, my dear, the army would never stand *that!*"

"Never," said the mother quietly, and the conversation came to an end.

Meanwhile, the subject of these remarks was lying wide awake upstairs in the bed with the yellow iron railing round it. His elder brother was asleep in the opposite corner of the room, snoring peacefully. He could just see the brass knobs of the bedstead as the dying firelight quivered and shone on them. The walls and ceiling were draped in shadows that altered their shapes from time to time as the coals dropped softly into the grate. Gradually the fire sank, and the room darkened. A feeling of delight and awe stole into his heart.

Jimbo loved these early hours of the night before sleep came. He felt no fear of the dark; its mystery thrilled his soul; but he liked the summer dark, with its soft, warm silences better than the chill winter shadows. Presently the firelight sprang up into a brief flame and then died away altogether with an odd little gulp. He knew the sound well; he often watched the fire out, and now, as he lay in bed waiting for he knew not what, the moonlight filtered in through the baize curtains and gradually gave to the room a wholly new character.

Jimbo sat up in bed and listened. The house was very still. He slipped into his red dressing-gown and crept noiselessly over to the window. For a moment he paused by his brother's bed to make sure that he really was asleep; then, evidently satisfied, he drew aside a corner of the curtain and peered out.

"Oh!" he said, drawing in his breath with delight, and again "oh!"

It was difficult to understand why the sea of white moonlight that covered the lawn should fill him with such joy, and at the same time bring a lump into his throat. It made him feel as if he were swelling out into something very much greater than the actual limits of his little person. And the sensation was one of mingled pain and delight, too intense for him to feel for very long. The unhappiness passed gradually away, he always noticed, and the happiness merged after a while into a sort of dreamy ecstasy in which he neither thought nor wished much, but was conscious only of one single unmanageable yearning.

The huge cedars on the lawn reared themselves up like giants in silver cloaks, and the horse-chestnut—the Umbrella Tree, as the children called it—loomed with motionless branches that were frosted and shining. Beyond it, in a blue mist of moonlight and distance, lay the kitchen-garden; he could just make out the line of the high wall where the fruit-trees grew. Immediately below him the gravel of the carriage drive sparkled with frost.

The bars of the windows were cold to his hands, yet he stood there for a long time with his nose flattened against the pane and his bare feet on the cane chair. He felt both happy and sad; his heart longed dreadfully for something he had not got, something that seemed out of his reach because he could not name it. No one seemed to believe all the things he *knew* in quite the same way as he did. His brothers and sisters played up to a certain point, and then put the things aside as if they had only been assumed for the time and were not real. To him they were always real. His father's words, too, that evening had sorely puzzled him when he came to think over them afterwards: "They're a baby's notions... They're silly, silly, silly." Were these things real or were they not? And, as he pondered, yearning dumbly, as only these little souls can yearn, the wistfulness in his heart went out to meet the moonlight in the air. Together they wove a spell that seemed to summon before him a fairy of the night, who whispered an answer into his heart: "We are real so long as you believe in us. It is your imagination that makes us real and gives us life. Please, never, never stop believing."

Jimbo was not quite sure that he understood the message, but he liked it all the same, and felt comforted. So long as they believed in one another, the rest did not matter very much after all. And when at last, shivering with cold, he crept back to bed, it was only to find through the Gates of Sleep a more direct way to the things he had been thinking about, and to wander for the rest of the night, unwatched and free, through the wonders of an Enchanted Land.

Jimbo, as his father had said, was an imaginative child. Most children are—more or less; and he was "more," at least, "more" than his brothers and sisters. The Colonel thought he had made a penetrating discovery, but his wife had known it always. His head, indeed, was "full of things,"— things that, unless trained into a channel where they could be controlled and properly schooled, would certainly interfere with his success in a practical world, and be a source of mingled pain and joy to him all through life. To have trained these forces, ever bursting out towards creation, in his little soul,—to have explained, interpreted, and dealt fairly by them, would perhaps have been the best and wisest way; to have suppressed them altogether, cleaned them out by the process of substitution, this might have succeeded too in less measure; but to turn them into a veritable rout of horror by the common method of "frightening the nonsense out of the boy," this was surely the very worst way of dealing with such a case, and the most cruel. Yet, this was the method adopted by the Colonel in the robust good-nature of his heart, and the utter ignorance of his soul.

So it came about that three months later, when May was melting into June, Miss Ethel Lake arrived upon the scene as a result of the Colonel's blundering good intentions. She brought with her a kind disposition, a supreme ignorance of unordinary children, a large store of self-confidence—and a corded yellow tin box.

CHAPTER II

MISS LAKE COMES—AND GOES

The conversation took place suddenly one afternoon, and no one knew anything about it except the two who took part in it: the Colonel asked the governess to try and knock the nonsense out of Jimbo's head, and the governess promised eagerly to do her very best. It was her first "place"; and by "nonsense" they both understood imagination. True enough, Jimbo's mother had given her rather different instructions as to the treatment of the boy, but she mistook the soldier's bluster for authority, and deemed it best to obey him. This was her first mistake.

In reality she was not devoid of imaginative insight; it was simply that her anxiety to prove a success permitted her better judgment to be overborne by the Colonel's boisterous manner.

The wisdom of the mother was greater than that of her husband. For the safe development of that tender and imaginative little boy of hers, she had been at great pains to engage a girl—a clergyman's daughter—who possessed sufficient sympathy with the poetic and dreamy nature to be of real help to him; for true help, she knew, can only come from true understanding. And Miss Lake was a good girl. She was entirely well-meaning—which is the beginning of well-doing, and her principal weakness lay in her judgment, which led her to obey the Colonel too literally.

"She seems most sensible," he declared to his wife.

"Yes, dear."

"And practical."

"I think so."

"And firm and—er—wise with children."

"I hope so."

"Just the sort for young Jimbo," added the Colonel with decision.

"I trust so; she's a little young, perhaps."

"Possibly, but one can't get everything," said her husband, in his horse-and-dog voice. "A year with her should clean out that fanciful brain of his, and prepare him for school with other boys. He'll be all right once he gets to school. My dear," he added, spreading out his right hand, fingers extended, "you've made a most wise selection. I congratulate you. I'm delighted."

"I'm so glad."

"Capital, I repeat, capital. You're a clever little woman. I knew you'd find the right party, once I showed you how the land lay."

❧

The Empty House, that stood in its neglected garden not far from the Park gates, was built on a point of land that entered wedgewise into the Colonel's estate. Though something of an eyesore, therefore, he could do nothing with it.

To the children it had always been an object of peculiar, though not unwholesome, mystery. None of them cared to pass it on a stormy day—the wind made such odd noises in its empty corridors and rooms—and they refused point-blank to go within hailing distance of it after dark. But in Jimbo's imagination it was especially haunted, and if he had ceased to reveal to the others what he *knew* went on under its roof, it was only because they were unable to follow him, and were inclined to greet his extravagant recitals with "Now, Jimbo, you know *perfectly* well you're only making up."

The House had been empty for many years; but, to the children, it had been empty since the beginning of the world, since what they called the "*very* beginning." They believed—well, each child believed according to his own mind and powers, but there was at least one belief they all held in common: for it was generally accepted as an article of faith that the Indians, encamped among the shrubberies on the back lawn, secretly buried their dead behind the crumbling walls of its weedy garden—the "dead" provided by the children's battles, be it understood. Wakeful ears in the night-nursery had heard strange sounds coming from that direction when the windows were open on hot summer nights; and the gardener, supreme authority on all that happened in the night (since they believed that he sat up to watch the vegetables and fruit-trees ripen, and never went to bed at all), was evidently of the same persuasion.

When appealed to for an explanation of the mournful wind-voices, he knew what was expected of him, and rose manfully to the occasion.

"It's either them Redskins aburin' wot you killed of 'em yesterday," he declared, pointing towards the Empty House with a bit of broken flower-pot, "or else it's the ones you killed last week, and who was always astealin' of my strorbriz." He looked very wise as he said this, and his wand of office—a dirty trowel—which he held in his hand, gave him tremendous dignity.

"That's just what we thought, and of course if you say so too, that settles it," said Nixie.

"It's more'n likely, missie, leastways from wot you describes, which it is a hempty house all the same, though I can't say as I've heard no sounds, not very distinct that is, myself."

The gardener may have been anxious to hedge a bit, for fear of a scolding from headquarters, but his cryptic remarks pleased the children greatly, because it showed, they thought, that they knew more than the gardener did.

Thus the Empty House remained an object of somewhat dreadful delight, lending a touch of wonderland to that part of the lane where it stood, and forming the background for many an enchanting story over the nursery fire in winter-time. It appealed vividly to their imaginations, especially to Jimbo's. Its dark windows, without blinds, were sometimes full of faces that retreated the moment they were looked at. That tangled ivy did not grow over the roof so thickly for nothing; and those high elms on the western side had not been planted years ago in a semicircle without a reason. Thus, at least, the children argued, not knowing exactly what they meant, nor caring much, so long as they proved to their own satisfaction that the place was properly haunted, and therefore worthy of their attention.

It was natural they should lead Miss Lake in that direction on one of their first walks together, and it was natural, too, that she should at once discover from their manner that the place was of some importance to them.

"What a queer-looking old house," she remarked, when they turned the corner of the lane and it came into view. "Almost a ruin, isn't it?"

The children exchanged glances. A "ruin" did not seem the right sort of word at all; and, besides, was a little disrespectful. Also, they were not sure whether the new governess ought to be told everything so soon. She had not really won their confidence yet. After a slight pause—and a children's pause is the most eloquent imaginable—Nixie, being the eldest, said in a stiff little voice: "It's the Empty House, Miss Lake. We know it very well indeed."

"It looks empty," observed Miss Lake briskly.

"But it's not a ruin, of course," added the child, with the cold dignity of chosen spokesman.

"Oh!" said the governess, quite missing the point. She was talking lightly on the surface of things, wholly ignorant of the depths beneath her feet, intuition with her having always been sternly repressed.

"It's a gamekeeper's cottage, or something like that, I suppose," she said.

"Oh, no; it isn't a bit."

"Doesn't it belong to your father, then?"

"No. It's somebody else's, you see."

"Then you can't have it pulled down?"

"Rather not! Of course not! " exclaimed several indignant voices at once.

Miss Lake perceived for the first time that it held more than ordinary importance in their mind.

"Tell me about it," she said. "What is its history, and who used to live in it?"

There came another pause. The children looked into each others' faces. They gazed at the blue sky overhead; then they stared at the dusty road at their feet. But no one volunteered an answer. Miss Lake, they felt, was approaching the subject in an offensive manner.

"Why are you all so mysterious about it?" she went on. "It's only a tumble-down old place, and must be very draughty to live in, even for a gameskeeper."

Silence.

"Come, children, don't you hear me ? I'm asking you a question."

A couple of startled birds flew out of the ivy with a great whirring of wings. This was followed by a faint sound of rumbling, that seemed to come from the interior of the house. Outside all was still, and the hot sunshine lay over everything. The sound was repeated. The children looked at each other with large, expectant eyes. Something in the house was moving—was coming nearer.

"Have you *all* lost your tongues?" asked the governess impatiently.

"But you see," Nixie said at length, "somebody *does* live in it now."

"And who is he?"

"I didn't say it was a *man.*"

"Whoever it is—tell me about the person," persisted Miss Lake.

"There's really nothing to tell," replied the child, without looking up.

"Oh, but there must be something," declared the logical young governess, "or you wouldn't object so much to its being pulled down."

Nixie looked puzzled, but Jimbo came to the rescue at once.

"But *you* wouldn't understand if we did tell you," he said, in a slow, respectful voice. His tone held a touch of that indescribable scorn heard sometimes in a child's tone—the utter contempt for the stupid grown-up creature. Miss Lake noticed, and felt annoyed. She recognised that she was not getting on well with the children, and it piqued her. She remembered the Colonel's words about "knocking the nonsense out" of James' head, and she saw that her first opportunity, in fact her first real test, was at hand.

"And why, pray, should I not understand?" she asked, with some sharpness. "Is the mystery so *very* great?"

For some reason the duty of spokesman now devolved unmistakably upon Jimbo; and very seriously too, he accepted the task, standing with his feet firmly planted in the road and his hands in his trousers' pockets.

"You see, Miss Lake," he began gravely, "we know such a lot of Things in there, that they might not like us to tell you about them. They don't know you yet. If they did it might be different. But—but—you see, it isn't."

This was rather crushing to the aspiring educator, and the Colonel's instructions gained additional point in the light of the boy's explanation.

"Fiddlesticks!" she laughed, "there's probably nothing at all in there, except rats and cobwebs. 'Things,' indeed!"

"I knew you wouldn't understand," said Jimbo coolly, with no sign of being offended. "How could you?" He glanced at his sisters, gaining so much support from their enigmatical faces that he added, for their especial benefit, " How could she?"

"The gard'ner said so too," chimed in a younger sister, with a vague notion that their precious Empty House was being robbed of its glory.

"Yes; but, James, dear, I do understand perfectly," continued Miss Lake more gently, and wisely ignoring the reference to the authority of the kitchen-garden. "Only, you see, I cannot really encourage you in such nonsense—"

"It isn't nonsense," interrupted Jimbo, with heat.

"But, believe me, children, it *is* nonsense. How do you know that there's anything inside? You've never been there!"

"You can know perfectly well what's inside a thing without having gone there," replied Jimbo with scorn. " At least, *we* can."

Miss Lake changed her tack a little—fatally, as it appeared afterwards.

"I know at any rate," she said with decision, "that there's nothing good in there. Whatever there may be is bad, thoroughly bad, and not fit for you to play with."

The other children moved away, but Jimbo stood his ground. They were all angry, disappointed, sore hurt and offended. But Jimbo suddenly began to feel something else besides anger and vexation. It was a new point of view to him that the Empty House might contain bad things as well as good, or perhaps, only bad things. His imagination seized upon the point at once and set to work vigorously to develop it. This was his way with all such things, and he could not prevent it.

"Bad Things?" he repeated, looking up at the governess. "You mean Things that could hurt?"

"Yes, of course," she said, noting the effect of her words and thinking how pleased the Colonel would be later, when he heard it. "Things that might run out and catch you some day when you're passing here alone, and take you back a prisoner. Then you'd be a prisoner in the Empty House all your life. Think of that!"

Miss Lake mistook the boy's silence as proof that she was taking the right line. She enlarged upon this view of the matter, now she was so successfully launched, and described the *Inmate of the House* with such wealth of detail that she felt sure her listener would never have anything to do with the place again, and that she had "knocked out" this particular bit of "nonsense" for ever and a day.

But to Jimbo it was a new and horrible idea that the Empty House, haunted hitherto only by rather jolly and wonderful Red Indians, contained a Monster who might take him prisoner, and the thought made him feel afraid. The mischief had, of course, been done, and the terror in his eyes was unmistakable, when the foolish governess saw her mistake. Retreat was impossible: the boy was shaking with fear; and not all Miss Lake's genuine sympathy, or Nixie's explanations and soothings, were able to relieve his mind of its new burden.

Hitherto Jimbo's imagination had loved to dwell upon the pleasant side of things invisible; but now he had been severely frightened, and his imagination took a new turn. Not only the Empty House, but all his inner world, to which it was in some sense the key, underwent a distressing change. His sense of horror had been vividly aroused.

The governess would willingly have corrected her mistake, but was, of course, powerless to do so. Bitterly she regretted her tactlessness and folly. But she could do nothing, and to add to her distress, she saw that Jimbo shrank from her in a way that could not long escape the watchful eye of the mother. But, if the boy shed tears of fear that night in his bed, it must in justice be told that she, for her part, cried bitterly in her own room, not that she had endangered her "place," but that she had done a cruel injury to a child, and that she was helpless to undo it. For she loved children, though she was quite unsuited to take care of them. Her just reward, however, came swiftly upon her.

A few nights later, when Jimbo and Nixie were allowed to come down to dessert, the wind was heard to make a queer moaning sound in the ivy branches and hung over the dining-room windows. Jimbo heard it too. He held his breath for a minute; then he looked round the table in a frightened way, and the next minute gave a scream and burst into tears. He ran round and buried his face in his father's arms.

After the tears came the truth. It was a bad thing for Miss Ethel Lake, this little sighing of the wind and the ivy leaves, for the Djin of terror she had thoughtlessly evoked swept into the room and introduced himself to the parents without her leave.

"What new nonsense is this now?" growled the soldier, leaving his walnuts and lifting the boy on to his knee. "He shouldn't come down till he's a little older, and knows how to behave."

"What's the matter, darling child?" asked the mother, drying his eyes tenderly.

"I heard the bad Things crying in the Empty House."

"The Empty House is a mile away from here!" snorted the Colonel.

"Then it's come nearer," declared the frightened boy.

"Who told you there were bad things in the Empty House?" asked the mother.

"Yes, who told you, indeed, I should like to know!" demanded the Colonel.

And then it all came out. The Colonel's wife was very quiet, but very determined. Miss Lake went back to the clerical family whence she had come, and the children knew her no more.

"I'm glad," said Nixie, expressing the verdict of the nursery. "I thought she was awfully stupid."

"She wasn't a real lake at all," declared another, "she was only a sort of puddle."

Jimbo, however, said little, and the Colonel likewise held his peace.

But the governess, whether she was a lake or only a puddle, left her mark behind her. The Empty House was no longer harmless. It had a new lease of life. It was tenanted by some one who could never have friendly relations with children. The weeds in the old garden took on fantastic shapes; figures hid behind the doors and crept about the passages; the rooks in the high elms became birds of ill-omen; the ivy bristled upon the walls, and the trivial explanations of the gardener were no longer satisfactory.

Even in bright sunshine a Shadow lay crouching upon the broken roof. At any moment it might leap into life, and with immense striding legs chase the children down to the very Park gates.

There was no need to enforce the decree that the Empty House was a forbidden land. The children of their own accord declared it out of bounds, and avoided it as carefully as if all the wild animals from the Zoo were roaming its gardens, hungry and unchained.

CHAPTER III

THE SHOCK

One immediate result of Miss Lake's indiscretion was that the children preferred to play on the other side of the garden, the side farthest from the Empty House. A spiked railing here divided them from a field in which cows disported themselves, and as bulls also sometimes were admitted to the cows, the field was strictly out of bounds.

In this spiked railing, not far from the great shrubberies where the Indians increased and multiplied, there was a swinging gate. The children swung on it whenever they could. They called it Express Trains, and the fact that it was forbidden only added to their pleasure. When opened at its widest it would swing them with a rush through the air, past the pillars with a click, out into the field, and then back again into the garden. It was bad for the hinges, and it was also bad for the garden, because it was frequently left open after these carnivals, and the cows got in and trod the flowers down. The children were not afraid of the cows, but they held the bull in great horror. And these trivial things have been mentioned here because of the part they played in Jimbo's subsequent adventures.

It was only ten days or so after Miss Lake's sudden departure when Jimbo managed one evening to elude the vigilance of his lawful guardians, and wandered off unnoticed among the laburnums on the front lawn. From the laburnums he passed successfully to the first laurel shrubbery, and thence he executed a clever flank movement and entered the carriage drive in the rear. The rest was easy, and he soon found himself at the Lodge gate.

For some moments he peered through the iron grating, and pondered on the seductiveness of the dusty road and of the ditch beyond. To his surprise he found, presently, that the gate was moving outwards; it was yielding to his weight. One thing leads easily to another sometimes, and the open gate led easily on to the seductive road. The result was that a minute later Jimbo was chasing butterflies along the green lane, and throwing stones into the water of the ditch.

It was the evening of a hot summer's day, and the butterflies were still out in force. Jimbo's delight was intense. The joy of finding himself alone where he had no right to be put everything else out of his head, and for some time he wandered on, oblivious of all but the intoxicating sense of freedom and the difficulty of choosing between so many butterflies and such a magnificently dirty ditch.

At first he yielded to the seductions of the ditch. He caught a big, sleepy beetle and put it on a violet leaf, and sent it sailing out to sea; and when it landed on the farther shore he found a still bigger leaf, and sent it forth on a voyage in another direction, with a cargo of daisy petals, and a hairy caterpillar for a bo'sun's mate. But, just as the vessel was getting under way, a butterfly of amazing brilliance floated past insolently under his very nose. Leaving the beetle and the caterpillar to navigate the currents as best they could, he at once gave chase. Cap in hand, he flew after the butterfly down the lane, and a dozen times when his cap was just upon it, it sailed away sideways without the least effort and escaped him.

Then, suddenly, the lane took a familiar turning; the ditch stopped abruptly; the hedge on his right fell away altogether; the butterfly danced out of sight into a field, and Jimbo found himself face to face with the one thing in the whole world that could, at that time, fill him with abject terror—the Empty House.

He came to a full stop in the middle of the road and stared up at the windows. He realised for the first time that he was alone, and that it was possible for brilliant sunshine, even on a cloudless day, to become somehow lustreless and dull. The walls showed a deep red in the sunset light. The house was still as the grave. His feet were rooted to the ground, and it seemed as if he could not move a single muscle; and as he stood there, the blood ebbing quickly from his heart, the words of the governess a few days before rushed back into his mind, and turned his fear into a dreadful, all-possessing horror. In another minute the battered door would slowly open and the horrible Inmate come out to seize him. Already there was a sound of something moving within, and as he gazed, fascinated with terror, a shuddering movement ran over the ivy leaves hanging down from the roof. Then they parted in the middle, and something—he could not in his agony see what—flew out with a whirring sound into his face, and then vanished over his shoulder towards the fields.

Jimbo did not pause a single second to find out what it was, or to reflect that any ordinary thrush would have made just the same sound. The shock it gave to his heart immediately loosened the muscles of his little legs, and he ran for his very life. But before he actually began to run he gave one piercing scream for help, and the person he screamed to was the very person who was unwittingly the cause of his distress. It was as though he knew instinctively that the person who had created for him the terror of the Empty House, with its horrible Inmate, was also the person who could properly banish it, and undo the mischief before it was too late. He shrieked for help to the governess, Miss Ethel Lake.

Of course, there was no answer but the noise of the air whistling in his ears as his feet flew over the road in a cloud of dust; there was no friendly butcher's cart, no baker's boy, or farmer with his dog and gun; the road was deserted. There was not even the beetle or the caterpillar; he was beyond reach of help.

Jimbo ran for his life, but unfortunately he ran in the wrong direction. Instead of going the way he had come, where the Lodge gates were ready to receive him not a quarter of a mile away, he fled in the opposite direction.

It so happened that the lane flanked the field where the cows lived; but cows were nothing compared to a Creature from the Empty House, and even bulls seemed friendly. The boy was over the five-barred gate in a twinkling and half-way across the field before he heard a heavy, thunderous sound behind him. Either the Thing had followed him into the field, or it was the bull. As he raced, he managed to throw a glance over his shoulder and saw a huge, dark mass bearing down upon him at terrific speed. It must be the bull, he reflected—the bull grown to the size of an elephant. And it appeared to him to have two immense black wings that flapped at its sides and helped it forward, making a whirring noise like the arms of a great windmill.

This sight added to his speed, but he could not last very much longer. Already his body ached all over, and the frantic effort to get breath nearly choked him.

There, before him, not so very far away now, was the swinging gate. If only he could get there in time to scramble over into the garden, he would be safe. It seemed almost impossible, and behind him, meanwhile, the sound of the following creature came closer and closer; the ground seemed to tremble; he could almost feel the breath on his neck.

The swinging gate was only twenty yards off; now ten; now only five. Now he had reached it—at last. He stretched out his hands to seize the top bar, and in another moment he would have been safe in the garden and within easy reach of the house. But, before he actually touched the iron rail, a sharp, stinging pain shot across his back;—he drew one final breath as he felt himself being lifted, lifted up into the air. The horns had caught him just behind the shoulders!

There seemed to be no pain after the first shock. He rose high into the air, while the bushes and spiked railing he knew so well sank out of sight beneath him, dwindling curiously in size. At first he thought his head must bump against the sky, but suddenly he stopped rising, and the green earth rushed up as if it would strike him in the face. This meant he was sinking again. The gate and railing flew by underneath him, and the next second he fell with a crash upon the soft grass of the lawn—upon the other side. He had been tossed over the gate into the garden, and the bull could no longer reach him.

Before he became wholly unconscious, a composite picture, vivid in its detail, engraved itself deeply, with exceeding swiftness, line by line, upon the waxen tablets of his mind. In this picture the thrush that had flown out of the ivy, the Empty House itself, and its horrible, pursuing Inmate were all somehow curiously mingled together with the black wings of the bull, and with his own sensation of rushing—flying headlong—through space, as he rose and fell in a curve from the creature's horns.

And behind it he was conscious that the real author of it all was somewhere in the shadowy background, looking on as though to watch the result of her unfortunate mistake. Miss Lake, surely, was not very far away. He associated her with the horror of the Empty House as inevitably as taste and smell join together in the memory of a certain food; and the very last thought in his mind, as he sank away into the blackness of unconsciousness, was a sort of bitter surprise that the governess had not turned up to save him before it was actually too late.

Moreover, a certain sense of disappointment mingled with the terror of the shock; for he was dimly aware that Miss Lake had not acted as worthily as she might have done, and had not played the game as well as might have been expected of her. And, somehow, it didn't all seem quite fair.

CHAPTER IV

ON THE EDGE OF UNCONSCIOUSNESS

Jimbo had fallen on his head. Inside that head lay the mass of highly sensitive matter called the brain, on which were recorded, of course, the impressions of everything that had yet come to him in life. A severe shock, such as he had just sustained, was bound to throw these impressions into confusion and disorder, jumbling them up into new and strange combinations, obliterating some, and exaggerating others. Jimbo himself was helpless in the matter; he could exercise no control over their antics until the doctors had once again reduced them to order; he would have to wander, lost and lonely, through the comparative chaos of disproportioned visions, generally known as the region of delirium, until the doctor, assisted by mother nature, restored him once more to normal consciousness.

For a time everything was a blank, but presently he stirred uneasily in the grass, and the pictures graven on the tablets of his mind began to come back to him line by line.

Yet, with certain changes: the bull, for instance, had so far vanished into the background of his thoughts that it had practically disappeared altogether, and he recalled nothing of it but the wings—the huge, flapping wings. Of the creature to whom the wings belonged he had no recollection beyond that it was very large, and that it was chasing him from the Empty House. The pain in his shoulders had also gone; but what remained with undiminished vividness were the sensations of flight without escape, the breathless race up into the sky, and the swift, tumbling drop again through the air on to the lawn.

This impression of rushing through space—short though the actual distance had been—was the dominating memory. All else was apparently oblivion. He forgot where he came from, and he forgot what he had been doing. The events leading up to the catastrophe, indeed everything connected with his existence previously as "Master James," had entirely vanished; and the slate of memory had been wiped so clean that he had forgotten even his own name!

Jimbo was lying, so to speak, on the edge of unconsciousness, and for a time it seemed uncertain whether he would cross the line into the region of delirium and dreams, or fall back again into his natural world. Terror, assisted by the horns of the black bull, had tossed him into the borderland.

His last scream, however, had reached the ears of the ubiquitous gardener, and help was near at hand. He heard voices that seemed to come from beyond the stars, and was aware that shadowy forms were standing over him and talking in whispers. But it was all very unreal; one minute the voices sounded up in the sky, and the next in his very ears, while the figures moved about, sometimes bending over him, sometimes retreating and melting away like shadows on a shifting screen.

Suddenly a blaze of light flashed upon him, and his eyes flew open; he tumbled back for a moment into his normal world. He wasn't on the grass at all, but was lying upon his own bed in the night nursery. His mother was bending over him with a very white face, and a tall man dressed in black stood beside her, holding some kind of shining instrument in his fingers. A little behind them he saw Nixie, shading a lamp with her hand. Then the white face came close over the pillow, and a voice full of tenderness whispered,

"My darling boy, don't you know me? It's mother! No one will hurt you. Speak to me, if you can, dear."

She stretched out her hands, and Jimbo knew her and made an effort to answer. But it seemed to him as if his whole body had suddenly become a solid mass of iron, and he could control no part of it; his lips and his hands both refused to move. Before he could make a sign that he had understood and was trying to reply, a fierce flame rushed between them and blinded him, his eyes closed, and he dropped back again into utter darkness. The walls flew asunder and the ceiling melted into air, while the bed sank away beneath him, down, down, down into an abyss of shadows. The lamp in Nixie's hands dwindled into a star, and his mother's anxious face became a tiny patch of white in the distance, blurred out of all semblance of a human countenance. For a time the man in black seemed to hover over the bed as it sank, as though he were trying to follow it down; but it, too, presently joined the general enveloping blackness and lost its outline. The pain had blotted out everything, and the return to consciousness had been only momentary.

Not all the doctors in the world could have made things otherwise. Jimbo was off on his travels at last—travels in which the chief incidents were directly traceable to the causes and details of his accident: the terror of the Empty House, the pursuit of its Inmate, the pain of the bull's horns, and, above all, the flight through the air.

For everything in his subsequent adventures found its inspiration in the events described, and a singular parallel ran ever between the Jimbo upon the bed in the night-nursery and the other emancipated Jimbo wandering in the regions of unconsciousness and delirium.

CHAPTER V

INTO THE EMPTY HOUSE

The darkness lasted a long time without a break, and when it lifted all recollection of the bedroom scene had vanished.

Jimbo found himself back again on the grass. The swinging gate was just in front of him, but he did not recognise it; no suggestion of "Express Trains" came back to him as his eyes rested without remembrance upon the bars where he had so often swung, in defiance of orders, with his brothers and sisters. Recollection of his home, family, and previous life he had absolutely none; or at least, it was buried so deeply in his inner consciousness that it amounted to the same thing, and he looked out upon the garden, the gate, and the field beyond as upon an entirely new piece of the world.

The stars, he saw, were nearly all gone, and a very faint light was beginning to spread from the woods beyond the field. The eastern horizon was slowly brightening, and soon the night would be gone. Jimbo was glad of this. He began to be conscious of little thrills of expectation, for with the light surely help would also come. The light always brought relief, and he already felt that strange excitement that comes with the first signs of dawn. In the distance cocks were crowing, horses began to stamp in the barns not far away, and a hundred little stirrings of life ran over the surface of the earth as the light crept slowly up the sky and dropped down again upon the world with its message of coming day.

Of course, help would come by the time the sun was really up, and it was partly this certainty, and partly because he was a little too dazed to realise the seriousness of the situation, that prevented his giving way to a fit of fear and weeping. Yet a feeling of vague terror lay only a little way below the surface, and when, a few moments later, he saw that he was no longer alone, and that an odd-looking figure was creeping towards him from the shrubberies, he sprang to his feet, prepared to run unless it at once showed the most friendly intentions.

This figure seemed to have come from nowhere. Apparently it had risen out of the earth. It was too large to have been concealed by the low shrubberies; yet he had not been aware of its approach, and it had appeared without making any noise. Probably it was friendly, he felt, in spite of its curious shape and the stealthy way it had come. At least, he hoped so; and if he could only have told whether it was a man or an animal he would easily have made up his mind. But the uncertain light, and the way it crouched half-hidden behind the bushes, prevented this. So he stood, poised ready to run, and yet waiting, hoping, indeed expecting every minute a sign of friendliness and help.

In this way the two faced each other silently for some time, until the feeling of terror gradually stole deeper into the boy's heart and began to rob him of full power over his muscles. He wondered if he would be able to run when the time came, and whether he could run fast enough. This was how it first showed itself, this suggestion of insidious fear. Would he be able to keep up the start he had? Would it chase him? Would it run like a man or like an animal, on four legs or on two? He wished he could see more clearly what it was. He still stood his ground pluckily, facing it and waiting, but the fear, once admitted to his mind, was gaining strength, and he began to feel cold and shivery. Then suddenly the tension came to an end. In two strides the figure came up close to his side, and the same second Jimbo was lifted off his feet and borne swiftly away across the field.

He felt quite unable to offer the least resistance, and at the same time he felt a sense of relief that something had happened at last. He was still not sure that the figure was unkind; only its shape filled him with a feeling that was certainly the beginning of real horror. It was the shape of a man, he thought, but of a very large and ill-constructed man; for it certainly had moved on two legs and had caught him up in a pair of tremendously strong arms. But there was something else it had besides arms, for a kind of soft cloak hung all round it and wrapped the boy from head to foot, preventing him seeing his captor properly, and at the same time filling his body with a kind of warm drowsiness that mitigated his active fear and made him rather like the sensation of being carried along so easily and so fast.

But was he being carried? The pace they were going was amazing, and he moved as easily as a sailing boat, and with the same swinging motion. Could it be some animal like a horse after all? Jimbo tried to see more, but found it impossible to free himself from the folds of the enveloping substance, and meanwhile they were swinging forward at what seemed a tremendous pace over fields and ditches, through hedges, and down long lanes.

The odours of earth, and dew-drenched grass, and opening flowers came to him. He heard the birds singing, and felt the cool morning air sting his cheeks as they raced along. There was no jolting or jarring, and the figure seemed to cover the ground as lightly as though it hardly touched the earth. It was certainly not a dream, he was sure of that; but the longer they went on the drowsier he became, and the less he wondered whether the figure was going to help him or to do something dreadful to him. He was now thoroughly afraid, and yet, strange contradiction, he didn't care a bit. Let the figure do what it liked; it was only a sort of nightmare person after all, and might vanish as suddenly as it had arrived.

For a long time they raced forward at this great speed, and then with a bump and a crash they stopped suddenly short, and Jimbo felt himself let down upon the solid earth. He tried to free himself at once from the folds of the clinging substance that enveloped him, but, before he could do so and see what his captor was really like, he heard a door slam and felt himself pushed along what seemed to be the hallways of a house. His eyes were clear now and he could see, but the darkness had come down again so thickly that all he could discover was that the figure was urging him along the floor of a large empty hall, and that they were in a dark and empty building.

Jimbo tried hard to see his captor, but the figure, dim enough in the uncertain light, always managed to hide its face and keep itself bunched up in such a way that he could never see more than a great, dark mass of a body, from which long legs and arms shot out like telescopes, draped in a sort of clinging cloak. Now that the rapid motion through the air had ceased, the boy's drowsiness passed a little, and he began to shiver with fear and to feel that the tears could not be kept back much longer.

Probably in another minute he would have started to run for his life, when a new sound caught his ears and made him listen intently, while a feeling of wonder and delight caught his heart, and made him momentarily forget the figure pushing him forward from behind.

Was it the wind he heard? Or was it the voices of children all singing together very low? It was a gentle, sighing sound that rose and fell with mournful modulations and seemed to come from the very centre of the building; it held, too, a strange, far-away murmur, like the surge of a faint breeze moving in the tree-tops. It might be the wind playing round the walls of the building, or it might be children singing in hushed voices. One minute he thought it was outside the house, and the next he was certain it came from somewhere in the upper part of the building. He glanced up, and fancied for one moment that he saw in the darkness a crowd of little faces peering down at him over the banisters, and that as they disappeared he heard the sound of many little feet moving, and then a door hurriedly closing. But a push from the figure behind that nearly sent him sprawling at the foot of the stairs, prevented his hearing very clearly, and the light was far too dim to let him feel sure of what he had seen.

They passed quickly along deserted corridors and through winding passages. No one seemed about. The interior of the house was chilly, and the keen air nipped. After going up several flights of stairs they stopped at last in front of a door, and before Jimbo had a moment to turn and dash downstairs again past the figure, as he had meant to do, he was pushed violently forward into a room.

The door slammed after him, and he heard the heavy tread of the figure as it went down the staircase again into the bottom of the house. Then he saw that the room was full of light and of small moving beings.

Curiosity and astonishment now for a moment took the place of fear, and Jimbo, with a thumping heart and clenched fists, stood and stared at the scene before him. He stiffened his little legs and leaned against the wall for support, but he felt full of fight in case anything happened, and with wide-open eyes he tried to take in the whole scene at once and be ready for whatever might come.

But there seemed no immediate cause for alarm, and when he realised that the beings in the room were apparently children, and only children, his rather mixed sensations of astonishment and fear gave place to an emotion of overpowering shyness. He became exceedingly embarrassed, for he was surrounded by children of all ages and sizes, staring at him just as hard as he was staring at them.

The children, he began to take in, were all dressed in black; they looked frightened and unhappy; their bodies were thin and their faces very white. There was something else about them he could not quite name, but it inspired him with the same sense of horror that he had felt in the arms of the Figure who had trapped him. For he now realised definitely that he had been trapped; and he also began to realise for the first time that, though he still had the body of a little boy, his way of thinking and judging was sometimes more like that of a grown-up person. The two alternated, and the result was an odd confusion; for sometimes he felt like a child and thought like a man, while at others he felt like a man and thought like a child. Something had gone wrong, very much wrong; and, as he watched this group of silent children facing him, he knew suddenly that what was just beginning to happen to him *had happened to them long, long ago.*

For they looked as if they had been a long, long time in the world, yet their bodies had not kept pace with their minds. Something had happened to stop the growth of the body, while allowing the mind to go on developing. The bodies were not stunted or deformed; they were well-formed, nice little children's bodies, but the minds within them were grown-up, and the incongruity was distressing. All this he suddenly realised in a flash, intuitively, just as though it had been most elaborately explained to him; yet he could not have put the least part of it into words or have explained what he saw and felt to another.

He saw that they had the hands and figures of children, the heads of children, the unlined faces and smooth foreheads of children, but their gestures, and something in their movements, belonged to grown-up people, and the expression of their eyes in meaning and intelligence was the expression of old people and not of children. And the expression in the eyes of every one of them he saw was the expression of terror and of pain. The effect was so singular that he seemed face to face with an entirely new order of creatures: a child's features with a man's eyes; a child's figure with a woman's movements; full-grown souls cramped and cribbed in absurdly inadequate bodies and little, puny frames; the old trying uncouthly to express itself in the young.

The grown-up, old portion of him had been uppermost as he stared and received these impressions, but now suddenly it passed away, and he felt as a little boy again. He glanced quickly down at his own little body in the alpaca knickerbockers and sailor blouse, and then, with a sigh of relief, looked up again at the strange group facing him. So far, at any rate, he had not changed, and there was nothing yet to suggest that he was becoming like them in appearance at least.

With his back against the door he faced the roomful of children who stood there motionless and staring; and as he looked, wild feelings rushed over him and made him tremble. Who was he? Where had he come from? Where in the world had he spent the other years of his life, the forgotten years? There seemed to be no one to whom he could go for comfort, no one to answer questions; and there was such a lot he wanted to ask. He seemed to be so much older, and to know so much more than he ought to have known, and yet to have forgotten so much that he ought not to have forgotten.

His loss of memory, however, was of course only partial. He had forgotten his own identity, and all the people with whom he had so far in life had to do; yet at the same time he was dimly conscious that he had just left all these people, and that some day he would find them again. It was only the surface-layers of memory that had vanished, and these had not vanished for ever, but only sunk down a little below the horizon.

Then, presently, the children began to range themselves in rows between him and the opposite wall, without once taking their horrible, intelligent eyes off him as they moved. He watched them with growing dread, but at last his curiosity became so strong that it overcame everything else, and in a voice that he meant to be very brave, but that sounded hardly above a whisper, he said:

"Who are you? And what's been done to you?"

The answer came at once in a whisper as low as his own, though he could not distinguish who spoke:

"Listen and you shall know. You, too, are now one of us."

Immediately the children began a slow, impish sort of dance before him, moving almost with silent feet over the boards, yet with a sedateness and formality that had none of the unconscious grace of children. And, as they danced, they sang, but in voices so low, that it was more like the mournful sighing of wind among branches than human voices. It was the sound he had already heard outside the building.

"We are the children of the whispering night,
Who live eternally in dreadful fright
Of stories told us in the grey twilight
                    By—*nurserymaids!*

We are the children of a winter's day;
Under our breath we chant this mournful lay;
We dance with phantoms and with shadows play,
                    And have no rest.

We have no joy in any children's game,
For happiness to us is but a name,
Since Terror kissed us with his lips of flame
                    In wicked jest.

We hear the little voices in the wind
Singing of freedom we may never find,
Victims of fate so cruelly unkind,
                    We are unblest,

We hear the little footsteps in the rain
Running to help us, though they run in vain,
Tapping in hundreds on the window-pane
                    In vain behest,

We are the children of the whispering night,
Who dwell unrescued in eternal fright
Of stories told us in the dim twilight
                    By—*nurserymaids!*"

The plaintive song and the dance ceased together, and before Jimbo could find any words to clothe even one of the thoughts that crowded through his mind, he saw them moving towards a door he had not hitherto noticed on the other side of the room. A moment later they had opened it and passed out, sedate, mournful, unhurried; and the boy found that in some way he could not understand the light had gone with them, and he was standing with his back against the wall in almost total darkness.

Once out of the room, no sound followed them, and he crossed over and tried the handle of the door. It was locked. Then he went back and tried the other door; that, too, was locked. He was shut in. There was no longer any doubt as to the Figure's intentions; he was a prisoner, trapped like an animal in a cage.

The only thought in his mind just then was an intense desire for freedom. Whatever happened he must escape. He crossed the floor to the only window in the room; it was without blinds, and he looked out. But instantly he recoiled with a fresh and overpowering sense of helplessness, for it was three storeys from the ground, and down below in the shadows he saw a paved courtyard that rendered jumping utterly out of the question.

He stood for a long time, fighting down the tears, and staring as if his heart would break at the field and trees beyond. A high wall enclosed the yard, but beyond that was freedom and open space. Feelings of loneliness and helplessness, terror and dismay overwhelmed him. His eyes burned and smarted, yet, strange to say, the tears now refused to come and bring him relief. He could only stand there with his elbows on the window-sill, and watch the outline of the trees and hedges grow clearer and clearer as the light drew across the sky, and the moment of sunrise came close.

But when at last he turned back into the room, he saw that he was no longer alone. Crouching against the opposite wall there was a hooded figure steadily watching him.

CHAPTER VI

HIS COMPANION IN PRISON

Shocks of terror, as they increase in number, apparently lessen in effect; the repeated calls made upon Jimbo's soul by the emotions of fear and astonishment had numbed it; otherwise the knowledge that he was locked in the room with this mysterious creature beyond all possibility of escape must have frightened him, as the saying is, out of his skin.

As it was, however, he kept his head in a wonderful manner, and simply stared at the silent intruder as hard as ever he could stare. How in the world it got in was the principal thought in his mind, and after that: what in the world was it?

The dawn must have come very swiftly, or else he had been staring longer than he knew, for just then the sun topped the edge of the world and the window-sill simultaneously, and sent a welcome ray of sunshine into the dingy room. It turned the grey light to silver, and fell full upon the huddled figure crouching against the opposite wall. Jimbo caught his breath, and stared harder than ever.

It was a human figure, the figure, apparently, of a man, sitting crumpled up in a very uncomfortable sort of position on his haunches. It sat perfectly still. A black cloak, with loose sleeves, and a cowl or hood that completely concealed the face, covered it from head to foot. The material of the cloak could not have been very thick, for inside the hood he caught the gleam of eyes as they roamed about the room and followed his movements. But for this glitter of the moving eyes it might have been a figure carved in wood. Was it going to sit there for ever watching him? At first he was afraid it was going to speak; then he was afraid it wasn't. It might rise suddenly and come towards him; yet the thought that it would not move at all was worse still.

In this way the two faced each other for several minutes until, just as the position was becoming simply unbearable, a low whisper ran round the room: "At last! Oh! I've found him at last! " Jimbo was not quite sure of the words, though it was certainly a human voice that had spoken; but, the suspense once broken, the boy could not stand it any longer, and with a rush of desperate courage he found his voice—a very husky one—and moved a step forward.

"Who are you, please, and how *did* you get in?" he ventured with a great effort.

Then he fell back against the wall, amazed at his own daring, and waited with tightlyclenched fists for an answer. But he had not to wait very long, for almost immediately the figure rose awkwardly to its feet, and came over to where he stood. Its manner of moving may best be described as shuffling; and it stretched in front of it a long cloaked arm, on which the sleeve hung, he thought, like clothes on a washing line.

He breathed hard, and waited. Like many other people with strong wills and sensitive nerves, Jimbo was both brave and a coward: he hoped nothing horrid was going to happen, but he was quite ready if it should. Yet, now that the actual moment had come, he had no particular fear, and when he felt the touch of the hand on his shoulder, the words sprang naturally to his lips with a little trembling laugh, more of wonder perhaps than anything else.

"You do look a horrid... *brute*," he was going to say, but at the last moment he changed it to "*thing*," for, with the true intuition of a child, he recognised that the creature inside the cloak was a kind creature and well disposed towards him. "But how did you get in?" he added, looking up bravely into the black visage, "because the doors are both locked on the outside, and I couldn't get out?"

By way of reply the figure shuffled to one side, and, taking the hand from his shoulder, pointed silently to a trap-door in the floor behind him. As he looked, he saw it was being shut down stealthily by some one beneath.

"Hush!" whispered the figure, almost inaudibly. "He's watching!"

"Who's watching?" he cried, curiosity taking the place of every other emotion. "I want to see." He ran forward to the spot where the trap-door now lay flush with the floor, but, before he had gone two steps, the black arms shot out and caught him. He turned, struggling, and in the scuffle that followed the cloak shrouding the figure became disarranged; the hood dropped from the face, and he found himself looking straight into the eyes, not of a man, but of a woman!

"It's you!" he cried. "YOU—!"

A shock ran right through his body from his head to his feet, like a current of electricity, and he caught his breath as though he had been struck. For one brief instant the sinister face of some one who had terrified him in the past came back vividly to his mind, and he shrank away in terror. But it was only for an instant, the twentieth part of an instant. Immediately, before he could even remember the name, recognition passed into darkness and his memory shut down with a snap. He was staring into the face of an utter stranger, about whom he knew nothing and had no feelings particularly one way or another.

"I thought I knew you," he gasped, "but I've forgotten you again—and I thought you were going to be a man, too."

"Jimbo!" cried the other, and in her voice was such unmistakable tenderness and yearning that the boy knew at once beyond doubt that she was his friend, "Jimbo!"

She knelt down on the floor beside him, so that her face was on a level with his, and then opened both her arms to him. But though Jimbo was glad to have found a friend who was going to help him, he felt no particular desire to be embraced, and he stood obstinately where he was with his back to the window.

The morning sunshine fell upon her features and touched the thick coils of her hair with glory. It was not, strictly speaking, a pretty face, but the look of real human tenderness there was very welcome and comforting, and in the kind brown eyes there shone a strange light that was not merely the reflection of the sunlight. The boy felt his heart warm to her as he looked, but her expression puzzled him, and he would not accept the invitation of her arms.

"Won't you come to me?" she said, her arms still outstretched.

"I want to know who you are, and what I'm doing here," he said. "I feel so funny—so old and so young—and all mixed up. I can't make out who I am a bit. What's that funny name you call me?"

"Jimbo is your name," she said softly.

"Then what's *your* name?" he asked quickly.

" My name," she repeated slowly after a pause, "is not—as nice as yours. Besides, you need not know my name—you might dislike it."

"But I must have something to call you," he persisted.

"But if I told you, and you disliked the name, you might dislike *me* too," she said, still hesitating.

Jimbo saw the expression of sadness in her eyes, and it won his confidence though he hardly knew why. He came up closer to her and put his puzzled little face next to hers.

"I like you very much already," he whispered, "and if your name is a horrid one I'll change it for you at once. Please tell me what it is."

She drew the boy to her and gave him a little hug, and he did not resist. For a long time she did not answer. He felt vaguely that something of dreadful importance hung about this revelation of her name. He repeated his question, and at length she replied, speaking in a very low voice, and with her eyes fixed intently upon his face.

"My name," she said, "is Ethel Lake."

"Ethel Lake," he repeated after her. The words sounded somehow familiar to him; surely he had heard that name before. Were not the words associated with something in his past that had been unpleasant? A curious sinking sensation came over him as he heard them.

His companion watched him intently while he repeated the words over to himself several times, as if to make sure he had got them right. There was a moment's hesitation as he slowly went over them once again. Then he turned to her, laughing.

"I like your name, Ethel Lake," he said. "It's a nice name—Miss—Miss— " Again he hesitated, while a little warning tremor ran through his mind, and he wondered for an instant why he said "Miss." But it passed as suddenly as it had come, and he finished the sentence—"Miss Lake, I shall call you." He stared into her eyes as he said it.

"Then you don't remember me at all?" she cried, with a sigh of intense relief. "You've quite forgotten?"

"I never saw you before, did I? How can I remember you? I don't remember any of the things I've forgotten. Are you one of them?"

For reply she caught him to her breast and kissed him. "You precious little boy!" she said. "I'm so glad, oh, so glad!"

"But do you remember *me?*" he asked, sorely puzzled. "Who am I?
Haven't I been born yet, or something funny like that?"

"If you don't remember *me,*" said the other, her face happy with smiles
that had evidently come only just in time to prevent tears, "there's not
much good telling you who *you* are. But your name, if you really want to
know, is—" She hesitated a moment.

"Be quick, Eth—Miss Lake, or you'll forget it again."

She laughed rather bitterly. "Oh, I never forget. I can't!" she said. "I wish
I could. Your name is James Stone, and Jimbo is 'short' for James. Now you
know."

She might just as well have said Bill Sykes for all the boy knew or
remembered.

"What a silly name!" he laughed. "But it can't be my real name, or I
should know it. I never heard it before." After a moment he added, "Am I
an old man? I feel just like one. I suppose I'm grown up—grown up so fast
that I've forgotten what came before—"

"You're not grown up, dear, at least, not exactly—" She glanced down at
his alpaca knickerbockers and brown stockings; and as he followed her
eyes and saw the dirty buttoned-boots there came into his mind some dim
memory of where he had last put them on, and of some one who had
helped him. But it all passed like a swift meteor across the dark night of
his forgetfulness and was lost in mist.

"You mustn't judge by these silly clothes," he laughed. "I shall change
them as soon as I get—as soon as I can find—" he stopped short. No words
came. A feeling of utter loneliness and despair swept suddenly over him,
drenching him from head to foot. He felt lost and friendless, naked, home-
less, cold. He was ever on the brink of regaining a whole lot of knowledge
and experience that he had known once long ago, ever so long ago, but it
always kept just out of his reach. He glanced at Miss Lake, feeling that she
was his only possible comfort in a terrible situation. She met his look and
drew him tenderly towards her.

"Now, listen to me," she said gently, "I've something to tell you—about
myself."

He was all attention in a minute.

"I am a discharged governess," she began, holding her breath when once
the words were out.

"Discharged!" he repeated vaguely. "What's that? What for?"

"For frightening a child. I told a little boy awful stories that weren't true.
They terrified him so much that I was sent away. That's why I'm here now.
It's my punishment. I am a prisoner here until I can find him—and help
him to escape—"

"Oh, I say!" he exclaimed quickly, as though remembering something.
But it passed, and he looked up at her half-bored, half-politely. "Escape
from what?" he asked.

"From here. This is the Empty House I told the stories about; *and you are the little boy I frightened*. Now, at last, I've found you, and am going to save you." She paused, watching him with eyes that never left his face for an instant.

Jimbo was delighted to hear he was going to be rescued, but he felt no interest at all in her story of having frightened a little boy, who was himself. He thought it was very nice of her to take so much trouble, and he told her so, and when he went up and kissed her and thanked her, he saw to his surprise that she was crying. For the life of him he could not understand why a discharged governess whom he met, apparently, for the first time in the Empty House, should weep over him and show him so much affection. But he could think of nothing to say, so he just waited till she had finished.

"You see, if I can save you," she said between her sobs, "it will be all right again, and I shall be forgiven, and shall be able to escape with you. I want you to escape, so that you can get back to life again."

"Oh, then I'm dead, am I?"

"Not exactly dead," she said, drying her eyes with the corner of her black hood. "You've had a funny accident, you know. If your body gets all right, so that you can go back and live in it again, then you're not dead. But if it's so badly injured that you can't work in it any more, then you are dead, and will have to stay dead. You're still joined to the body in a fashion, you see."

He stared and listened, not understanding much. It all bored him. She talked without explaining, he thought. An immense sponge had passed over the slate of the past and wiped it clean beyond recall. He was utterly perplexed.

"How funny you are!" he said vaguely, thinking more of her tears than her explanations.

"Water won't stay in a cracked bottle," she went on, "and you can't stay in a broken body. But they're trying to mend it now, and if we can escape in time you can be an ordinary, happy little boy in the world again."

"Then are you dead, too?" he asked, "or nearly dead?"

"I am out of my body, like you," she answered evasively, after a moment's pause.

He was still looking at her in a dazed sort of way, when she suddenly sprang to her feet and let the hood drop back over her face.

"Hush!" she whispered, "he's listening again."

At the same moment a sound came from beneath the floor on the other side of the room, and Jimbo saw the trap-door being slowly raised above the level of the floor.

"Your number is 102," said a voice that sounded like the rushing of a river.

Instantly the trap-door dropped again, and he heard heavy steps rumbling away into the interior of the house. He looked at his companion and saw her terrified face as she lifted her hood.

"He always blunders along like that," she whispered, bending her head on one side to listen. "He can't see properly in the daylight. He hates sunshine, and usually only goes out after dark." She was white and trembling.

"Is that the person who brought me in here this morning at such a frightful pace?" he asked, bewildered.

She nodded. "He wanted to get in before it was light, so that you couldn't see his face."

"Is he such a fright?" asked the boy, beginning to share her evident feeling of horror.

"He *is* Fright!" she said in an awed whisper. "But never talk about him again unless you can't help it; he always knows when he's being talked about, and he likes it, because it gives him more power."

Jimbo only stared at her without comprehending. Then his mind jumped to something else he wanted badly to have explained, and he asked her about his number, and why he was called No. 102.

"Oh, that's easier," she said, "102 is your number among the Frightened Children; there are 101 of them, and you are the last arrival. Haven't you seen them yet? It is also the temperature of your broken little body lying on the bed in the night nursery at home," she added, though he hardly caught her words, so low were they spoken.

Jimbo then described how the children had sung and danced to him, and went on to ask a hundred questions about them. But Miss Lake would give him very little information, and said he would not have very much to do with them. Most of them had been in the House for years and years—so long that they could probably never escape at all.

"They are all frightened children," she said. "Little ones scared out of their wits by silly people who meant to amuse them with stories, or to frighten them into being well behaved—nursery-maids, elder sisters, and even governesses!"

"And they can never escape?"

"Not unless the people who frightened them come to their rescue and *run the risk of being caught themselves.*"

As she spoke there rose from the depths of the house the sound of muffled voices, children's voices singing faintly together; it rose and fell exactly like the wind, and with as little tune; it was weird and magical, but so utterly mournful that the boy felt the tears start to his eyes. It drifted away, too, just as the wind does over the tops of the trees, dying into the distance; and all became still again.

"It's just like the wind," he said, "and I do love the wind. It makes me feel so sad and so happy. Why is it?"

The governess did not answer.

"How old am I *really?*" he went on. "How can I be so old and so ignorant? I've forgotten such an awful lot of knowledge."

"The fact is—well, perhaps, you won't quite understand—but you're really two ages at once. Sometimes you feel as old as your body, and sometimes as old as your soul. You're still connected with your body; so you get the sensations of both mixed up."

"Then is the body younger than the soul?"

"The soul—that is yourself," she answered, "is, oh, so old, awfully old, as old as the stars, and older. But the body is no older than itself—of course, how could it be?"

"Of course," repeated the boy, who was not listening to a word she said. "How could it be?"

"But it doesn't matter how old you are or how young you feel, as long as you don't hate me for having frightened you," she said after a pause. "That's the chief thing."

He was very, very puzzled. He could not help feeling it had been rather unkind of her to frighten him so badly that he had literally been frightened out of his skin; but he couldn't remember anything about it, and she was taking so much trouble to save him now that he quite forgave her. He nestled up against her, and said of course he liked her, and she stroked his curly head and mumbled a lot of things to herself that he couldn't understand a bit.

But in spite of his new-found friend the feeling of over-mastering loneliness would suddenly rush over him. She might be a protector, but she was not a *real* companion; and he knew that somewhere or other he had left a lot of other *real* companions whom he now missed dreadfully. He longed more than he could say for freedom; he wanted to be able to come and go as he pleased; to play about in a garden somewhere as of old; to wander over soft green lawns among laburnums and sweet-smelling lilac trees, and to be up to all his old tricks and mischief—though he could not remember in detail what they were.

In a word, he wanted to escape; his whole being yearned to escape and be free again; yet here he was a wretched prisoner in a room like a prison-cell, with a sort of monster for a keeper, and a troop of horrible frightened children somewhere else in the house to keep him company. And outside there was only a hard, narrow, paved courtyard with a high wall round it. Oh, it was too terrible to think of, and his heart sank down within him till he felt as if he could do nothing else but cry.

"I shall save you in time," whispered the governess, as though she read his thoughts. "You must be patient, and do what I tell you, and I promise to get you out. Only be brave, and don't ask too many questions. We shall win in the end and escape."

Suddenly he looked up, with quite a new expression in his face. "But I say, Miss Lake, I'm frightfully hungry. I've had nothing to eat since—I can't remember when, but ever so long ago."

"You needn't call me Miss Cake, though," she laughed.

"I suppose it's because I'm so hungry."

"Then you'll call me Miss Lake when you're thirsty, perhaps," she said. " But, anyhow, I'll see what I can get you. Only, you must eat as little as possible. I want you to get very thin. What you feel is not really hunger—it's only a memory of hunger, and you'll soon get used to it."

He stared at her with a very distressful little face as she crossed the room making this new announcement; and just as she disappeared through the trap-door, only her head being visible, she added with great emphasis, "The thinner you get the better; because the thinner you are the lighter you are, and the lighter you are the easier it will be to escape. Remember, the thinner the better—the lighter the better—and don't ask a lot of questions about it."

With that the trap-door closed over her, and Jimbo was left alone with her last strange words ringing in his ears.

CHAPTER VII

THE SPELL OF THE EMPTY HOUSE

It was not long before Jimbo realised that the House, and everything connected with it, spelt for him one message, and one only—a message of fear. From the first day of his imprisonment the forces of his whole being shaped themselves without further ado into one intense, single, concentrated desire to *escape.*

Freedom, escape into the world beyond that terrible high wall, was his only object, and Miss Lake, the governess, as its symbol, was his only hope. He asked a lot of questions and listened to a lot of answers, but all he really cared about was how he was going to escape, and when. All her other explanations were tedious, and he only half-listened to them. His faith in her was absolute, his patience unbounded; she had come to save him, and he knew that before long she would accomplish her end. He felt a blind and perfect confidence. But, meanwhile, his fear of the House, and his horror for the secret Being who meant to keep him prisoner till at length he became one of the troop of Frightened Children, increased by leaps and bounds.

Presently the trap-door creaked again, and the governess reappeared; in her hand was a small white jug and a soup plate.

"Thin gruel and skim milk," she explained, pouring out a substance like paste into the soup plate, and handing him a big wooden spoon.

But Jimbo's hunger had somehow vanished.

"It wasn't real hunger," she told him, "but only a sort of memory of being hungry. They're trying to feed your broken body now in the night-nursery, and so you feel a sort of ghostly hunger here even though you're out of the body."

"It's easily satisfied, at any rate," he said, looking at the paste in the soup plate.

"So one actually eats or drinks here—"

"But I'm solid," he said, "am I not?"

"People always think they're solid everywhere," she laughed. "It's only a question of degree; solidity *here* means a different thing to solidity *there.*"

"I can get thinner though, can't I?" he asked, thinking of her remark about escape being easier the lighter he grew.

She assured him there would be no difficulty about that, and after replying evasively to a lot more questions, she gathered up the dishes and once more disappeared through the trapdoor.

Jimbo watched her going down the ladder into the black gulf below, and wondered greatly where she went to and what she did down there; but on these points the governess had refused to satisfy his curiosity, and every time she appeared or disappeared the atmosphere of mystery came and went with her.

As he stared, wondering, a sound suddenly made itself heard behind him, and on turning quickly round he saw to his great surprise that the door into the passage was open. This was more than he could resist, and in another minute, with mingled feelings of dread and delight, he was out in the passage.

When he was first brought to the house, two hours before, it had been too dark to see properly, but now the sun was high in the heavens, and the light still increasing. He crept cautiously to the head of the stairs and peered over into the well of the house. It was still too dark to make things out clearly; but, as he looked, he thought something moved among the shadows below, and for a moment his heart stood still with fear. A large grey face seemed to be staring up at him out of the gloom. He clutched the banisters and felt as if he hardly had strength enough in his legs to get back to the room he had just left; but almost immediately the terror passed, for he saw that the face resolved itself into the mingling of light and shadow, and the features, after all, were of his own creation. He went on slowly and stealthily down the staircase.

It was certainly an empty house. There were no carpets; the passages were cold and draughty; the paper curled from the damp walls, leaving ugly discoloured patches about; cobwebs hung in many places from the ceiling, the windows were more or less broken, and all were coated so thickly with dirt that the rain had traced little furrows from top to bottom. Shadows hung about everywhere, and Jimbo thought every minute he saw moving figures; but the figures always resolved themselves into nothing when he looked closely.

He began to wonder how far it was safe to go, and why the governess had arranged for the door to be opened—for he felt sure it was she who had done this, and that it was all right for him to come out. Fright, she had said, was never about in the daylight. But, at the same time, something warned him to be ready at a moment's notice to turn and dash up the stairs again to the room where he was at least comparatively safe.

So he moved along very quietly and very cautiously. He passed many rooms with the doors open—all empty and silent; some of them had tables and chairs, but no sign of occupation; the grates were black and empty, the walls blank, the windows unshuttered. Everywhere was only silence and shadows; there was no sign of the frightened children, or of where they lived; no trace of another staircase leading to the region where the governess went when she disappeared down the ladder through the trapdoor—only hushed, listening, cold silence, and shadows that seemed for ever shifting from place to place as he moved past them. This illusion of people peering at him from corners, and behind doors just ajar, was very strong; yet whenever he turned his head to face them, lo, they were gone, and the shadows rushed in to fill their places.

The spell of the Empty House was weaving itself slowly and surely about his heart.

Yet he went on pluckily, full of a dreadful curiosity, continuing his search, and at length, after passing through another gloomy passage, he was in the act of crossing the threshold of an open door leading out into the courtyard, when he stopped short and clutched the doorposts with both hands.

Some one had laughed!

He turned, trying to look in every direction at once, but there was no sign of any living being. Yet the sound was close beside him; he could still hear it ringing in his ears—a mocking sort of laugh, in a harsh, guttural voice. The blood froze in his veins, and he hardly knew which way to turn, when another voice sounded, and his terror disappeared as if by magic.

It was Miss Lake's voice calling to him over the banisters at the top of the house, and its tone was so cheerful that all his courage came back in a twinkling.

"Go out into the yard," she called, "and play in the sunshine. But don't stay too long."

Jimbo answered "All right" in a rather feeble little voice, and went on down the passage and out into the yard.

The June sunshine lay hot and still over the paved court, and he looked up into the blue sky overhead. As he looked at the high wall that closed it in on three sides, he realised more than ever that he was caught in a monstrous trap from which there could be no ordinary means of escape. He could never climb over such a wall even with a ladder. He walked out a little way and noticed the rank weeds growing in patches in the corners; decay and neglect left everywhere their dismal signs; the yard, in spite of the sunlight, seemed as gloomy and cheerless as the house itself.

In one corner stood several little white upright stones, each about three feet high; there seemed to be some writing on them, and he was in the act of going nearer to inspect, when a window opened and he heard some one calling to him in a loud, excited whisper:

"Hst! Come in, Jimbo, at once. Quick! Run for your life!"

He glanced up, quaking with fear, and saw the governess leaning out of the open window. At another window, a little beyond her, he thought a number of white little faces pressed against the glass, but he had no time to look more closely, for something in Miss Lake's voice made him turn and run into the house and up the stairs as though Fright himself were close at his heels. He flew up the three flights, and found the governess coming out on the top landing to meet him. She caught him in her arms and dashed back into the room, as if there was not a moment to be lost, slamming the door behind her.

"How in the world did you get out?" she gasped, breathless as himself almost, and pale with alarm. "Another second and He'd have had you—!"

"I found the door open—"

"He opened it on purpose," she whispered, looking quickly round the room. "He meant you to go out."

"But you called to me to play in the yard," he said. "I heard you. So of course I thought it was safe."

"No," she declared, "I never called to you. That wasn't my voice. That was one of his tricks. I only this minute found the door open and you gone. Oh, Jimbo, that was a narrow escape; you must never go out of this room till— till I tell you. And never believe any of these voices you hear—you'll hear lots of them, saying all sorts of things—but unless you *see* me, don't believe it's my voice."

Jimbo promised. He was very frightened; but she would not tell him any more, saying it would only make it more difficult to escape if he knew too much in advance. He told her about the laugh, and the gravestones, and the faces at the other window, but she would not tell him what he wanted to know, and at last he gave up asking. A very deep impression had been made on his mind, however, and he began to realise, more than he had hitherto done, the horror of his prison and the power of his dreadful keeper.

But when he began to look about him again, he noticed that there was a new thing in the room. The governess had left him, and was bending over it. She was doing something very busily indeed. He asked her what it was.

"I'm making your bed," she said.

It was, indeed, a bed, and he felt as he looked at it that there was something very familiar and friendly about the yellow framework and the little brass knobs.

"I brought it up just now," she explained. "But it's not for sleeping in. It's only for you to lie down on, and also partly to deceive Him."

"Why not for sleeping?"

"There's no sleeping at all here," she went on calmly.

"Why not?"

"You can't sleep out of your body," she laughed.

"Why not?" he asked again.

"Your body goes to sleep, but you don't," she explained.

"Oh, I see." His head was whirling. "And my body—my real body—"

"Is lying asleep—unconscious they call it—in the night-nursery at home. It's sound asleep. That's why you're here. It can't wake up till you go back to it, and you can't go back to it till you escape—even if it's ready for you before then. The bed is only for you to rest on, for you can *rest* though you can't *sleep*."

Jimbo stared blankly at the governess for some minutes. He was debating something in his mind, something very important, and just then it was his Older Self, and not the child, that was uppermost. Apparently it was soon decided, for he walked sedately up to her and said very gravely, with her serious eyes fixed on his face,

"Miss Lake, are you *really* Miss Lake?"

"Of course I am."

"You're not a trick of His, like the voices, I mean?"

"No, Jimbo, I am really Miss Lake, the discharged governess who frightened you." There was profound anxiety in every word.

Jimbo waited a minute, still looking steadily into her eyes. Then he put out his hand cautiously and touched her. He rose a little on tiptoe to be on a level with her face, taking a fold of her cloak in each hand. The soul-knowledge was in his eyes just then, not the mere curiosity of the child.

"And are you—*dead?*" he asked, sinking his voice to a whisper.

For a moment the woman's eyes wavered. She turned white and tried to move away; but the boy seized her hand and peered more closely into her face.

"I mean, if we escape and I get back into my body," he whispered, "will you get back into yours too?"

The governess made no reply, and shifted uneasily on her feet. But the boy would not let her go.

"Please answer," he urged, still in a whisper.

"Jimbo, what funny questions you ask!" she said at last, in a husky voice, but trying to smile.

"But I want to know," he said. "I must know. I believe you are giving up everything just to save me—*everything;* and I don't want to be saved unless you come too. Tell me!"

The colour came back to her cheeks a little, and her eyes grew moist. Again she tried to slip past him, but he prevented her.

"You must tell me," he urged; "I would rather stay here with you than escape back into my body and leave you behind."

Jimbo knew it was his Older Self speaking—the freed spirit rather than the broken body—but he felt the strain was very great; he could not keep it up much longer; any minute he might slip back into the child again, and lose interest, and be unequal to the task he now saw so clearly before him.

"Quick!" he cried in a louder voice. "Tell me! You are giving up everything to save me, aren't you? And if I escape you will be left alone—quick, answer me! Oh, be quick, I'm slipping back—"

Already he felt his thoughts becoming confused again, as the spirit merged back into the child; in another minute the boy would usurp the older self.

"You see," began the governess at length, speaking very gently and sadly, "I am bound to make amends whatever happens. I must atone—"

But already he found it hard to follow.

"Atone," he asked, "what does '*atone*' mean?" He moved back a step, and glanced about the room. The moment of concentration had passed without bearing fruit; his thoughts began to wander again like a child's. "Anyhow, we shall escape together when the chance comes, shan't we?" he said.

"Yes, darling, we shall," she said in a broken voice. "And if you do what I tell you, it will come very soon, I hope." She drew him towards her and kissed him, and though he didn't respond very heartily, he felt he liked it, and was sure that she was good, and meant to do the best possible for him.

Jimbo asked nothing more for some time; he turned to the bed where he found a mattress and a blanket, but no sheets, and sat down on the edge and waited. The governess was standing by the window looking out; her back was turned to him. He heard an occasional deep sigh come from her, but he was too busy now with his own sensations to trouble much about her. Looking past her he saw the sea of green leaves dancing lazily in the sunshine. Something seemed to beckon him from beyond the high wall, and he longed to go out and play in the shade of the elms and hawthorns; for the horror of the Empty House was closing in upon him steadily but surely, and he longed for escape into a bright, unhaunted atmosphere, more than anything else in the whole world.

His thoughts ran on and on in this vein, till presently he noticed that the governess was moving about the room. She crossed over and tried first one door and then the other; both were fastened. Next she lifted the trap-door and peered down into the black hole below. That, too, apparently was satisfactory. Then she came over to the bedside on tiptoe.

"Jimbo, I've got something very important to ask you," she began.

"All right," he said, full of curiosity.

"You must answer me very exactly. Everything depends on it."

"I will."

She took another long look round the room, and then, in a still lower whisper, bent over him, and asked:

"Have you any pain?"

"Where?" he asked, remembering to be exact.

"Anywhere."

He thought a moment.

"None, thank you."

"None at all—anywhere?" she insisted.

"None at all—anywhere," he said with decision.

She seemed disappointed.

"Never mind; it's a little soon yet, perhaps," she said. "We must have patience. It will come in time."

"But I don't want any pain," he said, rather ruefully.

"You can't escape till it comes."

"I don't understand a bit what you mean." He began to feel alarmed at the notion of escape and pain going together.

"You'll understand later, though," she said soothingly, "and it won't hurt *very* much. The sooner the pain comes, the sooner we can try to escape. Nowhere can there be escape without it."

And with that she left him, disappearing without another word into the hole below the trap, and leaving him, disconsolate yet excited, alone in the room.

CHAPTER VIII

THE GALLERY OF
ANCIENT MEMORIES

With every one, of course, the measurement of time depends largely
upon the state of the emotions, but in Jimbo's case it was curiously exaggerated. This may have been because he had no standard of memory by
which to test the succession of minutes; but, whatever it was, the hours
passed very quickly, and the evening shadows were already darkening the
room when at length he got up from the mattress and went over to the
window.

Outside the high elms were growing dim; soon the stars would be out in
the sky. The afternoon had passed away like magic, and the governess still
left him alone; he could not quite understand why she went away for such
long periods.

The darkness came down very swiftly, and it was night almost before he
knew it. Yet he felt no drowsiness, no desire to yawn and get under sheets
and blankets; sleep was evidently out of the question, and the hours
slipped away so rapidly that it made little difference whether he sat up all
night or whether he slept.

It was his first night in the Empty House, and he wondered how many
more he would spend there before escape came. He stood at the window,
peering out into the growing darkness and thinking long, long thoughts.
Below him yawned the black gulf of the yard, and the outline of the
enclosing wall was only just visible, but beyond the elms rose far into the
sky, and he could hear the wind singing softly in their branches. The
sound was very sweet; it suggested freedom, and the flight of birds, and all
that was wild and unrestrained. The wind could never really be a prisoner; its voice sang of open spaces and unbounded distances, of flying clouds
and mountains, of mighty woods and dancing waves; above all, of wings—
free, swift, and unconquerable wings.

But this rushing song of wind among the leaves made him feel too sad
to listen long, and he lay down upon the bed again, still thinking, thinking.

The house was utterly still. Not a thing stirred within its walls. He felt
lonely, and began to long for the companionship of the governess; he
would have called aloud for her to come only he was afraid to break the
appalling silence. He wondered where she was all this time and how she
spent the long, dark hours of the sleepless nights. Were all these things
really true that she told him? Was he actually out of his body, and was his
name really Jimbo? His thoughts kept groping backwards, ever seeking the

other companions he had lost; but, like a piece of stretched elastic too short to reach its object, they always came back with a snap just when he seemed on the point of finding them. He wanted these companions very badly indeed, but the struggling of his memory was painful, and he could not keep the effort up for very long at one time.

The effort once relaxed, however, his thoughts wandered freely where they would; and there rose before his mind's eye dim suggestions of memories far more distant—ghostly scenes and faces that passed before him in endless succession, but always faded away before he could properly seize and name then.

This memory, so stubborn as regards quite recent events, began to play strange tricks with him. It carried him away into a Past so remote that he could not connect it with himself at all, and it was like dreaming of scenes and events that had happened to some one else; yet, all the time, he knew quite well those things had happened to him, and to none else. It was the memory of the soul asserting itself now that the clamour of the body was low. It was an underground river coming to the surface, for odd minutes, here and there, showing its waters to the stars just long enough to catch their ghostly reflections before it rolled away underground again.

Yet, swift and transitory as they were, these glimpses brought in their train sensations that were too powerful ever to have troubled his child-mind in its present body. They stirred in him the strong emotions, the ecstasies, the terrors, the yearnings of a much more distant past; whispering to him, could he but have understood, of an infinitely deeper layer of memories and experiences which, now released from the burden of the immediate years, strove to awaken into life again. The soul in that little body covered with alpaca knickerbockers and a sailor blouse seemed suddenly to have access to a storehouse of knowledge that must have taken centuries, rather than a few short years, to acquire.

It was all very queer. The feeling of tremendous age grew mysteriously over him. He realised that he had been wandering for ages. He had been to the stars and also to the deeps; he had roamed over strange mountains far away from cities or inhabited places of the earth, and had lived by streams whose waves were silvered by moonlight dropping softly through whispering palm branches....

Some of these ghostly memories brought him sensations of keenest happiness—icy, silver, radiant; others swept through his heart like a cold wave, leaving behind a feeling of unutterable woe, and a sense of loneliness that almost made him cry aloud. And there came Voices too—Voices that had slept so long in the inner kingdoms of silence that they failed to rouse in him the very slightest emotion of recognition....

Worn out at length with the surging of these strange hosts through him, he got up and went to the open window again. The night was very dark and warm, but the stars had disappeared, and there was the hush and the faint odour of coming rain in the air. He smelt leaves and the earth and the moist things of the ground, the wonderful perfume of the life of the soil.

The wind had dropped; all was silent as the grave; the leaves of the elm trees were motionless; no bird or insect raised its voice; everything slept; he alone was watchful, awake. Leaning over the window-sill, his thoughts searched for the governess, and he wondered anew where she was spending the dark hours. She, too, he felt sure, was wakeful somewhere, watching with him, plotting their escape together, and always mindful of his safety....

His reverie was suddenly interrupted by the flight of an immense night-bird dropping through the air just above his head. He sprang back into the room with a startled cry, as it rushed past in the darkness with a great swishing of wings. The size of the creature filled him with awe; it was so close that the wind it made lifted the hair on his forehead, and he could almost feel the feathers brush his cheeks. He strained his eyes to try and follow it, but the shadows were too deep and he could see nothing; only in the distance, growing every moment fainter, he could hear the noise of big wings threshing the air. He waited a little, wondering if another bird would follow it, or if it would presently return to its perch on the roof; and then his thoughts passed on to uncertain memories of other big birds—hawks, owls, eagles—that he had seen somewhere in places now beyond the reach of distinct recollections....

Soon the light began to dawn in the east, and he made out the shape of the elm trees and the dreadful prison wall; and with the first real touch of morning light he heard a familiar creaking sound in the room behind him, and saw the black hood of the governess rising through the trap-door in the floor.

"But you've left me alone all night!" he said at once reproachfully, as she kissed him.

"On purpose," she answered. "He'd get suspicious if I stayed too much with you. It's different in the daytime, when he can't see properly."

"Where's he been all night, then?" asked the boy.

"Last night he was out most of the time—hunting—"

"Hunting!" he repeated, with excitement. "Hunting what?"

"Children—frightened children," she replied, lowering her voice. "That's how he found you."

It was a horrible thought—Fright hunting for victims to bring to his dreadful prison—and Jimbo shivered as he heard it.

"And how did you get on all this time?" she asked, hurriedly changing the subject.

"I've been remembering, that is half-remembering, an awful lot of things, and feeling, oh, so old. I never want to remember anything again," he said wearily.

"You'll forget quick enough when you get back into your body, and have only the body-memories," she said, with a sigh that he did not understand. "But, now tell me," she added, in a more serious voice, "have you had any pain yet?"

He shook his head. She stepped up beside him.

"None *there?*" she asked, touching him lightly just behind the shoulder blades.

Jimbo jumped as if he had been shot, and uttered a piercing yell.

"That hurts!" he screamed.

"I'm so glad," cried the governess. "That's the pains coming at last." Her face was beaming.

"Coming!" he echoed, "I think they've *come*. But if they hurt as much as that, I think I'd rather not escape," he added ruefully.

"The pain won't last more than a minute," she said calmly. "You must be brave and stand it. There's no escape without pain—from anything."

"If there's no other way," he said pluckily, " I'll try,—but—"

"You see," she went on, rather absently, "at this very moment the doctor is probing the wounds in your back where the horns went in—"

But he was not listening. Her explanations always made him want either to cry or to laugh. This time he laughed, and the governess joined him, while they sat on the edge of the bed together talking of many things. He did not understand all her explanations, but it comforted him to hear them. So long as somebody understood, no matter who, he felt it was all right.

In this way several days and nights passed quickly away. The pains were apparently no nearer, but as Miss Lake showed no particular anxiety about their non-arrival, he waited patiently too, dreading the moment, yet also looking forward to it exceedingly.

During the day the governess spent most of the time in the room with him; but at night, when he was alone, the darkness became enchanted, the room haunted, and he passed into the long, long Gallery of Ancient Memories.

CHAPTER IX

THE MEANS OF ESCAPE

A week passed, and Jimbo began to wonder if the pains he so much dreaded, yet so eagerly longed for, were ever coming at all. The imprisonment was telling upon him, and he grew very thin, and consequently very light.

The nights, though he spent them alone, were easily borne, for he was then intensely occupied, and the time passed swiftly; the moment it was dark he stepped into the Gallery of Memories, and in a little while passed into a new world of wonder and delight. But the daytime seemed always long. He stood for hours by the window watching the trees and the sky, and what he saw always set painful currents running through his blood—unsatisfied longings, yearnings, and immense desires he never could understand.

The white clouds on their swift journeys took with them something from his heart every time he looked upon them; they melted into air and blue sky, and lo! that "something" carne back to him charged with all the wild freedom and magic of open spaces, distance, and rushing winds.

But the change was close at hand.

One night, as he was standing by the open window listening to the drip of the rain, he felt a deadly weakness steal over him; the strength went out of his legs. First he turned hot, and then he turned cold; clammy perspiration broke out all over him, and it was all he could do to crawl across the room and throw himself on to the bed. But no sooner was he stretched out on the mattress than the feelings passed entirely, and left behind them an intoxicating sense of strength and lightness. His muscles became like steel springs; his bones were strong as iron and light as cork; a wonderful vigour had suddenly come into him, and he felt as if he had just stepped from a dungeon into fresh air. He was ready to face anything in the world.

But, before he had time to realise the full enjoyment of these new sensations, a stinging, blinding pain shot suddenly through his right shoulder as if a red-hot iron had pierced to the very bone. He screamed out in agony; though, even while he screamed, the pain passed. Then the same thing happened in his other shoulder. It shot through his back with equal swiftness, and was gone, leaving him lying on the bed trembling with pain. But the instant it was gone the delightful sensations of strength and lightness returned, and he felt as if his whole body were charged with some new and potent force.

The pains had come at last! Jimbo had no notion how they could possibly be connected with escape, but Miss Lake—his kind and faithful friend, Miss Lake—had said that no escape was possible without them; and had promised that they should be brief. And this was true, for the entire episode had not taken a minute of time.

"ESCAPE, ESCAPE!"—the words rushed through him like a flame of fire. Out of this dreadful Empty House, into the open spaces; beyond the prison wall; out where the wind and the rain could touch him; where he could feel the grass beneath his feet, and could see the whole sky at once, instead of this narrow strip through the window. His thoughts flew to the stars and the clouds....

But a strange humming of voices interrupted his flight of imagination, and he saw that the room was suddenly full of moving figures. They were passing before him with silent footsteps, across the window from door to door. How they had come in, or how they went out, he never knew; but his heart stood still for an instant as he recognised the mournful figures of the Frightened Children filing before him in a slow procession. They were singing—though it sounded more like a chorus of whispering than actual singing—and as they moved past with the measured steps of their sorrowful dance, he caught the words of the song he had heard them sing when he first came into the house:—

"We hear the little voices in the wind
Singing of freedom we may never find."

Jimbo put his fingers into his ears, but still the sound came through. He heard the words almost as if they were inside himself—his own thoughts singing:—

"We hear the little footsteps in the rain
Running to help us, though they run in vain,
Tapping in hundreds on the window-pane."

The horrible procession filed past and melted away near the door. They were gone as mysteriously as they had come, and almost before he realised it.

He sprang from the bed and tried the doors; both were locked. How in the world had the children got in and out? The whispering voices rose again on the night air, and this time he was sure they came from outside. He ran to the open window and thrust his head out cautiously. Sure enough, the procession was moving slowly, still with the steps of that impish dance across the courtyard stones. He could just make out the slow waving arms, the thin bodies, and the white little faces as they passed on silent feet through the darkness, and again a fragment of the song rose to his ears as he watched, and filled him with an overpowering sadness:—

"We have no joy in any children's game,
For happiness to us is but a name,
Since Terror kissed us with his lips of flame."

Then he noticed that the group was growing smaller. Already the numbers were less. Somewhere, over there in the dark corner of the yard, the children disappeared, though it was too dark to see precisely how or where.

"We dance with phantoms, and with shadows play," rose to his ears.

Suddenly he remembered the little white upright stones he had seen in that corner of the yard, and understood. One by one they vanished just behind those stones.

Jimbo shivered, and drew his head in. He did not like those upright stones; they made him uncomfortable and afraid. Now, however, the last child had disappeared and the song had ceased. He realised what his fate would be if the escape were not successful; he would become one of this band of Frightened Children; dwelling somewhere behind the upright stones; a terrified shadow, waiting in vain to be rescued, waiting perhaps for ever and ever. The thought brought the tears to his eyes, but he somehow managed to choke them down. He knew it was the young portion of him only that felt afraid—the body; the older self could not feel fear, and had nothing to do with tears.

He lay down again upon the hard mattress and waited; and soon afterwards the first crimson streaks of sunrise appeared behind the high elms, and rooks began to caw and shake their wings in the upper branches. A little later the governess came in.

Before he could move out of the way—for he disliked being embraced—she had her arms round his neck, and was covering him with kisses. He saw tears in her eyes.

"You darling Jimbo!" she cried, "they've come at last."

"How do you know?" he asked, surprised at her knowledge and puzzled by her display of emotion.

"I heard you scream to begin with. Besides, I've been watching."

"Watching?"

"Yes, and listening too, every night, every single night. You've hardly been a minute out of my sight," she added.

"I think it's awfully good of you," he said doubtfully, "but—"

A flood of questions followed—about the upright stones, the shadowy children, where she spent the night "watching him," and a hundred other things besides. But he got little satisfaction out of her. He never did when it was Jimbo, the child, that asked; and he remained Jimbo, the child, all that day. She only told him that all was going well. The pains had come; he had grown nice and thin, and light; the children had come into his room as a hint that he belonged to their band, and other things had happened about which she would tell him later. The crisis was close at hand. That was all he could get out of her.

"It won't be long now," she said excitedly. "They'll come to-night, I expect."

"What will come to-night?" he asked, with querulous wonder.

"Wait and see!" was all the answer he got. "Wait and see!"

She told him to lie quietly on the bed and to have patience.

With asking questions, and thinking, and wondering, the day passed very quickly. With the lengthening shadows his excitement began to grow. Presently Miss Lake took her departure and went off to her unknown and mysterious abode; he watched her disappear through the floor with mingled feelings, wondering what would have happened before he saw her again. She gave him a long, last look as she sank away below the boards, but it was a look that brought him fresh courage, and her eyes were happy and smiling.

Tingling already with expectancy he got into the bed and lay down, his brain alive with one word—ESCAPE.

From where he lay he saw the stars in the narrow strip of sky; he heard the wind whispering in the branches; he even smelt the perfume of the fields and hedges-grass, flowers, dew, and the sweet earth—the odours of freedom.

The governess had, for some reason she refused to explain, taken his blouse away with her. For a long time he puzzled over this, seeking reasons and finding none. But, while in the act of stroking his bare arms, the pains of the night before suddenly returned to both shoulders at once. Fire seemed to run down his back, splitting his bones apart, and then passed even more quickly than before, leaving him with the same wonderful sensations of lightness and strength. He felt inclined to shout and run and jump, and it was only the memory of the governess's earnest caution to "lie quietly" that prevented his new emotions passing into acts.

With very great effort he lay still all night long; and it was only when the room at last began to get light again that he turned on his side, preparatory to getting up.

But there was something new—something different! He rested on his elbow, waiting. Something had happened to him. Cautiously he sat on the edge of the bed, and stretched out one foot and touched the floor. Excitement ran through him like a wave. There was a great change, a tremendous change; for as he stepped out gingerly on to the floor *something followed him from the bed*. It clung to his back; it touched both shoulders at once; it stroked his ribs, and tickled the skin of his arms.

Half frightened, he brought the other leg over, and stood boldly upright on both feet. But the weight still clung to his back. He looked over his shoulder. Yes! it was trailing after him from the bed; it was fan-shaped, and brilliant in colour. He put out a hand and touched it; it was soft and glossy; then he took it deliberately between his fingers; it was smooth as velvet, and had numerous tiny ribs running along it.

Seizing it at last with all his courage, he pulled it forward in front of him for a better view, only to discover that it would not come out beyond a certain distance, and seemed to have got caught somehow between his shoulders—just where the pains had been. A second pull, more vigorous than the first, showed that it was not caught, but *fastened* to his skin; it divided itself, moreover, into two portions, one half coming from each shoulder.

"I do believe they're feathers!" he exclaimed, his eyes almost popping out of his head.

Then, with a sudden flash of comprehension, he saw it all, and understood. They were, indeed, feathers; but they were something more than feathers merely. *They were wings!*

Jimbo caught his breath and stared in silence. He felt dazed. Then bit by bit the fragments of the weird mosaic fell into their proper places, and he began to understand. Escape was to be by flight. It filled him with such a whirlwind of delight and excitement that he could scarcely keep from screaming aloud.

Lost in wonder, he took a step forward, and watched with bulging eyes how the wings followed him, their tips trailing along the floor. They were a beautiful deep red, and hung down close and warm beside his body; glossy, sleek, magical. And when, later, the sun burst into the room and turned their colour into living flame, he could not resist the temptation to kiss them. He seized them, and rubbed their soft surfaces over his face. Such colours he had never seen before, and he wanted to be sure that they really belonged to him and were intended for actual use.

Slowly, without using his hands, he raised them into the air. The effort was a perfectly easy muscular effort from the shoulders that came naturally, though he did not quite understand how he accomplished it. The wings rose in a fine, graceful sweep, curving over his head till the tips of the feathers met, touching the walls as they rose, and almost reaching to the ceiling.

He gave a howl of delight, for this sight was more than he could manage without some outlet for his pent-up emotion; and at the same moment the trap-door shot open, and the governess came into the room with such a bang and a clatter that Jimbo knew at once her excitement was as great as his own. In her hands she carried the blouse she had taken away the night before. She held it out to him without a word. Her eyes were shining like electric lamps. In less than a second he had slipped his wings through the neatly-made slits, but before he could practise them again, Miss Lake rushed over to him, her face radiant with happiness.

"Jimbo! My darling Jimbo!" she cried—and then stopped short, apparently unable to express her emotion.

The next instant he was enveloped, wings and all, in a warm confusion of kisses, congratulations and folds of hood.

When they became disentangled again the governess went down on her knees and made a careful examination; she pulled the wings out to their full extent and found that they stretched about four feet and a half from tip to tip.

"They *are* beauties!" she exclaimed enthusiastically, "and full grown and strong. I'm not surprised they took so long coming."

"Long!" he echoed, "I thought they came awfully quickly."

"Not half so quickly as they'll go," she interrupted; adding, when she saw his expression of dismay, "I mean, you'll fly like the wind with them."

Jimbo was simply breathless with excitement. He wanted to jump out of the window and escape at once. The blue sky and the sunshine and the white flying clouds sent him an irresistible invitation. He could not wait a minute longer.

"Quick," he cried, "I can't wait! They may go again. Show me how to use them. Oh! do show me."

"I'll show you everything in tine," she answered. There was something in her voice that made him pause in his excitement. He looked at her in silence for some minutes.

"But how are *you* going to escape?" he asked at length. "You haven't got"—he stopped short.

The governess stepped back a few paces from him. She threw back the hood from her face. Then she lifted the long black cloak that hung like a cassock almost to her ankles and had always enveloped her hitherto.

Jimbo stared. Falling from her shoulders, and folding over her hips, he saw long red feathers clinging to her; and when he dashed forward to touch them with his hands, he found they were just as sleek and smooth and glossy as his own.

"And you never told me all this time?" he gasped.

"It was safer not," she said. "You'd have been stroking and feeling your shoulders the whole time, and the wings might never have come at all."

She spread out her wings as she spoke to their full extent; they were nearly six feet across, and the deep crimson on the under side was so exquisite, gleaming in the sunlight, that Jimbo ran in and nestled beneath the feathers, tickling his checks with the fluffy surface and running his fingers with childish delight along the slender red quills.

"You precious child," she said, tenderly folding her wings round him and kissing the top of his head. "Always remember that I really love you; no matter what happens, remember that, and I'll save you."

"And we shall escape together?" he asked, submitting for once to the caresses with a good grace.

"We shall escape from the Empty House together," she replied evasively. "How far we can go after that depends—on you."

"On me?"

"If you love me enough—as I love you, Jimbo—we can never separate again, because love ties us together for ever. Only," she added, " it must be mutual."

"I love you very much," he said, puzzled a little. "Of course I do."

"If you've really forgiven me for being the cause of your coming here," she said, " we can always be together, but—"

"I don't remember, but I've forgiven you—that *other you*—long ago," he said simply. "If you hadn't brought me here, I should never have met you."

"That's not real forgiveness—quite," she sighed, half to herself.

But Jimbo could not follow this sort of conversation for long; he was too anxious to try his wings for one thing.

"Is it *very* difficult to use them?" he asked.

"Try," she said.

He stood in the centre of the floor and raised them again and again. They swept up easily, meeting over his head, and the air whistled musically through them. Evidently, they had their proper muscles, for it was no great effort, and when he folded them again by his side they fell into natural curves over his arms as if they had been there all his life. The sound of the feathers threshing the air filled him with delight and made him think of the big night-bird that had flown past the window during the night. He told the governess about it, and she burst out laughing.

"I was that big bird!" she said.

"You!"

"I perched on the roof every night to watch over you. I flew down that time because I was afraid you were trying to climb out of the window."

This was indeed a proof of devotion, and Jimbo felt that he could never doubt her again; and when she went on to tell him about his wings and how to use them he listened with his very best attention and tried hard to learn and understand.

"The great difficulty is that you can't practise properly," she explained. "There's no room in here, and yet you can't get out till you *fly* out. It's the first swoop that decides all. You have to drop straight out of this window, and if you use the wings properly they will carry you in a single swoop over the wall and right up into the sky."

"But if I miss—?"

"You can't miss," she said with decision, "but, if you did, you would be a prisoner here for ever. HE would catch you in the yard and tear your wings off. It is just as well that you should know this at once."

Jimbo shuddered as he heard her.

"When can we try?" he asked anxiously.

"Very soon now. The muscles must harden first, and that takes a little time. You must practise flapping your wings until you can do it easily four hundred times a minute. When you can do that it will be time for the first start. You must keep your head steady and not get giddy; the novelty of the motion—the ground rushing up into your face and the whistling of the wind—are apt to confuse at first, but it soon passes, and you must have confidence. I can only help you up to a certain point; the rest depends on you."

"And the first jump?"

"You'll have to make that by yourself," she said; "but you'll do it all right. You're very light, and won't go too near the ground. You see, we're like bats, and cannot rise from the earth. We can only fly by dropping from a height, and that's what makes the first plunge rather trying. But you won't fall," she added, "and remember, I shall always be within reach."

"You're awfully kind to me," said Jimbo, feeling his little soul more than ever invaded by the force of her unselfish care. "I promise you I'll do my best." He climbed on to her knee and stared into her anxious face.

"Then you are beginning to love me a little, aren't you?" she asked softly, putting her arms round him.

"Yes," he said decidedly. "I love you very much already."

Four hundred times a minute sounded a very great deal of wing-flapping; but Jimbo practised eagerly, and though at first he could only manage about twice a second, or one hundred and twenty times a minute, he found this increased very soon to a great deal more, and before long he was able to do the full four hundred, though only for a few minutes at a time.

He stuck to it pluckily, getting stronger every day. The governess encouraged him as much as possible, but there was very little room for her while he was at work, and he found the best way to practise was at night when she was out of the way. She told him that a large bird moved its wings about four times a second, two up-strokes and two down-strokes; but a small bird like a partridge moved its wings so rapidly it was impossible for the eye to distinguish or count the strokes. A middle course of four hundred suited his own case best, and he bent all his energies to acquire it.

He also learned that the convex outside curve of wings allowed the wind to escape over them, while the under side, being concave, held every breath. Thus the upward stroke did not simply counterbalance the downward and keep him stationary. Moreover, she showed him how the feathers under-lapped each other so that the downward stroke pressed them closely together to hold the wind, whereas in the upward stroke they opened and separated, letting the air slip easily through them, thus offering less resistance to the atmosphere.

By the end of a week Jimbo had practised so hard that he could keep himself off the floor in mid-air for half an hour at a time, and even then without feeling any great fatigue. His excitement became intense; and, meanwhile, in his body on the nursery bed, though he did not know it, the fever was reaching its crisis. He could think of nothing else but the joys of flying, and what the first, awful plunge would be like, and when Miss Lake came up to him one afternoon and whispered something in his ear, he was so wildly happy that he hugged her for several minutes without the slightest coaxing.

"It's bright and clear," she explained, "and Fright will not come after us, for he fears the light, and can only fly on dark and gloomy nights."

"So we can start—?" he stammered joyfully.

"To-night," she answered, "for our first practice-flight."

CHAPTER X

THE PLUNGE

To enter the world of wings is to enter a new state of existence. The apparent loss of weight; the ability to attain full speed in a few seconds, and to stop suddenly in a headlong rush without fear of collapse; the power to steer instantly in any direction by merely changing the angle of the body; the altered and enormous view of the green world below—looking down upon forests, seas and clouds; the easy voluptuous rhythm of rising and falling in long, swinging undulations; and a hundred other things that simply defy description and can be appreciated only by actual experience, these are some of the delights of the new world of wings and flying. And the fearful joy of very high speed, especially when the exhilaration of escape is added to it, means a condition little short of real ecstasy.

Yet Jimbo's first flight, the governess had been careful to tell him, could not be the flight of final escape; for, even if the wings proved equal to a prolonged effort, escape was impossible until there was somewhere safe to escape to. So it was understood that the practice flights might be long, or might be short; the important thing, meanwhile, was to learn to fly as well as possible. For skilled flying is very different to mere headlong rushing, and both courage and perseverance are necessary to acquire it.

With rare common sense Miss Lake had said very little about the possibility of failure. Having warned him about the importance of not falling, she had then stopped, and the power of suggestion had been allowed to work only in the right direction of certain success. While the boy knew that the first plunge from the window would be a moment fraught with the highest danger, his mind only recognised the mere off-chance of falling and being caught. He felt confidence in himself, and by so much, therefore, were the chances of disaster lessened.

For the rest of the afternoon Jimbo saw nothing of his faithful companion; he spent the time practising and resting, and when weary of everything else, he went to the window and indulged in thrilling calculations about the exact height from the ground. A drop of three storeys into a paved courtyard with a monster waiting to catch him, and a high wall too close to allow a proper swing, was an alarming matter from any point of view. Fortunately, his mind dwelt more on the delight of prospective flight and freedom than on the chances of being caught.

The yard lay hot and naked in the afternoon glare and the enclosing wall had never looked more formidable; but from his lofty perch Jimbo could see beyond into soft hayfields and smiling meadows, yellow with cowslips and buttercups. Everything that flew he watched with absorbing interest:

swift blackbirds, whistling as they went, and crows, their wings purple in the sunshine. The song of the larks, invisible in the sea of blue air sent a thrill of happiness through him—he, too, might soon know something of that glad music—and even the stately flight of the butterflies, which occasionally ventured over into the yard, stirred anticipation in him of joys to come.

The day waned slowly. The butterflies vanished; the rooks sailed homewards through the sunset; the wind dropped away, and the shadows of the high elms lengthened gradually and fell across the window.

The mysterious hour of the dusk, when the standard of reality changes and other worlds come close and listen, began to work its subtle spell upon his soul. Imperceptibly the shadows deepened as the veil of night drew silently across the sky. A gentle breathing filled the air; trees and fields were composing themselves to sleep; stars were peeping; wings were being folded.

But the boy's wings, trembling with life to the very tips of their long feathers, these were not being folded. Charged with excitement, like himself, they were gathering all their forces for the supreme effort of their first journey out into the open spaces where they might touch the secret sources of their own magical life.

For a long, long time he waited; but at last the trap-door lifted and Miss Lake appeared above the floor. The moment she stood in the room he noticed that her wings came through two little slits in her gown and folded down close to the body. They almost touched the ground.

"Hush!" she whispered, holding up a warning finger.

She came over on tiptoe and they began to talk in low whispers.

"He's on the watch; we must speak very quietly. We couldn't have a better night for it. The wind's in the south and the moon won't be up till we're well on our way."

Now that the actual moment was so near the boy felt something of fear steal over him. The night seemed so vast and terrible all of a sudden—like an immense black ocean with no friendly islands where they could fold their wings and rest.

"Don't waste your strength thinking," whispered the governess. "When the time comes, act quickly, that's all!"

She went over to the window and peered out cautiously, after a while beckoning the child to join her.

"He is there," she murmured in his ear. Jimbo could only make out an indistinct shadowy object crouching under the wall, and he was not even positive of that.

"Does he know we're going?" he asked in an awed whisper.

"He's there on the chance," she muttered, drawing back into the room. "When there's a possibility of any one getting frightened he's bound to be lurking about somewhere near. That's Fright all over. But he can't hurt you," she added, "because you're not going to get frightened. Besides, he can only fly when it's dark; and to-night we shall have the moon."

"I'm not afraid," declared the boy in spite of a rather fluttering heart.

"Are you ready?" was all she said.

At last, then, the moment had come. It was actually beside him, waiting, full of mystery and wonder, with alarm not far behind. The sun was buried below the horizon of the world, and the dusk had deepened into night. Stars were shining overhead; the leaves were motionless; not a breath stirred; the earth was silent and waiting.

"Yes, I'm ready," he whispered, almost inaudibly.

"Then listen," she said, "and I'll tell you exactly what to do: Jump upwards from the window ledge as high as you can, and the moment you begin to drop, open your wings and strike with all your might. You'll rise at once. The thing to remember is to *rise as quickly as possible,* because the wall prevents a long, easy, sweeping rise; and, whatever happens, you must clear that wall!"

"I shan't touch the ground then?" asked a faint little voice.

"Of course not! You'll get near it, but the moment you use your wings you'll stop sinking, and rise up, up, up, ever so quickly."

"And where to?"

"To me. You'll see me waiting for you above the trees. Steering will come naturally; it's quite easy."

Jimbo was already shaking with excitement. He could not help it. And he knew, in spite of all Miss Lake's care, that fright was waiting in the yard to catch him if he fell, or sank too near the ground.

"I'll go first," added the governess, "and the moment you see that I've cleared the wall you must jump after me. Only do not keep me waiting!"

The girl stood for a minute in silence, arranging her wings. Her fingers were trembling a little. Suddenly she drew the boy to her and kissed him passionately.

"Be brave!" she whispered, looking searchingly into his eyes, "and strike hard—you can't possibly fail."

In another minute she was climbing out of the window. For one second he saw her standing on the narrow ledge with black space at her feet; the next, without even a cry, she sprang out into the darkness, and was gone.

Jimbo caught his breath and ran up to see. She dropped like a stone, turning over sideways in the air, and then at once her wings opened on both sides and she righted. The darkness swallowed her up for a moment so that he could not see clearly, and only heard the threshing of the huge feathers; but it was easy to tell from the sound that she was rising.

Then suddenly a black form cleared the wall and rose swiftly in a magnificent sweep into the sky, and he saw her outlined darkly against the stars above the high elm tree. She was safe. Now it was his turn.

"Act quickly! Don't think!" rang in his ears. If only he could do it all as quickly as she had done it. But insidious fear had been working all the time below the surface, and his refusal to recognise it could not prevent it weakening his muscles and checking his power of decision. Fortunately something of his Older Self came to the rescue. The emotions of fear, excitement, and intense anticipation combined to call up the powers of his deeper being: the boy trembled horribly, but the old, experienced part of him sang with joy.

Cautiously he began to climb out on to the window-sill; first one foot and then the other hung over the edge. He sat there, staring down into black space beneath.

For a minute he hesitated; despair rushed over him in a wave; he could never take that awful jump into emptiness and darkness. It was impossible. Better be a prisoner for ever than risk so fearful a plunge. He felt cold, weak, frightened, and made a half-movement back into the room. The wings caught somehow between his legs and nearly flung him headlong into the yard.

"Jimbo! I'm waiting for you!" came at that moment in a faint cry from the stars, and the sound gave him just the impetus he needed before it was too late. He could not disappoint her—his faithful friend. Such a thing was impossible.

He stood upright on the ledge, his hands clutching the window-sash behind, balancing as best he could. He clenched his fists, drew a deep, long breath, and jumped upwards and forwards into the air.

Up rushed the darkness with a shriek; the air whistled in his ears; he dropped at fearful speed into nothingness.

At first everything was forgotten—wings, instructions, warnings, and all. He even forgot to open his wings at all, and in another second he would have been dashed upon the hard paving-stones of the courtyard where his great enemy lay waiting to seize him.

But just in the nick of time he remembered, and the long hours of practice bore fruit. Out flew the great red wings in a tremendous sweep on both sides of him, and he began to strike with every atom of strength he possessed. He had dropped to within six feet of the ground; but at once the strokes began to tell, and oh, magical sensation! he felt himself rising easily, lightly, swiftly.

A very slight effort of those big wings would have been sufficient to lift him out of danger, but in his terror and excitement he quite miscalculated their power, and in a single moment he was far out of reach of the dangerous yard and anything it contained. But the mad rush of it all made his head swim; he felt dizzy and confused, and, instead of clearing the wall, he landed on the top of it and clung to the crumbling coping with hands and feet, panting and breathless.

The dizziness was only momentary, however. In less than a minute he was on his feet and in the act of taking his second leap into space. This time it came more easily. He dropped, and the field swung up to meet him. Soon the powerful strokes of his wings drove him at great speed upwards, and he bounded ever higher towards the stars.

Overhead, the governess hovered like an immense bird, and as he rose up he caught the sound of her wings beating the air, while far beneath him, he heard with a shudder a voice like the rushing of a great river. It made him increase his pace, and in another minute he found himself among the little whirlwinds that raced about from the beating of Miss Lake's great wings.

"Well done!" cried the delighted governess. "Safe at last! Now we can fly to our heart's content!"

Jimbo flew up alongside, and together they dashed forward into the night.

CHAPTER XI

THE FIRST FLIGHT

There was not much talking at first. The stress of conflicting emotions was so fierce that the words choked themselves in his throat, and the desire for utterance found its only vent in hard breathing.

The intoxication of rapid motion carried him away headlong in more senses than one. At first he felt as if he never would be able to keep up; then it seemed as if he never would get down again. For with wings it is almost easier to rise than to fall, and a first flight is, before anything else, a series of vivid and audacious surprises.

For a long time Jimbo was so dizzy with excitement and the novelty of the sensation that he forgot his deliverer altogether.

And what a flight it was! Instead of the steady race of the carrier pigeon, or of the rooks homeward bound at evening, it was the see-saw motion of the wren's swinging journey across the lawn; only heavier, faster, and with more terrific impetus. Up and down, each time with a rise and fall of twenty feet, he careered, whistling through the summer night; at the drop of each curve, so low that the scents of dewy grass rose into his face; at the crest of it, so high that the trees and hedges often became mere blots upon the dark surface of the earth.

The fields rushed by beneath him; the white roads flashed past like streaks of snow. Sometimes he shot across sheets of water and felt the cooler air strike his cheeks; sometimes over sheltered meadows, where the sunshine had slept all day and the air was still soft and warm; on and on, as easily as rain dropping from the sky, or wind rushing earthwards from between the clouds. Everything flew past him at an astonishing rate— everything but the bright stars that gazed calmly down overhead; and when he looked up and saw their steadfastness it helped to keep within bounds the fine alarm of this first excursion into the great vault of the sky.

"Gently, child!" gasped Miss Lake behind him. "We shall never keep it up at this rate."

"Oh! but it's so wonderful," he cried, drawing in the air loudly between his teeth, and shaking his wings rapidly like a hawk before it drops.

The pace slackened a little and the girl drew up alongside. For some time they flew forward together in silence.

They had been skirting the edge of a wood, when suddenly the trees fell away and Jimbo gave a scream and rose fifty feet into the air with a single bound. Straight in front of him loomed an immense, glaring disc that seemed to swim suddenly up into the sky above the trees. It hung there before his eyes and dazzled him.

"It's only the moon," cried Miss Lake from below.

Jimbo dropped through the air to her side again with a gasp.

"I thought it was a big hole in the sky with fire rushing through," he explained breathlessly.

The boy stared, full of wonder and delight, at the huge flaming circle that seemed to fill half the heavens in front of him.

"Look out!" cried the governess, seizing his hand.

Whish! whew! whirr! A large bird whipped past them like some winged imp of darkness, vanishing among the trees far below. There would certainly have been a collision but for the girl's energetic interference.

"You must be on the look-out for these night-birds," she said. "They fly so unexpectedly, and, of course, they don't see us properly. Telegraph wires and church steeples are bad too, but then we shan't fly over cities much. Keep a good height, it's safer."

They altered their course a little, flying at a different angle, so that the moon no longer dazzled them. Steering came quite easily by turning the body, and Jimbo still led the way, the governess following heavily and with a mighty business of wings and flapping.

It was something to remember, the glory of that first journey through the air. Sixty miles an hour, and scarcely an effort! Skimming the long ridges of the hills and rushing through the pure air of mountain tops; threading the star-beams; bathing themselves from head to foot in an ocean of cool, clean wind; swimming on the waves of viewless currents— currents warmed only by the magic of the stars, and kissed by the burning lips of flying meteors.

Far below them the moonlight touched the fields with silver and the murmur of the world rose faintly to their ears, trembling, as it were, with the inarticulate dreams of millions. Everywhere about them thrilled and sang the unspeakable power of the night. The mystery of its great heart seemed laid bare before them.

It was like a wonder-journey in some Eastern fairy tale. Sometimes they passed through zones of sweeter air, perfumed with the scents of hay and wild flowers; at others, the fresh, damp odour of ploughed fields rose up to them; or, again, they went spinning over leagues of forest where the tree-tops stretched beneath them like the surface of a wide, green sea, sleeping in the moonlight. And, when they crossed open water, the stars shone reflected in their faces; and all the while the wings, whirring and purring softly through the darkness, made pleasant music in their ears.

"I'm tired," declared Jimbo presently.

"Then we'll go down and rest," said his breathless companion with obvious relief.

She showed him how to spread his wings, sloping them towards the ground at an angle that enabled him to shoot rapidly downwards, at the same time regulating his speed by the least upward tilt. It was a glorious motion, without effort or difficulty, though the pace made it hard to keep the eyes open, and breathing became almost impossible. They dropped to within ten feet of the ground and then shot forward again.

But, while the boy was watching his companion's movements, and paying too little attention to his own, there rose suddenly before him out of the ground a huge, bulky form of something—and crash—he flew headlong into it.

Fortunately it was only a haystack; but the speed at which he was going lodged his head several inches under the thatch, whence he projected horizontally into space, feet, arms, and wings gyrating furiously. The governess, however, soon released him with much laughter, and they dropped down into the fallen hay upon the ground with no worse result than a shaking.

"Oh, what a lark!" he cried, shaking the hay out of his feathers, and rubbing his head rather ruefully.

"Except that larks are hardly night-birds," she laughed, helping him.

They settled with folded wings in the shadow of the haystack; and the big moon, peeping over the edge at them, must have surely wondered to see such a funny couple, in such a place, and at such an hour.

"Mushrooms!" suddenly cried the governess, springing to her feet. "There must be lots in this field. I'll go and pick some while you rest a bit."

Off she went, trapesing over the field in the moonlight, her wings folded behind her, her body bent a little forward as she searched, and in ten minutes she came back with her hands full. That was undoubtedly the time to enjoy mushrooms at their best, with the dew still on their tight little jackets, and the sweet odour of the earth caught under their umbrellas.

Soon they were all eaten, and Jimbo was lying back on a pile of hay, his shoulders against the wall of the stack, and his wings gathered round him like a warm cloak of feathers. He felt cosy and dozy, full of mushrooms inside and covered with hay and feathers outside. The governess had once told him that a sort of open-air sleep sometimes came after a long flight. It was, of course, not a real sleep, but a state in which everything about oneself is forgotten; no dreams, no movement, no falling asleep and waking up in the ordinary sense, but a condition of deep repose in which recuperation is very great.

Jimbo would have been greatly interested, no doubt, to know that his real body on the bed had also just been receiving nourishment, and was now passing into a quieter and less feverish condition. The parallel always held true between himself and his body in the nursery, but he could not know anything about this, and only supposed that it was this open-air sleep that he felt gently stealing over him.

It brought at first strange thoughts that carried him far away to other woods and other fields. While Miss Lake sat beside him eating her mushrooms, his mind was drawn off to some other little folk. But it was always stopped just short of them. He never could quite see their faces. Yet his thoughts continued their search, groping in the darkness; he felt sure he ought to be sharing his adventures with these other little persons, whoever they were; they ought to have been sitting beside him at that very moment, eating mushrooms, combing their wings, comparing the length of their feathers, and snuggling with him into the warm hay.

But they obstinately hovered just outside his memory, and refused to come in and surrender themselves. He could not remember who they were, and his yearnings went unsatisfied up to the stars, as yearnings generally do, while his thoughts returned weary from their search and he yielded to the seductions of the soothing open-air sleep.

The moon, meanwhile, rose higher and higher, drawing a silver veil over the stars. Upon the field the dews of midnight fell silently. A faint mist rose from the ground and covered the flowers in their dim seclusion under the hedgerows. The hours slipped away swiftly.

"Come on, Jimbo, boy!" cried the governess at length. "The moon's below the hills, and we must be off!"

The boy turned and stared sleepily at her from his nest in the hay.

"We've got miles to go. Remember the speed we came at!" she explained, getting up and arranging her wings.

Jumbo got up slowly and shook himself.

"I've been miles away," he said dreamily, "miles and miles. But I'm ready to start at once."

They looked about for a raised place to jump from. A ladder stood against the other side of the haystack. The governess climbed up it and Jimbo followed her drowsily. Hand in hand they sprang into the air from the edge of the thatched roof, and their wings spread out like sails to catch the wind. It smote their faces pleasantly as they plunged downwards and forwards, and the exhilarating rush of cool air banished from the boy's head the last vestige of the open-air sleep.

"We must keep up a good pace," cried the governess, taking a stream and the hedge beyond in a single sweep. "There's a light in the east already."

As she spoke a dog howled in a farmyard beneath them, and she shot upwards as though lifted by a sudden gust of wind.

"We're too low," she shouted from above. "That dog felt us near. Come up higher. It's easier flying, and we've got a long way to go."

Jimbo followed her up till they were several hundred feet above the earth and the keen air stung their cheeks. Then she led him still higher, till the meadows looked like the squares on a chess-board and the trees were like little toy shrubs. Here they rushed along at a tremendous speed, too fast to speak, their wings churning the air into little whirlwinds and eddies as they passed, whizzing, whistling, tearing through space.

The fields, however, were still dim in the shadows that precede the dawn, and the stars only just beginning to fade, when they saw the dark outline of the Empty House below them, and began carefully to descend. Soon they topped the high clues, startling the rooks into noisy cawing, and then, skimming the wall, sailed stealthily on outspread wings across the yard.

Cautiously dropping down to the level of the window, they crawled over the sill into the dark little room, and folded their wings.

CHAPTER XII

THE FOUR WINDS

The governess left the boy to his own reflections almost immediately. He spent the hours thinking and resting; going over again in his mind every incident of the great flight and wondering when the real, final escape would come, and what it would be like. Thus, between the two states of excitement he forgot for a while that he was still a prisoner, and the spell of horror was lifted temporarily from his heart.

The day passed quickly, and when Miss Lake appeared in the evening, she announced that there could be no flying again that night, and that she wished instead to give him important instruction for the future. There were rules, and signs, and times which he must learn carefully. The time might come when he would have to fly alone, and he must be prepared for everything.

"And the first thing I have to tell you," she said, exactly as though it was a school-room," is: *Never fly over the sea.* Our kind of wings quickly absorb the finer particles of water and get clogged and heavy over the sea. You finally cannot resist the drawing power of the water, and you will be dragged down and drowned. So be very careful! When you are flying high it is often difficult to know where the land ends and the sea begins, especially on moonless nights. But you can always be certain of one thing: if there are no sounds below you—hoofs, voices, wheels, wind in trees—you are over the sea."

"Yes," said the child, listening with great attention. "And what else?"

"The next thing is: *Don't fly too high.* Though we fly like birds, remember we are not birds, and we can fly where they can't. We can fly in the ether—"

"Where's that?" he interrupted, half afraid of the sound.

She stooped and kissed him, laughing at his fear.

"There is nothing to be frightened about," she explained. "The air gets lighter and lighter as you go higher, till at last it stops altogether. Then there's only ether left. Birds can't fly in ether because it's too thin. We can, because—"

"Is that why it was good for me to get lighter and thinner?" he interrupted again in a puzzled voice.

"Partly, yes."

"And what happens in the ether, please?" It still frightened him a little.

"Nothing—except that if you fly too high you reach a point where the earth ceases to hold you, and you dash off into space. Weight leaves you then, and the wings move without effort. Faster and faster you rush upwards, till you lose all control of your movements, and then—"

Miss Lake hesitated a moment.

"And then—?" asked the fascinated child.

"You may never come down again," she said slowly. "You may be sucked into anything that happens to come your way—a comet, or a shooting star, or the moon."

"I should like a shooting star best," observed the boy, deeply interested. "The moon frightens me, I think. It looks so dreadfully clean."

"You won't like any of them when the time comes," she laughed. " No one ever gets out again who once gets in. But you'll never be caught that way after what I've told you," she added, with decision.

"I shall never want to fly as high as that, I'm sure," said Jimbo. "And now, please, what comes next?"

The next thing, she went on to explain, was the *weather*, which, to all flying creatures, was of the utmost importance. Before starting for a flight he must always carefully consider the state of the sky, and the direction in which he wished to go. For this purpose he must master the meaning and character of the Four Winds and be able to recognise them in a moment.

"Once you know these," she said, "you cannot possibly go wrong. To make it easier, I've put each Wind into a little simple rhyme, for you."

"I'm listening," he said eagerly.

"The North Wind is one of the worst and most dangerous, because it blows so much faster than you think. It's taken you ten miles before you think you've gone two. In starting with a North Wind, always fly *against* it; then it will bring you home easily. If you fly *with* it, you may be swept so far that the day will catch you before you can get home; and then you're as good as lost. Even birds fly warily when this wind is about. It has no lulls or resting-places in it; it blows steadily on and on, and conquers everything it comes against—everything except the mountains."

"And its rhyme?" asked Jimbo, all ears.

> "It will show you the joy of the birds, my child,
> You shall know their terrible bliss;
> It will teach you to hide, when the night is wild,
> From the storm's too passionate kiss.
>> For the Wind of the North
>> Is a volleying forth
>> That will lift you with springs
>> In the heart of your wings,
>> And may sweep you away
>> To the edge of the day.
> So, beware of the Wind of the North, my child,
> Fly not with the Wind of the North!"

"I think I like him all the same," said Jimbo. "But I'll remember always to fly against him."

"The East Wind is worse still, for it hurts," continued the governess. "It stings and cuts. It's like the breath of an ice-creature; it brings hail and sleet and cold rain that beat down wings and blind the eyes. Like the North Wind, too, it is dreadfully swift and full of little whirlwinds, and may easily carry you into the light of day that would prove your destruction. Avoid it always; no hiding-place is safe from it. This is the rhyme:

> It will teach you the secrets the eagles know
> Of the tempests' and whirlwinds' birth;
> And the magical weaving of rain and snow
> As they fall from the sky to the earth.
>> But an Easterly wind
>> Is for ever unkind;
>> It will torture and twist you
>> And never assist you,
>> But will drive you with might
>> To the verge of the night.
> So, beware of the wind of the East, my child,
> Fly not with the Wind of the East."

"The West Wind is really a very nice and jolly wind in itself," she went on, "but it's dangerous for a special reason: *it will carry you out to sea.* The Empty House is only a few miles from the coast, and a strong West Wind would take you there almost before you had time to get down to earth again. And there's no use struggling against a really steady West Wind, for it's simply tireless. Luckily, it rarely blows at night, but goes down with the sun. Often, too, it blows hard to the coast, and then drops suddenly, leaving you among the fogs and mists of the sea."

"Rather a nice, exciting sort of wind though," remarked Jimbo, waiting for the rhyme.

> "So, at last, you shall know from their lightest breath
> To which heaven each wind belongs;
> And shall master their meaning for life or death
> By the shout of their splendid songs.
>> Yet the Wind of the West
>> Is a wind unblest;
>> It is lifted and kissed
>> By the spirits of mist;
>> It will clasp you and flee
>> To the wastes of the sea.
> So, beware of the Wind of the West, my child,
> Fly not with the Wind of the West!"

"A jolly wind," observed Jimbo again. "But that doesn't leave much over to fly with," he added sadly. "They all seem dangerous or cruel."

"Yes," she laughed, "and so they are till you can master them—then they're kind. The only one that's really always safe and kind is the Wind of the South. It's a sweet, gentle wind, beloved of all that flies, and you can't possibly mistake it. You can tell it at once by the murmuring way it stirs the grasses and the tops of the trees. Its taste is soft and sweet in the mouth like wine, and there's always a faint perfume about it like gardens in summer. It is the joy of this wind that makes all flying things sing. With a South Wind you can go anywhere and no harm can come to you."

"Dear old South Wind," cried Jimbo, rubbing his hands with delight. "I hope it will blow soon."

"Its rhyme is very easy, too, though you will always be able to tell it without that," she added.

> "For this is the favourite Wind of all,
>   Beloved of the stars and night;
> In the rustle of leaves you shall hear it call
>   To the passionate joys of flight.
> It will carry you forth in its wonderful hair
>   To the far-away courts of the sky,
> And the breath of its lips is a murmuring prayer
>   For the safety of all who fly.
>   For the Wind of the South
>   Is like wine in the mouth,
>   With its whispering showers
>   And perfume of flowers,
>   When it falls like a sigh
>   From the heart of the sky."

"Oh!" interrupted Jimbo, rubbing his hands, "that *is* nice. That's *my* wind!"

> "It will bear you aloft
>   with a pressure so soft
>   That you hardly shall guess
>   Whose the gentle caress."

"Hooray!" he cried again.

> "It's the kindest of weathers
>   For our red feathers,
>   And blows open the way
>   To the Gardens of Play.
> So, fly out with the Wind of the South, my child,
> With the wonderful Wind of the South."

"Oh, I love the South Wind already," he shouted, clapping his hands again. "I hope it will blow very, *very* soon."

"It may be rising even now," answered the governess, leading him to the window. But, as they gazed at the summer landscape lying in the fading light of the sunset, all was still and resting. The air was hushed, the leaves motionless. There was no call just then to flight from among the tree-tops, and he went back into the room disappointed.

"But why can't we escape at once?" he asked again, after he had given his promise to remember all she had told him, and to be extra careful if he ever went out flying alone.

"Jimbo, dear, I've told you before, it's because your body isn't ready for you yet," she answered patiently. "There's hardly any circulation in it, and if you forced your way back now the shock might stop your heart beating altogether. Then you'd be really dead, and escape would be impossible."

The boy sat on the edge of the bed staring intently at her while she spoke. Something clutched at his heart. He felt his Older Self, with its greater knowledge, rising up out of the depths within him. The child struggled with the old soul for possession.

"Have *you* got any circulation?" he asked abruptly at length. "I mean, has your heart stopped beating?"

But the smile called up by his words froze on her lips. She crossed to the window and stood with her back to the fading light, avoiding his eyes.

"My case, Jimbo, is a little different from yours," she said presently. "The important thing is to make certain about your escape. Never mind about me."

"But escape without you is nothing," he said, the Older Self now wholly in possession. "I simply wouldn't go. I'd rather stay here—with you."

The governess made no reply, but she turned her back to the room and leaned out of the window. Jimbo fancied he heard a sob. He felt a great big heart swelling up within his little body, and he crossed over beside her. For some minutes they stood there in silence, watching the stars that were already shining faintly in the sky.

"Whatever happens," he said, nestling against her, "I shan't go from here without you. Remember that!"

He was going to say a lot more, but somehow or other, when she stooped over to kiss his head—he hardly came up to her shoulder—it all ran suddenly out of his mind, and the little child dropped back into possession again. The tide of his thoughts that seemed about to rise, fast and furious, sank away completely, leaving his mind a clean-washed slate without a single image; and presently, without any more words, the governess left him and went through the trap-door into the silence and mystery of the house below.

Several hours later, about the middle of the night, there came over him a most disagreeable sensation of nausea and dizziness. The ground rose and fell beneath his feet, the walls swam about sideways, and the ceiling slid off into the air. It only lasted a few minutes, however, and Jimbo knew from what she had told him that it was the Flying Sickness which always followed the first long flight,

But, about the same time, another little body, lying in a night-nursery bed, was being convulsed with a similar attack; and the sickness of the little prisoner in the Empty House had its parallel, strangely enough, in the half-tenanted body miles away in a different world.

CHAPTER XIII

PLEASURES OF FLIGHT

Since the night when Jimbo had nearly fallen into the yard and risked capture, Fright, the horrible owner of the house, had kept himself well out of the way, and had allowed himself to be neither seen nor heard.

But the boy was not foolish enough to fall into the other trap, and imagine, therefore, that He did not know what was going on. Jimbo felt quite sure that He was only waiting his chance; and the governess's avoidance of the subject tended to confirm this supposition.

"He's disappeared somewhere and taken the children with him," she declared when he questioned her. "And now you know almost as much as I do."

"But not quite!" he laughed mischievously.

"Enough, though," she replied. "We want all our energy for escape when it comes. Don't bother about anything else for the moment."

During the day, when he was alone, his thoughts and fancies often terrified him; but at night, when he was rushing through the heavens, the intense delight of flying drove all minor emotions out of his consciousness, and he even forgot his one great desire—to escape. One night, however, something happened that brought it back more keenly than ever.

He had been out flying alone, but had not gone far when he noticed that an easterly wind had begun to rise and was blowing steadily behind him. With the recent instructions fresh in his head, he thought it wiser to turn homewards rather than fight his way back later against a really strong wind from this quarter. Flying low along the surface of the fields so as to avoid its full force, he suddenly rose up with a good sweep and settled on the top of the wall enclosing the yard.

The moonlight lay bright over everything. His approach had been very quiet. He was just about to sail across to the window when something caught his eye, and he hesitated a moment, and stared.

Something was moving at the other end of the courtyard.

It seemed to him that the moonlight suddenly grew pale and ghastly; the night air turned chilly; shivers began to run up and down his back.

He folded his wings and watched.

At the end of the yard he saw several figures moving busily to and fro in the shadow of the wall. They were very small; but close beside them all the time stood a much larger figure which seemed to be directing their movements. There was no need to look twice; it was impossible to mistake these terrible little people and their hideous overseer. Horror rushed over the boy, and a wild scream was out in the night before he could possibly prevent it. At the same moment a cloud passed over the face of the moon and the yard was shrouded in darkness.

A minute later the cloud passed off; but while it was still too dark to see clearly, Jimbo was conscious of a rushing, whispering sound in the air, and something went past him at a tremendous pace into the sky. The wind stirred his hair as it passed, and a moment later he heard voices far away in the distance—up in the sky or within the house he could not tell—singing mournfully the song he now knew so well:—

We dance with phantoms and with shadows play.

But when he looked down at the yard he saw that it was deserted, and the corner by the little upright stones lay in the clear moonlight, empty of figures, large or small.

Shivering with fright, he flew across to the window ledge, and almost tumbled into the arms of the governess who was standing close inside.

"What's the matter, child?" she asked in a voice that trembled a little.

And, still shuddering, he told her how he thought he had seen the children working by the gravestones. All her efforts to calm him at first failed, but after a bit she drew his thoughts to pleasanter things, and he was not so certain after all that he had not been deceived by the cunning of the moonlight and the shadows.

A long interval passed, and no further sign was given by the owner of the house or his band of frightened children. Jimbo soon lost himself again in the delights of flying and the joy of his increasing powers.

Most of all he enjoyed the quiet, starlit nights before the moon was up; for the moon dazzled the eyes in the rarefied air where they flew, whereas the stars gave just enough light to steer by without making it uncomfortable.

Moreover, the moon often filled him with a kind of faint terror, as of death; he could never gaze at her white face for long without feeling that something entered his heart with those silver rays—something that boded him no good. He never spoke of this to the governess; indeed, he only recognised it himself when the moon was near the full; but it lay always in the depths of his being, and he felt dimly that it would have to be reckoned with before he could really escape for good. He took no liberties when the moon was at the full.

He loved to hover—for he had learned by this time that most difficult of all flying feats; to hold the body vertical and whirr the wings without rising or advancing—he loved to hover on windless nights over ponds and rivers and see the stars reflected in their still pools. Indeed, sometimes he hovered till he dropped, and only saved himself from a wetting by sweeping up in a tremendous curve along the surface of the water, and thus up into the branches of the trees where the governess sat waiting for him. And then, after a little rest, they would launch forth again and fly over fields and woods, sometimes even as far as the hills that ran down the coast of the sea itself.

They usually flew at a height of about a thousand feet, and the earth passed beneath them like a great streaked shadow. But as soon as the moon was up the whole country turned into a fairyland of wonder. Her light touched the woods with a softened magic, and the fields and hedges became frosted most delicately. Beneath a thin transparency of mist the water shone with a silvery brilliance that always enabled them to distinguish it from the land at any height; while the farms and country houses were swathed in tender grey shadows through which the trees and chimneys pierced in slender lines of black. It was wonderful to watch the shadows everywhere spinning their blue veil of distance that lent even to the commonest objects something of enchantment and mystery.

Those were wonderful journeys they made together into the pathways of the silent night, along the unknown courses, into that hushed centre where they could almost hear the beatings of her great heart—like winged thoughts searching the huge vault, till the boy ached with the sensations of speed and distance, and the old yellow moon seemed to stagger across the sky.

Sometimes they rose very high into freezing air, so high that the earth became a dull shadow specked with light. They saw the trains running in all directions with thin threads of smoke shining in the glare of the open fire-boxes. But they seemed very tiny trains indeed, and stirred in him no recollections of the semi-annual visits to London town when he went to the dentist, and lunched with the dreaded grandmother or the stiff and fashionable aunts.

And when they came down again from these perilous heights, the scents of the earth rose to meet them, the perfume of woods and fields, and the smells of the open country.

There was, too, the delight, the curious delight of windy nights, when the wind smote and buffeted them, knocking them suddenly sideways, whistling through their feathers as if it wanted to tear then from their sockets; rushing furiously up underneath their wings with repeated blows; turning them round, and backwards and forwards, washing them from head to foot in a tempestuous sea of rapid and unexpected motion.

It was, of course, far easier to fly with a wind than without one. The difficulty with a violent wind was to get down—not to keep up. The gusts drove up against the undersurfaces of their wings and kept them afloat, so that by merely spreading them like sails they could sweep and circle without a single stroke. Jimbo soon learned to manoeuvre so that he could turn the strength of a great wind to his own purposes, and revel in its boisterous waves and currents like a strong swimmer in a rough sea.

And to listen to the wind as it swept backwards and forwards over the surface of the earth below was another pleasure; for everything it touched gave out a definite note. He soon got to know the long sad cry from the willows, and the little whispering in the tops of the poplar trees; the crisp, silvery rattle of the birches, and the deep roar from oaks and beech woods. The sound of a forest was like the shouting of the sea.

But far more lovely, when they descended a little, and the wind was more gentle, were the low pipings among the reeds and the little wayward murmurs under the hedgerows.

The pine trees, however, drew them most, with their weird voices, now far away, now near, rising upwards with a wind of sighs.

There was a grove of these trees that trooped down to the waters of a little lake in the hills, and to this spot they often flew when the wind was low and the music likely, therefore, to be to their taste. For, even when there was no perceptible wind, these trees seemed always full of mysterious, mournful whisperings; their branches held soft music that never quite died away, even when all other trees were silent and motionless.

Besides these special expeditions, they flew everywhere and anywhere. They visited the birds in their nests in lofty trees, and exchanged the time of night with wise-eyed owls staring out upon them from the ivy. They hovered up the face of great cliffs, and passed the hawks asleep on perilous ledges; skimmed over lonely marshes, frightening the water-birds paddling in and out among the reeds. They followed the windings of streams, singing among the meadows, and flew along the wet sands as they watched the moon rise out of the sea.

These flights were unadulterated pleasure, and Jimbo thought he could never have enough of them.

He soon began to notice, too, that the trees emanated something that affected his own condition. When he sat in their branches this was very noticeable. Currents of force passed from them into himself. And even when he flew over their crests he was aware that some woods exhaled vigorous, life-giving forces, while others tired and depleted him. Nothing was visible actually, but fine waves seemed to beat up against his eyes and thoughts, making him stronger or weaker, happy or melancholy, full of hope and courage, or listless and indifferent.

These emanations of the trees—this giving-forth of their own personal forces—were, of course, very varied in strength and character. Oaks and pines were the best combination, he found, before the stress of a long flight, the former giving him steadiness, and the latter steely endurance and the power to steer in sinuous, swift curves, without taking thought or trouble.

Other trees gave other powers. All gave something. It was impossible to sit among their branches without absorbing some of the subtle and exhilarating tree-life. He soon learned how to gather it all into himself, and turn it to account in his own being.

"Sit quietly," the governess said. "Let the forces creep in and stir about. Do nothing yourself. Give them time to become part of yourself and mix properly with your own currents. Effort on your part prevents this, and you weaken them without gaining anything yourself."

Jimbo made all sorts of experiments with trees and rocks and water and fields, learning gradually the different qualities of force they gave forth, and how to use them for himself. Nothing, he found, was really dead. And sometimes he got himself into strange difficulties in the beginning of his attempts to master and absorb these nature-forces.

"Remember," the governess warned him more than once, when he was inclined to play tricks, "they are in quite a different world to ours. You cannot take liberties with them. Even a sympathetic soul like yourself only touches the fringe of their world. You exchange surface-messages with them, nothing more. Some trees have terrible forces just below the surface. They could extinguish you altogether—absorb you into themselves. Others are naturally hostile. Some are mere tricksters. Others are shifty and treacherous, like the hollies, that move about too much.

The oak and the pine and the elm are friendly, and you can always trust them absolutely. But there are others—!"

She held up a warning finger, and Jimbo's eyes nearly dropped out of his head.

"No," she added, in reply to his questions, "you can't learn all this at once. Perhaps—" She hesitated a little. "Perhaps, if you don't escape, we should have time for all manner of adventures among the trees and other things—but then, we *are* going to escape, so there's no good wasting time over *that!*"

CHAPTER XIV

AN ADVENTURE

But Miss Lake did not always accompany him on these excursions into the night; sometimes he took long flights by himself, and she rather encouraged him in this, saying it would give him confidence in case he ever lost her and was obliged to find his way about alone.

"But I couldn't get really lost," he said once to her. "I know the winds perfectly now and the country round for miles, and I never go out in fog—"

"But these are only practice flights," she replied. "The flight of escape is a very different matter. I want you to learn all you possibly can so as to be prepared for anything."

Jimbo felt vaguely uncomfortable when she talked like this.

"But you'll be with me in the Escape Flight—the final one of all," he said; "and nothing ever goes wrong when you're with me."

"I should like to be always with you," she answered tenderly, "but it's well to be prepared for anything, just the same."

And more than this the boy could never get out of her.

On one of these lonely flights, however, he made the unpleasant discovery that he was being followed.

At first he only imagined there was somebody after him because of the curious vibrations of the very rarefied air in which he flew. Every time his flight slackened and the noise of his own wings grew less, there reached him from some other corner of the sky a sound like the vibrations of large wings beating the air. It seemed behind, and generally below him, but the swishing of his own feathers made it difficult to hear with distinctness, or to be certain of the direction.

Evidently it was a long way off; but now and again, when he took a spurt and then sailed silently for several minutes on outstretched wings, the beating of distant, following feathers seemed unmistakably clear, and he raced on again at full speed more than terrified. Other times, however, when he tried to listen, there was no trace of this other flyer, and then his fear would disappear, and he would persuade himself that it had been imagination. So much on these flights he knew to be imagination—the sentences, voices, and laughter, for instance, that filled the air and sounded so real, yet were actually caused by the wind rushing past his ears, the rhythm of the wing-beats, and the tips of the feathers occasionally rubbing against the sides of his body.

But at last one night the suspicion that he was followed became a certainty.

He was flying far up in the sky, passing over some big city, when the sound rose to his ears, and he paused, sailing on stretched wings, to listen. Looking down into the immense space below, he saw, plainly outlined against the luminous patch above the city, the form of a large flying creature moving by with rapid strokes. The pulsations of its great wings made the air tremble so that he both heard and felt them. It may have been that the vapours of the city distorted the thing, just as the earth's atmosphere magnifies the rising or setting of the moon; but, even so, it was easy to see that it was something a good deal larger than himself, and with a much more powerful flight.

Fortunately, it did not seem this time to be actually on his trail, for it swept by at a great pace, and was soon lost in the darkness far ahead. Perhaps it was only searching for him, and his great height had proved his safety. But in any case he was exceedingly terrified, and at once turned round, pointed his head for the earth, and shot downwards in the direction of the Empty House as fast as ever he could.

But when he spoke to the governess she made light of it, and told him there was nothing to be afraid of. It might have been a flock of hurrying night-birds, she said, or an owl distorted by the city's light, or even his own reflection magnified in water. Anyhow, she felt sure it was not chasing him, and he need pay no attention to it.

Jimbo felt reassured, but not quite satisfied. He knew a flying monster when he saw one; and it was only when he had been for many more flights alone, without its reappearance, that his confidence was fully restored, and he began to forget about it.

Certainly these lonely flights were very much to his taste. His Older Self, with its dim hauntings of a great memory somewhere behind him, took possession then, and he was able to commune with nature in a way that the presence of the governess made impossible. With her his Older Self rarely showed itself above the surface for long; he was always the child. But, when alone, Nature became alive; he drew force from the trees and flowers, and felt that they all shared a common life together. Had he been imprisoned by some wizard of old in a tree-form, knowing of the sunset and the dawn only by the sweet messages that rustled in his branches, the wind could hardly have spoken to him with a more intimate meaning; or the life of the fields, eternally patient, have touched him more nearly with their joys and sorrows. It seemed almost as if, from his leafy cell, he had gazed before this into the shining pools with which the summer rains jewelled the meadows, sending his soul in a stream of unsatisfied yearning up to the stars. It all came back dimly when he heard the wind among the leaves, and carried him off to the woods and fields of an existence far antedating this one—

And on gentle nights, when the wind itself was half asleep and dreaming, the pine trees drew him most of all, for theirs was the song he loved above all others. He would fly round and round the little grove by the mountain lake, listening for hours together to their sighing voices. But the governess was never told of this, whatever she may have guessed; for it seemed to him a joy too deep for words, the pains and sweetness being mingled too mysteriously for him ever to express in awkward sentences. Moreover, it all passed away and was forgotten the moment the child took possession and usurped the older memory.

One night, when the moon was high and the air was cool and fragrant after the heat of the day, Jimbo felt a strong desire to get off by himself for a long flight. He was full of energy, and the space-craving cried to be satisfied. For several days he had been content with slow, stupid expeditions with the governess,

"I'm off alone to-night," he cried, balancing on the window ledge, "but I'll be back before dawn. Good-bye!"

She kissed him, as she always did now, and with her good-bye ringing in his ears, he dropped from the window and rose rapidly over the elms and away from earth.

This night, for some reason, the stars and the moon seemed to draw him, and with tireless wings he mounted up, up, up, to a height he had never reached before. The intoxication of the strong night air rose into his brain and he dashed forward ever faster, with a mad delight, into the endless space before him.

Mile upon mile lay behind him as he rushed onwards, always pointing a little on the upward slope, drunk with speed. The earth faded away to a dark expanse of shadow beneath him, and he no longer was conscious of the deep murmur that usually flowed steadily upwards from its surface. He had often before risen out of reach of the earth noises, but never so far that this dull reverberating sound, combined of all the voices of the world merged together, failed to make itself heard. To-night, however, he heard nothing. The stars above his head changed from yellow to diamond white, and the cold air stung his cheeks and brought the water to his eyes.

But at length the governess's warning, as he explored these forbidden regions, came back to him, and in a series of gigantic bounds that took his breath away completely, he dropped nearer to the earth again and kept on at a much lower level.

The hours passed and the position of the moon began to alter noticeably. Some of the constellations that were overhead when he started were now dipping below the horizon. Never before had he ventured so far from home, and he began to realise that he had been flying much longer than he knew or intended. The speed had been terrific.

The change came imperceptibly. With the discovery that his wings were not moving quite so easily as before, he became suddenly aware that this had really been the case for some little time. He was flying with greater effort, and for a long time this effort had been increasing gradually before he actually recognised the fact.

Although no longer pointing towards the earth he seemed to be sinking. It became increasingly difficult to fly upwards. His wings did not seem to fail or weaken, nor was he conscious of feeling tired; but something was ever persuading him to fly lower, almost as if a million tiny threads were coaxing him downwards, drawing him gradually nearer to the world again. Whatever it was, the earth had come much closer to him in the last hour, and its familiar voices were pleasant to hear after the boundless heights he had just left.

But for some reason his speed grew insensibly less and less. His wings moved apparently as fast as before, but it was harder to keep up. In spite of himself he kept sinking. The sensation was quite new, and he could not understand it. It almost seemed as though he were being *pulled* downwards.

Jimbo began to feel uneasy. He had not lost his bearings, but he was a very long way from home, and quite beyond reach of the help he was so accustomed to. With a great effort he mounted several hundred feet into the air, and tried hard to stay there. For a short time he succeeded, but he soon felt himself sinking gradually downwards again. The force drawing him was a constant force without rise or fall; and with a deadly feeling of fear the boy began to realise that he would soon have to yield to it altogether. His heart beat faster and his thoughts turned to the friend who was then far away, but who alone could save him.

She, at least, could have explained it and told him what best to do. But the governess was beyond his reach. This problem he must face alone.

Something, however, had to be done quickly, and Jimbo, acting more as the man than as the boy, turned and flew hurriedly forward in another direction. He hoped this might somehow counteract the force that still drew him downwards; and for a time it apparently did so, and he flew level. But the strain increased every minute, and he looked down with something of a shudder as he realised that before very long he would be obliged to yield to this deadly force—and drop!

It was then for the first time he noticed a change had come over the surface of the earth below. Instead of the patchwork of field and wood and road, he saw a vast cloud stretching out, white and smooth in the moonlight. The world was hidden beneath a snowy fog, dense and impenetrable. It was no longer even possible to tell in what direction he was flying, for there was nothing to steer by. This was a new and unexpected complication, and the boy could not understand how the change had come about so quickly; the last time he had glanced down for indications to steer by, everything had been clear and easily visible.

It was very beautiful, this carpet of white mist with the silver moon shining upon it, but it thrilled him now with an unpleasant sense of dread. And, still more unpleasant, was a new sound which suddenly broke in upon the stillness and turned his blood into ice. He was certain that he heard wings behind him. He was being followed, and this meant that it was impossible to turn and fly back.

There was nothing now to do but fly forwards and hope to distance the huge wings; but if he was being followed by the powerful flyer he had seen a few nights before, the boy knew that he stood little chance of success, and he only did it because it seemed the one thing possible.

The cloud was dense and chill as he entered it; its moisture clung to his wings and made them heavy; his muscles seemed to stiffen, and motion became more and more difficult. The wings behind him meanwhile came closer.

He was flying along the surface of the mist now his body and wings hidden, and his head just above the level. He could see along its white, even top. If he sank a few more inches it would be impossible to see at all, or even to judge where he was going. Soon it rose level with his lips, and at the same time he noticed a new smell in the air, faint at first, but growing every moment stronger. It was a fresh, sweet odour, yet it somehow added to his alarm, and stirred in him new centres of uneasiness. He tried vainly to increase his speed and distance the wings which continued to gain so steadily upon him from behind.

The cloud, apparently, was not everywhere of the same density, for here and there he saw the tops of green hills below him as he flew. But he could not understand why each green hill seemed to have a little lake on its summit—a little lake in which the reflected moon stared straight up into his face. Nor could he quite make out what the sounds were which rose to his ears through the muffling of the cloud—sounds of tumultuous rushing, hissing, and tumbling. They were continuous, these sounds, and once or twice he thought he heard with them a deep, thunderous roar that almost made his heart stop beating as he listened.

Was he, perhaps, over a range of high mountains, and was this the sound of the tumbling torrents?

Then, suddenly, it came to him with a shock that the ordinary sounds of the earth had wholly ceased.

Jimbo felt his head beginning to whirl. He grew weaker every minute; less able to offer resistance to the remorseless forces that were sucking him down. Now the mist had closed over his head, and he could no longer see the moonlight. He turned again, shaking with terror, and drove forward headlong through the clinging vapour. A sensation of choking rose in his throat; he was tired out, ready to drop with exhaustion. The wings of the following creature were now so close that he thought every minute he would be seized from behind and plunged into the abyss to his death.

It was just then that he made the awful discovery that the world below him was not stationary: the *green hills were moving.* They were sweeping past with a rushing, thundering sound in regular procession; and their huge sides were streaked with white. The reflection of the moon leaped up into his face as each hill rolled hissing and gurgling by, and he knew at last with a shock of unutterable horror that it was THE SEA!

He was flying over the sea, and the waters were drawing him down. The immense, green waves that rolled along through the sea fog, carrying the moon's face on their crests, foaming and gurgling as they went, were already leaping up to seize him by the feet and drag him into their depths.

He dropped several feet deeper into the mist, and towards the sea, terror-stricken and blinded. Then, turning frantically, not knowing what else

JIMBO   91

to do, he struck out, with his last strength, for the upper surface and the moonlight. But as he did so, turning his face towards the sky he saw a dark form hovering just above him, covering his retreat with huge outstretched wings. It was too late; he was hemmed in on all sides.

At that moment a huge, rolling wave, bigger than all the rest, swept past and wet him to the knees. His heart failed him. The next wave would cover him. Already it was rushing towards him with foaming crest. He was in its shadow; he heard its thunder. Darkness rushed over him—he saw the vast sides streaked with grey and white—when suddenly, the owner of the wings plucked him in the back, mid-way between the shoulders, and lifted him bodily out of the fog, so that the wave swept by without even wetting his feet.

The next minute he saw a dun, white sheet of silvery mist at his feet, and found himself far above it in the sweet, clean moonlight; and when he turned, almost dead with terror, to look upon his captor, he found himself looking straight into the eyes of—the governess.

The sense of relief was so great that Jimbo simply closed his wings, and hung, a dead weight, in the air.

"Use your wings!" cried the governess sharply; and, still holding him, while he began to flap feebly, she turned and flew in the direction of the land.

"You!" he gasped at last. "It was you following me!"

"Of course it was me! I never let you out of my sight. I've always followed you—every time you've been out alone."

Jimbo was still conscious of the drawing power of the sea, but he felt that his companion was too strong for it. After fifteen minutes of fierce flight he heard the sounds of earth again, and knew that they were safe.

Then the governess loosened her hold, and they flew along side by side in the direction of home.

"I won't scold you, Jimbo," she said presently, "for you've suffered enough already." She was the first to break the silence, and her voice trembled a little. "But remember, the sea draws you down, just as surely as the moon draws you up. Nothing would please Him better than to see you destroyed by one or the other."

Jimbo said nothing. But, when once they were safe inside the room again, he went up and cried his eyes out on her arm, while she folded him in to her heart as if he were the only thing in the whole world she had to love.

CHAPTER XV

THE CALL OF THE BODY

One night, towards the end of the practice flights, a strange thing happened, which showed that the time for the final flight of escape was drawing near.

They had been out for several hours flying through a rainstorm, the thousand little drops of which stung their faces like tiny gun-shot. About two in the morning the wind shifted and drove the clouds away as by magic; the stars came out, at first like the eyes of children still dim with crying, but later with a clear brilliance that filled Jimbo and the governess with keen pleasure. The air was washed and perfumed; the night luminous, alive, singing. All its tenderness and passion entered their hearts and filled them with the wonder of its glory.

"Come down, Jimbo," said the governess, "and we'll lie in the trees and smell the air after the rain."

"Yes," added the boy, whose Older Self had been whispering mysterious things to him, "and watch the stars and hear them singing."

He led the way to some beech trees that lined a secluded lane, and settled himself comfortably in the top branches of the largest, while the governess soon found a resting-place beside him. It was a deserted spot, far from human habitation. Here and there through the foliage they could see little pools of rainwater reflecting the sky. The group of trees swung in the wind, dreaming great woodland dreams, and overhead the stars looked like a thousand orchards in the sky, filling the air with the radiance of their blossoms.

"How brilliant they are to-night," said the governess, after watching the boy attentively for some minutes as they lay side by side in the great forked branch. "I never saw the constellations so clear."

"But they have so little shape," he answered dreamily; "if we wore lights when we flew about we should make much better constellations than they do."

"The Big and Little Child instead of the Big and Little Bear," she laughed, still watching him.

"I'm slipping away—" he began, and then stopped suddenly. He saw the expression of his companion's eyes, which were looking him through and through with the most poignant love and yearning mingled in their gaze, and something clutched at his heart that he could not understand.

"—not slipping out of the tree," he went on vaguely, "but slipping into some new place or condition. I don't understand it, Am I—going off somewhere—where you can't follow? I thought suddenly—I was losing you."

The governess smiled at him sadly and said nothing. She stroked his wings and then raised them to her lips and kissed them. Jimbo watched her, and folded his other wing across into her hands; he felt unhappy, and his heart began to swell within him; but he didn't know what to say, and the Older Self began slowly to fade away again.

"But the stars," he went on, "have they got things they send out too—forces, I mean, like the trees? Do they send out something that makes us feel sad, or happy, or strong, or weak?"

She did not answer for some time; she lay watching his face and fondling his smooth red wings; and, presently, when she did begin to explain, Jimbo found that the child in him was then paramount again, and he could not quite follow what she said.

He tried to answer properly and seem interested, but her words were very long and hard to understand, and after a time he thought she was talking to herself more than to him, and he gave up all serious effort to follow. Then he became aware that her voice had changed. The words seemed to drop down upon him from a great height. He imagined she was standing on one of those far stars he had been asking about, and was shouting at him through an immense tube of sky and darkness. The words pricked his ears like needle-points, only he no longer heard them as words, but as tiny explosions of sound, meaningless and distant. Swift flashes of light began to dance before his eyes, and suddenly from underneath the tree, a wind rose up and rushed, laughing, across his face. Darkness in a mass dropped over his eyes, and he sank backwards somewhere into another corner of space altogether.

The governess, meanwhile, lay quite still, watching the limp form in the branches beside her and still holding the tips of his red wings. Presently tears stole into her eyes, and began to run down her checks. One deep sigh after another escaped from her lips; but the little boy, or the old soul, who was the cause of all her emotion, apparently was far away and knew nothing of it. For a long time she lay in silence, and then leaned a little nearer to him, so as to see his full face. The eyes were wide open and staring, but they were looking at nothing she could see, for the consciousness cannot be in two places at the same time, and Jimbo just then was off on a little journey of his own, a journey that was but preliminary to the great final one of all.

"Jimbo," whispered the girl between her tears and sighs, "Jimbo! Where have you gone to? Tell me, are they getting ready for you at last, and am I to lose you after all? Is this the only way I can save you—by losing you?"

There was no answer, no sign of movement and the governess hid her face in her hands and cried quietly to herself, while her tears dropped down through the branches of the tree and fell into the rain-pools beneath.

For Jimbo's state of oblivion in the tree was in reality a momentary return to consciousness in his body on the bed, and the repaired mechanism of the brain and muscles had summoned him back on a sort of trial visit. He remembered nothing of it afterwards, any more than one remembers the experiences of deep sleep; but the fact was that, with the descent of the darkness upon him in the branches, he had opened his eyes once again on the scene in the night-nursery bedroom where his body lay.

He saw figures standing round the bed and about the room; his mother with the same white face as before, was still bending over the bed asking him if he knew her; a tall man in a long black coat moved noiselessly to and fro; and he saw a shaded lamp on a table a little to the right of the bed. Nothing seemed to have changed very much, though there had probably been time enough since he last opened his eyes for the black-coated doctor to have gone and come again for a second visit. He held an instrument in his hands that shone brightly in the lamplight. Jimbo saw this plainly and wondered what it was. He felt as if he were just waking out of a nice, deep sleep—dreamless and undisturbed. The Empty House, the Governess, Fright and the Children had all vanished from his memory, and he knew no more about wings and feathers than he did about the science of meteorology.

But the bedroom scene was a mere glimpse after all; his eyes were already beginning to close again. First they shut out the figure of the doctor; then the bed-curtains; and then the nurse moved her arm, making the whole scene quiver for an instant, like some huge jelly-shape, before it dipped into profound darkness and disappeared altogether. His mother's voice ran off into a thin trickle of sound, miles and miles away, and the light from the lamp followed him with its glare for less than half a second. All had vanished.

"Jimbo, dear, where have you been? Can you remember anything?" asked the soft voice beside him, as he looked first at the stars overhead, and then from the tracery of branches and leaves beneath him to the great sea of tree-tops and open country all round.

But he could tell her nothing; he seemed dreamy and absent-minded, lying and staring at her as if he hardly knew who she was or what she was saying. His mind was still hovering near the border-line of the two states of consciousness, like the region between sleeping and waking, where both worlds seem unreal and wholly wonderful.

He could not answer her questions, but he evidently caught some reflex of her emotions, for he leaned towards her across the branches, and said he was happy and never wanted to leave her. Then he crawled to the end of the big bough and sprang out into the air with a shout of delight. He was the child again—the flying child, wild with the excitement of tearing through the night air at fifty miles an hour.

The governess soon followed him and they flew home together, taking a long turn by the sea and past the great chalk cliffs, where the sea sang loud beneath them.

These lapses became with time more frequent, as well as of longer duration; and with them the boy noticed that the longing to escape became once again intense. He wanted *to get home,* wherever home was; he experienced a sort of nostalgia for the body, though he could not remember where that body lay. But when he asked the governess what this feeling meant, she only mystified him by her answers, saying that every one, in the body or out of it, felt a deep longing for their final *home*, though they might not have the least idea where it lay, or even to be able to recognise, much less to label, their longing.

His normal feelings, too, were slowly returning to him. The Older Self became more and more submerged. As he approached the state of ordinary, superficial consciousness, the characteristics of that state reflected themselves more and more in his thoughts and feelings. His memory still remained a complete blank; but he somehow felt that the things, places, and people he wanted to remember, had moved much nearer to him than before. Every day brought them more within his reach.

All these forgotten things will come back to me soon, I know," he said one day to the governess, "and then I'll tell you all about them."

"Perhaps you'll remember me too then," she answered, a shadow passing across her face.

Jimbo clapped his hands with delight.

"Oh," he cried, "I should like to remember you, because that would make you a sort of two-people governess, and I should love you twice as much."

But with the gradual return to former conditions the feelings of age and experience grew dim and indefinite, his knowledge lessened, becoming obscure and confused, showing itself only in vague impressions and impulses, until at last it became quite the exception for the child-consciousness to be broken through by flashes of intuition and inspiration from the more deeply hidden memories.

For one thing, the deep horror of the Empty House and its owner now returned to him with full force. Fear settled down again over the room, and lurked in the shadows over the yard. A vivid dread seized him of the *other door* in the room—the door through which the Frightened Children had disappeared, but which had never opened since. It gradually became for him a personality in the room, a staring, silent, listening thing, always watching, always waiting. One day it would open and he would be caught! In a dozen ways like this the horror of the house entered his heart and made him long for escape with all the force of his being.

But the governess, too, seemed changing; she was becoming more vague and more mysterious. Her face was always sad now, and her eyes wistful; her manner became restless and uneasy, and in many little ways the child could not fail to notice that her mind was intent upon other things. He begged her to name the day for the final flight, but she always seemed to have some good excuse for putting it off.

"I feel frightened when you don't tell me what's going on," he said to her.

"It's the preparations for the last flight," she answered, "the flight of escape. He'll try to prevent us going together so that you should get lost. But it's better you shouldn't know too much," she added. "Trust me and have patience."

"Oh, that's what you're so afraid of," he said, *"separation!"* He was very proud indeed of the long word, and said it over several times to himself.

And the governess, looking out of the window at the fading sunlight, repeated to herself more than to him the word he was so proud of.

"Yes, that's what I'm so afraid of—separation; but if it means your salvation—" and her sentence remained unfinished as her eyes wandered far above the tops of the trees into the shadows of the sky.

And Jimbo, drawn by the sadness of her voice, turned towards the window and noticed to his utter amazement that he could *see right through her.* He could see the branches of the trees *beyond* her body.

But the next instant she turned and was no longer transparent, and before the boy could say a word, she crossed the floor and disappeared from the room.

CHAPTER XVI

PREPARATION

Now that he was preparing to leave it, Jimbo began to realise more fully how things in this world of delirium—so the governess sometimes called it—were all terribly out of order and confused. So long as he was wholly in it and of it, everything had seemed all right; but, as he approached his normal condition again, the disorder became more and more apparent.

And the next few hours brought it home with startling clearness, and increased to fever heat the desire for final escape.

It was not so much a nonsense-world—it was too alarming for that—as a world of nightmare, wherein everything was distorted. Events in it were all out of proportion; effects no longer sprang from adequate causes; things happened in a dislocated sort of way, and there was so sequence in the order of their happening. Tiny occurrences filled him with disproportionate, inconceivable horror; and great events, on the other hand, passed him scathless. The spirit of disorder—monstrous, uncouth, terrifying—reigned supreme; and Jimbo's whole desire, though inarticulate, was to escape back into order and harmony again.

In contrast to all this dreadful uncertainty, the conduct of the governess stood out alone as the one thing he could count upon: she was sure and unfailing; he felt absolute confidence in her plans for his safety, and when he thought of her his mind was at rest. Come what might, she would always be there in time to help. The adventure over the sea had proved that; but, childlike, he thought chiefly of his own safety, and had ceased to care very much whether she escaped with him or not. It was the older Jimbo that preferred captivity to escape without her, whereas every minute now he was sinking deeper into the normal child state in which the intuitive flashes from the buried soul became more and more rare.

Meanwhile, there was preparation going on, secret and mysterious. He could feel it. Some one else besides the governess was making plans, and the boy began to dread the moment of escape almost as much as he desired it. The alternative appalled him—to live for ever in the horror of this house, bounded by the narrow yard, watched by Fright listening ever at his elbow, and visited by the horrible Frightened Children. Even the governess herself began to inspire him with something akin to fear, as her personality grew more and more mysterious. He thought of her as she stood by the window, with the branches of the tree visible through her body, and the thought filled him with a dreadful and haunting distress.

But this was only when she was absent; the moment she came into the room, and he looked into her kind eyes, the old feeling of security returned, and he felt safe and happy.

Once, during the day, she came up to see him, and this time with final instructions. Jimbo listened with rapt attention.

"To-night, or to-morrow night we start," she said in a quiet voice. "You must wait till you hear me calling—"

"But sha'n't we start together?" he interrupted.

"Not exactly," she replied. "I'm doing everything possible to put him off the scent, but it's not easy, for once Fright knows you he's always on the watch. Even if he can't prevent your escape, he'll try to send you home to your body with such a shock that you'll be only 'half there' for the rest of your life."

Jimbo did not quite understand what she meant by this, and returned at once to the main point.

"Then the moment you call I'm to start?"

"Yes. I shall be outside somewhere. It depends on the wind and weather a little, but probably I shall be hovering above the trees. You must dash out of the window and join me the moment you hear me call. Clear the wall without sinking into the yard, and mind he doesn't tear your wings off as you fly by."

"What will happen, though, if I don't find you?" he asked.

"You might get lost. If he succeeds in getting me out of the way first, you're sure to get lost—"

"But I've had long flights without getting lost," he objected.

"Nothing to this one," she replied. "It will be tremendous. You see, Jimbo, it's not only distance; it's change of condition as well."

"I don't mind what it is so long as we escape together," he said, puzzled by her words.

He kept his eyes fixed on her face. It seemed to him she was changing even as he looked at her. A sort of veil lifted from her features. He fancied he could see the shape of the door through her body.

"Oh, please, Miss Lake—" he began in a frightened voice, taking a step towards her. "What is the matter? You look so different!"

"Nothing, dearest boy, is the matter," she replied faintly. "I feel sad at the thought of your—of our going, that's all. But that's nothing," she added more briskly, "and remember, I've told you exactly what to do so you can't make any mistake. Now goodbye for the present."

There was a smile on her face that he had never seen there before, and an expression of tenderness and love that he could not fail to understand. But even as he looked she seemed to fade away into a delicate, thin shadow as she moved slowly towards the trap-door. Jimbo stretched out his arms to touch her, for the moment of dread had passed, and he wanted to kiss her.

"No!" she cried sharply. "Don't touch me, child; don't touch me!"

But he was already close beside her, and in another second would have had his arms round her, when his foot stumbled over something, and he fell forward into her with his full weight. Instead of saving himself against her body, however, he fell *clean through her!* Nothing stopped him; there was no resistance; he met nothing more solid than air, and fell full length upon the floor. Before he could recover from his surprise and pick himself up, something touched him on the lips, and he heard a voice that was faint as a whisper saying, "Good-bye, darling child, and bless you." The next moment he was on his feet again and the room was empty. The governess had gone through the trap-door, and he was alone.

It was all very strange and confusing, and he could not understand what was happening to her. He never for a moment realised that the change was in himself, and that as the tie between himself and his body became closer, the things of this other world he had been living in for so long must fade gradually away into shadows and emptiness.

But Jimbo was a brave boy; there was nothing of the coward in him, though his sensitive temperament made him sometimes hesitate where an ordinary child with less imagination would have acted promptly. The desire to cry he thrust down and repressed, fighting his depression by the thought that within a few hours the voice might sound that should call him to the excitement of the last flight—and freedom.

The rest of the daylight slipped away very quickly, and the room was full of shadows almost before he knew it. Then came the darkness. Outside, the wind rose and fell fitfully, booming in the chimney with hollow music, and sighing round the walls of the house. A few stars peeped between the branches of the elms, but masses of cloud hid most of the sky, and the air felt heavy with coming rain.

He lay down on the bed and waited. At the least sound he started, thinking it might be the call from the governess. But the few sounds he did hear always resolved themselves into the moaning of the wind, and no voice came. With his eyes on the open window, trying to pierce the gloom and find the stars, he lay motionless for hours, while the night wore on and the shadows deepened.

And during those long hours of darkness and silence he was conscious that a change was going on within him. Name it he could not, but somehow it made him feel that living people like himself were standing near, trying to speak, beckoning, anxious to bring bin back into their own particular world. The darkness was so great that he could see only the square outline of the open window, but he felt sure that any sudden flash of light would have revealed a group of persons round his bed with arms outstretched, trying to reach him. The emotion they roused in him was not fear, for he felt sure they were kind, and eager only to help him; and the more he realised their presence, the less he thought about the governess who had been doing so much to make his escape possible.

Then, too, voices began to sound somewhere in the air, but he could not tell whether they were actually in the room, or outside in the night, or only within himself—in his own head—strange, faint voices, whispering, laughing, shouting, crying; fragments of stories, rhymes, riddles, odd names of people and places jostled one another with varying degrees of clearness, now loud, now soft, till he wondered what it all meant, and longed for the light to come.

But besides all this, something else, too, was abroad that night—something he could not name or even think about without shaking with terror down at the very roots of his being. And when he thought of this, his heart called loudly for the governess, and the people hidden in the shadows of the room seemed quite useless and unable to help.

Thus he hovered between the two worlds and the two memories, phantoms and realities shifting and changing places every few minutes.

A little light would have saved him much suffering. If only the moon were up! Moonlight would have made all the difference. Even a moon half hidden and misty would have put the shadows farther away from him.

"Dear old misty moon!" he cried half aloud to himself upon the bed, "why aren't you here to-night? My last night!"

Misty Moon, Misty Moon! The words kept ringing in his head. Misty Moon, Misty Moon! They swam round in his blood in an odd, tumultuous rhythm. Every time the current of blood passed through his brain in the course of its circulation it brought the words with it, altered a little, and singing like a voice.

Like a voice! Suddenly he made the discovery that it actually *was* a voice—and not his own. It was no longer the blood singing in his veins, it was some one singing outside the window. The sound began faintly and far away, up above the trees; then it came gradually nearer, only to die away again almost to a whisper.

If it was not the voice of the governess, he could only say it was a very good imitation of it.

The words forming out of the empty air rose and fell with the wind, and, taking his thoughts, flung them in a stream through the dark sky towards the hidden, misty moon:

> "O misty moon,
> Dear, misty moon,
> The nights are long without thee;
> The shadows creep
> Across my sleep,
> And fold their wings about me!"

And another silvery voice, that might have been the voice of a star, took it up faintly, evidently from a much greater distance:

> "O misty moon,
> Sweet, misty moon,
> The stars are dim behind thee;
> And, lo, thy beams
> Spin through my dreams
> And weave a veil to blind me!"

The sound of this beautiful voice so delighted Jimbo that he sprang from his bed and rushed to the window, hoping that he might be able to hear it more clearly. But, before he got half-way across the room, he stopped short, trembling with terror. Underneath his very feet, in the depths of the house, he heard the awful voice he dreaded more than anything else. It roared out the lines with a sound like the rushing of a great river:

> "O misty moon,
> Pale misty moon,
> Thy songs are nightly driven,
> Eternally,
> From sky to sky,
> O'er the old, grey Hills of heaven!"

And after the verse Jimbo heard a great peal of laughter that seemed to shake the walls of the house, and rooted his feet to the floor. It rolled away with thundering echoes into the very bowels of the earth. He just managed to crawl back to his mattress and lie down, when another voice took up the song, but this time in accents so tender, that the child felt something within him melt into tears of joy, and he was on the verge of recognising, for the first time since his accident, the voice of his mother:

> "O misty moon,
> Shy, misty moon,
> Whence comes the blush that trembles
> In sweet disgrace
> O'er half thy face
> When Night her stars assembles?"

But his memory, of course, failed him just as he seemed about to grasp it, and he was left wondering why the sound of that one voice had brought him a moment of radiant happiness in the midst of so much horror and pain. Meanwhile the answering voices went on, each time different, and in new directions.

But the next verse somehow brought back to him all the terror he had felt in his flight over the sea, when the sound of the hissing waters had reached his ears through the carpet of fog:

> "O misty moon,
> Persuasive moon,
> Earth's tides are ever rising;
> By the awful grace
> Of thy weird white face
> Leap the seas to thy enticing!"

Then followed the voice that had started the horrid song. This time he was sure it was not Miss Lake's voice, but only a very clever imitation of it. Moreover, it again ended in a shriek of laughter that froze his blood:

> "O misty moon,
> Deceiving moon,
> Thy silvery glance brings sadness;
> Who flies to thee,
> From land or sea,
> Shall end—his—days—in—MADNESS!"

Other voices began to laugh and sing, but Jimbo stopped his ears, for he simply could not bear any more. He felt certain, too, that these strange words to the moon had all been part of a trap—a device to draw him to the window. He shuddered to think how nearly he had fallen into it, and determined to lie on the bed and wait till he heard his companion calling, and knew beyond all doubt that it was she.

But the night passed away and the dawn came, and no voice had called him forth to the last flight.

Hitherto, in all his experiences, there had been only one absolute certainty: the appearance of the governess with the morning light. But this time sunrise came and the clouds cleared away, and the sweet smells of field and air stole into the little room, yet without any sign of the governess. The hours passed, and she did not come, till finally he realised that she was not coming at all, and he would have to spend the whole day alone. Something had happened to prevent her, or else it was all part of her mysterious "plan." He did not know, and all he could do was to wait, and wonder, and hope.

All day long he lay and waited, and all day long he was alone. The trap-door never once moved; the courtyard remained empty and deserted; there was no sound on the landing or on the stairs; no wind stirred the leaves outside, and the hot sun poured down out of a cloudless sky. He stood by the open window for hours watching the motionless branches. Everything seemed dead; not even a bird crossed his field of vision. The loneliness, the awful silence, and above all, the dread of the approaching night, were sometimes more than he seemed able to bear; and he wanted to put his head out of the window and scream, or lie down on the bed and cry his heart out. But he yielded to neither impulse; he kept a brave heart, knowing that this would be his last night in prison, and that in a few hours' time he would hear his name called out of the sky, and would dash through the window to liberty and the last wild flight. This thought gave him courage, and he kept all his energy for the great effort.

Gradually, once more, the sunlight faded, and the darkness began to creep over the land. Never before had the shadows under the elms looked so fantastic, nor the bushes in the field beyond assumed such sinister shapes. The Empty House was being gradually invested; the enemy was masquerading already under cover of these very shadows.

Very soon, he felt, the attack would begin, and he must be ready to act.

The night came down at last with a strange suddenness, and with it the warning of the governess came back to him; he thought quakingly of the stricken children who had been caught and deprived of their wings; and then he pulled out his long red feathers and tried their strength, and gained thus fresh confidence in their power to save him when the time came.

CHAPTER XVII

OFF!

With the full darkness a whole army of horrors crept nearer. He felt sure of this, though he could actually see nothing. The house was surrounded, the courtyard crowded. Outside, on the stairs, in the other rooms, even on the roof itself, waited dreadful things ready to catch him, to tear off his wings, to make him prisoner for ever and ever.

The possibility that something had happened to the governess now became a probability. Imperceptibly the change was wrought; he could not say how or when exactly; but he now felt almost certain that the effort to keep her out of the way had succeeded. If this were true, the boy's only hope lay in his wings, and he pulled them out to their full length and kissed them passionately, speaking to the strong red feathers as if they were living little persons.

"You must save me! You will save me, won't you?" he cried in his anguish. And every time he did this and looked at them he gained fresh hope and courage.

The problem *where he was to fly to* had not yet insisted on a solution, though it lay always at the back of his mind; for the final flight of escape without a guide had never been even a possibility before.

Lying there alone in the darkness, waiting for the sound of the voice so longed for, he found his thoughts turning again to the moon, and the strange words of the song that had puzzled him the night before. What in the world did it all mean? Why all this about the moon? Why was it a cruel moon, and why should it attract and persuade and entice him? He felt sure, the more he thought of it, that this had all been a device to draw him to the window—and perhaps even farther.

The darkness began to terrify him; he dreaded more and more the waiting, listening things that it concealed. Oh, when would the governess call to him? When would he be able to dash through the open window and join her in the sky?

He thought of the sunlight that had flooded the yard all day—so bright it seemed to have come from a sun fresh made and shining for the first time. He thought of the exquisite flowers that grew in the fields just beyond the high wall, and the night smells of the earth reached him through the window, wafted in upon a wind heavy with secrets of woods and fields. They all came from a Land of Magic that after to-night might be for ever beyond his reach, and they went straight to his heart and immediately turned something solid there into tears. But the tears did not find their natural expression, and Jimbo lay there fighting with his pain, keeping all his strength for the one great effort, and waiting for the voice that at any minute now might sound above the tree-tops.

But the hours passed and the voice did not come.

How he loathed the room and everything in it. The ceiling stretched like a white, staring countenance above him; the walls watched and listened; and even the mantelpiece grew into the semblance of a creature with drawn-up shoulders bending over him. The whole room, indeed, seemed to his frightened soul to run into the shape of a monstrous person whose arms were outstretched in all directions to prevent his escape.

His hands never left his wings now. He stroked and fondled them, arranging the feathers smoothly and speaking to them under his breath just as though they were living things. To him they were indeed alive, and he knew when the time came they would not fail him. The fierce passion for the open spaces took possession of his soul, and his whole being began to cry out for freedom, rushing wind, the stars, and a pathless sky.

Slowly the power of the great, open Night entered his heart, bringing with it a courage that enabled him to keep the terrors of the House at a distance.

So far, the boy's strength had been equal to the task, but a moment was approaching when the tension would be too great to bear, and the long pent-up force would rush forth into an act. Jimbo realised this quite clearly; though he could not exactly express it in words, he felt that his real hope of escape lay in the success of that act. Meanwhile, with more than a child's wisdom, he stored up every particle of strength he had for the great moment when it should come.

A light wind had risen soon after sunset, but as the night wore on it began to fail, dropping away into little silences that grew each time longer. In the heart of one of these spells of silence Jimbo presently noticed a new sound—a sound that he recognised.

Far away at first, but growing in distinctness with every dropping of the wind, this new sound rose from the interior of the house below and came gradually upon him. It was voices faintly singing, and the tread of stealthy footsteps.

Nearer and nearer came the sound, till at length they reached the door, and there passed into the room a wave of fine, gentle sound that woke no echo and scarcely seemed to stir the air into vibration at all. The door had opened, and a number of voices were singing softly under their breath.

And after the sounds, creeping slowly like some timid animal, there came into the room a small black figure just visible in the faint starlight. It peered round the edge of the door, hesitated a moment, and then advanced with an odd rhythmical sort of motion. And after the first figure came a second, and after the second a third; and then several entered together, till a whole group of them stood on the floor between Jimbo and the open window.

Then he recognised the Frightened Children and his heart sank. Even they, he saw, were arrayed against him, and took it for granted that he already belonged to them.

Oh, why did not the governess come for him ? Why was there no voice in the sky? He glanced with longing towards the heavens, and as the children moved past, he was almost certain that he saw the stars *through* their bodies too.

Slowly they shuffled across the floor till they formed a semicircle round the bed; and then they began a silent, impish dance that made the flesh creep. Their thin forms were dressed in black gowns like shrouds, and as they moved through the steps of the bizarre measure he saw that their legs were little more than mere skin and bone. Their faces—what he could see of them when he dared to open his eyes—were pale as ashes, and their beady little eyes shone like the facets of cut stones, flashing in all directions. And while they danced in and out amongst each other, never breaking the semicircle round the bed, they sang a low, mournful song that sounded like the wind whispering through a leafless wood.

And the words stirred in him that vague yet terrible fear known to all children who have been frightened and made to feel afraid of the dark. Evidently his sensations were being merged very rapidly now into those of the little boy in the night-nursery bed.

> "There is Someone in the Nursery
> Whom we never saw before;
> —Why hangs the moon so red?—
> And he came not by the passage,
> Or the window, or the door;
> —Why hangs the moon so red?—
> And he stands there in the darkness,
> In the centre of the floor.
> —See, where the moon hangs red!—
>
> Someone's hiding in the passage
> Where the door begins to swing;
> —Why drive the clouds so fast?—
> In the corner by the staircase
> There's a dreadful waiting thing:
> —Why drive the clouds so fast?—
> Past the curtain creeps a monster
> With a black and fluttering wing;
> —See, where the clouds drive fast!
>
> In the chilly dusk of evening;
> In the hush before the dawn;
> —Why drips the rain so cold?—
> In the twilight of the garden,
> In the mist upon the lawn,
> —Why drips the rain so cold?—
> Faces stare, and mouth upon us,

Faces white and weird and drawn;
—See, how the rain drips cold!—

Close beside us in the night-time,
Waiting for us in the gloom,
—O! Why sings the wind so shrill?—
In the shadows by the cupboard,
In the corners of the room,
—O! Why sings the wind so shrill?—
From the corridors and landings
Voices call us to our doom.
—O! how the wind sings shrill!"—

By this time the dreadful dancers had come much closer to him, shifting stealthily nearer to the bed under cover of their dancing, and *always between him and the window.*

Suddenly their intention flashed upon him; they meant to prevent his escape!

With a tremendous effort he sprang from the bed. As he did so a dozen pairs of thin, shadowy arms shot out towards him as though to seize his wings; but with an agility born of fright he dodged them, and ran swiftly into the corner by the mantelpiece. Standing with his back against the wall he faced the children, and strove to call out for help to the governess; but this time there was an entirely new difficulty in the way, for he found to his utter dismay that his voice refused to make itself heard. His mouth was dry and his tongue would hardly stir.

Not a sound issued from his lips, but the children instantly moved forwards and hemmed him in between them and the wall; and to reach the window he would have to break through this semicircle of whispering, shadowy forms. Above their heads he could see the stars shining, and any moment he might hear Miss Lake's voice calling to him to come out. His heart rose with passionate longing within him, and he gathered his wings tightly about him ready for the final dash. It would take more than the Frightened Children to hold him prisoner when once he heard that voice, or even without it!

Whether they were astonished at his boldness, or merely waiting their opportunity later, he could not tell; but anyhow they kept their distance for a time and made no further attempt to seize his feathers. Whispering together under their breath, sometimes singing their mournful, sighing songs, sometimes sinking their voices to a confused murmur, they moved in and out amongst each other with soundless feet like the shadows of branches swaying in the wind.

Then, suddenly, they moved closer and stretched out their arms towards him, their bodies swaying rhythmically together, while their combined voices, raised just above a whisper, sang to him—

"Dare you fly out to-night,
When the Moon is so strong?
Though the stars are so bright,
There is death in their song;
You're a hostage to Fright,
And to us you belong!

Dare you fly out alone
Through the shadows that wave,
When the course is unknown
And there's no one to save?
You are bone of our bone,
And for ever His slave!"

And, following these words, came from somewhere in the air that voice like the thunder of a river. Jimbo knew only too well to whom it belonged as he listened to the rhyme of the West Wind—

"For the Wind of the West
Is a wind unblest,
And its dangerous breath
Will entice you to death!
Fly not with the Wind of the West, O child,
With the terrible Wind of the West!"

But the boy knew perfectly well that these efforts to stop him were all part of a trap. They were lying to him. It was not the Wind of the West at all; *it was the South Wind!* That at least he knew by the odours that were wafted in through the window. Again he tried to call to the governess, but his tongue lay stiff in his mouth and no sound came.

Meanwhile the children began to draw closer, hemming him in. They moved almost imperceptibly, but he saw plainly that the circle was growing smaller and smaller. His legs began to tremble, and he felt that soon he would collapse and drop at their feet, for his strength was failing and the power to act and move was slowly leaving him.

The little shadowy figures were almost touching him, when suddenly a new sound broke the stillness and set every nerve tingling in his body.

Something was shuffling along the landing. He heard it outside, pushing against the door. The handle turned with a rattle, and a moment later the door slowly opened.

For a second Jimbo's breath failed him, and he nearly fell in a heap upon the floor. Round the edge of the door he saw a dim huge figure come crawling into the room—creeping along the floor—and trailing behind it a pair of immense black wings that stretched along the boards. For one brief second he stared, horror-stricken, and wondering what it was. But before the whole length of the creature was in, he knew. It was Fright himself! *And he was making steadily for the window!*

The shock instantly galvanised the boy into a state of activity again. He recovered the use of all his muscles and all his faculties. His voice, released by terror, rang out in a wild shriek for help to the governess, and he dashed forward across the room in a mad rush for the window. Unless he could reach it before the other, he would be a prisoner for the rest of his life. It was now or never.

The instant he moved, the children came straight at him with hands outstretched to stop him; but he passed through them as if they were smoke, and with almost a single bound sprang upon the narrow window-sill. To do this he had to clear the head and shoulders of the creature on the floor, and though he accomplished it successfully, he felt himself clutched from behind. For a second he balanced doubtfully on the window ledge. He felt himself being pulled back into the room, and he combined all his forces into one tremendous effort to rush forward.

There was a ripping, tearing sound as he sprang into the air with a yell of mingled terror and exultation. His prompt action and the fierce impetus had saved him. He was free. But in the awful hand that seized him he had left behind the end feathers of his right wing. A few inches more and it would have been not merely the feathers, but the entire wing itself.

He dropped to within three feet of the stones in the yard, and then, borne aloft by the kind, rushing Wind of the South, he rose in a tremendous sweep far over the tops of the high elms and out into the heart of the night.

Only there was no governess's voice to guide him; and behind him, a little lower down, a black pursuing figure with huge wings flapped heavily as it followed with laborious flight through the darkness.

CHAPTER XVIII

HOME

But it was the sound of something crashing heavily through the top branches of the elms that made the boy realise he was actually being followed; and all his efforts became concentrated into the desire to put as much distance as possible between himself and the horror of the Empty House.

He heard the noise of big wings far beneath him, and his one idea was to out-distance his pursuer and then come down again to earth and rest his wings in the branches of a tree till he could devise some plan how to find the governess. So at first he raced at full speed through the air, taking no thought of direction.

When he looked down, all he could see was that something vague and shadowy, shaking out a pair of enormous wings between him and the earth, move along with him. Its path was parallel with his own, but apparently it made no effort to rise up to his higher level. It thundered along far beneath him, and instinctively he raised his head and steered more and more upwards and away from the world.

The gap at the end of his right wing where the feathers had been torn out seemed to make no difference in his power of flight or steering, and he went tearing through the night at a pace he had never dared to try before, and at a height he had never yet reached in any of the practice flights. He soared higher even than he knew; and perhaps this was fortunate, for the friction of the lower atmosphere might have heated him to the point of igniting, and some watcher at one of earth's windows might have suddenly seen a brilliant little meteor flash through the night and vanish into dust.

At first the joy of escape was the only idea his mind seemed able to grasp; he revelled in a passionate sense of freedom, and all his energies poured themselves into one concentrated effort to fly faster, faster, faster. But after a time, when the pursuer had been apparently outflown, and he realised that escape was an accomplished fact, he began to search for the governess, calling to her, rising and falling, darting in all directions, and then hovering on outstretched wings to try and catch some sound of a friendly voice.

But no answer came, either from the stars that crowded the vault above, or from the dark surface of the world below; only silence answered his cries, and his voice was swallowed up and lost in the immensity of space almost the moment it left his lips.

Presently he began to realise to what an appalling distance he had risen above the world, and with anxious eyes he tried to pierce the gaping emptiness beneath him and on all sides. But this vast sea of air had nothing to reveal. The stars shone like pinholes of gold pricked in a deep black curtain; and the moon, now rising slowly, spread a veil of silver between him and the upper regions. There was not a cloud anywhere and the winds were all asleep. He was alone in space. Yet, as the swishing of his feathers slackened and the roar in his ears died away, he heard in the short pause the ominous beating of great wings somewhere in the depths beneath him, and knew that the great pursuer was still on his track.

The glare of the moon now made it impossible to distinguish anything properly, and in these huge spaces, with nothing to guide the eye, it was difficult to know exactly from what direction the sound came. He was only sure of one thing—that it was far below him, and that for the present it did not seem to come much nearer. The cry for help that kept rising to his lips he suppressed, for it would only have served to guide his pursuer; and, moreover, a cry—a little thin, despairing cry—was instantly lost in these great heavens. It was less than a drop in an ocean.

On and on he flew, always pointing away from the earth, and trying hard to think where he would find safety. Would this awful creature hunt him all night long into the daylight, or would he be forced back into the Empty House in sheer exhaustion? The thought gave him new impetus, and with powerful strokes he dashed onwards and upwards through the wilderness of space in which the only pathways were the little golden tracks of the starbeams. The governess would turn up somewhere; he was positive of that. She had never failed him yet.

So, alone and breathless, he pursued his flight, and the higher he went the more the tremendous vault opened up into inconceivable and untold distances. His speed kept increasing; he thought he had never found flying so easy before; and the thunder of the following wings that held persistently on his track made it dangerous for him to slacken up for more than a minute here and there. The earth became a dark blot beneath him, while the moor, rising higher and higher, grew weirdly bright and close. How black the sky was; how piercing the points of starlight; how stimulating the strong, new odours of these lofty regions! He realised with a thrill of genuine awe that he had flown over the very edge of the world, and the moment the thought entered his mind it was flung back at him by a voice that seemed close to his ear one moment, and the next was miles away in the space overhead. Light thoughts, born of the stars and the moon and of his great speed, danced before his mind in fanciful array. Once he laughed aloud at them, but once only. The sound of his voice in these echoless spaces made him afraid.

The speed, too, affected his vision, for at one moment thin clouds stretched across his face, and the next he was whirling through perfectly clear air again with no vestige of a cloud in sight. The same reason doubtless explained the sudden presence of sheets of light in the air that reflected the moonlight like particles of glittering ice, and then suddenly disappeared again. The terrific speed would explain a good many things, but

certainly it was curious how creatures formed out of the hollow darkness,
like foam before a steamer's bows, and moved noiselessly away on either
side to join the army of dim life that crowded everywhere and watched his
passage. For, in front and on both sides, there gathered a vast assembly of
silent forms more than shadows, less than bodily shapes, that opened up
a pathway as he rushed through them, and then immediately closed up
their ranks again when he had passed. The air seemed packed with living
creatures. Space was filled with them. They surrounded him on all sides.
Yet his passage through them was like the passage of a hand through
smoke; it was easy to make a pathway, but the pathway left no traces
behind it. More smoke rushed in and filled the void.

He could never see these things properly, face to face; they always kept
just out of the line of vision, like shadows that follow a lonely walker in a
wood and vanish the moment he turns to look at them over his shoulder.
But ever by his side, with a steady, effortless motion, he knew they kept up
with him—strange inhabitants of the airless heights, immense and misty-
winged, with veiled, flaming eyes and silent feathers. He was not afraid of
them; for they were neither friendly nor hostile; they were simply the
beings of another world, alien and unknown.

But what puzzled him more was that the light and the darkness seemed
separate things, each distinctly visible. After each stroke of his wings he
saw the darkness sift downwards past him through the air like dust. It floated all round him in thinnest diaphanous texture—visible, not because the
moonlight made it so, but because in its inmost soul it was itself luminous.
It rose and fell in eddies, swirling wreaths, and undulations; inwoven with
starbeams, as with golden thread, it clothed him about in circles of some
magical primordial substance.

Even the stars, looking down upon him from terrifying heights, seemed
now draped, now undraped, as if by the sweeping of enormous wings that
stirred these sheets of visible darkness into a vast system of circulation
through the heavens. Everything in these oceans of upper space apparently made use of wings, or the idea of wings. Perhaps even the great earth
itself, rolling from star to star, was moved by the power of gigantic, invisible wings! .   . .

Jimbo realised he had entered a forbidden region. He began to feel afraid.

But the only possible expression of his fear, and its only possible relief,
lay in his own wings—and he used them with redoubled energy. He
dashed forward so fast that his face begun to burn, and he kept turning his
head in every direction for a sign of the governess, or for some indication
of where he could *escape to*. In the pauses of the wild flight he heard the
thunder of the following wings below. They were still on his trail, and it
seemed that they were gaining on him.

He took a new angle, realising that his only chance was to fly high; and
the new course took him perpendicularly away from the earth and straight
towards the moon. Later, when he had out-distanced the other creature, he
would drop down again to safer levels.

Yet the hours passed and it never overtook him. A measured distance was steadily kept up between them as though with calculated purpose.

Curious distant voices shouted from time to time all manner of sentences and rhymes in his ears, but he could neither understand nor remember them. More and more the awful stillness of the vast regions that lie between the world and the moon appalled him.

Then, suddenly, a new sound reached him that at first he could not in the least understand. It reached him, however, not through the ears, but by a steady trembling of the whole surface of his body. It set him in vibration all over, and for some time he had no idea what it meant. The trembling ran deeper and deeper into his body, till at last a single, powerful, regular vibration took complete possession of his whole being, and he felt as though he was being wrapped round and absorbed by this vast and gigantic sound. He had always thought that the voice of Fright, like the roar of a river, was the loudest and deepest sound he had ever heard. Even that set his soul a-trembling. But this new, tremendous, rolling-ocean of a voice came not that way, and could not be compared to it. The voice of the other was a mere tickling of the ear compared to this awful crashing of seas and mountains and falling worlds. It must break him to pieces, he felt.

Suddenly he knew what it was,—and for a second his wings failed him:—he had reached such a height that he could hear the roar of the world as it thundered along its journey through space! That was the meaning of this voice of majesty that set him all a-trembling. And before long he would probably hear, too, the voices of the planets, and the singing of the great moon. The governess had warned him about this. At the first sound of these awful voices she told him to turn instantly and drop back to the earth as fast as ever he could drop.

Jimbo turned instinctively and began to fall. But, before he had dropped half a mile, he met once again the ascending sound of the wings that had followed him from the Empty House.

It was no good flying straight into destruction. He summoned all his courage and turned once more towards the stars. Anything was better than being caught and held for ever by Fright, and with a wild cry for help that fell dead in the empty spaces, he renewed his unending flight towards the stars,

But, meanwhile, the pursuer had distinctly gained. Appalled by the mighty thunder of the stars' voices above, and by the prospect of immediate capture if he turned back, Jimbo flew blindly on towards the moon, regardless of consequences. And below him the pursuer came closer and closer. The strokes of its wings were no longer mere distant thuds that he heard when he paused in his own flight to listen; they were the audible swishing of feathers. It was near enough for that.

Jimbo could never properly see what was following him. A shadow between him and the earth was all he could distinguish, but in the centre of that shadow there seemed to burn two glowing eyes. Two brilliant lights flashed whenever he looked down, like the lamps of a revolving lighthouse. But other things he saw, too, when he looked down, and once the earth rose close to his face so that he could have touched it with his hands. The same instant it dropped away again with a rush of whirlwinds, and became a distant shadow miles and miles below him. But before it went, he had time to see the Empty House standing within its gloomy yard, and the horror of it gave him fresh impetus.

Another time when the world raced up close to his eyes he saw a scene of a different kind that stirred a passionately deep yearning within him— a house overgrown with ivy and standing among trees and gardens, with laburnums and lilacs flowering on smooth green lawns, and a clean gravel drive leading down to a big pair of iron gates. Oh, it all seemed so familiar! Perhaps in another minute the well-known figures would have appeared and spoken to him. Already he heard their voices behind the bushes. But, just before they appeared, the earth dropped back with a roar of a thousand winds, and Jimbo saw instead the shadow of the Pursuer mounting, mounting, mounting towards him. Up he shot again with terror in his heart, and all trembling with the thunder of the great star-voices above. He felt like a leaf in a hurricane, "lost, dizzy, shelterless."

Voices, too, now began to be heard more frequently. They dropped upon him out of the reaches of this endless void; and with them sometimes came forms that shot past him with amazing swiftness, racing into the empty Beyond as though sucked into a vast vacuum. The very stars seemed to move. He became part of some much larger movement in which he was engulfed and merged. He could no longer think of himself as Jimbo. When he uttered his own name he saw merely a mass of wind and colour through which the great pulses of space and the planets beat tumultuously, lapping him round with the currents of a terrific motion that seemed to swallow up his own little personality entirely, while giving him something infinitely greater....

But surely these small voices, shrill and trumpet-like, did not come from the stars! these deep whispers that ran round the immense vault overhead and sounded almost familiarly in his ears—

"Give it him the moment he wakes."

"Bring the ice-bag... quick!"

"Put the hot bottle to his feet IMMEDIATELY!"

The voices shrieked all round him, turning suddenly into soft whispers that died away somewhere among his feathers. The soles of his feet began to glow, and he felt a gigantic hand laid upon his throat and head. Almost it seemed as if he were lying somewhere on his back, and people were bending over him, shouting and whispering.

"Why hangs the moon so red?" cried a voice that was instantly drowned in a chorus of unintelligible whispering.

"The black cow must be killed," whispered some one deep within the sky.

"Why drips the rain so cold?" yelled one of the hideous children close behind him. And a third called with a distant laughter from behind a star—

"Why sings the wind so shrill?"

"QUIET!" roared an appalling voice below, as if all the rivers of the world had suddenly turned loose into the sky. "QUIET!"

Instantly a star, that had been hovering for some time on the edge of a fantastic dance, dropped down close in front of his face. It had a glaring disc, with mouth and eyes. An icy hand seemed laid on his head, and the star rushed back into its place in the sky, leaving a trail of red flame behind it. A little voice seemed to go with it, growing fainter and fainter in the distance—

"We dance with phantoms and with shadows play."

But, regardless of everything, Jimbo flew onwards and upwards, terrified and helpless though he was. His thoughts turned without ceasing to the governess, and he felt sure that she would yet turn up in time to save him from being caught by the Fright that pursued, or lost among the fearful spaces that lay beyond the stars.

For a long time, however, his wings had been growing more and more tired, and the prospect of being destroyed from sheer exhaustion now presented itself to the boy vaguely as a possible alternative—vaguely only, because he was no longer able to think, properly speaking, and things came to him more by way of dull feeling than anything else.

It was all the more with something of a positive shock, therefore, that he realised the change. For a change had come. He was now suddenly conscious of an influx of new power—greater than anything he had ever known before in any of his flights. His wings now suddenly worked as if by magic. Never had the motion been so easy, and it became every minute easier and easier. He simply flashed along without apparent effort. An immense driving power had entered into him. He realised that he could fly for ever without getting tired. His pace increased tenfold—increased alarmingly. The possibility of exhaustion vanished utterly. Jimbo knew now that something was wrong. This new driving power was something wholly outside himself. His wings were working far too easily. Then, suddenly, he understood: *His wings were not working at all!*

He was not being driven forward from behind; he was being drawn forward from in front.

He saw it all in a flash: Miss Lake's warning long ago about the danger of flying too high; the last song of the Frightened Children, "Dare you fly out alone through the shadows that wave, when the course is unknown and there's no one to save?" the strange words sung to him about the "relentless misty moon," and the object of the dreadful Pursuer in steadily forcing him upwards and away from the earth. It all flashed across his poor little dazed mind. He understood at last.

He had soared too high and had entered the sphere of the moon's attraction.

"The moon is too strong, and there's death in the stars!" a voice bellowed below him like the roar of a falling mountain, shaking the sky.

The child flew screaming on. There was nothing else he could do. But hardly had the roar died away when another voice was heard, a tender voice, a whispering, sympathetic voice, though from what part of the sky it came he could not tell—

"Arrange the pillows for his little head."

But below him the wings of the Pursuer were mounting closer and closer. He could almost feel the mighty wind from their feathers, and hear the rush of the great body between them. It was impossible to slacken his speed even had he wished; no strength on earth could have resisted that terrible power drawing upwards towards the moon. Instinctively, however, he realised that he would rather have gone forwards than backwards. He never could have faced capture by that dreadful creature behind. All the efforts of the past weeks to escape from Fright, the owner of the Empty House, now acted upon him with a cumulative effect, and added to the suction of the moon-life. He shot forward at a pace that increased with every second.

At the back of his mind, too, lay some kind of faint perception that the governess would, after all, be there to help him. She had always turned up before when he was in danger, and she would not fail him now. But this was a mere ghost of a thought that brought little comfort, and merely added its quota of force to the speed that whipped him on, ever faster, into the huge white moon-world in front.

For this, then, he had escaped from the horror of the Empty House! To be sucked up into the moon, the "relentless, misty moon"—to be drawn into its cruel, silver web, and destroyed. The Song to the Misty Moon outside the window came back in snatches and added to his terror; only it seemed now weeks ago since he had heard it. Something of its real meaning, too, filtered down into his heart, and he trembled anew to think that the moon could be a great, vast, moving Being, alive and with a purpose....

But why, oh, why did they keep shouting these horrid snatches of the song through the sky? Trapped! Trapped! The word haunted him through the night:

> Thy songs are nightly driven,
> From sky to sky,
> Eternally,
> O'er the old, grey hills of heaven!

Caught! Caught at last! The moon's prisoner, a captive in her airless caves; alone on her dead white plains; searching for ever in vain for the governess; wandering alone and terrified.

> By the awful grace
> Of thy weird white face.

The thought crazed him, and he struggled like a bird caught in a net. But he might as well have struggled to push the worlds out of their courses.

The power against him was the power of the universe in which he was nothing but a little, lost, whirling atom. It was all of no avail, and the moon did not even smile at his feeble efforts. He was too light to revolve round her, too impalpable to create his own orbit; he had not even the consistency of a cornet; he had reached the point of stagnation, as it were—the dead level—the neutral zone where the attractions of the earth and moon meet and counterbalance one another—where bodies have no weight and existence no meaning.

Now the moon was close upon him; he could see nothing else. There lay the vast, shining sea of light in front of him. Behind, the roar of the following creature grew fainter and fainter, as he outdistanced it in the awful swiftness of the huge drop down upon the moon mountains.

Already he was close enough to its surface to hear nothing of its great singing but a deep, confused murmur. And, as the distance increased, he realised that the change in his own condition increased. He felt as if he were flying off into a million tiny particles—breaking up under the effects of the deadly speed and the action of the new moon-forces. Immense, invisible arms, half-silver and half-shadow, grew out of the white disc and drew him downwards upon her surface. He was being merged into the life of the moon.

There was a pause. For a moment his wings stopped dead. Their vain fluttering was all but over....

Hark! Was that a voice borne on the wings of some lost wind? Why should his heart beat so tumultuously all at once?

He turned and stared into the ocean of black air overhead till it turned him dizzy. A violent trembling ran through his tired being from head to foot. He had heard a voice—a voice that he knew and loved—a voice of help and deliverance. It rang in shrill syllables up the empty spaces, and it reached new centres of force within him that touched his last store of courage and strength.

"Jimbo, hold on!" it cried, like a faint, thin, pricking current of sound almost unable to reach him through the seas of distance. "I'm coming; hold on a little longer!"

It was the governess. She was true to the end. Jimbo felt his heart swell within him. She was mounting, mounting behind him with incredible swiftness. The sound of his own name in these terrible regions recalled to him some degree of concentration, and he strove hard to fight against the drawing power that was seeking his destruction.

He struggled frantically with his wings. But between him and the governess there was still the power of Fright to be overcome—the very Power she had long ago invoked. It was following him still, preventing his turning back, and driving him ever forward to his death.

Again the voice sounded in the night; and this time it was closer. He could not quite distinguish the words. They buzzed oddly in his ears... other voices mingled with them... the hideous children began to shriek somewhere underneath him... wings with eyes among their burning feathers flashed past him.

His own wings folded close over his little body, drooping like dead things. His eyes closed, and he turned on his side. A huge face that was one-half the governess and the other half the head gardener at home, thrust itself close against his own, and blew upon his eyelids till he opened there. Already he was falling, sinking, tumbling headlong through a space that offered no resistance.

"Jimbo!" shrieked a voice that instantly died away into a wail behind him.

He opened his eyes once more—for it was that loved voice again—but the glare from the moon so dazzled him that he could only fancy he saw the figure of the governess, not a hundred feet away, struggling and floundering in the clutch of a black creature that beat the air with enormous wings all round her. He saw her hair streaming out into the night, and one wing seemed to hang broken and useless at her side.

He was turning over and over, like a piece of wood in the waves of the sea, and the governess, caught by Fright, the monster of her own creation, drifted away from his consciousness as a dream melts away in the light of the morning.... From the gleaming mountains and treeless plains below Jimbo thought there rose a hollow roar like the mocking laughter of an immense multitude of people, shaking with mirth. The Moon had got him at last, and her laughter ran through the heavens like a wave. Revolving upon his own little axis so swiftly that he neither saw nor heard anything more, he dropped straight down upon the great satellite.

The light of the moon fanned up into his eyes and dazzled him.

But what in the world was this?

How could the moon dwindle so suddenly to the size of a mere lamp flame?

How could the whole expanse of the heavens shrink in an instant to the limits of a little, cramped room?

In a single second, before he had time to realise that he felt surprise, the entire memory of his recent experiences vanished from his mind. The past became an utter blank. Like a wreath of smoke everything melted away as if it had never been at all. The functions of the brain resumed their normal course. The delirium of the past few hours was over.

Jimbo was lying at home on his bed in the night-nursery, and his mother was bending over him. At the foot of the bed stood the doctor in black. The nurse held a lamp, only half shaded by her hand, as she approached the bedside.

This lamp was the moon of his delirium—only he had quite forgotten now that there had ever been any moon at all.

The little thermometer, thrust into his teeth among the stars, was still in his mouth. A hot-water bottle made his feet glow and burn. And from the walls of the sick-room came as it were the echoes of recently-uttered sentences "Take his temperature! Give him the medicine the moment he wakes! Put the hot bottle to his feet... Fetch the ice-bag.... Quick!"

"Where am I, mother?" he asked in a whisper.

"You're in bed, darling, and must keep quite quiet. You'll soon be all right again. It was the old black cow that tossed you. The gardener found you by the swinging gate and carried you in.... You've been unconscious!"

"How long have I been uncon—?" Jimbo could not manage the whole word.

"About three hours, darling."

Then he fell into a deep, dreamless sleep, and when he woke long after it was early morning, and there was no one in the room but the old family nurse, who sat watching beside the bed. Something—some dim memory—that had stirred his brain in sleep, immediately rushed to his lips in the form of an inconsequent question. But before he could even frame the sentence, the thought that prompted it had slipped back into the deeper consciousness he had just left behind with the trance of deep sleep.

But the old nurse, watching every movement, waiting upon the child's very breath, had caught the question, and she answered soothingly in a whisper—

"Oh, Miss Lake died a few days after she left here," she said in a very low voice. "But don't think about her any more, dearie! She'll never frighten children again with her silly stories."

"*DIED!*"

Jimbo sat up in bed and stared into the shadows behind her, as though his eyes saw something she could not see. But his voice seemed almost to belong to some one else.

"She was really dead all the time, then," he said below his breath.

Then the child fell back without another word, and dropped off into the sleep which was the first step to final recovery.

THE END

THE
EDUCATION
OF UNCLE
PAUL

By Algernon Blackwood

To
All Those Children
Between the Ages of Eight and Eighty
Who Led Me to "The Crack";
And Have Since Journeyed With Me Through It
Into
The Land "Between Yesterday and To-Morrow"

CHAPTER I

...I stand as mute
As one with full strong music in his heart
Whose fingers stray upon a shattered lute.
ALICE MEYNELL

All night the big liner had been plunging heavily, but towards morning she entered quieter water, and when the passengers woke, her rising and falling over the great swells was so easy that even the sea-sick women admitted the relief.

"Land in sight, sir! We shall see Liverpool within twenty hours now, barring fog."

The friendly bathroom steward passed the open door of Stateroom No. 28, and the big, brown-bearded man in the blue serge suit who was sitting, already dressed, on the edge of the port-hole berth, started as though he had been shot, and ran up on deck without waiting to finish tying the laces of his india-rubber shoes.

"By Jove!" he said, as he thundered along the stuffy passages of the rolling vessel, and "By Gad!"

He emerged on the upper deck in the sunlight, having nearly injured several persons in his impetuous journey, and, taking a great gulp of the salt air with keen satisfaction, he crossed to the side in a couple of strides, the shoe-laces clicking against the deck as he went.

"Twenty years ago," he muttered, "when I was barely out of my teens. And now—!"

The big man was distinctly excited, though "moved" perhaps is the better word, seeing that the emotion was a little too searching, too tinged with sadness, to include elation. He plunged both hands into his coat pockets with a violence that threatened to tear the bottoms out, and leaned over the railing.

Far away a faint blue line, tinged delicately with green, rose out of the sea. He saw it instantly, and his throat tightened unexpectedly, almost like a reflex action. For, about that simple little blue line on the distant horizon there was something strangely seizing, something absolutely arresting. The sight of it was a hundred times more poignant than he had imagined it would be; it touched a thousand springs of secret life in him, and a mist rose faintly before his eyes.

Paul Rivers had not realised that his emotion would be so intense; but from that instant everything on the ship, otherwise familiar and rather boring, looked different. A new sense of locality came to him. The steamer became strange and new; he "recognised" bits of it as though he had just come aboard a ship known aforetime. It was the steamer that was merely crossing the Atlantic; it was the boat that was bringing him home. And there, trimming the horizon in a thin ribbon of most arresting beauty, was the coast-line of the first Island.

"But it seems so much more solid—and so much more real than I expected!"

Though it was barely seven o'clock a few early passengers were already astir, and he made his way back again to the lower deck and thence climbed up into the bows. He wished to be alone. Another man, apparently from the steerage, was there before him, leaning over the rail and peering fixedly under one hand at the horizon. The saloon passenger took up his position a few feet farther on and stared hard. He, too, stared with the eyes of memory, now grown a little dim. The air was fresh and sweet, fragrant of long sea distances; there was a soft warmth in it too, for it was late April and the spring made its presence known even on the great waters where there was nothing to hang its fairy banners on.

"So that's land! That's the Old Country!"

The words dropped out of their own accord ; he could not help himself. The sky seemed to come down a little closer, with a more familiar and friendly touch; the very air, he fancied, had a new taste in it,—a whiff of his boyhood days—a smell of childhood and the things of childhood—ages ago, it seemed, in another life.

The huge ship rose and fell on the regular, sweeping swells, and sea-birds from the land already came out to meet her. He easily imagined that the thrills in the depths of his own being somehow communicated themselves to the mighty vessel that tore the seas asunder in her great desire to reach the land.

"Twenty years," he repeated aloud, oblivious of his neighbour, "twenty years since I last saw it!"

" And it's gol-darned nearer fifty since *I* seen it," exclaimed a harsh voice just behind him.

He turned with a start. The steerage passenger beside him, he saw, was an old man with a rough, grey face, and hair turning white; the hand that shaded his eyes was thick and worn; there was a heavy gold ring on the little finger, and the dirty cuff of a dark flannel shirt tumbled, loosely and unbuttoned, over the very solid wrist. The face, he noticed, at a second glance, was rugged, beaten, scored, the face of a man who had tumbled terribly about life, battered from pillar to post; and it was only the light in the hard blue eyes—eyes still fixed unwaveringly on the distant line of the land—that redeemed it from a kind of grim savagery. Beaten and battered, yes! Yet at the same time triumphant. The atmosphere of the man proclaimed in some vibrant fashion beyond analysis that he had failed in all he undertook—failed from stupidity rather than character, and always doggedly beginning over again with the same lack of intelligence—but yet had never given in, and never would give in.

It was not difficult to reconstruct his history from his appearance; or to realise his feelings as he saw the Old Country after fifty years—a returned failure. Although the voice had vibrated with emotion, the face remained expressionless and unmoved; but down both cheeks large tears ran slowly, in sudden jerks, to drop with a splash upon the railing. And Paul Rivers, after his intuitive fashion, grasped the whole drama of the man with a sudden completeness that touched him with swift sympathy. At the same time he could not help thinking of rain-drops running down the face of a statue. He recognised with shame that he was conscious of a desire to laugh.

"Fifty years! That's a long time indeed," he said kindly. "It's half-a-century."

"That's so, Boss," returned the other in a dead voice that betrayed Ireland overlaid with acquired American twang and intonation; "and I guess now I'll never be able to stick it over here. Jest see it—and then git back again."

He kept his eyes fixed on the horizon, and never once turned his head towards the man he was speaking to; only his lips moved; he did not even lift a finger to brush off the great tears that fell one by one from his cheeks to the deck. He seemed unconscious of them; as though it was so long since those hard eyes had melted that they had forgotten how to do it properly and the skin no longer registered the sensation of the trickling. The tears continued to fall at intervals; Paul Rivers actually heard them splash.

"I went out steerage," the man continued to himself, or to the sea, or to any one else who cared to listen, "and I come back steerage. That's my trouble. And now"—his eye shifted for a fraction of a second and watched a huge wave go thundering by—"I'm grave-huntin', I guess. And that's about the size of it. Jest see it and—git back again!"

The first-class passenger made some kind and appropriate reply—words with genuine sympathy in them—and then, getting no further answer, found it difficult to continue the conversation. The man, he realised, had only wanted a peg to hang his emotion on. It had to be a living peg, but any other living peg would do equally well, and before long he would find some one in the steerage who would listen with delight to the flood that was bound to come. And, presently, he took his departure to his own quarters where the sailors, with bare feet, were still swabbing the slippery decks.

A couple of hours later, after breakfast, he leaned over the rail and again saw the man on the steerage deck, and heard him talking volubly. The tears were gone, but the smudges were still visible on the cheeks, where they had traced a zigzag pattern. He was telling the history of his fifty years' disappointments and failures to one and all who cared to listen.

And, apparently, many cared to listen. The man's emotion was real; it found vigorous expression. The sight of the old, loved shore, not seen for half-a-century, but the subject of ten thousand yearnings, had been too much for him. He told in detail the substance of these ten thousand dreams—ever one and the same dream, of course—and in the telling of it he found the relief his soul sought. He got it all out; it did him a world of good, saving his inner being from a whole army of severe mental fevers and spiritual pains. The man revelled in a delirium of self-expression, and in so doing found sanity and health for his overburdened soul.

And the picture of that hard-faced old man crying accompanied Paul Rivers to the upper decks, and remained insistently with him for a long time. It portrayed with such neat emphasis precisely what was so deplorably lacking in his own character. There, in concrete form, though not precisely his own case, still near enough to be extremely illuminating, he had seen a grown-up man finding abundant and natural expression for his emotion. The man was not ashamed of his tears, and would doubtless have let them splash on the deck before a hundred passengers, whereas he, Paul Rivers, was, it seemed, constitutionally unable to reveal himself, to tell his deep longings, to find expression through any sensible medium for the ten thousand dreams that choked his life to the brim. He was unable, perhaps ashamed, to splash on the deck.

It was not that the big, bronzed Englishman wanted to cry, or to wash his soul in sentiment, but that the sight of this old man's passion, and its frank and easy utterance, touched with dramatic intensity the crying need of his whole temperament. The need of the steerage passenger was the need of a moment; his own was the need of an existence.

"Lucky devil!" he exclaimed, half laughing, half sighing, as he went to his cabin for the field-glasses; "he knows how to get it out—and does get it out! while I—with my impossible yearnings and my absurd diffidence in speaking of them to others—I haven't got a single safety-valve of any sort or kind. I can't get it out of me—all this ocean in my heart and soul—not a drop, not even a blessed tear!"

He laughed again and, stooping to pick up the glasses, he caught a glimpse of his sunburned, bearded face in the cabin mirror.

"Even my appearance is against me," he went on with mournful humour; "I look like a healthy lumberman more than anything else in God's world!"

He bent forward and examined himself carefully in detail.

"What has such a face as that to do with beauty, and the stars, and the moon sinking over a summer sea, or those night-winds I know rising faintly from their hiding-places in the dim forests and stealing on soft tip-toe about the sleeping world until the dawn gives them leave to run and sing? Yet I know—though I can never tell it to another—what so many do not know! Who could ever believe that *that* man"—he pointed to himself in the glass, laughing—"wants above all else in life, above wealth, fame, success, the knowledge of spiritual things, which is Reality—which is God?"

A flash of light from nowhere ran over his face, making it for one instant like the face of a boy, shining, wonderful, radiantly young.

"I know, for instance," he went on, the strange flush of enthusiasm rising into his eyes, "that the pine-trees hold wind in their arms as cups hold rare wine, and that when it spills I hear the exquisite trickling of its music—but I can't tell any one *that!* And I can't even put the wild magic of it into verse or music. Or even into conduct," he concluded with a laugh, "conduct that's sane, that is. For, if I could, I should find what I'm for ever seeking behind all life and behind all expressions of beauty—I should find the Reality I seek!"

"I've no safety-valves," he added, swinging the glasses round by their strap to the imminent danger of various articles of furniture, "that's the long and short of it. Like a giraffe that can't make any sound at all although it has the longest throat in all creation. Everything in me accumulates and accumulates. If only"—and the strange light came back for a second to his brown eyes—"I could write, or sing, or pray—live as the saints did, or do something to—to express adequately the sense of beauty and wonder and delight that lives, like the presence of a God, in my soul!"

The lamp in his eyes faded slowly and he sat back on the little cabin sofa, screwing and unscrewing his glasses till it was surprising that the thread didn't wear out. And as he screwed, a hundred fugitive pictures passed thronging through his mind; moments of yearning and of pain, of sudden happiness and of equally sudden despondency, vivid moods of all kinds provoked by the smallest imaginable fancies, as the way ever was with him. For the moods of the sky were his moods; the swift, coloured changes of sea and cloud were mirrored in his heart as with all too impressionable people, and he was for ever trying to seize the secret of their loveliness and to give it form—in vain. Like many another mystical soul he saw the invisible foundations of the visible world—longed to communicate it to others—found he couldn't—then suffered all the pain and fever of repression that seeks in vain for adequate utterance. Too shy to stammer his profound yearnings to ears that would not hear, and, never having known the blessed relief of a sympathetic audience, he perforce remained choked and dumb, the only mitigation he knew being that loss of self which follows prolonged contemplation. In his contemplation of Nature, for instance, he would gaze upon the landscape, the sky, a tree or flower, until their essential beauty passed into his own nature. For the moment he *felt with* these things. He *was* them. He took their qualities literally into himself. He lost his ordinary personality by changing its centre, merging it into those remoter phases of consciousness which extended from himself mysteriously to include the landscape, the sky, the tree, the flower.

For him everywhere in Nature there was psychic energy. And it was difficult to say which was with him the master passion: to find Reality— God—through Nature, or to explain Nature through God.

Then the busy faces of America, now left behind after twenty years, gradually receded, and others, dimly seen through mist, rose above the horizon of his thoughts. And among them he saw that two stood forth with more clearness than the rest. One of these was Dick Messenger, the friend of his boyhood, now dead but a few years; and the other, the face of his sister, Margaret, whom Dick had left a widow, and whose children he would now see for the first time at their country home in the South of England.

The "Old Country!" He repeated the words softly to himself, weaving it like a coloured thread through all his reverie. He had lived away long— long enough to understand the poignant magic that lies in the little phrase, and to appreciate the seizing and pathetic beauty lying along that faint blue line of sea and sky.

And presently he took his field-glasses again and went up on deck and hid himself in the bows alone. Leaning over the bulwarks he took the scented wind of spring full in the face, and watched with a curious exhilaration the huge rollers, charging and bellowing like wild bulls of the sea as the ship drew nearer and nearer to the coast, plunging, leaping, and thundering as she moved.

CHAPTER II

Justice is not done to the versatility and the unplumbed childishness of man's imagination. His life from without may seem but a rude mound of mud, there will be some golden chamber at the heart of it, in which he dwells delighted; and for as dark as his pathway seems to the observer, he will have some kind of a bull's-eye at his belt. —R. L. S.

The case of Paul Rivers after all was very simple, though perhaps in some respects uncommon. Circumstances—to sum it up roughly—had so conspired that the most impressionable portion of his character—half of his mind and most of his soul, that is—had never found utterance. He had never discovered the medium that could carry forth into the relief of expression all the inner turmoil and delight of a soul that was very much alive and singularly in touch with the simple and primitive forces of the world.

It was not, as with the returned emigrant, grief that he felt, but something far more troublesome: Joy. For the beauty of the world, of character as of nature, laid a spell upon him that set his heart in the glow and fever of an inner furnace, while the play of his imagination among the "common" things of life which the rest of the world apparently thought dull set him often upon the borders of an ecstasy whereof he found himself unable to communicate one single letter to his fellow-beings. Thus, in later years, and out of due season, he was afflicted and perplexed by a luxuriant growth that by rights should have been harvested before he was twenty-five; and a great part of him had neglected to grow up at all.

This result was due to no fault—no neglect, that is—of his own, but to circumstances and temperament combined. It explains, however, why, after twenty years in the backwoods of America, he saw the coast of the Old Country with a deep emotion that was not all delight, but held something also of dismay.

Left an orphan, with his younger sister, at an early age, the blundering of trustees had forced him out into the world before his first term at Cambridge was over, and after various vicissitudes he had found his way to America and had been drawn into the lumber trade. Here his knowledge and love of trees—it was a veritable passion with him—soon resulted in a transfer from the Minneapolis office to the woods, and after an interesting apprenticeship, he came to hold an important post in which he was strangely at home. He was appointed to the post of "Wood Cruiser"—forest-traveller, *commis voyageur* of the primeval woods. His duties, well paid too, were to survey, judge, mark, and report upon the qualities and values of the immense timber limits owned by his Company. And he loved the work. It was a life of solitude, but a life close to Nature; borne in his canoe down swift wilderness streams; meeting the wild animals in their secret haunts; becoming intimate with dawns and sunsets, great winds, the magic of storms and stars, and being initiated into the profound mysteries of the clean and haunted regions of the world.

And the effect of this kind of life upon him—especially at an age when most men are busy learning more common values in the strife of cities— was of course significant. For here, in this solitary existence, the beauty of the world, virgin and glorious, struck the eyes of his soul and nearly blinded them.

His whole being threw itself inwards upon his thoughts, and outwards upon what fed his thoughts—the wonder of Nature. Even as a boy he had been mystically minded, a poet if ever there was one, though a poet without a lyre; but at school he had chanced to come under the influence of masters who had sought to curb the exuberance of his imagination, so that he started into life with the rooted idea that it was something of a disgrace for a man to be too sensitive to beauty, and to possess a vivid and coloured imagination was almost a thing to he ashamed of.

This view of his only "silver talent," moreover, was never permitted by the nature of his life to alter. His early American experiences stiffened it into a conviction which he yet despised. The fires ran hidden, if unchecked. Had he dwelt in cities, they might have suffered total extinction perhaps, but here, in the heart of the free woods, they speedily rose to the surface again and flamed. He grew up singularly unspoilt, the shyness of the original nature utterly uncorrected, the stores of a poetic imagination accumulating steadily, but always unuttered.

For his sole companions all these years when he had any at all were the "Bosses" of the lumber camps he inspected, the "Cookee" who looked after his stew-pot in the "home-shack," and the half-breed Indian who accompanied him in the stern-seat of the bark canoe during the month-long trips about the wilderness: these—with the animals, winds, stars, and the forms of beauty his imagination for ever conjured out of them.

For twenty years he lived thus, knowing all the secrets of the woods and streams. In the summer he never slept under cover at all, so that even in sleep he understood, through closed eyelids, the motions of the stars behind the tangled network of branches overhead. In winter his snow-shoes carried him into the heart of the most dazzling scenes imaginable— the forest lying under many feet of snow with a cloudless sun lifting it all into an appearance of magic that took the breath away. Moreover, the fierce spring, when the streams became impassable floods, and the autumn, with a flaming glory of gold and scarlet unknown anywhere else in the world, he knew as intimately as the dryads themselves.

And all these moods became the intimate companions of his life, taking the place of men and women. He came to personify Nature as a matter of course.

Without knowing it, too, the place of children was taken somehow by the wild animals. He knew them all. He surprised them in their haunts in the course of his silent journeys into the heart of their playgrounds; and his headquarters—a one-story shanty on the height of land between his two chief "limits"—was never without a tamed baby bear, a young moose to draw him on his snow-shoes with the manners of a well-bred pony, and a dozen other animals reclaimed from savagery and turned by some mysterious system of his own into real companions and confidants.

And the only books he read in the long winter nights, besides a few modern American novels that puzzled and vaguely distressed him, were Blake, his loved Greek plays, and the Bible.

He rarely saw a woman. Sides of his nature that ought to have developed under the influences of normal life at home lay dormant altogether, or were filled as best might be by his intercourse with Nature. He wrote few letters. After Dick Messenger died, the formal correspondence he kept up at long intervals with his sister—Dick's widow—hardly deserved the name of letters. Great slabs of him, so to speak, stopped growing up, sinking down into the subconscious region to await conditions favourable for calling them to the surface again, and eventually coming to life—this was his tragic little secret—at a time when they were long overdue.

To the end of life he remained shy, shy in the sense that most of his thoughts and emotions he was afraid to reveal to others; with the shyness, too, of the utterly modest soul that cannot believe the world will give it the very things it has most right to claim, yet never dares to claim. And to the end Nature never lifted the spell laid upon him during those twenty years of initiation in her solitudes. To see the new moon tilting her silver horns in the west; to hear the wind rustling in high trees, like old Indians telling one another secrets of the early world; and to see the first stars looking down from the height of sky through spaces of watery blue—these, and a hundred other things that the majority seemed to ignore, were to him a more moving and terrible delight than anything he could imagine. For him such things could never be explained away, but remained living and uncorrected to the end.

Thus when, at forty-five, he inherited the fortune of his aunt (which he had always known must one day come to him), he returned to England with the shy, bursting, dream-laden heart of a boy, young as only those are young whom life has kept clean and sweet in the wilderness; and the question that sprang to life in his heart when he saw the blue line of coast was a vague wonder as to what would become of his full-blooded dreams when tested by the conventional English life that he remembered as a boy. To whom could he speak of his child-like yearning after God; of his swift divinations, his passionate intuitions into the very things that the majority put away with childhood? What modern priest—so he felt, at least—what befuddled mystic, could possibly enter into the essential nature of these cravings as he did, or understand, without a sneer, the unspoilt passions of a man who had never "grown up"?

"I shall be out of touch with it all," he thought as he stood there in the bows and watched the blue line grow nearer, "utterly out of touch. What shall I find to say to the men of my own age—I, who stopped growing up twenty years ago? How shall I ever link on with them? Children are the only things I can talk to, and children!"—he shrugged his shoulders and laughed—"children will find me out at once and give me away to the others."

"Dick's children, though, may be different!" came the sudden reflection. "Only—I've had nothing to do with children for such ages. Dick had real imagination. By George,"—and his eyes glowed a moment—"what if they took after him!"

And for the fiftieth time, as he pictured the meeting with his stranger sister, his heart sank, and he found refuge in the knowledge that he had not altogether burned his boats behind him. For he had been wise in his generation. He had arranged with his Company, who were only too glad of the chance of keeping his services, that he should go to England on a year's leave, and that if in the end he decided to return he should have a share in the business, while still continuing the work of forest-inspection that he loved.

"I'm nothing but a wood-cruiser. I shall go back. In the big world I might lose all my vision!"

And, having lived so long out of the world, he now came back to it with this simple, innocent, imaginative heart of a great boy, a boy still dreaming, for all his five-and-forty years. Fully realising that something was wrong with him, that he ought to be more sedate, more cynical, more prosaic and sober, he yet could not quite explain to himself wherein lay the source of his disability. His thoughts stumbled and blundered when he tried to lay his finger on it, with the only result that he felt he would be "out of touch " with his new world, not knowing exactly how or why.

"It's a regular log-jam," he said, using the phraseology he was accustomed to, "and I'm sorry for the chap that breaks it."

It never occurred to him that in this simple thrill that Nature still gave him he possessed one of the greatest secrets for the preservation of genuine youth; indeed, had he understood this, it would have meant that he was already old. For with the majority such dreams die young, brushed rudely from the soul by the iron hand of experience, whereas in his case it was their persistent survival that lent such a childlike quality to his shyness, and made him secretly ashamed of not feeling as grown-up as he realised he ought to feel.

Paul Rivers, in a word, belonged to a comprehensible though perhaps not over common type, and one not often recognised owing to the elaborate care with which its "specimens" conceal themselves from the world under all manner of brave disguises. He was destitute of that nameless quality that constitutes a human being, not mature necessarily, but grown up. Sources of inner enthusiasm that most men lose when life brings to them the fruit of the Tree of Good and Evil, had kept alive; and though on the one hand he was secretly ashamed of the very simplicity of his great delights, on the other hand he longed intensely for some means by which he could express them and relieve his burdened soul.

He envied the emigrant who could let fall hot tears on the deck without further ado, while at the same time he dreaded the laughter of the world into which he was about to move when they learned the cause of the emotions that produced them. A boy at forty-five! A dreamer of children's dreams with fifty in sight—and no practical results!

These were some of the thoughts still tumbling vaguely about his mind when the tug brought letters aboard at Queenstown, and on the dining-room table where they were spread out he found one for himself in a handwriting that he both welcomed and dreaded.

CHAPTER III

He welcomed it, because for years it had been the one remaining link with the life of his old home—these formal epistles that reached him at long intervals; and he dreaded it, because he knew it would contain a definite invitation of an embarrassing description.

"She's bound to ask me," he reflected as he opened it in his cabin; "she can't help herself. And I am bound to accept, for I can't help myself either." He was far too honest to think of inventing elaborate excuses. "I've got to go and spend a month with her right away whether I like it or not."

It was not by any means that he disliked his sister, for indeed he hardly knew her; after all these years he barely remembered what she looked like, the slim girl of eighteen he had left behind. It was simply that in his mind she stood for the conventional life, so alien to his vision, to which he had returned.

He would try to like her, certainly. Very warm impulses stirred in his heart as he thought of her—his only near relative in the world, and the widow of his old school and Cambridge friend, Dick Messenger. It was in her handwriting that he first learned of Dick's love for her, as it was in hers that the news of his friend's death reached him—after his long tour—two months old. The handwriting was a symbol of the deepest human emotions he had known. And for that reason, too, he dreaded it.

He never realised quite what kind of woman she had become; in his thoughts she had always remained simply the girl, of eighteen—grown up—married. Her letters had been very kind and gentle, if in the nature of the case more and more formal. She became shadowy and vague in his mind as the years passed, and more and more he had come to think of her as wholly out of his own world. Reading between the lines it was not difficult to see that she attached importance to much in life that seemed to him unreal and trivial, whereas the things that he thought vital she never referred to at all. It might, of course, be merely restraint concealing great depths. He could not tell. The letters, after a few years, had become like formal government reports. He had written fully, however, to announce his home-coming, and her reply had been full of genuine pleasure.

"I don't think she'll make very much of me," was the thought in his mind whenever he dwelt upon it. "I'm afraid my world must seem foreign—unreal to her; the things I know rubbish."

So, in the privacy of his cabin, his heart already strangely astir by the emotion of that blue line on the horizon, he read his sister's invitation and found it charming. There was spontaneous affection in it.

"We shall fix things up between us so that no one would ever know." He did not explain what it was "no one would ever know," but went on to finish the letter. He was to make his home with her in the country, he read, until he decided what to do with himself. The tone of the letter made his heart bound. It was a real welcome, and he responded to it instantly like a boy. Only one thing in it seriously disturbed his equanimity. Absurd as it may seem, the fact that his sister's welcome included also that of the children, had a subtly disquieting effect upon him.

"...for they are dying to see you and to find out for themselves what the big old uncle they have heard so much about is really like. All their animals are being cleaned and swept so as to be ready for your arrival, and, in anticipation of your stories of the backwoods, no other tales find favour with them any more."

An expression of perplexity puckered his face. "I declare, I'm afraid of those children—Dick's children!" he thought, holding the open letter to his mouth and squinting down the page, while his eyebrows rose and his forehead broke into lines. "They'll find out what I am. They'll betray me. I shall never be able to hold out against them." He knew only too well how searching was the appeal that all growing and immature life made to him. It touched the very centre of him that had refused to grow up and that made him young with itself. "I can no more resist them than I could resist the baby bears, or that little lynx that used to eat out of my hand." He shrugged his big shoulders, looking genuinely distressed. "And then every one will know what I am—an overgrown boy—a dumb poet—a dreamer of dreams that bear no fruit!"

He was not morbidly introspective. He was merely trying to face the little problem squarely. He got up and staggered across the cabin, steadying himself against the rolling of the ship in front of the looking-glass.

"Big Old Uncle!"

He stuffed the letter into his pocket and surveyed himself critically. Big he certainly was, but that other adjective brought with it a sensation of weariness that had never yet troubled him in his wilderness existence. He was only a little, just a very little, on the shady side of forty-five, but to the children he might seem really old, *aged,* and to his sister, who was considerably his junior, as elderly, and perhaps in need of the comforts of the elderly."

He squared his shoulders and looked more closely into the glass. There, opposite to him, stood a tall, dignified man in a blue suit, with a spotless linen collar and a neat tie passing through a gold ring, instead of the unkempt fellow he was accustomed to in a flannel shirt, red handkerchief and big sombrero hat pulled over his eyes; a man weighing the best part of fifteen stones, lean, well-knit, vigorous, and nearly six feet three in his socks. A pair of brown eyes, kindly brown eyes he thought, met his own questioningly and a brown beard—yes, it was still brown—covered the lower part of the face. He put up a hand to stroke it, and noticed that it was a strong, muscular hand, sunburnt but well kept, with neat fingernails, and a heavy signet ring on one finger. It brushed across the rather deep lines on the bronzed forehead, without brushing them away, however, and then travelled higher to the rough parting in the dark-brown hair, and the hair, he noticed, was brushed in a particular way evidently, a way he thought no one would notice but himself and the lumber-camp barber who first taught him, so as to cover up a few places where the wind made little chilly feelings in winter-time under his fur cap.

Old? No, not old yet—but "getting on" was a gentler phrase he could not deny, and there were certainly odd traces where the crows had walked on his skin while he slept in the forest, and had hopped up even to the corners of his eyes to see if he were really asleep. There were other lines, too—lines of exposure, traced by wind and sun, and one or two queer marks that are said only to come from prolonged hardship and severest want. For he had known both sides of the wilderness life, and on his long journeys Nature had not always been kind to him.

He stared for a long time at his reflection in the glass, lost in reverie. This coming back to England after so many years was like looking at a picture of himself as he was when he had left; it furnished him with a ready standard of comparison; the changes of the years stood out very sharply, as though they had come about in a single night.

Yes, his face and figure had aged a good deal. He admitted it. And when he frowned he had distinctly an appearance of middle age. This, of course, was the absurd part of it, for in spirit he had remained as young as he was at twenty, as enthusiastic, hopeful, spontaneous as ever, just as much in love with the world, and just as full of boyhood's dreams as when he went to Cambridge. And in his eyes still burned the strange flames that sought to pierce behind the veil of appearances.

"And those children will find it out and make one look ridiculous before I've been there a week!" he exclaimed again, sitting down on his bunk with a crash as the steamer gave a sudden lurch; "and then where shall I be, I'd like to know?"

He lay on his back for an hour thinking out a plan of action. For, of course, he decided that he must go; only—he must go *disguised*. And he spent hours inventing the disguise, and more hours perfecting it. For the first time in his life he would adopt a distinct attitude, and, having carefully thought out the attitude he intended to adopt by way of disguise, he buckled it on like armour and fastened it very securely indeed to his large person.

He would be kind; he would even meet the children half-way, kiss them if necessary at stated times, in a stated way, and perhaps occasionally unbend a little as opportunity served and circumstances permitted. But never must he forget, or allow them to forget, that he was a stiff and elderly man, a little grim and gruff sometimes even severe and short-tempered, and never to be trifled with at any time, or under any conditions.

Over the tenderer emotions he must keep especial watch; these were a direct channel to his secrets, and once the old unsatisfied enthusiasms escaped, there was no saying what might happen. The thought frightened him, for the pain involved might be very great indeed.

With people of his own age, he realised, the danger would be less. Silence and reserve cover a multitude of shortcomings. But children, he knew, had a simple audacity, a merciless penetration, that no mere pose could ever withstand. And this he felt intuitively, knowing nothing of children, but being taught by these very qualities in himself. Like little animals they would soon find the direct channel to his heart unless well guarded, and come tumbling along it without delay. And then—!

So Paul Rivers left London the very next day, glad in many ways to think that he had this haven of refuge to go to from the noisy horror of the huge strange city; yet with a sinking of his heart lest his true self should be discovered, and held up to scorn.

Moreover, the strange part of it was that as he sped down through the smiling green country that spring afternoon, armed from head to foot in the rigid steel casings of his disguise, he seemed to hear a faint singing deep within him, a singing that belonged to the youngest part of him and yet sprang from that which was vastly ancient, but as to the cause of which he was so puzzled that, in his efforts to analyse it, he forgot about his journey altogether, and was nearly carried past the station where he had to get out.

CHAPTER IV

No man worth his spiritual salt can ever become really entangled in locality.
                                                              —A.H.L.

The house, like the description of himself in the letter, was big and old.
It consisted of three rambling wings, each added at a different period to an
original farmhouse, and was thus full of unexpected staircases, sudden rising passages, and rooms of queer shapes. It resembled, indeed, the structure of a mind that has grown by chance and not by system, and was just
as difficult for a stranger to find his way in.

It stood among pine-woods, at the foot of hills that ran on another five
miles to drop their chalk cliffs abruptly into the sea. Where the lawns
stopped on one side and the kitchen-garden on the other began an
expanse of undulating heather-land, dotted with pools of brown water
and yellow with patches of gorse and broom. Here rabbits increased and
multiplied; sea-gulls screamed and flew, using some of the more secluded
ponds for their annual breeding places; foxes lived happily, unhunted and
very bold; and the dainty hoof-marks of deer were sometimes found in the
sandy margins of the freshwater springs.

It was beautiful country, a bit of wild England, out of the world as very
few parts of it now are, and haunted by a loveliness that laid its spell on
the heart of the returned exile the moment he topped the hill in the dog-
cart and saw it spread out before him like a softly coloured map. The
scenery from the train window had somehow disheartened him a little,
producing a curious sense of confinement, almost of imprisonment, in his
mind: the neat meadows holding wooden cattle; the careful boundaries of
ditch and hedge; the five-barred gates, strong to enclose, the countless
notices to warn trespassers, and the universal network of barbed wire.
Accustomed as he was to the vast, unhedged landscapes of a primitive
country, it all looked to him, with its precise divisions, like a toy garden,
combed, washed, swept—exquisitely cared for, but a little too sweet and
perfumed to be quite wholesome. Only tame things, he felt, could enjoy so
gentle a playground, and the call of his own forests—for this really was
what worked in him—sang out to him with a sterner cry.

But this view from the ridge pleased him more: there were but few
hedges visible; the eye was led to an open horizon and the sea; an impression of space and freedom rose from the hills and moorlands. Here his
thoughts, accustomed to deal with leagues rather than acres, could at least
find room to turn about in. And although the perfume that rose to his nostrils was like the perfume of flowers preserved by some artificial process
rather than the great clean smells of a virgin world such as he was used to,
it was nevertheless the smell of his boyhood and it moved him powerful-

ly. Odour is the one thing that is impossible to recall in exile. Sights and sounds the imagination can always reconstruct after a fashion, but odour is too elusive. It rose now to his nostrils as something long forgotten, and swept him with a wave of memory that was extraordinarily keen.

"That's a smell to take me back twenty-five years," he thought, inhaling the scent of the heather. He caught his breath sharply, uncertain whether it was pain or pleasure that predominated. A profound yearning, too fugitive to be seized, too vague to be definitely labelled, stirred in the depths of him as his eye roamed over the miles of sunlight and blue shadow at his feet; again something sang within him as he gazed over the long ridges of heathland, sprinkled with silvery pools, and bearing soft purple masses of pine-woods on their sides as they melted away through haze to the summer sea beyond.

Only when his gaze fell upon the smoke rising from the grey stone roof of the house nestling far below did the joy of his emotion chill a little. A vague sense of alarm and nervousness touched him as he wondered what that grey old building might hold in store for him.

"It's silly, I know," his thought ran, "but I feel like a lost sheep here. It's Nature that calls me, not people. I don't know how I shall get on in this chess-board sort of a country. They'll never care for the things that I care for."

For a moment a sort of panic came over him. He could almost have turned and run. Vaguely he felt that he was an unfinished, uncouth article in a shop of dainty china. He sent the dog-cart on ahead, and walked down the hill-side towards the house, thinking, thinking—wondering almost why he had ever consented to come, and already conscious of a sense of imprisonment. He was still impressionable as a boy, with sharp, fleeting moods like a boy's.

Then, quite suddenly it seemed, he had walked up the drive and passed through the house, and a figure moved across a lawn to meet him. The first sight of his sister he had known for twenty years was a tall woman in white serge, with a prim, still girlish figure and a quiet, smiling face, moving graciously through patches of sunshine between flower-beds of formal outline. There was no spontaneous rush of welcome, no gush, or flood of questions. He felt relieved. With a flash, too, he realised that her dominant note was still grief for her lost husband. It was written all over her.

Instantly, however, shyness descended upon him like a cloud. The scene he had rehearsed so often in imagination vanished before the reality. He slipped down inside himself, as his habit sometimes was, and watched the performance curiously, as though he were a spectator of it instead of an actor.

He saw himself, hot and rather red in the face, walking awkwardly across the lawn with both hands out, offering his bearded face clumsily to be kissed. And it was kissed, first on one cheek, then on the other, calmly, soberly, delicately. He felt the tingling of it for a long time afterwards. That kiss confused him ridiculously.

At first he could think of nothing to say except the form of address he always used to the Bosses of the lumber camps—"How's everything up your way?"—which he felt was not quite the most suitable phrase for the occasion. Then his sister spoke, and quickly set him more at his ease.

"But you don't look one little bit like an American, Paul!"

He gazed at her in admiration, just as he might have gazed at a complete stranger. The soft intonation of her voice was a keen delight to him. And her matter-of-fact speech put his shyness to flight.

"Of course not," he replied, leaving out her name after a second's hesitation, "but my voice, I guess—"

"Not a bit either," she repeated, surveying him very critically. "You look like a sailor home from the sea more than anything else."

She wore a wide garden hat of Panama straw, charmingly trimmed with flowers. Her face beneath it, Paul thought, was the most refined and exquisitely delicate he had ever seen. It was like chiselled porcelain. He thought of Hank Davis's woman at Deep Bay Camp—whose face he used to think wonderful rather—and it suddenly seemed by comparison to have been chopped with a blunt axe out of wood.

They moved to the long chairs upon the lawn, and her brother realised for the first time that his boots were enormous, and that his Minneapolis clothes did not sit upon him quite as they might have done. He trod on a corner of a geranium bed as they went, crushing an entire plant with one foot. But his sister appeared not to notice it.

"It's an awful long time, M—Margaret," he stammered as they went.

They both sat down and turned to stare at each other. It was, of course, idle to pretend that after so long an absence they could feel any very profound affection. Dick, he realised quickly with a flash of intuition, was the truer link. And, on the whole, it was all much easier than he had expected. His mind began to work very quickly in several directions at once. The beauty of the English garden in its quiet way touched him keenly, stirring in him little whirls of inner delight, fugitive but wonderful. Only a portion of him, after all, went out to his sister.

"I believe you expected a Red Indian, or a bear," he said at length.

She laughed gently, returning his stare of genuine admiration. "One couldn't help wondering a little, Paul dear,—after so many years—could one?" She always said "one" instead of the obvious personal pronoun. "You had no beard, for instance, when you left?"

"And more hair, perhaps!"

"You look splendid. I *shall* be proud of you!"

Paul blushed furiously. It was the first compliment ever paid to him by a woman.

"Oh, I feel all right," he stammered. "The healthy life in the woods, open air, and constant moving keep a fellow "fixed-up" to concert pitch all the time. I've never once—consulted a doctor m my life." He was careful to keep the slang out. He felt he managed it admirably. He said "consulted."

"And you wrote such nice letters, Paul. It *was* dear of you."

"I was lonely," he said bluntly. And after a pause he added, " I got all yours."

"I'm so glad." And then another pause. In which fashion they talked on for half an hour, each secretly estimating the other—wondering a little why they did not feel all kind of poignant emotions they had rather expected to feel.

It was a perfectly natural scene between a brother and sister who had grown up entirely apart, who were quite honest, who were utterly different types, and who yet wished to hold to one another as the nearest blood ties they possessed. They skimmed pleasantly and, so far as he was concerned, more and more easily, over the surface of things. Her talk, like her letters, was sincere, simple, shallow; it concealed no hidden depths, he felt at once. And by degrees, even in this first conversation, crept a shadow of other things, so that he realised they were in reality leagues apart, and could never have anything much in common below the pleasant surface relations of life.

Yet, even while he sheered off, as oil declines from its very nature to mingle with water, he felt genuinely drawn to her in another way. She was his own sister; she was his nearest tie; and she was Dick's widow. They would get along together all right; they would be good friends.

"Twenty years, Margaret."

"Twenty years, Paul."

And then another pause of several minutes during which something that was too vague to be a real thought passed like a shadow through his mind. What could his friend Dick have seen in her that was necessary to his life and happiness—Dick Messenger, who was scholar, poet, thinker—who sought the everlasting things—God? He instantly suppressed it as unworthy, something of which he was ashamed, but not before it had left a definite little trace in his imagination.

"So at last, Paul, you've really come home," she resumed; "I can hardly believe it,—and are going to settle down. You are a rich man."

"Aunt Alice did her duty," he laughed. He ignored the reference to settling down. It vaguely displeased him. "It's for you as well as me," he added, meaning the money. "I want to share with you whatever you need."

"Not a penny," she said quickly; "I have all I need. I live with my memories, you know. I am only so glad for your sake,—after all your hard life out there."

"The life wasn't hard; it was rather wonderful," he said simply. "I liked it."

"For a time perhaps; but you must have had curious experiences and lived with very rough people in those—lumber camp places you wrote about."

He shrugged his shoulders. "Simple kind of men, but very decent, very genuine. Few signs of city polish, I admit, but then you know I never cared for frills, Margaret."

"Frills!" she exclaimed, without any expression on her face. "Of course not. Still, I am very glad you have left it all. The life must often have been unsuitable and lonely; one always felt that for you. You can't have had any of the society that one's accustomed to."

"Not of that kind," he put in hurriedly with a short laugh, "but of other kinds. I struck a pretty good crowd of men on the whole."

She turned her face slightly away from him; her eyes, he divined, had been fixed for a moment on his hands. For the first time in his life he realised that they were large and rough and brown. Her own were so pale and dainty—like china hands, glossy and smooth—and the gold bangle on her thin wrist looked as though every second it must slip over her fingers. His own hands disappeared swiftly into the pockets of his coat.

She turned to him with a gentle smile. "Anyhow," she said, "it is simply too delightful to know that you really are here at last. It must seem strange to you at first, and there are so many things to talk over—such a lot to tell. I want to hear all your plans. You'll get used to us after a bit, and there are lots of nice people in the neighbourhood who are dying to meet you."

Her brother felt inclined to explain that he had no wish to interfere with their "dying"; but, instead, he returned her smile. "I'm a poor hand at meeting people, I'm afraid," he said. "I'm not as sociable as I might be."

"But you'll get over that. Of course, living so long in the backwoods makes one unsociable. But we'll try and make you happy and comfortable. You have no idea how very, very glad I am that you've come home."

Paul believed her. He leaned over and patted her hand, and she smiled frankly and sweetly in his face. She was a very shadowy sort of personality, he felt. If he blew hard she might blow away altogether, or disappear like a soap-bubble.

"I'm glad too, of course," he replied. "Only at my age, you know, it's not easy to tackle new habits."

"No one could take you for a day more than thirty-five," she said with truth; "so that shall be our own little private secret. You look quite absurdly young."

They laughed together easily and naturally. Paul felt more at home and soothed than he had thought possible. It had not been in the least formidable after all, and for the first time in his life he knew a little of that enervating kind of happiness that comes from being made a fuss of. As there was still a considerable interval before tea, they left their chairs and strolled through the garden, and as they went, the talk turned upon the past, and his sister spoke of Dick and of all he had meant to do in the world, had he lived. Paul heard the details of his sudden death for the first time. Her voice and manner were evidence of the melancholy she still felt, but her brother's heart was deeply stirred; he asked for all the particulars he had so often wondered about, and in her quiet, soothing tone, tinged now with tender sadness, she supplied the information. Clearly she had never arisen from the blow. She had worshipped Dick without understanding him.

"Death always frightens me, I think," she said with a faint smile. "I try not to think about it."

She passed on to speak of the children, and told him how difficult she found it to cope with them—she suffered from frequent headaches and could not endure noise—and how she hoped when they were a little older to be more with them. Mademoiselle Fleury, meanwhile, was such an excellent woman and was teaching them all they should know.

"Though, of course, I keep a close eye on them so far as I am able," she explained, "and only wish I were stronger."

They sauntered through the rose-garden and down the neat gravel paths that led to the wilder parts of the grounds where the rhododendron bushes stood in rounded domes and masses. It was very peaceful, very beautiful. He trod softly and carefully. The hush of centuries of cultivation lay over it all. Even the butterflies flew gently, as to the measure of a leisurely dance that deprecated undue animation. Paul caught his thoughts wandering to the open spaces of untamed moorland he had seen from the hilltop. More and more, as his sister's personality revealed itself, he got the impression that she lived enclosed like the wooden cows he had seen from the train, in a little green field, with precise and neatly trimmed borders. Strong emotions, as all other symptoms of plain and vigorous life, she shrank from. There were notice-boards set about her to warn trespassers, stating clearly that she did not wish to be let out. Yet in her way she was true, loving, and sweet—only it was such a conventional way, he felt.

Leaving the world of rhododendron bushes behind them, they came to the beginning of a pine-wood leading to the heather-land beyond. There was a touch of primitive wildness here. The trees grew straight and tall, filling the glade, and a stream ran brawling among their roots.

"This is the Gwyle," she said, as they entered the shade, "it was Dick's favourite part of the whole grounds. I rarely come here; it's dark even in summer, and rather damp and draughty, I always think."

Paul looked about him and drew a long breath. The air was strong with open-air scents of earth and bark and branches. Far overhead the tufted pines swayed, murmuring to the sky; the ground ran away downhill, becoming broken up and uneven; nothing but dark, slender stems rose everywhere about him, like giant seaweeds, he thought, rising from the pools of a deep sea. And the soft wind, moving mysteriously between the shadows and the sunlight, completed the spell. He passed suddenly—willy-nilly, as his nature would have it—into that mood when the simplest things about him turned their faces upwards so that he caught their eyes and their meaning; when the well-known and common things of the world shone out and revealed the infinite. Something in this quiet pine-wood that was mighty, and utterly wonderful, entered his soul, linking him on at a single stroke with the majesty of the great spirit of the earth. What lay behind it? What was its informing spirit? How and where could it link on so intimately with his soul? And could it not be a channel, as he always felt it must be, to the God behind it? Beauty seized him by the throat and made him tremble.

This sudden rush came over him, sea-like. His moods were ever like the sea, some strange touch of colour shifting the entire key. Something, too, made him feel lonely and oppressed. He, who was accustomed to space in bulk—the space the stars and winds live in—had come to this little, parceled-out place. He felt clipped already. He turned to the shadowy personality beside him, the boyish impulse bursting its way out. After all, she was his own sister; he could reveal himself to no one if not to her.

"By Gosh, Margaret," he cried, "this is the real thing. This wood must be alive and haunted just as the James Bay forests are. It's simply full of wonder."

"It's the Gwyle wood," she said quietly. "It's usually rather damp. But Dick loved it."

Her brother hardly heard what she said. "Listen," he said in a hushed tone; "do you hear the wind up there aloft? The trees are talking. The wood is full of whispers. There's no sound in the world like that murmur of a soft breeze in pine branches. It's like the old gods sighing, which only their true worshippers hear! Isn't it fine and melancholy? Margaret, d'you know, it goes through me like a fever."

His sister stopped and stared at him. She wore a little frightened expression. His sudden enthusiasm puzzled her evidently.

"It's the Gwyle wood," she repeated mechanically. "It's very pretty, I think. Dick always thought so too."

Her brother, surprised at his own rush of ready words, and already ashamed of the impulse that had prompted him to reveal himself, fell into silence.

"Nature excites me sometimes," he said presently. "I suppose it's because I've known nothing else."

"That's quite natural, I'm sure, Paul dear," she rejoined, turning to lead the way back to the sunshine of the open garden; "it's very pretty; I love it too. But it rather alarms me, I think, sometimes."

"Perhaps the natural tendency in solitude is to personify nature, and make it take the place of men and women. It has become a profound need of my being certainly." He spoke more quietly, chilled by her utter absence of comprehension.

"In its place I think it is ever so nice. But, Paul, you surprise me. I had no idea you were clever like that." She was perfectly sincere in what she said.

Her brother blushed like a boy. "It's my foolishness, I suppose, Margaret," he said with a shy laugh. "I am certainly not clever."

"Anyhow, you can be foolish or clever here to your heart's content. You must use the place as though it were your own exactly."

"Thank you, Margaret."

"Only I don't think I quite understand all those things," she added vaguely after a pause. "Nixie talks rather like that. She has all poor Dick's ideas and strange fancies. I really can't keep up with her at all."

Paul stiffened at the reference to the children; he remembered his attitude. Already he had been guilty of a serious lapse from his good intentions.

"She comes down to this wood far too much, and I'm sure it's not quite healthy for her. I always forget to speak to Mlle. Fleury." Then she turned to him and smiled. "But they are all so excited about your coming. They will simply devour you."

"I'm a poor hand at children, I'm afraid," he said, falling back upon his usual formula, "but, of course, I shall be delighted to see them."

She gathered up her white skirts about her trim ankles and led the way out of the wood, her brother following and thinking how slim and grace-ful she was, and what a charming figure she made among the rose-trees. He got the impression of her as something unreal and shadowy, a creature but half alive. It would hardly have surprised him to see her suddenly flit off into mist and sunshine and disappear from view, leaving him with the cer-tainty that he had been talking with a phantasm of a dream. Between him-self and her, however, he realised now, there was a gulf fixed. They looked at one another as it were down the large end of a telescope, and talked down a long-distance telephone that changed all their words and made the sense unintelligible and meaningless. The scale of values between them had no common denominator. Yet he could love her, and he meant to.

They crossed the lawns and went through the French window into the cool of the drawing-room, and while he was sipping his first cup of after-noon English tea, struggling with a dozen complex emotions that stirred within him, there suddenly darted across the lawn a vision of flying chil-dren, with a string of animals at their heels. They swept out of some lau-rel shrubberies into the slanting evening sunlight, and came to a dead stop on the gravel path in front of the window.

Their eyes met. They had seen him.

There they stood, figures of suddenly arrested motion, staring at him through the glass. "So that's Uncle Paul!" was the thought in the mind of each. He was being inspected, weighed, labelled. The meeting with his sis-ter was nothing compared to this critical examination, conducted though it was from a distance.

But it lasted only a moment. With a sudden quietness the children passed away from the window towards another door round the corner, and so out of sight.

"They've gone up to get tidy before coming to see you," explained his sis-ter; and Paul used the short respite to the best possible advantage by col-lecting his thoughts, remembering his "attitude and disguise," and seeing to it that his armour was properly fastened on, leaving no loopholes for sudden attack. He retired cautiously to the only place in a room where a shy man feels really safe—the mat before the fireplace. He almost wished for his gun and hunting-knife. The idea made him laugh.

"They already love you," he heard his sister's gentle whispering voice, "and I know you'll love them too. You must never let them annoy you, of course."

"They're your children—and Dick's," he answered quietly. "I shall get on with them famously, I'm sure."

CHAPTER V

I kiss you and the world begins to fade.
Land of Heart's Desire. —YEATS.

A few minutes later the door opened softly, and a procession, solemn of face and silent of foot, marched slowly into the room. The moment had come at last for his introduction, and, by a single stroke of unintentional diplomacy, his sister did more to winning her brother's shy heart than by anything else she could possibly have devised. She went out.

"They will prefer to make your acquaintance by themselves," she said in her gentle way, "and without any assistance from me."

The procession advanced to the middle of the room and then stopped short. Evidently, for them, the departure of their mother somewhat complicated matters. They had depended upon her to explain them to their uncle. There they stood, overcome by shyness, moving from one foot to another, with flushed and rosy faces, hair brushed, skin shining, and eyes all prepared to laugh as soon as somebody gave the signal, but not the least knowing how to begin.

And their uncle faced them in similar plight, as, for the second time that afternoon, shyness descended upon him like a cloud, and he could think of nothing to say. His size overwhelmed him; he felt like an elephant. With a sudden rush all his self-possession deserted him. He almost wished that his sister might return so that they should be brought up to him *seriatim,* named just as Adam named the beasts, and dismissed—which Adam did not do—with a kiss. It was really, of course—and he knew it to his secret mortification—a meeting on both sides of children; they all felt the shyness and self-consciousness of children, he as much as they, and at any moment might take the sudden plunge into careless intimacy, as the way with children ever is.

Meanwhile, however, he took rapid and careful note of them as they stood in that silent, fidgety group before him, with solemn, wide-open eyes fixed upon his face.

The youngest, being in his view little more than a baby, needs no description beyond the fact that it stared quite unintelligently without winking an eye. Its eyes, in fact, looked as though they were not made to close at all. And this is its one and only appearance.

Standing next to the baby, holding its hand, was a boy in a striped suit of knickerbockers, with a big brown curl like a breaking wave on the top of his forehead; he was between eight and nine years old, and his names— for, of course, he had two—were Richard Jonathan, shortened, as Paul learned later, into Jonah. He balanced himself with the utmost care in the centre of a particular square of carpet as though half an inch to either side would send him tumbling into a bottomless abyss. The fingers not claimed by the baby travelled slowly to and fro along the sticky line of his lower lip.

Close behind him, treating similarly another square of carpet, stood a rotund little girl, slightly younger than himself, named Arabella Lucy. There was a touch of audacity in her eyes, and an expression about the mouth that indicated the imminent approach of laughter. She had been distinctly washed and brushed-up for the occasion. Her face shone like a polished onion skin. She had the same sort of brown hair that Jonah considered fashionable, and her name for all common daily purposes was Toby.

The eldest and most formidable of his tormentors, standing a little in advance of the rest, was Margaret Christina, shortened by her father (who, indeed, had been responsible for all the nicknames) into Nixie. And the name fitted her like a skin, for she was the true figure of a sprite, and looked as if she had just stepped out of the water and her hair had stolen the yellow of the sand. Her eyes ran about the room like sunshine from the surface of a stream, and her movements instantly made Paul think of water gliding over pebbles or ribbed sand with easy and gentle undulations. Flashlike he saw her in a clearing of his lonely woods, a creature of the elements. Her big blue eyes, too, were full of wonder and pensive intelligence, and she stood there in a motherly and protective manner as though she were quite equal to the occasion and would presently know how to act with both courage and wisdom.

And Nixie, indeed, it was, after this prolonged and critical pause, who commenced operations. There was a sudden movement in the group, and the next minute Paul was aware that she had left it and was walking slowly towards him. He noticed her graceful, flowing way of moving, and saw a sunburnt arm and hand extended in his direction. The next second she kissed him. And that kiss acted like an electric shock. Something in her that was magical met its kind in his own soul and, flamelike, leaped towards it. A little tide of hot life poured into him, troubling the deeps with a momentary sense of delicious bewilderment.

"How do you do, Uncle Paul," she said; "we are *very* glad you have come—at last."

The blood ran ridiculously to his head. He found his tongue, and pulled himself sharply together.

"So am I, dear. Of course, it's a long way to come—America." He stooped and bestowed the necessary kisses upon the others, who had followed their leader and now stood close beside him, staring like little owls in a row.

"I know," she replied gravely. "It takes weeks, doesn't it? And mother has told us such a lot about you. We've been waiting a very long time, I think," she added as though stating a grievance.

"I suppose it is rather a long time to wait," he said sheepishly. He stroked his beard and waited.

"All of us," she went on. She included the others in this last observation by bending her head at them, and into her uncle's memory leaped the vision of a slender silver birch-tree that grew on the edge of the Big Beaver Pond near the Canadian border. She moved just as that silver birch moved when the breeze caught it.

Her manner was very demure, but she looked so piercingly into the very middle of his eyes that Paul felt as though she had already discovered everything about him. They all stood quite close to him now, touching his knees; ready, there and then, to take him wholly into their confidence.

An impulse that he only just managed to control stirred in him and a curious pang accompanied it. He remembered his "attitude," however, and stiffened slightly.

"No, it only takes ten days roughly from where I've come," he said, leaving the mat and dropping into a deep arm-chair a little farther off. "The big steamers go very fast, you know, nowadays."

Their eyes remained simply glued to his face. They switched round a few points to follow his movement, but did not leave their squares of carpet.

"Madmerzelle said"—it was Toby, *née* Arabella Lucy, speaking for the first time—"you knew lots of stories about deers and wolves and things, and would look like a Polar bear for us sometimes."

"Oh yes, and beavers and Indians in snowstorms, and the roarer boryalis," chimed in Jonah, giving a little hop of excitement that brought him still closer. "And the songs they sing in canoes when there are rapids," he added with intense excitement. "Madmizelle sings them sometimes, but they're not a bit the real thing, because she hasn't enough bass in her voice."

Paul bit his lip and looked at the carpet. Something in the atmosphere of the room seemed to have changed in the last few minutes. Jolly thrills ran through him such as he knew in the woods with his animals sometimes.

"I'm afraid I can't sing much," he said, "but I can tell you a bear story sometimes—if you're good." He added the condition as an afterthought.

"We *are* good," Jonah said disappointedly, "almost always."

Again that curious pang shot through him. He did not wish to be unkind to them. He pulled back his coat-sleeve suddenly and showed them a scar on his arm.

"That was made by a bear," he said, "years ago."

"Oh, look at the fur!" cried Toby.

"Don"t be silly! All proper men have hair on their arms," put in Jonah. "Does it still hurt, Uncle Paul?" he asked, examining the place with intense interest.

"Not now. We rolled down a hill together head over heels. Such a big brute, too, he was, and growled like a thunderstorm; it's a wonder he didn't squash me. I've got his claws upstairs. I think, really, he was more frightened than I was."

They clapped their hands. "Tell us, oh, do tell us!"

But Nixie intervened in her stately fashion, leaning over a little and stroking the scar with fingers that were like the touch of leaves.

"Uncle Paul's tired after coming such a long way," she said gravely with sympathy. "He hasn't even unpacked his luggage yet, have you, Uncle?"

Paul admitted that this was the case. He made the least possible motion to push them off and clear a space round his chair.

"Are you tired? Oh, I'm so sorry," said Jonah.

"Then he ought to see the animals at once," decided Toby, "before they go to bed,"—she seemed to have a vague idea that the whole world must go to bed earlier than usual if Uncle Paul was tired—or they'll be awfully disappointed." Her face expressed the disappointment of the animals as well as her own; her uncle's fatigue had already taken a second place. "Oughtn't he?" she added, turning to the others.

Paul remembered his intention to remain stiffly grown up.

He made a great effort. Oh, but why did they tug and tear at his heart so, these little fatherless children? And why did he feel at once that he was in their own world, comfortably "at home" in it? Did this world of children, then, link on so easily and naturally with the poet's region of imagination and wonder in which he himself still dwelt for all his many years, bringing him close to his main passion—to know Reality?

"Of course, I'll come and say good-night to them before they turn in," he decided kindly, letting Nixie and Toby take his hands, while Jonah followed in the rear to show that he considered this a girl's affair yet did not wholly disapprove.

"Hadn't we better tell your mother where we're going?" he asked as they started.

"Oh, mother won't mind," came the answer in chorus. "She hardly ever comes up to the nursery, and, besides, she doesn't care for the animals, you see."

"They're rather 'noying for mother," Nixie added by way of explanation. She decapitated many of her long words in this way, and invariably omitted difficult consonants.

It was a long journey, and the explanations about the animals, their characteristics, names, and habits, occupied every minute of the way. He gathered that they were chiefly cats and kittens, to what number he dared not calculate, and that puppies, at least one parrot, a squirrel, a multitude of white mice, and various larger beasts of a parental and aged description, were indiscriminately all mixed up together. Evidently it was a private menagerie that he was invited to say good-night to, and the torrent of outlandish names that poured into his ears produced a feeling of confusion in his mind that made him wonder if he was not turning into some sort of animal himself, and thus becoming free of their language.

It was the beginning of a very trying ordeal for him, this being half pulled, half shoved along the intricate passages of the old house; now down a couple of unexpected steps that made him stumble; now up another which made him trip; through narrow doorways, where Jonah had the audacity to push him from behind lest he should stick half-way; and, final-

ly, at full speed, the girls tugging at his arms in front, down a long corridor which proved to be the home-stretch to the nursery.

"I was afraid we'd lost the trail," he gasped. "It's poorly blazed."

"Oh, but we haven't got any tails to lose," laughed Toby, misunderstand-
ing him. "And they wouldn't blaze if we had."

"Look out, Nixie! Not so fast! Uncle Paul's losing his wind as well as his
trail," shouted Jonah from the rear. And at that moment they reached the
door of the nursery and came to an abrupt halt, Paul puffing like a lumberman.

It was impossible for him to remain sedate, but he did the next best
thing—he remained silent.

Then Jonah, pushing past him, turned the handle, and he was ushered,
still panting, into so typical a nursery-schoolroom that the scenes of his
forgotten boyhood rushed hack to him with a vividness that seemed to
destroy the passage of time at a single stroke. The past stood reconstructed. The actual, living mood of his own childhood rose out of the depths of
blurred memories and caused a mist to rise before his eyes. An emotion he
was utterly unable to define shook his heart.

The room was filled with the slanting rays of the setting sun, and the air
from the open windows smelt of garden trees, lawns, and flower-beds. Sea
and heather, too, added their own sharper perfumes. It caught him away
for a moment—oh, that strange power of old perfumes—to the earliest
scenes of his own life, the boyhood in the gardens of Kent before America had claimed him. And then the details of the room itself became so
insistent that he almost lost his head and turned back without more ado
into a boy of fifteen.

He looked swiftly about him. There was the old-fashioned upright piano
against the wall, the highly coloured pictures hanging crooked on the wall,
the cane chairs, the crowded mantelpiece, the high wire fender before the
empty grate, the general atmosphere of toys, untidiness and broken articles of every sort and kind—and, above all, the figures of these excited
children all bustling recklessly about him with their glowing and expectant faces.

There was Toby, her blue sash all awry, running busily about the room;
and Nixie, now in sunshine, now in shadow, with her hair of yellow sand
and her blue dreaming eyes that saw into the Beyond; and little Jonah,
moving about somewhat pompously to prepare the performance that was
to follow. It all combined to produce a sudden shock that swept down
upon him so savagely, that he was within an ace of bolting through the
door and making his escape into safer quarters.

The False Paul, that is, was within an ace of running away with all his
elaborate armour, and leaving the True Paul dancing on the floor, a child
among children, a spirit of impulse, enthusiasm and imagination, laughing with the sheer happiness of his perpetual youth.

It was a dangerous moment; he was within measurable distance of
revealing himself. For a moment his clothes felt far too large for him; and

only just in time did he remember his "attitude," and the danger of being young when he really was old, and the absurdity of being anything else than a large, sedate man of forty-five. Only he wished that Nixie would not watch him so appealingly with those starry eyes of hers... and look so strangely like the forms that haunted his own wild forests and streams on the other side of the Atlantic.

He stiffened quickly, drew himself up, and turned to give his elderly attention to the chorus of explanation and introduction that was already rising about him with the sound and murmur of the sea.

Something was happening.

For the floor of the room, he now perceived, had become suddenly full of movement, as though the carpet had turned alive. He felt a rubbing against his legs and ankles; with a soft thud something leaped upon the table and covered his hand with smooth, warm fur, uttering little sounds of pleasure at the same time. On the top of the piano, a thing he had taken for a heap of toys rose and stretched itself into an odd shape of straight lines and arching curves. From the window-sill, where the sun poured in, a round grey substance dropped noiselessly down upon the carpet and advanced with measured and calculated step towards him; while, from holes and hiding-places undivined, three or four little fluffy things, with padded feet and stiff pointing tails, shot out like shadows and headed straight for a row of saucers that he now noticed for the first time against the farther wall. The whole room seemed to fill with soft and graceful movement; and, mingled with the voices of the children, he caught a fine composite murmur that was soothing as the sound of flowing wind and water.

It was the sound and the movement of many animals.

"Here they are," said a voice—"some of them. The others are lost, or out hunting."

For the moment Paul did not stop to ask how many "others" there were. He stood rigidly still for fear that if he moved he might tread on something living.

There came a scratching sound at the door, and Toby dashed forward to open it.

"Silly, naughty babies!" she cried, nearly tumbling over the fender in her attempt to seize two round bouncing things that came tearing into the room like a couple of yellow puddings. "Uncle Paul has come to see you all the way from America! And then you're late like this! For shame!"

With a series of thuds and bangs that must have bruised anything not unusually well padded, the new arrivals, who looked for all the world like small fat bears, or sable muffs on short brown legs with feet of black velvet, dashed round the room in a mad chase after nothing at all. A hissing and spitting issued from dark corners and from beneath various pieces of furniture, but the two balls confined their attentions almost at once to the honoured guest. They charged up against his legs as though determined to upset his balance—this mountain of a man—and then careered clumsily round the room, knocking over anything small enough that came in their way, and behaving generally as though they wanted to clear the whole place in the shortest possible time for their own particular and immediate benefit.

Next, lifting his eyes for a moment from this impetuous attack, he saw a brilliantly coloured thing behind bars, standing apparently on its head and looking upside-down at him with an expression of undisguised and scornful amusement; while not far from it, in a cage hanging by the cuckoo clock, some one with a tail as large as his body, shot round and round on a swinging trapeze that made Paul think of a midget practising in a miniature gymnasium.

"These are our animals, you see, Uncle Paul," Jonah announced proudly from his position by the door. There was a trace of condescension in his tone.

"We have lots of out-of-door animals as well, though," Toby hastened to explain, lest her uncle should be disappointed.

"I suppose they're out of doors?" said Paul lamely.

"Of course they are," replied Jonah; "in the stables and all about." He turned to Nixie, who stood quietly by her uncle's side in a protective way, superintending. Nixie nodded corroboration.

"Now, we'll introduce you—gradgilly," announced Toby, stooping down and lifting with immense effort the large grey Persian that had been sleeping on the window-sill when they came in. She held it with great difficulty in her arms and hands, but in spite of her best efforts only a portion of it found actual support, the rest straggling away like a loosely stuffed bolster she could not encompass.

It was evidently accustomed to being dealt with thus in sections, for it continued to purr sleepily, blinking its large eyes with the usual cat-smile, and letting its head fall backwards as though it suddenly desired to examine the ceiling from an entirely fresh point of view. None of its real attention, of course, was given to the actual proceeding. It merely suffered the absurd affair—absent-mindedly and with condescension. Its whiskers moved gently.

"What's its name?" he asked kindly.

"*Her* name," whispered Nixie.

"We call her Mrs. Tompkyns, because it's old now," Toby explained, ignoring genders.

After the head-gardener's gra'mother," Nixie explained hastily in his ear; "but we might change it to Uncle Paul in honour of you now, mightn't we?"

"Mrs. Uncle Paul," corrected Jonah, looking on with slight disapproval, and anxious to get to the white mice and the squirrel.

"It would be a pity to change the name, I think," Paul said, straightening himself up dizzily from the introduction, and watching the splendid creature fall upon its head from Toby's weakening grasp, and then march away with unperturbed dignity to its former throne upon the window-sill. "I feel rather afraid of Mrs. Tompkyns," he added; "she's so very majestic."

"Oh, you needn't be," they cried in chorus. "It's all put on, you know, that sort of grand manner. *We* knew her when she was a kitten."

The object-lesson was not lost upon him. Of all creatures in the world, he reflected as he watched her, cats have the truest dignity. They absolutely refuse to be laughed at. No cat would ever betray its real self, yet here was he, a grown-up, intelligent man, vacillating, and on the verge already of hopeless capitulation.

"And what's the name of *these* persons?" he asked quickly, turning for safety to Nixie, who had her arms full of a writhing heap she had been diligently collecting from the corners of the room.

"Oh, that's only Mrs. Tompkyns' family," exclaimed Jonah impatiently; "the last family, I mean. She's had lots of others."

"The last family before this was only two," Nixie told him. "We called them Ping and Pong. They live in the stables now. But these we call Pouf, Sambo, Spritey, Zezette, and Dumps—"

"And the next ones," Toby broke in excitedly, "we're going to call with the names on the engines when we go up to London to see the dentist."

"Or the names of the Atlantic steamers wouldn't be bad," said Paul.

"Not bad," Jonah said, with lukewarm approval; "only the engines would be much better."

"There may not be any next ones," opined Toby, emerging from beneath a sofa after a frantic, but vain, attempt to catch something alive.

Jonah snorted with contempt. "Of course there will. They come in bunches all the time, just like grapes and chestnuts and things. Madmizelle told me so. There's no end to them. Don't they, Uncle Paul?"

"I believe so," said the authority appealed to, extracting his finger with difficulty from the teeth and claws of several kittens.

There came a lull in the proceedings, the majority of the animals having escaped, and successfully concealed themselves among what Toby called "the furchinur." Paul was still following a prior train of reflection.

"Yes, cats are really rather wonderful creatures," he mused aloud in spite of himself, turning instinctively in the direction of Nixie. "They possess a mysterious and superior kind of intelligence."

For a moment it was exactly as if he had tapped his armour and said, "Look! It's all sham!"

The child peered sharply up in his face. There was a sudden light in her eyes, and her lips were parted. He had not exactly expected her to answer, but somehow or other he was not surprised when she did. And the answer she made was just the kind of thing he knew she would say. He was annoyed with himself for having said so much.

"And they lead secret little lives somewhere else, and only let us see what they want us to see. I knew you understood *really.*" She said it with an elfin smile that was certainly borrowed from moonlight on a mountain stream. With one fell swoop it caught him away into a world where age simply did not exist. His mind wavered deliciously. The singing in his heart was almost loud enough to be audible.

But he just saved himself. With a sudden movement he leaned forward and buried his face in the pie of kittens that nestled in her arms, letting them lose their paws for a moment in his beard. The kittens might understand, but at least they could not betray him by putting it into words. It was a narrower escape than he cared for.

"And these are the Chow puppies," cried Jonah, breathless from a long chase after the sable muffs. "We call them China and Japan."

Paul welcomed the diversion. Their teeth were not nearly so sharp as the kittens', and they burrowed with their black noses into his sleeves. So thick was their fur that they seemed to have no bones at all; their dark eyes literally dripped laughter.

With an effort he put on a more sedate manner.

"You *have* got a lot of beasts," he said.

"Animals," Nixie corrected him. "Only toads, rats, and hedgehogs are beasts. And, remember, if you're rude to an animal, as Mademoiselle Fleury was once, it only 'spices you and then—"

"I beg their pardon," he put in hurriedly; "I quite understand, of course."

"You see it's rather important, as they want to like you, and unless you respect them they can't, can they?" she finished earnestly.

"I do respect them, believe me, Nixie, and I appreciate their affection. Affection and respect must always go together."

The children were wholly delighted. Paul had completely won their hearts from the very beginning. The parrot, the squirrel, and the white mice were all introduced in turn to him, and he heard sundry mysterious allusions to "the owl in the stables," "Juliet and her two kids," to say nothing of dogs, ponies, pigeons, and peacocks, that apparently dwelt in the regions of outer space, and were to be reserved for the morrow.

The performance was coming to an end. Paul was already congratulating himself upon having passed safely, if not with full credit, through a severe ordeal, when the door opened and a woman of about twenty-five, with a pleasant face full of character and intelligence, stood in the doorway. A torrent of French instantly broke loose on all sides. The woman started a little when she perceived that the children were not alone.

"Oh, Mademoiselle, this is Uncle Paul," they cried, each in a different fashion. "This is *our* Uncle Paul! He's just been introduced to the animals, and now he must be introduced to you."

Paul shook hands with her, and the introduction passed off easily enough; the woman was charming, he saw at the first glimpse, and possessed of tact. She at once took his side and pretended to scold her charges for having plagued and bothered him so long. Evidently she was something more to them than a mere governess. The lassitude of his sister, no doubt, gave her rights and responsibilities.

But what impressed Paul when he was alone—for her simple remark that it was past bedtime was followed by sudden kisses and disappearance—was the remarkable change that her arrival had brought about in the room. It came to him with a definite little shock. It was more than significant, he felt.

And it was this: that the children, though obviously they loved her, treated her as some one grown up and to be obeyed, whereas himself, he now realised, they had all along treated as one of themselves to whom they could be quite open and natural. His "attitude" they had treated with respect, just as he had treated the attitude of the animals with respect, but at the same time he had been made to feel one of themselves, in their world, part and parcel of their own peculiar region. There had been nothing forced about it whatever. Whether he liked it or not they accepted him. His "attitude" was not regarded seriously. It was not regarded at all. And this was grave.

He was so simple that he would never have thought of this but for the entrance of the governess. Her arrival threw it all into sharp relief. Clearly the children recognised no barrier between themselves and him; he had been taken without parley straight into their holy of holies. Nixie, as leader and judge, had carried him off at once.

And this was a very subtle and powerful compliment that made him think a great deal. He would either have to drop his armour altogether or make it very much more effective.

Indeed, it was the immediate problem in his mind as he slowly made his way downstairs to find his sister on the lawn, and satisfy her rather vague curiosity by telling her that the children had introduced him to the animals, and that he had got on famously with them all.

CHAPTER VI

Oh! Fairies, take me out of this dull world
For I would ride with you upon the wind,
Run on the top of the dishevelled tide,
And dance upon the mountains like a flame!
Land of Heart's Desire. —YEATS.

Paul went early to bed that night. It was his first night in an English country home for many years; strange forces were at work in him. His introduction to the children, his meeting with Nixie especially, had let loose powers in his soul that called for sober reflection; and he felt the need of being alone.

Another thing, too, urged him to seek the solitude of his chamber, for after dinner he had sat for a couple of hours with his sister, talking over the events and changes of the long interval since they had met,—the details that cannot be told in letters, the feelings that no one writes. And he came upstairs with his first impression of her character slightly modified. She had more in her than he first divined. Beneath that shadowy and silken manner he had caught traces of distinct purpose. For one thing she was determined to keep him in England.

He had told her frankly about his arrangement with the lumber Company, explaining that he regarded his present visit in the light of a holiday. "I suppose that is—er—wise of you," she said, but she had not been able to conceal her disappointment. She asked him presently if he really wanted to live all his life in such a place, and what it was in English life, or civilised, conventional life, that he so disliked, and Paul, feeling distinctly uncomfortable—for he loathed giving pain—had answered evasively, with more skill than he knew, " 'Where your treasure is, there shall your heart be also.' I suppose my treasure—the only kind I know—is out there in the great woods, Margaret."

"Paul, are you married, then?" she asked with a start; and when he laughed and assured her most emphatically that he was not, she looked exceedingly puzzled and a little shocked too. "Are you so very fond of this—er—treasure, then?" she asked point blank in her softest manner, "and is she so—I mean, can't you bring her home and acknowledge her?" And after his first surprise when he had gathered her meaning, it took him a long time to explain that there was no woman concerned at all, and that it was entirely a matter of his temperament.

"Everybody makes his own world, remember," he laughed, "and its size depends, I suppose, upon the power of the imagination."

"Then I fear one's imagination is a very poor one," she said solemnly, "or else I have none at all. I cannot pretend to understand your tastes for trees and woods and things; but you're exactly like poor Dick in that way, and I suppose one must be really clever to be like that."

"A year is a long time, Margaret," he said after a pause, to comfort her. "Much may happen before it's over."

"I hope so," she had answered, standing behind his chair and stroking his head. "By that time you may have met some one who will reconcile you to—to staying here—a little longer." She patted his head as though he were a Newfoundland dog, he thought. It made him laugh.

"Perhaps," he said.

And, now in his room, before the candles were lighted, he was standing by the open window, thinking it all over. Of women, of course, he knew little or nothing; to him they were all charming; some of them wonderful; and he was not conscious that his point of view might be considered by a man of the world—of the world that is little, sordid, matter-of-fact—distinctly humorous. At forty-five he believed in women just as he had believed in them at twenty, only more so, for nothing had ever entered his experience to trouble an exquisite picture in his mind. They stood nearer to God than men did, he felt, and the depravity of really bad women he explained by the fact that when they did fall they fell farther. The sex-fever, so far as he was concerned, had never mounted to his brain to obscure his vision.

He only knew—and knew it with a sacred wonder that was akin to worship—that women, like the angels, were beyond his reach and beyond his understanding. Comely they all were to him. He looked up to them in his thoughts, not for their reason or strength, but for the subtlety of their intuition, their power of sacrifice, and last but not least, for the beauty and grace of their mere presence in a world that was so often ugly and unclean.

"The flame—the lamp—the glory—whatever it may be called—keeps alight in their faces," he loved to say to himself, "almost to the end. With men it is gone at thirty—often at twenty."

And his sister, for all her light hold on life, and the strain in her that in his simplicity he regarded as rather "worldly," was no exception to the rule. He thought her entirely good and wonderful, and, perhaps, so far as she went, he was not too egregiously mistaken. He looked for the best in everybody, and so, of course, found it.

"Only she will never make much of me, or I of her, I'm afraid," he thought as he leaned out of the window, watching the scented darkness. "We shall get along best by leaving each other alone and being affectionate, so to speak, from a distance."

And, indeed, so far he had escaped the manifold seductions by which Nature seeks to attain her great object of perpetuating the race. As a potential father of many sons he was of course an object of legitimate prey; but his forest life had obviated all that; his whole forces had turned inwards for the creation of the poet's visions, and Nature in this respect, he believed, had passed him by. So far as he was aware there was no desire in him to come forth and perform a belated duty to the world by increasing its population. It was the first time any one had even suggested to him that he should consider such a matter, and the mere idea made him smile.

Gradually, however, these thoughts cleared away, and he turned to other things he deemed more important.

The night was still as imaginable; odours of earth and woods were wafted into the room with the scent of roses. Overhead, as he leaned on his elbow and gazed, the stars shone thickly, like points of gold pricked in a velvet curtain. A lost wind stirred the branches; he could distinguish their solemn dance against the constellations. Orion, slanting and immense, tilted across the sky, the two stars at the base resting upon the shoulder of the hill, and far off, in the deeps of the night, the murmur of the pines sounded like the breaking of invisible surf.

Something indescribably fresh and wild in the taste of the air carried him back again across the ocean. The ancient woods he knew so well rose before the horizon's rim, swimming with purple shadows and alive with continuous great murmur that stretched for a hundred leagues. The picture of those desolate places, lying in lonely grandeur beneath the glitter of the Northern Lights, with a thousand lakes echoing the laughter of the loons, came seductively before his inner eye. The thought of it all stirred emotions profound and primitive, emotions too closely married to instincts, perhaps, to be analysed; something in him that was ancestral, possibly pre-natal. There was nothing in this little England that could move him so in the same fashion. His thoughts carried him far, far away....

The faint sound of a church clock striking the hour—a sound utterly alien to the trend of his thoughts—brought him back again to the present. He heard it across many fields, fields that had been tilled for centuries, and there could have been no more vivid or eloquent reminder that he was no longer in a land where hedges, church bells, notice-boards, and so forth were not. He came back with a start, and a sensation almost akin to pain. He felt cramped, caught, caged. The tinkling church bells annoyed him.

His thoughts turned, with a sudden jerk, as it were, to the undeniable fact that he had been trying to go about in a disguise, with a clumsy mask over his face, so that he might appear decently grown up in his new surroundings.

A pair of owls began to hoot softly in the woods, answering one another like voices in a dream, and just then the lost wind left the pine branches and died away into the sky with a swift rush as of many small wings. In the sudden pool of silence that followed, he fancied he could hear across the dark miles of heathland the continuous low murmur of the sea.

The beauty of night, as ever, entered his soul, but with a joy that was too solemn, too moving, to be felt as pleasure. It touched something in him beyond the tears of either pain or delight: something that held in it a mysterious wonder so searching, so poignant, as to be almost terrible.

He caught his breath and waited.... The great woods of the world, mountains, the sea, stars, and the crying winds were always for him symbols of the gateways into a mightier and ideal region, a Beyond-world where he found rest for his yearnings and a strange peace. They were his means of losing himself in a temporary heaven.

And to-night it was the beauty of an English scene that carried him away; and this in spite of his having summoned the wilder vision from across the seas. Already the forces of his own country were insensibly at work upon an impressionable mind and temperament. The very air, so sweetly scented as he drew it in between his lips, was charged with the subtly-working influences of the "Old Country." A new web, soft but mighty, was being woven about his spirit. Even now his heart was conscious of its gossamer touch, as his dreams yielded imperceptibly to a new colour.

He followed vaguely, curiously, the leadings of delicate emotions that had been stirred in him by the events of the day. Symbols, fast-shifting, protean, passed in suggestive procession before his mind's eye, in the way that symbols ever will—in a poet's heart. He thought of children, of *the* children, and of the extraordinarily fresh appeal they had made to him. Children: how near they, too, stood to the great things of life, and all the nearer, perhaps, for not being aware of it. How their farseeing eyes and their simple, unlined souls pointed the way, like Nature, to the ideal region of which he was always dreaming: to Reality, to God.

All real children knew and understood; were ready to offer their timid yet unhesitating guidance, and without question or explanation.

Had, then, Nixie and her troupe already taken him prisoner? And were the soft chains already twined about his neck?...

Paul hardly acknowledged the question definitely to himself. He was merely dreaming, and his dreams, rising and falling like the tides of a sea, bore him to and fro among the shoals and inlands of the day's events. The spell of the English June night was very strong upon him, no doubt, for presently a door opened somewhere behind him, and the very children he was thinking about danced softly into the room. Nixie came up close and gazed into his very eyes, and again there began that odd singing in his heart that he had twice noticed during the day. An atmosphere of magic, shot with gold and silver, came with the child into the room.

For the fact was—though he realised it only dimly—the Fates were now making him a deliberate offer. Had he not been so absorbed, he would have perceived and appreciated the delicacy of their action. As a rule they command, whereas now they were only suggesting.

It was really his own heart asking. Here, in this rambling country house under the hills, was an opportunity of entering the region to which all that was best and truest in him naturally belonged. The experience might prove a stepping-stone to a final readjustment of his peculiar being with the normal busy world of common things. Here was a safety-valve, as he called it, a channel through which he might express much, if not all, of his accumulated stores. The guides, now fast asleep in their beds, had sent out their little dream-bodies to bring the invitation; they were ready and waiting.

And he, thinking there under the stars his queer, long thoughts, bred in years of solitude, dallied with the invitation, and—hesitated. The inevitable pain frightened him—the pain of being young when the world cries that you are old; the pang of the eternal contrast when the world would laugh at what seemed to it a foolish fantasy of youth—a pose, a dream that must bring a bitter awakening! He heard the voices but too plainly, and shrank quickly from the sound.

But Nixie, standing there beside him with such gentle persistence, certainly made him waver.... The temptation to yield was strong and seductive.... Yet, when the faint splendour of the summer moonrise dimmed the stars near the horizon, and the pines shone tipped with silver, he found himself borne down by the sense of caution that urged no revolutionary change, and advised him to keep his armour tightly buckled on in the disguise he had adopted.

He would wait and see—a little longer, at any rate; and meanwhile he must be firm and stern and dull; master of himself, and apparently normal.

He walked to the dressing-table and lit his candles, and, as he did so, caught a picture of himself in the glass. There was a gleam of subdued fire in his eyes, he thought, that was not naturally there. Something about him looked a little wild; it made him laugh.

He laughed to think how utterly absurd it was that a man of his size and age, and—But the idea refused to frame himself in Language—He did not know exactly why he laughed, for at the same time he felt sad. With him, as with all other children, tears and laughter are never far apart. It would have been just as intelligible if he had cried.

But when the candles were out and he was in bed, and the stars were peeping into the darkened room, the memory of his laughter seemed unreal, and the sound of it oddly remote.

For, after all, that laughter was rather mysterious. It was not the Outer Paul laughing at the Inner Paul. It was the Inner Paul laughing with himself.

CHAPTER VII

The imaginative process may be likened to the state of reverie.

—ALISON.

The psychology of sleep being apparently beyond all intelligible expla-nation, it was not surprising that he woke up next morning as though he had gone to bed without a single perplexity. He remembered none of the thoughts that had thronged his brain a few short hours before; perhaps they had all slipped down into the region of submerged consciousness, to crop out later in natural, and apparently spontaneous, action.

At any rate he remembered little enough of his troubles when he woke and saw the fair English sun streaming in through the open windows. Odours of woods and dew-drenched lawns came into the room, and the birds were singing with noise enough to waken all the country-side. It was impossible to lie in bed. He was up and dressed long before any servant came to call him.

Downstairs he found the house in darkness; doors barred and windows heavily shuttered as though the house had expected an attack. Not a soul was stirring. The air was close and musty. The idea of having to strike a match in a "country" house at 6 A.M. somehow oppressed him. Not know-ing his way about very well yet, he stumbled across the hall to find a door, and as he did so something soft came rubbing against his legs. He put his hand down in the darkness and felt a furry, warm body and a stiff upright tail that reached almost to his knees. The thing began to purr.

"I declare!" he exclaimed; "Mrs. Tompkyns!" and he struck a match and followed her to the drawing-room door. A moment later they had unfas-tened the shutters of the French window—Mrs. Tompkyns assisting by standing on her hind legs and tapping the swinging bell—and made their way out on to the lawn.

The sunshine came slanting between the cedars and lay in shining strips on the grass. Everything glistened with dew. The air was sweet and fresh as it only is in the early hours after the dawn. Very faintly, as though its mind was not yet made up, the air stirred among the bushes.

Paul's first impulse was to waken the entire household so that they might share with him this first glory of the morning. "Probably they don't know how splendid it is!" The thought of the sleeping family, many of them perhaps with closed windows, missing all the wonder, was a positive pain to him. But, fortunately for himself, he decided it might be better not to begin his visit in this way.

"I guess you and I, Mrs. Tompkyns, are the only people about," he said, looking down at the beautiful grey creature that sniffed the air calmly at his feet. "Come on, then. Let's make a raid together on the woods!"

He threw a disdainful glance at the sleeping house; no smoke came from the chimneys; most of the upper windows were closed. A delicious fragrance stole out of the woods to meet him as he strolled across the wet lawn. He felt like a schoolboy doing something out of bounds.

"You lead and I follow," he said, addressing his companion in mischief.

And at once his attention became absorbed in the animal's characteristic behaviour. Obviously it was delighted to be with him; yet it did not wish him to think so, or, if he did think so, to give any sign of the fact. Nothing could have been plainer. First it crept along by the stone wall delicately, with its body very close to the ground as though the weight of the atmosphere oppressed it; and when he spoke, it turned its head with an affectation of genuine surprise as though it would say, "You here! I thought I was alone." Then it sat down on the gravel path and began to wash its face and paws till he had passed, after which—when he was not looking, of course—it followed him condescendingly, sniffing at blades of grass *en route* without actually touching them, and flicking its tail upwards with sudden, electric jerks.

Paul understood in a general way what was expected of him. He watched it surreptitiously, pretending to examine the flowers. For this, he knew, was the great Cat Game of elaborate pretence. And Mrs. Tompkyns, true adept in the art, played up wonderfully, and incidentally taught him much about the ways and methods of simple disguise; it advanced stealthily when he wasn't looking; it stopped to wash, or gaze into the air, the moment he turned. It was very shy, and very affected, and very self-conscious. Inimitable was the way it kept to all the little rules of the game. It walked daintily down the path after him, shaking the dew from its paws with a rapid, quivering motion. Then, suddenly arching its back as though momentarily offended—at nothing—it stared up at him with an expression that seemed to question his very existence. "I guess I ought to fade away when you look at me like that!" was his thought.

"I'm here. I'm coming, Mrs. Tompkyns," he felt constrained to remark aloud before going forward again. "The grand morning excites my blood just as much as it excites your own."

It seemed necessary to assert his presence. No intelligent person can be conceited long in the presence of a cat. No living creature can so sublimely "ignore." But Paul was not conceited. He continued to watch it with delight.

One very important rule of the game appeared to be that plenty of bushes were necessary by way of cover, so that it could pretend it was not really coming farther than the particular bush where it was hiding at the moment. Instinctively, he never made the grave mistake of calling it to follow; and though it never trotted alongside, being always either behind or in front of him, the presence of the cat in his immediate neighbourhood provided all sorts of company imaginable. It had also provided him with an opportunity to play the hero.

Then, suddenly, the calm and peace of the morning was disturbed by a scene of strange violence. Mrs. Tompkyns, with spread legs, dashed past him at a surprising speed and flew up the trunk of a big tree as though all the dogs in the county were at her heels. From this position of vantage she looked back over her shoulder with hysterical and frightened eyes. There was a great show of terror, a vast noise of claws upon the bark. No actress could have created better the atmosphere of immediate danger and alarm.

Paul had an instinctive *flair* for this move of the game. He made a great pretence of running up to save the cat from its awful position, but of course long before he got there she had dropped laughingly to earth again, having thus impressed upon him the value of her life.

"A question of life or death that time, I think, Mrs. Tompkyns," he said soothingly, trying to stroke her back. "I wonder if the head-gardener's grandmother after whom you were named ever did this sort of thing. I doubt it!"

But the creature escaped from him easily. For no one is ever caught in the true Cat Game. It scuttled down the path at full speed in a sort of canter, but sideways, as though a violent wind blew it and desperate resistance was necessary to keep on its feet at all. After that its self-consciousness seemed to disappear a little. It behaved normally. It stalked birds that showed, however, no fear of its approach. It sniffed the tips of leaves. It played baby-fashion with various invisible companions; and finally it vanished in a thick jungle of laurels to hunt in savage earnest, and left Paul to his own devices. Like all its kind, it only wished to prove how charming it could be, in order to emphasise later its utter independence of human sympathy and companionship.

"If you *must* go, I suppose you must," he laughed, "and I shall try to enjoy myself without you."

He strolled on alone and lost himself in the pinewood that flanked the back lawn, stopping finally by a gate that led to the world of gorse and heather beyond. The brilliant patches of yellow wafted perfumes to his nostrils. Far in the distance a blue line hinted where the sea lay; and over all lay the radiance of the early morning. The old spell was there that never failed to make his heart leap. And, as he stood still, the cuckoo flitted, invisible and mischievous, from tree to tree, calling with its flutelike notes,—

> Sung beyond memory,
> When golden to the winds this world of ours
> Waved wild with boundless flowers;
> Sung in some past where wildernesses were,—

and his thoughts went roaming back to the great woods he had left behind, woods where the naked streams ran shouting and lawless, where the trees had not learned self-consciousness, and where no little tame folk trotted on velvet feet through trim and scented gardens.

And the virgin glory of the morning entered into him with that search-ing sweetness which is almost suffering, just as a few hours before the Night had bewitched him with the mystery of her haunted caverns. For the beauty of Nature that comes to most softly, with hints, came to him with an exquisite fierce fever that was pain,—with something of the full-fledged glory that burst upon Shelley—and to bear it, unrelieved by expression, was a perpetual torment to him.

But, after long musing that led he scarcely knew where, Paul came back to himself and laughed. Laughter was better than sighing, and he was too much of a child to go long without the sense of happiness coming upper-most. He lit his pipe—that most delicious of all, the pipe before break-fast—and wandered out into the sea of yellow gorse, thinking aloud, laughing, talking to himself.

Something in the performance of Mrs. Tompkyns awakened the train of thought of the night before. The sublime acting of the animal—he dared not call it "beast"—linked him on to the children's world. They, too, had a magnificent condescension for the mere grown-up person. But he—he was *not* grown up. It made him sigh and laugh to think of it. He was a great, over-grown child, playing with gorgeously coloured dreams while the world of ordinary life passed him by.

The animals and the children linked on again, of course, with the region of fantasy and make-believe, the world of creation, the world of eternity, the world where thoughts were alive, and strong belief was a creative act.

"That's where I still belong," he said aloud, picking his way among the waves of yellow sea, "and I shall never get out till I die, my visions unex-pressed, my singing dumb." He laughed and threw a stone at a bush that had no blossoms. "Oh, if only I knew how to link on with the normal world of fact *without losing the other! To* turn all these seething dreams within me to some account. To show them to others!"

He ran and cleared a low gorse-bush with a flying jump.

"That would be worth living for," he continued, panting; "to make these things real to all the people who live in little cages. By Jove, it would open doors and windows in thousands of cages all over the world, besides pro-viding me with the outlet I must find some day or"—he sprang over a ditch, slipped, and landed head first into prickles—or explode!" he con-cluded with a shout of laughter that no one heard but the cuckoos and the yellow-hammers. Then he fell into a reverie, and his thoughts travelled farther still—into the Beyond.

Quickly recovering himself, and picking up his pipe, he went on towards the house; and, as he emerged from the pine copse again, the sound of a gong, ringing faintly in the distance, brought him back to earth with a shock almost as abrupt as the ditch. Mrs. Tompkyns appeared simultane-ously, wearing an aspect of pristine innocence, admirably assumed the instant she caught sight of him.

"Fancy your being out here!" was the expression of her whole person, "and coming, too, in just as the gong sounds!"

"Breakfast, I suppose!" he observed. And she trotted behind him like a dog. For all her affectations of superiority she wanted her milk just as much as he wanted his coffee.

He walked into the dining-room, through the window, stiffening as he did so with the resolution of the night before. His armour fitted him tightly. Little animals, children, the too searching calls of Nature, occult, symbolic, magical—all these must be sternly resisted and suppressed in the company of others. The danger of letting his imagination loose was too alarming. The ridicule would overwhelm him. In the eyes of the world he now lived in he would seem simply mad. The risk was impossible.

Like the Christian Scientists, he felt the need of vigorous affirmation: "I am Paul Rivers. I am a grown-up man. I am an official in a lumber Company. I am forty-five. I have a beard. I am important and sedate."

Thus he fortified himself; and thus, like the persuasive Mrs. Tompkyns on the lawn, he imagined that he was deceiving both himself—and those who were *on the watch!*

CHAPTER VIII

And a little child shall lead them.

A week passed quickly away and found Paul still in his sister's house. The country air agreed with him, and he went for long walks over the heathery hills and down to the sea. The little private study provided for him,—remembering Mrs. Tompkyns' example, he made a brave pretence of having reports to write to his lumber Company—was admirable for his work. As a place of retreat when he felt temptation too strong upon him, or danger was near at hand, he used it constantly. He scented conditions in advance very often, though no one probably would have suspected it of him.

Once or twice he lunched out with neighbours, and sometimes people motored over to tea; companionship and society were at hand if he wanted them. And books of the kind he loved stood in precious rows upon the shelves of Dick's well-stored library. Here he browsed voraciously.

His sister, meanwhile, showed tact hardly to be expected of her. She tried him tentatively with many things to see if he liked them, but she made no conspicuous plans for him, and took good care that he was left entirely to his own devices. A kind of intelligent truce had established itself between them—these two persons who lived in different worlds and stared at one another with something like astonishment over the top of a high wall. Moreover, her languid interest in life made no claims upon him; there was pleasant companionship, gentle talks, and genuine, if thinly coloured, affection. He felt absolutely free, yet was conscious of being looked after with kindness and discretion. She managed him so well, in fact, that he hardly realised he was being managed at all.

He fell more easily than he had thought possible into the routine of the uneventful country life. From feeling "caged" he came to feel "comfortable." June, and the soft forces of the summer, purred about him, and almost without knowing it he began to purr with them.

For his superabundant energy he found relief in huge walks, early and late, and in all manner of unnecessary and invented labours of Hercules about the place. Thus, he dammed up the little stream that trickled harmlessly through the Gwyle pine-wood, making a series of deep pools in which he bathed when the spirit moved him; he erected a gigantic and very dangerous see-saw for the children (and himself) across a fallen trunk; and, by means of canvas, boards, and steps, he constructed a series of rooms and staircases in a spreading ilex tree, with rope railings and bells at each "floor" for visitors, so that even the gardeners admitted it was the most wonderful thing they had ever set eyes upon in a tree.

With the children he was, however, careful to play the part he had decided to play. He was kind and good-natured; he spent a good deal of time with them daily; he even submitted periodically to be introduced all over again to the out-of-door animals, but he went through it all soberly and deliberately, and flattered himself that he was quite successful in presenting to them the "Uncle Paul" whom it was best for his safety they should know.

Heart-searchings and temptations he had in plenty, but came through the ordeal with flying colours, and by the end of the first week he was satisfied that they accepted him as he wished—sedate, stolid, dull, and "grown up."

Yet, all the time, there was something that puzzled him. Under the leadership of Nixie the children played up almost too admirably. It was almost as though he had called them and explained everything in detail. In spite of himself, they seemed somehow or other to have got into his confidence, so that he felt his pretence was after all not so effective as he meant it to be.

Even—nay, especially—the way he was "accepted" by the animals was suspicious—for nothing can be more eloquent of the true relations between children and a grown-up than the terms they permit their animals to have towards him—and this easy acceptance of himself as he pretended to be constituted the most wearing and subtle kind of attack he could possibly conceive. He felt as if the steel casings of his armour were changing into cardboard; soon they would become mere tissue-paper, and then turn transparent and melt away altogether.

"They seem to think it's all put on, this stiffness of mine," he thought more than once. "Perhaps they're playing a sort of game with me. If once they find out I'm only acting—whew!" he whistled low—the game is up at once! I must keep an eye peeled!"

Consequently he kept that eye peeled; he made more use of his private study, and so often gave the excuse of having reports to write that, had it been true, his lumber Company would have been obliged to double its staff in order to read them.

Yet, even in the study, he was not absolutely safe.

The children penetrated there too. They knocked elaborately—always; but with the knock he invariably realised a roguish pair of eyes and a sly laugh on the other side of the door. It was like knocking on his heart direct. He always said—in a bored, unnatural tone:

"Oh, come in, whoever it is!" knowing quite well who it was. And, then, in they would come—one or the other of them.

They slipped in softly as shadows, like the coming of dusk, like stray puffs of wind, fragrant and summery, or like unexpected rays of light as the suit walked round the house in the afternoon. And when they were gone—swiftly, like the sun dipping behind a cloud—lo, the room seemed cold and empty again.

"Oh, they're up to something, they're up to something," he said wisely to himself with a sigh. "They're laying traps for me, bless their little insolences!"

And the more he thought about it, the more certain he felt that Nixie, Jonah, and Toby were simply playing the Cat Game—pretending to accept his attitude because they saw he wished it. Only, less occult and intelligent than the cat, they sometimes made odd little slips that betrayed them.

For instance, one evening Jonah penetrated into the study to say goodnight, and brought the Chow puppies, China and Japan, with him. Their tails curled over their backs like wire brushes; their vigorous round bodies, for ever on the move, were all he could manage. Having been duly kissed, the child waited, however, for something else, and at length, receiving no assistance from his uncle, he lifted each puppy in turn on to the table.

"You, Uncle, please hold them; I can't," he explained.

And, rather grimly, Paul tried to keep the two wriggling bodies still, while Jonah then came up a little closer to his chair.

"*They* have reports to write too, to their lumber-kings," he said, his face solemn as a gong—using a phrase culled heaven knows where. "So will you please see that they don't make blots either."

"But how did you know there were such things as lumber-kings?" Paul asked, surprised.

"I didn't know. They knew," with a jerk of his head toward the struggling puppies, who hated the elevation of the table and the proximity of Paul's bearded face. "They said you told them."

There was no trace of a smile in his eyes; nothing but the earnest expression of the child taking part in the ponderous make-believe of the grownup. Paul felt that by this simple expedient his reports and the safety they represented had been reduced in a single moment to the level of a paltry pretence.

He blushed. "Well, tell them to run after their tails more, and think less," he said.

"All right, Uncle Paul," and the boy was gone, grave as any judge.

And Toby, her small round face still shining like an onion skin, had a different but equally effective method of showing him that he belonged to their world in spite of his clumsy pretence. She gave him lessons in Natural History. One afternoon when a brightly-coloured creature darted across the page of his book, and he referred to it as a "beetle," she very smartly rebuked him.

"Not beetle, but beetie, *that* one," she corrected him.

He thought at first this was merely a child's abbreviation, but she went on to instruct him fully, and he discovered that the ordinary coleopterist has a great deal yet to learn in the proper classification of his species.

"There are beetles, and beedles, and beeties," she explained standing by his chair on the lawn, and twiddling with his watch-chain. "Beeties are all bright-coloured and little and very pretty—like ladybirds."

"And beedles?"

"Oh, b-e-e-e-d-d-les," pronouncing the word heavily and slowly, "are the stupid fat ones in the road that always get run over. They're always sleepy, you see, but quite nice, oh, quite nice;" she hastened to add lest Paul should dislike them from her description.

"And all the rest are beetles, I suppose, just ordinary beetles?" he asked.

"Beetles," she said, with the calmness of superior knowledge, "are fast, black things that scuttle about kitchens. Horrid and crawly! *Now* you know them all!"

She ran off with a burst of laughter upon that face of polished onion skin, and left her uncle to reflect deeply upon this new world of beetles.

The lesson was instructive and symbolic, though the choice of subject was not as poetic as might have been. With this new classification as a starting-point, the child, no doubt, had erected a vast superstructure of wonder, fun, beauty, and—why not? truth! For children, he mused, are ever the true idealists. In their games of make-believe they create the world anew—in six minutes. They scorn measurements, and deal directly with the eternal principles behind things. With a little mud on the end of a stick they trace the course of the angels, and with the wooden-blocks of their building-boxes they erect the towering palaces of a universe that shall never pass away.

Yet what they did, surely he also did! His world of imagination was identical with theirs of make-believe. Was, then, the difference between them one of expression merely?...

Toby came thundering up and fell upon him from nowhere.

"Uncle Paul," she said rather breathlessly.

"Yes, dear," he made answer, still thinking upon beedles and beeties.

"On the path down there by the rosydandrums there's a beedle now—a big one with horns—if you'd like to see it."

"Oh! By the rhododendrons, you mean?"

"Yes, by the rosydandrums," she repeated "Only we must be quick or he'll get home before we come."

He was far more keen to see that "beedle" than she was. Yet for the immediate safety of his soul he refused.

Nixie it was, however, who penetrated furthest into the fortress. She came with a fearless audacity that fairly made him tremble. She had only to approach for him to become aware how poorly his suit of armour fitted.

But she was so gentle and polite about it that she was harder to withstand than all the others put together. She was slim and insinuating in body, mind and soul. Often, before he realised what she was talking about, her slender little fingers were between the cracks of his breast-plate. For instance, after leaving Toby and her "beedle," he strolled down to the pinewood and stood upon the rustic bridge watching the play of sunlight and shadow, when suddenly, out of the very water it seemed, up rose a veritable water-sprite—hatless and stockingless—Nixie, the ubiquitous.

She scrambled lightly along the steep bank to his side, and leaned over the railing with him, staring at their reflections in the stream.

"I declare you startled me, child!" Paul exclaimed.

Her eyes met his in the running reflection beneath them. Of course, it may have been merely the trick of the glancing water, but to him it seemed that her expression was elfin and mischievous.

"Did I—*really*, Uncle Paul?" she said after a long silence, and without looking up. But woven through the simple words, as sunlight is woven through clearing mist, he divined all the other meanings of the child's subtle and curious personality. It amounted to this—she at once invited, nay included, him in her own particular tree and water world: included him because he belonged there with her, and she simply couldn't help herself. There was no favour about it one way or the other.

The compliment—the temptation—was overwhelming. Paul shivered a little, actually shivered, as he stood beside her in the sunshine. For several minutes they leaned there in silence, gazing at the flowing water.

'The woods are *very* busy—this evening," she said at length.

"I'm sure they are," he answered, before he quite realised what he was saying. Then he pulled himself together with an effort.

"But does Mlle. Fleury know, and approve—?"he asked a little stiffly, glancing down at her bare legs and splashed white frock.

"Oh, no," she laughed wickedly, "but then Mlle. only understands what she sees with her eyes! She is much too mixed-up and educated to know all *this* kind of thing!" She made a gesture to include the woods about them. "Her sort of knowledge is so stuffing, you know."

"Rather," he exclaimed. "I would far sooner know the trees themselves than know their Latin names."

It slipped out in spite of himself. The next minute he could have bitten his tongue off. But Nixie took no advantage of him. She let his words pass as something taken for granted.

"I mean—it's better to learn useful things while you can," he said hurriedly, blushing in his confusion like a child.

Nixie peered steadily down into the water for several minutes before she said anything more.

"Either she's found me out and knows everything," thought Paul; "or she hasn't found me out and knows nothing." But which it was, for the life of him, he couldn't be certain.

"Oh," she cried suddenly, looking up into his face, her eyes, to Paul's utter amazement, wet with tears, "Oh! how Daddy must have loved you!"

And, before he could think of a word to say, she was gone! Gone into the woods with a fluttering as of white wings.

"So apparently I am not too mixed-up and educated for their exquisite little world," he reflected, as soon as the emotion caused by her last words had subsided a little; "and the things I know are not of the "stuffing" kind!"

It all made him think a good deal—this attitude the children adopted towards *his* attitude, this unhesitating acceptance of him in spite of all his pretence. But he still valiantly maintained his studied aloofness of manner, and never allowed himself to overstep the danger line. He never forgot himself when he played with them, and the stories he told were just what they called "ornary " stories, and not tales of pure imagination and fantasy. The rules of the game, finely balanced, were observed between them just as between himself and Mrs. Tompkyns.

Yet somehow, by unregistered degrees and secretly, they loosened the joints of his armour day by day and hour by hour.

CHAPTER IX

All the Powers that vivify nature must be children, for all the fairies, and gnomes, the goblins, yes, and the great giants too, are only different sizes and shapes and characters of children. —GEORGE MACDONALD.

It was a week later, and Paul was smoking his evening pipe on the lawn before dinner. His sister was in London for a couple of days. Mlle. Fleury had gone to the dentist in the neighbouring town and had not yet returned. The children, consequently, had been running rather wild.

The sun had barely disappeared, when the full moon, rising huge and faint in the east, cast a silvery veil over the gardens and the wood. The night came treading softly down the sky, passing with an almost visible presence from the hills to the motionless trees in the valley, and then sinking gently and mysteriously down into the very roots of the grass and flowers.

During the day there had been rain—warm showers alternating with dazzling sunshine as in April—and now the earth, before going to sleep, was sending out great wafts of incense. Paul sniffed it in with keen enjoyment.

The odour of burning wood floated to him over the tree tops, hanging a little heavily in the moist atmosphere; he thought of a hundred fires of his own making—elsewhere, far away! "And grey dawns saw his camp-fires in the rain," he murmured.

He wandered down to the Larch Gate, so called by the children because the larches stood there about the entrance of the wood like the porch of some forest temple. He halted, listening to the faint drip-drip of the trees, and as he listened, he thought; and his thoughts, like stones falling through a deep sea, sank down into the depths of him where so little light was that no words came to give them form or substance.

Overhead, the blue lanes of the sky down which the sunlight had poured all day were slowly softening for the coming of the stars; and in himself the plastic depths, he felt, were a-stirring, as though some great change that he could not alter or control were about to take place in him. He was aware of an unwonted undercurrent of excitement in his blood. It seemed to him that there was "something afoot," although he had no evidence to warrant the suspicion.

"Something's up to-night," he murmured between the puffs of his pipe. "There's something in the air!"

He blew a long whiff of smoke and watched it melt away over a bed of mignonette among the blue shadows where the dusk gathered beneath the ilex trees. There, for a moment, his eye followed it, and just as it sifted off into transparency he became aware with a start of surprise that behind the bushes something was moving. He looked closer.

"It's stopped," he muttered; "but only a second ago it was moving—moving parallel with myself."

Paul was well accustomed to watching the motions of wild creatures in the forest; his eye was trained like the eye of an Indian. The gloom at first was too dense for anything to differentiate itself from their general mass, but after a short inspection his sight detected little bits of shadow that were lighter or darker than other little bits. The moving thing began to assume outline.

"It's a person!" he decided. "It's somebody watching—watching *me!*"

He took a step forward, and the figure likewise advanced, keeping even pace with him. He went faster, and the figure also went faster; it moved very silently, very softly, "like an Indian," he thought with admiration. Behind the Blue Summer-house, where they sometimes had tea on wet days, it disappeared.

"There are no cattle-stealers, or timber-sneaks in this country," he reflected, "but there are burglars. Perhaps this is a burglar who knows Margaret is away and thinks—"

He had not time to finish what the burglar thought, for at that moment, at the top of the Long Walk, where the moonlight already lay in a patch, the figure suddenly dashed out at full speed from the cover of the bushes, and he beheld, not a burglar, but—a little girl in a blue frock with a broad white collar, and long, black spindle legs.

"Nixie, my dear child!" he exclaimed. "But aren't you in bed?"

It was a stupid question of course, and she did not attempt to answer it, but came up close to him, picking her way neatly between the flower-beds. The moon gleamed on her shiny black shoes and on her shiny yellow hair; over her summer dress she wore a red cloak, but it was open and only held to her by two thin bands about the neck. Under the hood he saw her elf-like face, the expression grave, but the eyes bright with excitement, and she moved softly over the grass like a shadow, timidly, yet without hesitation. A small, warm hand stole into his.

Paul put his pipe, still alight, into his pocket like a naughty boy caught smoking, and turned to face her.

"'Pon my soul, Nixie, I believe you really *are* a sprite!"

She let go his hand and sprang away lightly over the lawn, laughing silently, her hood dropping off so that her hair flew out in a net to catch the moonlight, and for an instant he imagined he was looking at running water, swift and dancing; but the very next second she was back at his side again, the red hood replaced, the cloak gathered tightly about her slim person, feeling for his big hand again with both of her own.

"At night I *am* a sprite," she whispered laughing, "and mind I don't bewitch you altogether!"

She drew him gently across the lawn, choosing the direction with evident purpose, and he, curiously and suddenly bereft of all initiative, allowed her to do as she would.

"But, please, Uncle Paul," she went on with vast gravity, "I want you to be serious now. I've something to say to you, and that's why I'm not in bed when I ought to be. All the other Sprites are about too, you know, so be very careful how you answer."

The big man allowed himself to he led away. He felt his armour dropping off in great flakes as he went. No light is so magical as in that mingled hour of sun and moon when the west is still hurtling and the east just a-glimmer with the glory that is to come. Paul felt it strongly. He was half with the sun and half with the moon, and the gates of fantasy seemed somewhere close at hand. Curtains were being drawn aside, veils lifting, doors softly opening. He almost heard the rush of the wind behind, and tasted the keen, sweet excitement of another world.

He turned sharply to look at his companion. But first he put the hood back, for she seemed more human that way.

"Well, child!" he said, as gruffly as he could manage, "and what is it you have stayed up so late to ask me?"

"It's something I have to *say* to you, not to *ask*," she replied at once demurely. There was a delicious severity about her.

After a pause of twenty seconds she tripped round in front of him and stared full into his face. He felt as though she cried "Hands up" and held a six-shooter to his head. She pulled the trigger that same moment.

"Isn't it time now to stop writing all those Reports, and to take off your dressing-up things?" she asked with decision.

Paul stopped abruptly and tried to disengage his hand, but she held him so tightly that he could not escape without violence.

"What dressing-up things are you talking about?" he asked, forcing a laugh which, he admitted himself, sounded quite absurd.

"All this pretending that you're so old, and don't know about things—I mean *real* things—*our* things."

He searched as in a fever for the right words—words that should be true and wise, and safe—but before he could pick them out of the torrent of sentences that streamed through his mind, she had gone on again. She spoke calmly, but very gravely.

"We are so tired of helping to pretend with you; and we've been waiting patiently *so* long. Even Toby knows it's only 'sguise you put on to tease us."

"Even Toby?" he repeated foolishly, avoiding her brilliant eyes.

"And it really isn't quite fair, you know. There are so very few that care—and understand—"

There came a little quaver in her voice. She hardly came up to his shoulder. He felt as though a whole bathful of happiness had suddenly been upset inside him, and was running about deliciously through his whole being—as though he wanted to run and dance and sing. It was like the reaction after tight boots—collars—or tight armour—and the blood was beginning to flow again mightily. Nothing could stop it. Some keystone in the fabric of his being dropped or shifted. His whole inner world fell into a new pattern. Resistance was no longer possible or desirable. He had done his best. Now he would give in and enjoy himself at last.

"But, my dear child—my dear little Nixie—"

"No, really, Uncle, there's no good talking like that," she interrupted, her voice under command again, though still aggrieved, "because you know quite well we're all waiting for you to join us properly—our Society, I mean—and have our a'ventures with us—"

She called it "aventures." She left out all consonants when excited. The word caught him sharply. Nixie had wounded him better than she knew.

"Er—then do you have adventures?" he asked.

"Of course—wonderful."

"But not—er—the sort—er—I could join in?"

"Of course; very wonderfulindeedaventures. That's what Daddy used to call them—before he went away."

It was Dick himself speaking. Paul imagined he could hear the very voice. Another, and deeper, emotion surged through him, making all the heartstrings quiver.

He turned and looked about him, still holding the child tightly by the hand....

Behind him he heard the air moving in the larches, combing out their long green hair; the pampas grass rustled faintly on the lawn just beyond; and from the wood, now darkening, came the murmur of the brook. On his right, the old house looked shadowy and unreal. There stood the chimneys, like draped figures watching him, with the first stars peeping over their hunched shoulders. Dew glistened on the slates of the roof; beyond them he saw the clean outline of the hill, darkly sweeping up into the pallor of the sunset. There, too, past the wall of the house, he saw the great distances of heathland moving down through crowds of shadows to the sea. And the moon was higher.

"There's seats in the Blue Summer-house," the voice beside him said, with insinuation as well as command.

He found it impossible to resist; indeed, the very desire to resist had been spirited away. Slowly they made their way across the silvery patchwork of the lawn to the door of the Blue Summer-house. This was a tumble-down structure with a thatched roof; it had once been blue, but was now no colour at all. Low seats ran round the inside walls, and as Paul stood at the dark entrance he perceived that these seats were already occupied; and he hesitated. But Nixie pulled him gently in.

"This is a regular Meeting," she said, as naturally as though she had been wholly innocent of a part in the plot. "They've only been waiting for us. Please come in." She even pushed him.

"It may be regular, but it is most unexpected," he said, breathless rather, and curiously shy as he crossed the threshold and peered round at the silent faces about him. Eyes, he saw, were big and round and serious, shining with excitement. Clearly it was a very important occasion. He wondered what an "irregular" meeting would be like.

"We waited till mother was away," explained a candid voice, speaking with solemnity from the recesses.

"And till Madmerzelle had to go to the dentist and stay to tea," added another.

"So that it would be easier for *you* to come," concluded Nixie, lest he should think all these excuses were only on their own account.

She led him across the cobbled floor to a wooden arm-chair with crooked and shattered legs, and persuaded him to sit down. He did so.

"There was some sense in that, at any rate," he remarked irrelevantly, not quite sure whether he referred to the children, or Mademoiselle, or the chair, and landing at the same instant with a crash upon the rickety support which was much lower than he thought it was. The joints and angles of the wood entered his ribs. He lost all memory of how to be sedate after that. He began to enjoy himself absurdly.

Silvery laughter was heard, followed immediately by the sound of rushing little feet as a dozen small shadows shot out into the moonlight and tore across the lawn at top speed. China and Japan he recognised, and a cohort of furry creatures in their rear.

"Now you've frightened them *all* away," exclaimed the voice that had spoken first.

"Doesn't matter," replied the other, who evidently spoke with authority; "Uncle Paul was in before they left. They saw the introduction. That's enough. So now," it added with decision, "if you're quite ready we'd better begin."

Paul grasped by this time that he was the central figure in some secret ceremony of the children, that it was of vital importance to them, as well as a profound compliment to himself. The animals formed part of it so long as they could be persuaded to stay. Their own rituals, however, were so vastly more wonderful and dignified—especially the Ritual of the Cats— that they were somewhat contemptuous, and had escaped at the earliest opportunity. It was, of course, his formal initiation into their world of make-believe and imagination. He stood before them on the floor of this tumbled-down Blue Summer-house in the capacity of the Candidate. Strange chills began to chase one another down his long spine. A shy happiness swept through him and made him shiver. "Can they possibly guess," he wondered, "how far more important this is to me than to them?"

"Are you ready then?" Nixie asked again.

"Quite ready," he replied in a deep and tremulous voice.

"Go ahead then," said the voice of decision.

A little bell rang, manipulated by some invisible hand in the darkness, and Nixie darted forward and drew a curtain that bore a close resemblance to a carriage rug across the doorway, so that only the faintest gleam of moonlight filtered through the cracks on either side. Then the owner of the voice of authority left his throne on the back wall and stepped solemnly forward in the direction of the candidate. Paul recognised Jonah with some difficulty. He tripped twice on the way.

The stumbling was comprehensible. On his head he wore a sort of mitre that on ordinary occasions was evidently used to keep the tea hot on the schoolroom table; for it was beyond question a tea-cosy. A garment of variegated colours wrapped his figure down to the heels and trailed away some distance behind him. It was either a table-cloth or a housemaid's Sunday dress, and it invested him with a peculiar air of quaint majesty. He might have been King of the Gnomes. On his hands were large leathern gauntlets—very large indeed; and with loose fingers whose movements were clearly difficult to control, he grasped a stick that once may have been a hunting crop, but now was certainly a wand of office.

In front of Paul he came to a full stop, gathering his robes about him.

He made a little how, during which the mitre shifted dangerously to one side, and then tapped the candidate lightly with the wand on the head, shoulders, and breast.

"Please answer now," he said in a low tone, and then went backwards to his seat against the wall. His robe of office so impeded him that he was obliged to use the wand as a common walking-stick. Once or twice, too, he hopped.

"But you've forgotten to ask it," whispered Nixie from the door where she was holding up the curtains with both hands. "He's got nothing to answer."

Quickly correcting his mistake, Jonah then stood up on his seat and said, rather shyly, the following lines, evidently learned by heart with a good deal of trouble:—

> You've applied to our Secret Society,
> Which is full of unusual variety,
> And, in spite of your past,
> We admit you at last,
> But—we hope you'll behave with propriety.

"Now, stand up and answer, please," whispered Nixie. "Daddy made all this up, you know. It's your turn to answer now."

Paul rose with difficulty. At first it seemed as if the chair meant to rise with him, so tightly did it fit; but in the end he stood erect without it, and bowing to the President, he said in solemn tones—and the words came genuinely from his heart:

"I appreciate the honour done to me. I am very grateful indeed."

"That's very good, I think," Nixie whispered under her breath to him.

Then Toby advanced, climbing down laboriously from her perch on the broken bench, and stalked up to the spot just vacated by her brother. She, too, was suitably dressed for the occasion, but owing to her diminutive size, and the fact that she did not reach up to the patch of moonlight, it was not possible to distinguish more than the white cap pinned on to her hair. It looked like a housekeeper's cap. She, too, carried a wand of office. Was it a hunting crop or poker, Paul wondered?

Toby, then, with much more effort than Jonah, repeated the formula of admission. She got the lines a little mixed, however:—

You've applied to our Secret Society,
Which is full of unusual propriety,
And, in spite of your past,
We admit you at last,
But we hope you'll *behave with variety.*

"I will endeavour to do so," said Paul, replying with a low bow.

When he rose again to an upright position, Nixie was standing close in front of him. One arm still held up the curtains, but the other pointed directly into his face.

Your 'ficial position in the Society," she said in her thin, musical little voice, also repeating words learned by heart, "will be that of Recording Secretary, and your principal duties to keep a record of all the Aventures and to read them aloud at Regular Meetings. Any Meeting anywhere is a Regular Meeting. You must further promise on your living oath not to reveal the existence of the Society, or any detail of its proceedings, to any person not approved of by the Society as a whole."

She paused for his reply.

"I promise," he said.

"He promises," repeated three voices together.

There was a general clatter and movement in the summer-house. He was forced down again into the rickety chair and the three little officials were clambering upon his knees before he knew where he was. All talked breathlessly at once.

"Now you're in properly—at last!"

"You needn't pretend any more—"

"But we knew all along you were really trying hard to get in?"

"I really believe I was," said he, getting in a chance remark.

They covered him with kisses.

"We never thought you were as important as you pretended," Jonah said; "and your being so big made no difference."

"Or your beard, Uncle Paul," added Toby.

"And we never think people old till they're married," Jonah explained, putting the mitre on his uncle's head.

"So now we can have our aventures all together," exclaimed Nixie, kissing him swiftly, and leaping off his knee. The other two followed her example, and suddenly—he never quite understood how it happened so quickly—the summer-house was empty, and he was alone with the moonlight. A flash of white petticoats and slender black legs on the lawn, and lo, they were gone!

On the gravel path outside sounded a quick step. Paul started with surprise. The very next minute Mlle. Fleury, in her town clothes and hat, appeared round the corner.

"'Ow then!" she exclaimed sharply, "the little ones zey are no more 'ere? Mr. Rivairs.... !" She shook her finger at him.

Paul tried to look dignified. For the moment, however, he quite forgot the tea-cosy still balanced on his head.

"Mademoiselle Fleury," he said politely, "the children have gone to bed."

"It is 'igh time that they are already in bed, only I hear their voices now this minute," she went on excitedly. "They 'ide here, do they not?"

"I assure you, Mademoiselle, they have gone to bed," Paul said. The woman stared at him with amazement in her eyes. He wondered why. Then, with a crash, something fell from the skies, hitting his nose on the way down, and bounding on to the ground.

"Oh, the mitre!" he cried with a laugh, "I clean forgot it was there." He kicked it aside and stared with confusion at his companion. She looked very neat and trim in her smart town frock. He understood now why she stared so, and his cheeks flamed crimson, though it was too dark for them to be seen.

"Meester Reevairs," she said at length, the desire to laugh and the desire to scold having fought themselves to a standstill, so that her face betrayed no expression at all, "you lead zem astray, I think."

"On the contrary, it is they who lead me," he said self-consciously. "In fact, they have just deprived me of my very best armour—"

"Armour!" she interrupted, "*Armoire!* Ah! They 'ide upstairs in the cupboard,"—and she turned to run.

"Do not be harsh with them," he cried after her, "it is all my fault really. I am to blame, not they."

"'Arsh! Oh no!" she called back to him. "Only, you know, if your seester find them at this hour not in bed—"

Paul lost the end of the sentence as she turned the corner of the house. He gathered up the remnants of the ceremony and followed slowly in her footsteps.

"Now, really," he thought, "what a simple and charming woman! How her eyes twinkled! And how awfully nice her voice was!" He flung down the rugs and wands and tea-cosy in the hall. "Out there," with a jerk in the direction of the Atlantic Ocean, "the whole camp would make her a Queen."

Altogether the excitement of the last hour had been considerable. He felt that something must happen to him unless he could calm down a bit.

"I know," he exclaimed aloud, "I'll go and have a hot bath. There's just time before dinner. That'll take it out of me." And he went up the front stairs, singing like a boy.

CHAPTER X

Everything possible to be believed is an image of truth. —BLAKE.

For some days after that Paul walked on air. Incredible as it may seem to normally constituted persons, he was so delighted to have found a medium in which he could in some measure express himself without fear of ridicule, that the entire world was made anew for him. He thought about it a great deal. He even argued in his muddled fashion, but he got no farther that way. The only thing he really understood was the plain fact that he had found a region where his companions were about his own age, with his own tastes, ready to consider things that were *real,* and to let the trivial and vulgar world go by.

This was the fact that stared him in the face and made him happy. For the first time in his life he could play with others. Hitherto he had played alone.

"It's a safety-valve at last," he exclaimed, using his favourite word. "Now I can let myself go a bit. *They* will never laugh; on the contrary, they'll understand and love it. Hooray!"

"And, remember," Nixie had again explained to him, "you have to write down all the aventures. That's what keeping the records means. And you must read them out to us at the Meetings."

And he chuckled as he thought about it, for it meant having real Reports to write at last, reports that others would read and appreciate.

The aventures, moreover, began very quickly; they came thick and fast; and he lived in them so intensely that he carried them over into his other dull world, and sometimes hardly knew which world he was in at all. His imagination, hungry and untamed, had escaped, and was seeking all it could devour.

It was a hot afternoon in mid-June, and Paul was lying with his pipe upon the lawn. His sister was out driving. He was alone with the children and the smaller portion of the menagerie,—smaller in size, that is, not in numbers; cats, kittens, and puppies were either asleep, or on the hunt, all about them. And from an open window a parrot was talking ridiculously in mixed French and English.

The giant cedars spread their branches; in the limes the bees hummed drowsily; the world lay a scented garden around him, and a very soft wind stole to and fro, stirring the bushes with sleepy murmurs and making the Powers nod.

China and Japan lay panting in the shade behind him, and not far off reposed the big grey Persian, Mrs. Tompkyns. Regardless of the heat, Pouf, Zezette, and Dumps flitted here and there as though the whole lawn was specially made for their games; and Smoke, the black cat, dignified and mysterious, lay with eyes half-closed just near enough for Paul to stroke his sleek, hot sides when he felt so disposed. He—Smoke that is—blinked indifferently at passing butterflies, or twitched his great tail at the very tip when a bird settled in the branches overhead; but for the most part he was intent upon other matters—matters of genuine importance that concerned none but himself.

A few yards off Jonah and Toby were doing something with daisies—what it was Paul could not see; and on his other side Nixie lay flat upon the grass and gazed into the sky. The governess was—where all governesses should be out of lesson-time—elsewhere.

"Nixie, you're sleeping. Wake up."

She rolled over towards him. "No, Uncle Paul, I'm not. I was only thinking."

"Thinking of what?"

"Oh, clouds and things; chiefly clouds, I think." She pointed to the white battlements of summer that were passing very slowly over the heavens. "It's so funny that you can see them move, yet can't see the thing that pushes them along."

"Wind, you mean?"

"H'mmmmm."

They lay flat on their backs and watched. Nixie made a screen of her hair and peered through it. Paul did the same with his fingers.

"You can touch it, and smell it, and hear it," she went on, half to herself, "but you can't *see* it."

"I suspect there are creatures that can see the wind, though," he remarked sleepily.

"I 'spect so too," she said softly. "I think I could, if I really tried hard enough. If I was very, oh very kind and gentle and polite to it, I think—"

"Come and tell me quietly," Paul said with excitement. "I believe you're right."

He scented a delightful aventure. The child turned over on the grass twice, roller fashion, and landed against him, lying on her face with her chin in her hands and her heels clicking softly in the air.

She began to explain what she meant. "You must listen properly because it's rather difficult to explain, you know"; he heard her breathing into his ear, and then her voice grew softer and fainter as she went on. Lower and lower it grew, murmuring like a distant mill-wheel, softer and softer; wonderful sentences and words all running gently into each other without pause, somewhere below ground. It begun to sound far away, and it melted into the humming of the bees in the lime trees.... Once or twice it stopped altogether, Paul thought, so that he missed whole sentences.... Gaps came, gaps filled with no definite words, but only the inarticulate murmur of summer and summer life....

Then, without warning, he became conscious of a curious sinking sensation, as though the solid lawn beneath him had begun to undulate. The turf grew soft like air, and swam up over him in green waves till his head was covered. His ears became muffled; Nixie's voice no longer reached him as something outside himself; it was within—curiously running, so to speak, with his blood. He sank deeper and deeper into a delicious, soothing medium that both covered and penetrated him.

The child had him by the hand, that was all he knew, then—a long sliding motion, and forgetfulness.

"I'm off," he remembered thinking, "off at last into a real aventure!"

Down they sank, down, down; through soft darkness, and long, shadowy places, passing through endless scented caverns, and along dim avenues that stretched, for ever and ever it seemed, beneath the gloom of mighty trees. The air was cool and perfumed with earth. They were in some underworld, strangely muted, soundless, mysterious. It grew very dark.

"Where are we, Nixie?" He did not feel alarm; but a sense of wonder, touched delightfully by awe, had begun to send thrills along his nerves.

Her reply in his ear was like a voice in a tiny trumpet, far away, very soft. "Come along! Follow me!"

"I'm coming. But it's so dark."

"Hush," she whispered. "We're in a dream together. I'm not sure where exactly. Keep close to me."

"I'm coming," he repeated, blundering over the roots beside her; "but where are we? I can't see a bit."

"Tread softly. We're in a lost forest—just before the dawn," he heard her voice answer faintly.

"A forest underground—? You mean a coal measure?" he asked in amazement.

She made no answer. "I think we're going to see the wind," she added presently.

Her words thrilled him inexplicably. It was as if—in that other world of gross values—some one had said, "You're going to make a million!" It was all hushed and soft and subdued. Everything had a coating of plush.

"We've gone backwards somewhere—a great many years. But it's all right. There's no time in dreams."

"It's dreadfully dark," he whispered, tripping again.

The persuasion of her little hand led him along over roots and through places of deep moss. Great spaces, he felt, were about him. Shadows coated everything with silence. It was like the vast primeval forests of his country across the seas. The map of the world had somehow shifted, and here, in little England, he found the freedom of those splendid scenes of desolation that he craved. Millions of huge trees reared up about them through the gloom, and he felt their presence, though invisible.

"The sun isn't up yet," she added after a bit. He held her hand tightly, as they stumbled slowly forward together side by side. He began to feel extraordinarily alive. Exhilaration seized him. He could have shouted with excitement.

"Hush!" whispered his guide, "do be careful. You'll upset us both." The trembling of his hand betrayed him. "You stumble like an om'ibus!"

"I'm all right. Go ahead!" he replied under his breath. "I can see better now!"

"Now look," she said, stopping in front of him and turning round.

The darkness lifted somewhat as he bent down to follow the direction of her gaze. On every side, dim and thronging, he saw the stems of immense trees rising upwards into obscurity. There were hundreds upon hundreds of them. His eyes followed their outline till the endless number bewildered him. Overhead, the stars were shining faintly through the tangled network of their branches. Odours of earth and moss and leaves, cool and delicate, rose about them; vast depths of silence stretched away in every direction. Great ferns stood motionless, with all the magic of frosted window-panes, among their roots. All was still and dark and silent. It was the heart of a great forest before the dawn—prehistoric, unknown to man.

"Oh, I wonder—I wonder—" began Paul, groping about him clumsily with his hands to feel the way.

"Oh, please don't talk so loud," Nixie whispered, pinching his arm; "we shall wake up if you do. Only people in dreams come to places like this."

"You know the place?" he exclaimed with increasing excitement. "So do I almost. I'm sure this has all happened before, only I can't remember—"

"We must keep as still as mice."

"We are—still as mice."

"This is where the winds sleep when they're not blowing. It's their resting-place."

He looked about him, drawing a deep breath.

"Look out; you'll wake them if you breathe like *that*," whispered the child.

"Are they asleep now?"

"Of course. Can't you see?"

"Not much—yet!"

"Move like a cat, and speak in whispers. We may see them when they wake."

"How soon?"

"Dawn. The wind always wakes with the sun. It's getting closer now."

It was very wonderful. No words can describe adequately the still splendour of that vast forest as they stood there, waiting for the sunrise. Nothing stirred. The trees were carved out of some marvellous dream-stuff; motionless, yet conveying the impression of life. Paul knew it and recognised it. All primeval woods possess that quality—trees that know nothing of men and have never heard the ringing of the axe. The silence was of death, yet a sense of life that is far beyond death pulsed through it. Cisterns of quiet, gigantic, primitive life lay somewhere hidden in these shadowed glades. It seemed the counterpart of a man's soul before rude passion and power have stirred it into activity. Here all slept potentially, as in a human soul. The huge, sombre pines rose from their beds of golden moss to shake their crests faintly to the stars, awaiting the coming of the true passion—the great Sun of life, that should call them to splendour, to reality, and to the struggle of a bigger life than they yet knew, when they might even try to shake free from their roots in the hard, confining earth, and fly to the source of their existence—the sun.

And the sun was coming now. The dawn was at hand. The trees moved gently together, it seemed. The wood grew lighter. An almost imperceptible shudder ran through it as through a vast spider's web.

"Look!" cried Nixie. His simple, intuitive little guide was nearer, after all, to reality than he was, for all his subtle vision. "Look, Uncle Paul!"

His attempt to analyse wonder had prevented his seeing it sooner, but as she spoke he became aware that something very unusual was going forward about them. His skin began to tickle, and a strange sense of excitement took possession of him.

A pale, semi-transparent substance he saw hung everywhere in the air about them, clinging in spirals and circles to the trunks, and hanging down from the branches in long slender ribbons that reached almost to the ground. The colour was a delicate pearl-grey. It covered everything as with the softest of filtered light, and hung motionless in the air in painted streamers of thinnest possible vapour.

The silken threads of these gossamer ribbons dropped from the sky in millions upon millions. They wrapped themselves round the very starbeams, and lay in sheets upon the ground; they curled themselves round the stones and crept in among the tiniest crevices of moss and bark; they clothed the ferns with their fairy gauze. Paul could even feel them coiling about his hair and beard and eyelashes. They pervaded the entire scene as light does. The colour was uniform; whether in sheets or ribbons, it did not vary in shade or in degree of transparency. The entire atmosphere was pervaded by it, frozen into absolute stillness.

"That's the winds—all that stuff," Nixie whispered, her voice trembling with excitement. "They're asleep still. Aren't they awful and wonderful?"

As she spoke a faint vibration ran everywhere through the ribbons. Involuntarily he tightened his grasp on the child's hand.

"That's their beginning to wake," she said, drawing closer to him, "like people moving in sleep."

The vibration ran through the air again. It quivered as reflections in the surface of a pool quiver to a ghost of passing wind. They seated themselves on a fallen trunk and waited. The trees waited too; as gigantic notes in a set piece, Paul thought, that the coming sun would presently play upon like a hand upon a vast instrument. Then something moved a few feet away, and he jumped in spite of himself.

"Only Jonah," explained his guide. "He's asleep like us. Don't wake him; he's having a dream too."

It was indeed Jonah, wandering vaguely this way and that, disappearing and reappearing, wholly unaware, it seemed, of their presence. He looked like a gnome. His feet made no sound as he moved about, and after a few minutes he lost himself behind a big trunk and they saw him no more. But almost at once behind him the round figures of China and Japan emerged into view. They came, moving fast and busily, blundering against the trees, tumbling down, and butting into everything that came in their path as though they could not see properly. Paul watched them with astonishment.

"They're only half asleep, and that's why they see so badly," Nixie told him. "Aren't they silly and happy?"

Before he could answer, something else moved into their limited field of vision, and he was aware that a silent grey shadow was stalking solemnly by. All dignity and self-confidence it was; stately, proud, sure of itself, in a region where it was at home, conscious of its power to see and move better than any one else. Two wide-open and brilliant eyes, shining like dropped stars, were turned for a moment towards them where they sat on the log and watched. Then, silent and beautiful, it passed on into the darkness beyond, and vanished from their sight.

"Mrs. Tompkyns!" whispered Nixie. "*She* saw us all right!"

"Splendid!" he exclaimed under his breath, full of admiration.

Nixie pinched his arm. A change had come about in the last few minutes, and into this dense forest the light of approaching dawn began to steal most wonderfully. A universal murmuring filled the air.

"The sun's coming. They're going to wake now!" The child gave a little shiver of delight. Paul sat up. A general, indefinable motion, he saw, was beginning everywhere to run to and fro among the hanging streamers. More light penetrated every minute, and the tree stems began to turn from black to purple, and then from purple to faint grey. Vistas of shadowy glades began to open up on all sides; every instant the trees stood out more distinctly. The myriad threads and ribbons were astir.

"Look!" cried the child aloud; "they're uncurling as they wake."

He looked. The sense of wonder and beauty moved profoundly in his heart. Where, oh where, in all the dreams of his solitary years had he seen anything to equal this unearthly vision of the awakening winds ?

The winds moved in their sleep, and awoke.

In loops, folds, and spirals of indescribable grace they slowly began to unwrap themselves from the tree stems with a million little delicate undulations; like thin mist trembling, and then smoothing out the ruffled surface of their thousand serpentine eddies, they slid swiftly upwards from the moss and ferns, disentangled themselves without effort from roots and stones and bark, and then, reinforced by countless thousands from the lower branches, they rose up slowly in vast coloured sheets towards the region of the tree tops.

And, as they rose, the silence of the forest passed into sound—trembling and murmuring at first, and then rapidly increasing in volume as the distant glades sent their voices to swell it, and the note of every hollow and dell joined in with its contributory note. From all the shadowy recesses of the wood they heard it come, louder and louder, leaping to the centre like running great arpeggios, and finally merging all lesser notes in the wave of a single dominant chord—the song of the awakened winds to the dawn.

"They're singing to the sun," Nixie whispered. Her voice caught in her throat a little and she tightened her grasp on his big hand.

"They're changing colour too," he answered breathlessly. They stood up on their log to see.

"It's the rate they go does that," she tried to explain. She stood on tiptoe.

He understood what she meant, for he now saw that as the wind rose in ribbons, streams and spirals, the original pearl-grey changed chromatically into every shade of colour under the sun.

"Same as metals getting hot," she said. "Their colour comes 'cording to their speed."

Many of the tints he found it impossible to name, for they were such as he had never dreamed of. Crimsons, purples, soft yellows, exquisite greens and pinks ran to and fro in a perfect deluge of colour, as though a hundred sunsets had been let loose and were hunting wildly for the West to set in. And there were shades of opal and mother-of-pearl so delicate that he could only perceive them in his bewildered mind by translating them into the world of sound, and imagining it was the colour of their own singing.

Far too rapidly for description they changed their protean dress, moving faster and faster, glowing fiercely one minute and fading away the next, passing swiftly into new and dazzling brilliancies as the distant winds came to join them, and at length rushing upwards in one huge central draught through the trees, shouting their song with a roar like the sea.

Suddenly they swept up into the sky—sound, colour and all—and silence once more descended upon the forest. The winds were off and about their business of the day. The woods were empty. And the sun was at the very edge of the world.

"Watch the tops of the trees now," cried Nixie, still trembling from the strange wonder of the scene. "The Little Winds will wake the moment the sun touches them—the little winds in the tops of the trees."

As she spoke, the sun came up and his first rays touched the pointed crests above them with gold; and Paul noticed that there were thousands of tiny, slender ribbons streaming out like elastic threads from the tips of all the pines, and that these had only just begun to move. As at a word of command they trooped out to meet the sunshine, undulating like wee coloured serpents, and uttering their weird and gentle music at the same time. And Paul, as he listened, understood at last why the wind in the tree-tops is always more delicately sweet than any other kind, and why it touches so poignantly the heart of him who hears, and calls wonder from her deepest lair.

"The young winds, you see," Nixie said, peering up beneath her joined hands and finding it difficult to keep her balance as she did so. "They sleep longer than the others. And they're not loose either; they're fastened on, and can only go out and come back."

And, as he watched, he saw these young winds fly out miles into the brightening sky, making lines of flashing colour, and then tear back with

a whirring rush of music to curl up again round the twigs and pine needles.

"Though sometimes they *do* manage to get loose, and make funny storms
and hurricanes and things that no one expects at all in the sky."

Paul was on the point of replying to this explanation when something
struck against his legs, and he only just saved himself from falling by seizing Nixie and risking a flying leap with her from the log.

"It's that wicked Japan again," she laughed, clambering back on to the
tree.

The puppy was vigorously chasing its own tail, bumping as it did so into
everything within reach. Paul stooped to catch it. At the same instant it
rose up past his very nose, and floated off through the trees and was lost
to view in the sky.

Nixie laughed merrily. "It woke in the middle of its silly little dream," she
said. "It was only half-asleep really, and playing. It won't come back now."

"All puppies are absurd like that—"

But he did not finish his profound observation about puppies, for his
voice at that moment was drowned in a new and terrible noise that seemed
to come from the heart of the wood. It happened just as in a children's fairy
tale. It bore no resemblance to the roar the winds made; there was no music
in it; it was crude in quality—angry; a sound from another place.

It came swiftly nearer and nearer, increasing in volume as it came. A veil
seemed to spread suddenly over the scene; the trees grew shadowy and
dim; the glades melted off into mistiness; and ever the mass of sound came
pouring up towards them. Paul realised that the frontiers of consciousness
were shifting again in a most extraordinary fashion, so that the whole forest slipped off into the background and became a dim map in his memory, faint and unreal—and, with it, went both Nixie and himself. The
ground rose and fell under their feet. Her hand melted into something
fluid and slippery as he tried to keep his hold upon it. The child whispered
words he could not catch. Then, like the puppy, they both began to rise.

The roar came out to meet them and enveloped them furiously in mid
air.

"At any rate, we've seen the wind!" he heard the child's voice murmuring in his beard. She rose away from him, being lighter, and vanished
through the tops of the trees.

And then the roar drowned him and swept him away in a whirling tempest, so that he lost all consciousness of self and forgot everything he had
ever known....

The noise resolved itself gradually into the crunching sounds of the carriage wheels and the clatter of horses' hoofs coming up the gravel drive.

Paul looked about him with a sigh that was half a yawn. China and Japan
were still romping on the lawn, Mrs. Tompkyns and Smoke were curled up
in hot, soft circles precisely where they had been before, Toby and Jonah
were still busily engaged doing "something with daisies" in the full blaze

of the sunshine, and Nixie lay beside him, all innocence and peace, still gazing through the tangle of her yellow hair at the slow-sailing clouds overhead.

And the clouds, he noticed, had hardly altered a line of their shape and position since he saw them last.

He turned with a jump of excitement.

"Nixie," he exclaimed, "I've seen the wind!"

She rolled over lazily on her side and fixed her great blue eyes on his own, between two strands of her hair. From the expression of her brown face it was possible to surmise that she knew nothing—and everything.

"Have you?" she said very quietly. "I thought you might."

"Yes, but did I dream it, or imagine it, or just think it and make it up?" He still felt a little bewildered; the memory of that strangely beautiful picture-gallery still haunted him. Yonder, before the porch, the steaming horses and the smart coachman on the box, and his sister coming across the lawn from the carriage all belonged to another world, while he himself and Nixie and the other children still stayed with him, floating in a golden atmosphere where Wind was singing and alive.

"That doesn't matter a bit," she replied, peering at him gravely before she pulled her hair over both eyes. "The point is that it's really true! Now," she added, her face completely hidden by the yellow web, "all you have to do is to write it for our next Meeting—write the record of your Aventure—"

"And read it out?" he said, beginning to understand.

The yellow head nodded. He felt utterly and delightfully bewitched.

"All right," he said; "I will."

"And make it a verywonderfulindeed Aventure," she added, springing to her feet. "Hush! Here's mother!"

Paul rose dizzily to greet his sister, while the children ran off with their animals to other things.

"You've had a pleasant afternoon, Paul, dear?" she asked.

"Oh, very nice indeed—" His thoughts were still entangled with the wind and with the story he meant to write about it for the next Meeting.

She opened her parasol and held it over her head.

"Now, come indoors," he went on, collecting himself with an effort, "or into the shade. This heat is not good for you, Margaret." He looked at her pale, delicate face. "You're tired too."

"I enjoyed the drive," she replied, letting him take her arm and lead her towards the house. "I met the Burdons in their motor. They're coming over to luncheon one day, they said. You'll like *him*, I think."

"That's very nice," he remarked again, "very nice. Margaret," he exclaimed suddenly, ashamed of his utter want of interest in all she was planning for him, "I think you ought to have a motor too. I'm going to give you one."

"That is sweet of you, Paul," she smiled at him.

"But really, you know, one likes horses best. They're much quieter. Motors do shake one so."

"I don't think that matters; the point is that it's really true," he muttered to himself, thinking of Nixie's judgment of his Aventure.

His sister looked at him with her expression of faint amusement.

"You mustn't mind me," he laughed, planting her in a deck-chair by the shade of the house; "but the truth is, my mind is full just now of some work I've got to do—a report, in fact, I've got to write."

He went off into the house, humming a song. She followed him with her eyes.

"He is so strange. I do wish he would see more people and be a little more normal."

And in Paul's mind, as he raced along the passage to his private study in search of pen and paper, there ran a thought of very different kind in the shape of a sentence from the favourite of all his books:

"Everything possible to be believed is an image of truth."

CHAPTER XI

It is said that a poet has died young in the breast of the most stolid. It may be contended, rather, that this (somewhat minor bard) in almost every case survives, and is the spice of life to his possessor. —R. L. S.

Now that his first Aventure was an accomplished fact, and that he was writing it out for the Meeting, Paul carried about with him a kind of secret joy. At last he had found an audience, and an audience is unquestionably a very profound need of every human heart. Nixie was helping him to expression.

"I'll write them such an Aventure out of that Wind-Vision," he exclaimed, "that they'll fairly shiver with delight. And if *they* shiver, why shouldn't all the children in the world shiver too?"

He no longer made the mistake of thinking it trivial; if he could find an audience of children all about the world, children known or unknown, to whom he could show his little gallery of pictures, what could be more reasonable or delightful? What could be more useful and worth doing than to show the adventuring mind some meaning in all the beauty that filled his heart? And the Wind-Vision might be a small—a very small, beginning. It might be the first of a series of modern fairy tales. The idea thrilled him with pleasure. "A safety-valve at last!" he cried. "An audience that won't laugh!"

For, in reality, there was also a queer motherly quality in him which he had always tried more or less successfully to hide, and of which, perhaps, he was secretly half ashamed—a feeling that made him long to give of his strength and sympathy to all that was helpless, weary, immature.

He went about the house like a new man, for in proportion as he allowed his imagination to use its wings, life became extraordinarily alive. He sang, and the world sang with him. Everything turned up little smiling faces to him, whispering fairy contributions to his tale.

"The more I give out, the more I get in," he laughed. "I declare it's quite wonderful," as though he had really discovered a new truth all for himself. New forces began to course through his veins like fire. As in a great cistern tapped for the first time, this new outlet produced other little cross-currents everywhere throughout his being. Paul began to find a new confidence. Another stone had shifted in the fabric of his soul. He moved one stage nearer to the final pattern that it had been intended from the beginning of time he should assume.

A world within a world began to grow up in the old grey house under the hill, one consisting of Nixie and her troupe, with Paul trailing heavily in the rear, very eager; and the other, of the grownup members of the household, with Mlle. Fleury belonging to neither, yet in a sense belonging to both. The cats and animals again were in the former—an inner division of it, so that it was like a series of Chinese boxes, each fitting within the next in size.

And this admission of Paul into the innermost circle produced a change in the household, as well as in himself. After all, the children had not betrayed him; they had only divined his secret and put him right with himself. But this was everything; and who is there with a vestige of youth in his spirit that will not understand the cause of his mysterious exhilaration?

Outwardly, of course, no definite change was visible in the doings of the little household. The children said little; they made no direct reference to his conversion; but the change, though not easily described, was felt by all. Paul recognised it in every fibre of his being. Every one, he noticed, understood by some strange freemasonry that he had been initiated, for every one, he fancied, treated him a little differently. It was natural that the children should give signs of increased admiration and affection for their huge new member, but there was no obvious reason why his sister, and the servants, and the very animals into the bargain, should regard him with a strain of something that hesitated between tolerance and tenderness.

If truth were told, they probably did nothing of the sort; it was his own point of view that had changed. His imagination was responsible for the rest; yet he felt as though he had been caught into the heart of a great conspiracy, and the silent, unobtrusive way every one played his, her, or its part contrived to make him think it was all very real indeed.

The cats, furry and tender magicians that they are, perhaps interpreted the change more skilfully and easily than any one else. Without the least fuss or ceremony they made him instantly free of their world, and the way their protection and encouragement were extended to him in a hundred gentle ways gave him an extraordinarily vivid impression that they, too, had their plans and conferences just as much as the children had. They made everything seem alive and intelligent, from the bushes where they hunted to the furniture where they slept. They brought the whole world, animate and inanimate, into his scheme of existence. Everything had life, though not the same degree of life. It was all very subtle and wonderful. He, and the children, and the cats, all had imagination according to their kind and degree, and all equally used it to make the world haunted and splendid.

Formerly, for instance, he had often surprised Mrs. Tompkyns going about in the passages on secret business of her own, perhaps not altogether good, yet looking up with an assumption of innocence that made it quite impossible to chide or interfere. (It was, of course, only an *assumption* of innocence. A cat's eyes are too intent and purposeful for genuine innocence; they are a mask, a concealment of a thousand plans.) But now, when he met her, she at once stopped and sent her tail aloft by way of signal, and came to rub against his legs. Her eyes smiled—that pregnant, significant smile of the feline, shown by mere blinking of the lids—and she walked slowly by his side with arched back, as an invitation that he might—nay, that he should—accompany her.

On her great, dark journeys he might not of course yet go, but on the smaller, less important expeditions he was welcome, and she showed it plainly every time they met. He was led politely to numerous cupboards, corners, attics, and cellars, whose existence he had not hitherto suspected. There were wonderful and terrible places among the book-shelves and under massive pieces of furniture which she showed to him when no one was about; and she further taught him how to sit and stare for long periods until out of vacancy there issued a series of fascinating figures and scenes of strange loveliness. And he, laughing, obeyed.

All this, and much else besides, they taught him cleverly.

Some of them, too, came to visit him in his own quarters. They came into his study, and into his bedroom, and one of them—that black, thick-haired fellow called Smoke—the one with the ghostly eyes and very furry trousers—even took to tapping at his door late at night (by standing on tip-toe he could just reach the knob), and thus established the right to sleep on the sofa or even to curl up on the foot of the bed.

And all that the kittens, the puppies, and the out-of-door animals did to teach him as an equal is better left untold, since this is a story and not a work on natural history.

Mlle. Fleury, the little French governess, alone seemed curiously out of the picture. She made difficulties here and there, though not insuperable ones. The fact was, he saw, that she was not properly in either of the two worlds. She wanted to be in both at once, but, from the very nature of her position, succeeded in getting into neither; and to fall between two worlds is far more perplexing than to fall between two stools. Paul made allowances for her just as he might have made allowances for an over-trained animal that had learned too many human-taught tricks to make its presence quite acceptable to its own four-footed circle. The charming little person—he, at least, always thought her voice and her manners and her grace charming after a life where these were unknown—had to justify herself to the grown-up world where his sister belonged, as well as to the world of the children whom she taught. And, consequently, she was often compelled to scold when, perhaps, her soul cried out that she should bless.

His heart always hammered, if ever so slightly, when he made his way, as he now did more and more frequently, to the schoolroom or the nursery. Schoolroom-tea became a pleasure of almost irresistible attractions, and when it was over and the governess was legitimately out of the way, Nixie sometimes had a trick of announcing a Regular Meeting to which Paul was called upon to read out his latest "Aventure."

"Hulloa! Having tea, are you?" he exclaimed, looking in at the door one afternoon shortly after the wind episode. This feigned surprise, which deceived nobody, he felt was admirable. It was exactly the way Mrs. Tompkyns did it.

"Come in, Uncle Paul. *Do* stay. You *must* stay," came the chorus, while

Mlle. Fleury half smiled, half frowned at him across the table. "Here's just the stodgy kind of cake you like, with jam *and* honey!"

"Well," he said hesitatingly, as though he scorned such things, while Mademoiselle poured out a cup, and the children piled up a plate for him.

He stayed, as it were, by chance, and a minute later was as earnestly engaged with the cake and tea as if he had come with that special purpose. "It's all very well done," was his secret thought. "It's exactly the way Mrs. Tompkyns manages all her most important affairs."

"Nous avons réunion apres," Jonah informed the governess presently with a very grave face. The young woman glanced interrogatively at Paul.

"Oui, oui," he said in his Canadian French, "c'est vrai. Réunion régulière."

"Mais qu'elle idée, donc!"

"Il est le président," said Toby indignantly, pointing with a jam sandwich.

"Voilá vous êtes!" he exclaimed. "There you are! Je suis le président!" and he helped himself to more cake as though by accident.

For five seconds Mlle. Fleury kept her face. Then, in spite of herself, her lips parted and a row of white teeth appeared.

"Meester Reevairs, you spoil them," she said, "and I approve it not. Mais, voyons donc! Queues maniéres!" she added as Sambo and Pouf passed from Toby's lap on to the table and began to sniff at the water cress.... "Non, ça c'est *trop* fort!" She leaned across to smack them back into propriety.

"Abominable,"Paul cried, " abominable tout à fait."

"Alwaze when you come such things 'appen."

"'Pas mon faute," he said, helping to catch Pouf.

"They are deeficult enough without that you make them more," she said.

"Uncle Paul doesn't know his genders," cried Jonah; "hooray!"

"Ma faute," he corrected himself, pronouncing it "fote."

Then Toby, struggling with Smoke, whose nose she was trying to force into a saucer of milk which he did not want, upset the saucer all over her dress and the table, splashing one and all. Jonah sprang up and knocked his chair over backwards in the excitement. Mrs. Tompkyns, wakening from her sleep upon the piano stool, leaped on to the notes of the open keyboard with a horrible crash. A pandemonium reigned, all talking, laughing, shouting at once, and the governess scolding. Then Paul trod on a kitten's tail under the table and extraordinary shrieks were heard, whereupon Jonah, stooping to discover their cause, bumped his head and began to cry. Moving forward to comfort him, Paul's sleeve caught in the spout of the teapot and it fell with a clatter among the cups and plates, sending the sugar-tongs spinning into the air, and knocking the milk jug sideways so that a white sea flooded the whole tray and splashed up with white spots on to Paul's cheeks.

The cumulative effect of these disasters reached a culminating point, and a sudden hush fell upon the room. The children looked a trifle scared. Paul, with milk drops trickling down his nose, blushed and looked solemn. Very guilty and awkward he felt. Mlle. Fleury in fluent, rattling French explained her view of the situation, at first, however, without effect. At such moments mere sound and fury are vain; subtle, latent influences of the personality alone can calm a panic, and these the little person did not, of course, possess.

To Paul the whole picture appeared in very vivid detail. With the simplicity of the child and the larger vision of the man he perceived how closely tears and laughter moved before them; and it really pained him to see her confused and rather helpless amid all the debris. She was pretty, slim, and graceful; futile anger did not sit well upon her.

There she stood, little more than a girl herself, staring at him for a moment speechless, the dainty ruffles of her neat grey dress sticking up about her pretty throat, he thought, like the bristles of an enraged kitten. The hair, too, by her ears and neck suddenly seemed to project untidily and increased the effect. The sunlight from the window behind her spread through it, making it cloud-like.

"C'est tout mon—ma fote," he said, stretching out both hands impulsively, "tout!" in his villainous Quebec French. "Scold *me* first, please."

There was milk on his left eyebrow, and a crumb of cake in his beard as well. The governess stared at him, her eyes still blazing ominously. Her lips quivered. Then, fortunately, she laughed; no one really could have done otherwise. And that laugh saved the situation. The children, who had been standing motionless as statues awaiting their doom, sprang again into life. In a trice the milk had been moped up, the tongs replaced, and the tea-pot put to bed under its ornamented cosy.

"I forgeeve—this time," she said. "But you are vairy troublesome."

In future, none the less, she forgave always; her hostility, never quite sure of itself, vanished from that moment.

"Blue Summer'ouse," whispered Jonah in his ear, "and bring your Wind-Vision to read to us at the Meeting."

"But not too much Wind-Vision, please, Meester Reevairs," she said, overhearing the whisper. "They think of nothing else."

Paul stared at her. The thought in his mind was that she ought to come too, only he knew the children would not approve.

"Then I must moderate their enthusiasm," he said gravely at last.

Mlle. Fleury laughed in his face. "*You* are worst of ze lot, I know—worst of all. Your Aventures and plays trouble all their lesson-time."

"It is my education," he said, as Jonah tugged at his coat from behind to get him out of the room. "You educate *them;* they educate *me;* I improve slowly. Voila!"

"But vairy slowly, n'est-ce pas? And you make up all such *expériences* like ze Wind-Vision to fill their minds."

Nixie had told him that all their aventures filtered through to her, and that she kept a special *cahier* in her own room, where she wrote them all out in her own language. "Another soul, perhaps, looking about for a safety-valve," he thought swiftly.

"But, Mademoiselle, why not translate them into French? That's a good idea, and excellent practice for them."

"Per'aps," she laughed, "per'aps we do that. C'est une idée au moins."

She wanted so much, it was clear, to come into their happy little world of imagination and adventure. He realised suddenly how lonely her life might be in such a household.

"You write them, and I will correct them for you," he said.

"Come on, *do* come on, Uncle," cried the voices urgently from the door. The children were already in the passage. The little governess looked rather wistfully after them, and on a sudden impulse Paul did a thing he had never before done in his life. He took her hand and kissed the tips of her fingers, but so boyishly, and with such simple politeness and sincerity that there was hardly more in the act than if Jonah had done the same to Nixie in an aventure of another sort.

"An revoir then," he said laughingly; "chacun a son devoir, don't they? And now I go to do mine."

His sentence was somewhat mixed. He just had time to notice the pretty blush of confusion that spread over her face, and to hear her laugh "You are weecked children—vairy weecked—and you, Meester Reevairs, the biggest of all," when Nixie and Jonah had him by the hand and they were off out of the house to their Meeting in the Blue Summer-house.

Thus Mlle. Fleury ceased to be a difficulty in the household so far as his proceedings with the children were concerned. On the contrary, she became a helpful force, and often acted as a sort of sentry, or outpost, between one world and the other. Herself, she never came into their own private region, but hovered only along the borders of it. For though little over twenty years of age, she was French, and she understood exactly how much interest she might allow herself to take in the Society without endangering her own position,—or theirs—or his. She knew that she could not enter their world freely and still maintain authority in the other; but, meanwhile, she managed Paul precisely as though he were one of her own charges, and saw to it that he did nothing which could really be injurious to the responsibilities for which she was answerable.

Thus Paul, thundering along with his belated youth, enjoyed himself more and more, while he enjoyed, also learned, marked, and read.

CHAPTER XII

It haunted him a good deal, this Vision of the Winds. Now he never heard the stirring of the woods without thinking of those delicately brilliant streamers flying across the sky.

The satisfaction of spinning a fairy tale out of it for the children's Society was only equalled by the pleasure of the original inspiration. Here, too, was a means of expressing himself he had never dreamed of; the relief was great. Moreover, it brought him into close touch with the inexhaustible reservoirs which children draw upon for their endless world of Make-Believe, and he understood that the child and the poet live in the same region. His feet were now set upon that secret path trodden by the feet of children since the world began; and, for all his burden of years, there was no telling where it might lead him. For the springs of perennial youth have their sources in that region—the youth of the spirit, with the constant flow of enthusiasm, the touch of simple, ever-living beauty, and the whole magic of vision. No one with imagination can ever become *blasé*, perhaps need ever grow old in the true sense.

By this means he might at last turn his accumulated stores to some useful account. The great geysers of imagination that dry up too soon with the majority might keep bubbling for ever; and provided the pipes kept open for smaller visions, they might with time become channels for inspiration of a still higher order. His audience might grow too.

"I'm getting on," he observed to Nixie a few days later; "getting on pretty well for an old man!"

"I knew you would," she replied approvingly. "Only you wasted a lot of time over it. When you came you were so old that Toby thought you were going to die, you know."

"So bad as all that, was it?"

"H'mmmmm," she nodded, her blue eyes faintly troubled; "quite!"

Paul took her on his knee and stared at her. The world of elemental wonder came quite close. There was something of magic about the atmosphere of this child's presence that made it possible to believe anything and everything. She embodied exquisitely so many of his dreams—those dreams of God and Nature he had lived with all those lonely years in Canadian solitudes.

"You know, I think," he said slowly as he watched with delight the look of tender affection upon her face, "that, without knowing it, you're something of a little magician, Nixie. What do *you* think?"

But she only laughed and wriggled on his knee. Am I really?" she said presently. "Then what are you, I wonder?"

"I used to be a Wood Cruiser," he replied gravely; but what I am now it's rather difficult to say. You ought to know," he added, "as you're the magician who's changing me."

"I've not changed you," she laughed. "I only found you out. The day you came I saw you were simply full of our things—and that you'd be a sort of Daddy to us. And we shall want a lot more Aventures, please, as soon as ever you can write them out—"

She was off his knee and half-way to the house the same second, for the voice of Mlle. Fleury was heard in the land. He watched her flitting through the patches of sunshine across the lawn, and caught the mischievous glance she turned to throw at him as she disappeared through the open French window—a vision of white dress, black legs, and flying hair. And only when she was gone did his heavier machinery get to work with the crop of questions he always thought of too late.

"A beginning, at any rate!" he said to himself, thinking of all the things he was going to write for them. "Only I wish we were all in camp out there among the cedars and hemlocks on Beaver Creek, instead of boxed up in this toy garden where there are no wild animals, and you mayn't cut down trees for a big fire, and there are silly little Notice Boards all over the place about trespassers being prosecuted..."

The thought touched something in the centre of his being. He travelled; laughing and sighing as he went. "My wig!" he thought aloud, "but it's really extraordinary how that child brings those big places over here for me, and makes them seem alive with all kinds of things I could never have dreamed of—alone!"

"Paul, dear, what *are* you thinking about, here all by yourself—and without a hat on too, as usual? If the gardeners hear you talking aloud like this they will think—! Well, I hardly know quite what they *will* think!"

"Something Blake said—to be honest," he laughed, turning to his sister who had come silently down the path, dressed, as on the day he had first seen her, in white serge with a big flower-hat. Languid she looked, but delicate and wholly charming; she wore brown garden gauntlets over hands and wrists, and a red parasol she held aloft, shed a becoming pink glow upon her face.

"*Maurice* Blake!" she exclaimed. "Joan's cousin with the big farm on the Downs? But you don't know him!"

"Not that Blake," he laughed again; "and Joan, if you mean Joan Nicholson, Dick's niece who took up that rescue work, or something, in London, I have never seen in my life."

"Then it's a book you mean—one of those books you are always poring over in the library," she murmured half reproachfully.

"One of Dick's books, yes," he replied gently, linking his arm through hers and leading the way in the direction of the cedars. "One of my 'treasures,'" he added slyly, "that you once shamelessly imagined to be in petticoats."

She rather liked his teasing. The interests they shared were uncommonly small, perhaps, and the coinage of available words still smaller. Yet their differences never took on the slightest "edge." A genuine affection smoothed all their little talks.

"You do read such funny old books, Paul," she observed, as though somewhere in her heart lurked a vague desire to make him more modern. "Don't you ever try books of the day—novels, for instance?" She had one under her arm at the moment. He took it to carry for her.

"I have tried," he admitted, a little ashamed of his backwardness, "but I never can make out what they're driving at—half the time. What they described has never happened to me, or come into my world. I don't recognise it all as true, I mean—"He stopped abruptly for fear he might say something to wound her.

"One can always learn, though, and widen one's world, can't one? After all, we *are* all in the same world, aren't we?"

He realised the impossibility of correcting her; the invitation to be sententious could not catch him; his nature was too profound to contain the prig.

"Are we?" he said gently.

"Oh, I think so—more or less, Paul. There's only one *nice* world, at least." She arranged her hat and parasol to keep the sun off, for she was afraid of the sun, even the shy sun of England.

He pulled out the deck chair for her, and opened it.

"Here," she said pointing, "if you don't mind, dear; or perhaps over *there* where it looks drier; or just *there* under that tree, perhaps, is better still. It's more sheltered, and there's less sun, isn't there?"

"I think there is, yes," he replied, obeying her. The phrase "there's less sun" seemed to him so neatly descriptive of the mental state of persons without imagination.

"She'll come here for her summer holidays soon," his sister resumed, going back to Joan. "She works very hard at that 'Home' place in town, and Dick always liked her to use us here as if the place were her own. I promised that." She dropped gracefully into the wicker chair, and Paul sat down for a moment beside her on the grass. "He spent a lot of capital, you know, in the thing and made her superintendent or something. She has a sort of passion for this rescuing of slum children, and, I believe, works herself to death over it, though she has means of her own. So you will be nice to her when she comes, won't you, and look after her a bit? I do what I can, but I always feel I'm rather a failure. I never know what to talk to her about. She's so dreadfully in earnest about everything."

Paul promised. Joan sounded rather attractive, to tell the truth. He remembered something, too, of the big organisation his old friend had founded in London for the rescue and education of waif-boys. A thrill of pride ran through him, and close at its heels a secret sense of shame, that he himself did nothing in the great world of action—that his own life was a mass of selfish dreaming and refined self-seeking, that all his yearning for God and beauty was after all, perhaps, but a spiritual egoism. It was not the first time this thought had come to trouble and perplex. Of late—especially since he had begun to find these safety-valves of self-expression, and so a measure of relief—his mind had turned in the direction of some big-

ger field to work in outside self, perhaps more than he quite knew or
realised.

"Paul," his sister interrupted his reflections, after a prolonged fidgeting
to make herself comfortable so that the parasol should shade her, the hat
not tickle her, and the novel open easily for reading; "you are happy here,
aren't you? You're not too dull with us, I mean ?"

"It's quite delightful, Margaret," he answered at once. "In one sense I
have never been so happy in my life." He looked straight at her, the sun
catching his brown beard and face. "And I love the children; they're just
the kind of companions I need."

"I'm so glad, so glad," she said genuinely. "And it's very kind and good-
natured of you to be with them such a lot. You really almost fill Dick's
place for them." She sighed and half closed her eyes. "Some day you may
have children of your own; only you would spoil them quite atrociously,
I'm sure."

"Am I spoiling yours?" he asked solemnly.

"Dreadfully," she laughed; "and turning little Mademoiselle's head into
the bargain."

It was his turn to burst out laughing. "I think that young lady can take
care of herself without difficulty," he exclaimed; "and as for my spoiling the
children, I think it's they who are spoiling me!"

And, presently, with some easy excuse, he left her side and went off into
the woods. Margaret watched him charge across the lawn. A perplexed
expression came into her face as she picked up her novel and settled down
into the cushions, balancing the red parasol over her head at a very careful angle. Admiration was in her glance, too, as she saw him go. Evidently she was proud of her brother—proud that he was so different from
other people, yet puzzled to the verge of annoyance that he should be so.

"What a strange creature he is," was her somewhat indefinite reflection;
"I thought but one Dick could exist in the world! He's still a boy—not a
day over twenty-five. I wonder if he's ever been in love, or ever will be? I
think—I hope he won't; he's rather nice as he is after all."

She sighed faintly. Then she dipped again into her novel, wherein the
emotions, from love downwards, were turned on thick and violent as from
so many taps in a factory; got bored with it; looked on to the last chapter
to see what happened to everybody; and, finally—fell asleep.

CHAPTER XIII

To me alone there came a thought of grief:
A timely utterance gave that thought relief,
And I again am strong:

I hear the echoes through the mountains throng,
The winds come to me from the fields of sleep,
And all the earth is gay....

Ode, W. W.

For the rest of the day Paul was in peculiarly good spirits; he went about the place full of bedevilment of all kinds, to the astonishment of the household in general and of his sister in particular. The oppressive heat seemed to have no effect upon him. There was something in the air that excited him, and he was very busy getting rid of the excitement.

With bedtime came no desire to sleep. "I feel all worked-up, Margaret," he said as he lit her candle in the hall. "I think it must be an 'aventure' coming,"—though, of course, she had no idea what he meant.

"There's thunder about," she replied. "It's been so very close all day."

"Sleep well," Paul said when he left her at the top of the stairs; and the last thing he heard as he went down the long winding passage to his bedroom in the west wing was her voice faintly assuring him "One always does here, I'm glad to say."

Once inside, and the door shut, he gave himself up to his mood. It was a mood apparently that came from nowhere. A soft and mysterious excitement, all delicious, stirred in the depths of his being, rising slowly to the surface. Perhaps it was growing-pains somewhere in the structure of his personality, engineered subconsciously by his imagination; perhaps only "weather." He always followed the barometer like a strip of dried seaweed.

But on this particular night something more than mere "weather" was abroad; his nerves sent a succession of swift faint warnings to his brain. To begin with, the night herself claimed definite attention. Some nights are just ordinary nights; others touch the soul and whisper "I am the night. Look at me. Listen!"

He obeyed the summons and went to the window, leaning out as his habit was. The darkness pressed up in a solid wall, charged to the brim with mysteries waiting to reveal themselves. No trees were visible, no outline of moor or hill or garden. The sky was pinned down to the horizon more tightly than usual—keeping back all manner of things. Very little air crept beneath the edges, so that the atmosphere was oppressive. The day had been cloudless, but with the sunset whole continents of vapour had climbed upon the hills of the evening wind, driven slowly by high currents that had not yet come near enough the earth to be heard and felt.

He coughed—gently. The least noise, he felt, would shatter some soft and delicate structure that rose everywhere through the darkness—some web-like shadow—scaffolding that reared upwards, supporting the night.

"Something's going to happen," he said low to himself. "I can feel it coming."

He became very imaginative, enjoying his mood enormously, letting it act as a mental purge. Aventures that he would discover for the next Meeting swept through him. The stress and fever of creative fancy, stirred by the deep travailing of the elements behind that curtain of night, was upon him. Then, sleep being far away, he went to the writing-table, where Nixie's deft hands had everything prepared, lit a second candle, and began to write.

"I'll write 'How I climbed the Scaffolding of the Night,' " he murmured; "for I feel it true within me. I feel as if I were part of the night—part of all this beautiful soft darkness."

But, before he had written a dozen lines, he stopped and fell to listening again, staring past the steady candle-flames out into the open. The stillness was profound. A single ivy-leaf rattled sharply all by itself on the wall outside his window. He felt as if that leaf tapped faintly upon his own brain. By a curious process known only to the poetic temperament, he passed on to *feel with* everything about him—as though some portion of himself actually merged in with the silence, with the perfumes of trees and garden, with the voice of that little tapping leaf. And, in proportion as he realised this, he transferred the magic of it to his tale. He found the words that fitted his conception like a natural skin. He knew in some measure the satisfaction and relief of expression.

"A year ago—a month ago," he thought with delight, "this would have been impossible to me. Nixie has taught me so much already!"

What he really wanted, of course, were the living, flaming words of poetry. But this he knew was denied him; perhaps the fire of inspiration did not burn steadily enough; perhaps the intellectual foundation was not there. At any rate, he could only do his best and struggle with the prose, and this he did with intense pleasure.

After a time he laid his pen down and fell to thinking again—the kind of reverie that dramatises a mood before the inner vision. And another inspiration came upon him with its sudden little glory; he realised vividly that *within* himself a region existed where all that he desired might find fulfilment; where yearnings, dreams, desires might come true. There existed this inner place within where he might visualise all he most wished for into a state of reality. The workshop of the creative imagination was its vestibule....

Whether or not he could put it into words for others to realise was merely a question of craft....

He must have sat thinking in this way much longer than he knew, for the candles had burnt down quite low when at length he bestirred himself with a mighty yawn and rose to go to bed. But hardly had he begun to unfasten his crumpled black tie when something made him pause.

Far away, through the hush that covered the world, that "something" was astir—coming swiftly nearer. He stepped back into the middle of the room and waited. Smoke, the sleeping black cat on the sofa, sat up and waited too. Looking about it with brilliant green eyes, wide open, and whiskers twitching backwards and forwards, it understood even better than he did that a change in all that world of darkness had come to pass. The animal stared alternately at the window and the door.

For another minute the stillness held supreme. Then, from the silent reaches beyond, this new sound came suddenly close, dropping down through leagues of night. It began with a faint roar in the chimney; a tree outside uttered a soft, rushing cry; a thousand leaves, instead of one, rattled on the wall.

A Messenger, running headlong through the darkness, was calling aloud a warning as it ran, for all to understand who could. And, among the few who were awake and understood, Paul and his four-footed companion were certainly the first.

A sudden movement of the vast fabric of darkness came next. That scaffolding of shadows trembled, as though the same moment it would fall and let in—Light. In front of the bow window the muslin curtain that so long had hung motionless, now bellied out slowly into the room. The movement, mysterious and suggestive, claimed attention significantly. Paul and Smoke, watching it, exchanged glances. Then, with a long, sighing sound, it floated back again to its original position. It hung down straight and still as before.

But in that moment something had entered the room. Borne by this messenger of the coming storm, this stray Wind had left its warning—and was gone!

Smoke leapt softly down and padded over to sniff the curtain, and having done so, blinked up at Paul with eloquent eyes, and sat back to wait and—wash! No apparatus of speech ever said more plainly "Look out! Something's coming! Better be prepared as I am!"

And something did come—almost the same minute. The forces that had so long been trying to upset the tent of darkness, did upset it, and from one uplifted corner there rushed down upon the world a blue-white sheet of light that was utterly gorgeous. For one instant trees, moor, hill leaped into vivid outline. The hands that held the sheet of brilliance shook it from the four corners, and all the sky shook with it; and, immediately after, the scaffolding of night fell with a prodigious crash, as the true storm, following upon its herald, descended with a hundred thunders and the roar of ten hundred trumpets.

The true wind rushed headlong into the room and extinguished both candles. Smoke rubbed against Paul's feet in the darkness, thoroughly aroused; but Paul himself stood still, as the thrill and splendour of it all entered his heart and filled him with delight. Thunder, lightning, wind—

all passed mysteriously into his blood till he was almost conscious of a desire to add the sound of his own voice and shout aloud. The excitement of the elemental forces swept into himself. He understood now the signs of preparation that had been going forward in him during the day.

Splendid sensations, the most splendid he ever knew, raced to and fro in his being, till it almost seemed as if his consciousness transferred itself to the tempest. Surely, that great wind tore out of his heart, that lightning sprang from his brain, that river of rain washed, not merely out of the sky, but out of himself. The edges of his personality became fluid and melted off into the very nature of the elements....

"Now," he exclaimed aloud, pacing to and fro while Smoke followed him in the darkness and tried to play with the bows on his pumps, "had I but the means of expression, what a message I could give to the world, of beauty, splendour, power!" He laughed in his excitement. "If only the strings of my poor instrument had been tuned—!'

Sighing a little to himself at the thought, he went to the window. The first fury of the storm had passed; there was a sudden deep lull broken only by the rushing drip of rain; he smelt the wet foliage and soaking grass. Close to the window, it chanced, there was a dead tree, and in its leafless branches, outlined sharply by the lightning against the black sky, he traced what seemed the huge letters of some elemental alphabet; and at that moment, the returning wind passed through them like a hand on giant strings. It drew forth a wonderful sound in response, a sound that pierced as a two-edged sword to the centre of his being. It was a true singing wind—a Wind of Inspiration.

And, as he heard it, the great wave that fought for utterance rose within him and began to force and tear its way out in spite of everything. Words came pouring through him—like the stammering of torn strings upon a fiddle—clipped wings trying to fly—sparks streaming towards flame yet never achieving it. Similes and metaphors rushed, mixed and headlong, through his mind. In a moment he had dashed across the floor; the candles were again alight; and Paul, pencil in hand, was sitting at the table before a sheet of blank foolscap, the storm crashing about him, and Smoke watching him calmly with eyes full of expectant wonder.

And then was enacted a little drama—tragedy if ever there was one— that must often enough take place in the secret places of the world's houses, where the dumb poet seeks to transfer his genuine passion into the measure of halting and inadequate verse. Poignantly dramatic the spectacle must be, though never witnessed mercifully by an audience of more than one. Paul wrote fast, setting the words down almost as they came. It was that little passionate Wind of Inspiration that was the cause of all the trouble. Smoke jumped up on the table to watch the motion of the pencil across the paper. For some reason he hardly thought it worth while to play with it:

> The Winds of Inspiration blow,
>   Yet pass me ever by;
> And songs God taught me long ago,
>   Unuttered burn and—die.

He read the verse over, and with an impatient motion altered "burn" into "fade." Then he shook his head and continued:

> From all the far blue hills of heaven
>   The dews of beauty rain;
> Yet unto me no drops are given
>   To quench the ancient pain.

He scratched out "ancient" and wrote over the top "undying." Then he scratched out "undying" and put "ancient" back in its place. This time Smoke stretched out a long black paw with a velvet end to it and gave the pencil a deliberate dab. Paul either ignored, or did not notice it; but Smoke left the paw thrust forward upon the paper so as to be ready for the next dab.

> I know the passion of the night,
>   Full of all days unborn,—
> Full of the yearning of the light
>   For one undying Morn.

Smoke caught the tip of the pencil with a swift and accurate stroke, and the "M" of "Morn" was provided with an irregular tail Paul had not intended. Very quickly, however, without further interruption, he wrote on to the end.

> Above the embers of my heart,
>   Waiting the Living Breath;
> The sparks fly listlessly apart
>   Then circle to their death.

> Dead sparks that gathered ne'er to flame,
>   Nor felt the kiss of fire!
> Dead thoughts that never found the name
>   To spell their deep desire!

> Is then this instrument so poor
>   That it may never sound
> Songs that must pass for evermore
>   unuttered and uncrowned?

O soul that fain would'st steal heaven's fire,
    Who clipped thy golden wings?
Who made so passionate a lyre,
    Then never tuned the strings?

The Winds of Inspiration blow,
    Yet pass me ever by;
And songs God taught me long ago,
    Lost in the silence—die.

He rose from the table with a gesture of abrupt impatience and read the entire effusion through from beginning to end. First he laughed, then he sighed. He wondered for a moment how it was that so little of his passion had crept into the poor words. He crumpled up the paper and tossed it into the drawer; and then, blowing out the candles, moved over to the big arm-chair and dropped down into it. Again, as he sat there, his thoughts fell to dramatising his mood. He imagined that region within himself where all might come true, and all yearnings find adequate expression. The idea got more and more mingled with the storm. He pictured it to himself with extraordinarily vivid detail.

"There *is* such a place, such a state," he murmured, "and it is, it must be accessible."

He heard the clock in the stables—or was it the church—strike the quarter before midnight.

As he sat in the big chair, Smoke left the table and curled up again on the plat at his feet.

CHAPTER XIV

Vision or imagination is a representation of what actually exists, really and unchangeably. He who does not imagine in stronger and better lineaments, and in stronger and better light, than his perishing *mortal eye can see, does not imagine at all.* —W. B.

It was Smoke who first drew his attention to something near the door by "padding" slowly across the carpet and staring up at the handle. Paul's eyes, following him, perceived next that the brass knob was silently turning. Then the door opened quickly and on the threshold stood—Nixie. The open door made such a draught that the twenty winds tearing about inside the room almost lifted the mat at his feet. Behind her he saw the shadowy outline of a second figure, which he recognised as Jonah.

"Shut the door-quick!" he said, but they had done so and were already beside him almost before the words were out of his mouth. In spite of the darkness a very faint radiance came with them so that he could distinguish their faces plainly; and his amazement on seeing them at all at this late hour was instantly doubled when he perceived further that they were fully dressed for going out. At the same time, however, so deep had he been in his reverie, and so strongly did the excitement of it yet linger in his blood, that he hardly realised how wicked they were to be parading the house at such a time of the night, and that his obvious duty was to bundle them back to bed. In a strange, queer way they almost seemed part of his dream, part of his dramatised mood, part of the region of wonder into which his thoughts had been leading him. Moreover, he felt in some dim fashion that they had come with a purpose of great importance.

"It's awfully late, you know," he exclaimed under his breath, peering into their faces through the darkness.

"But not too late, if we start at once," Jonah whispered. For a moment Paul had almost thought that they would melt away and disappear as soon as he spoke to them, or that they would not answer at all. But now this settled it; these were no figures in a dream. He felt their hands upon his arms and neck; the very perfume of Nixie's hair and breath was about him. She was dressed, he noticed, in her red cloak with the hood over her head, and her eyes were popping with excitement. The expression on her face was earnest, almost grave. He saw the faint gleam of the gold buckle where the shiny black belt enclosed her little waist.

"If we start *at once,* I said," repeated Jonah in a nervous whisper, pulling at his hand.

Paul started to his feet and began fumbling with his black tie, feeling vaguely that either he ought to tie it properly or take it off altogether, and that it was a sort of indecent tinsel to wear at such a time. But he only succeeded in pricking his finger with the pin sticking out of the collar. He felt more than a little bewildered, if the truth were told.

"I'll do that for you," Nixie said under her breath; and in a twinkling her deft fingers had whipped the strip of satin from his neck.

"You don't want a tie where we're going," she laughed softly.

"Or a hat either," added Jonah. "But I wish you'd hurry, please."

"I'd better put on another coat or a dressing-gown, or something," he stammered.

"Coat's best," Jonah told him, and in a moment he had changed into a tweed Norfolk jacket that lay upon the chair.

They pulled him towards the door, Nixie holding one hand, Jonah the other, and Smoke following so closely at his heels that he almost seemed to be prodding him gently forward with his velvet padded boots. Paul understood that tremendous forces, elemental in character like the wind and rain and lightning, somehow added their immense suasion to the little hands that pulled his own. He made no resistance, but just allowed himself to go; and he went with a wild and boyish delight tearing through his mind.

"Are we going out then?" he asked, "out of doors?"

"What's the exact time, the *very* exact time?" Nixie asked hurriedly, ignoring his question; and though Paul had looked a few minutes before they came in, he had quite forgotten by now. She helped herself to his watch, burrowing under his coat to find it, and peering closely to read the position of the hands.

"Five minutes to twelve!" she exclaimed, addressing Jonah in excited whispers. "Oh, I say! We must be off at once, or we shall miss the crack altogether. Come on, Uncle, or your life won't be safe a minute."

"Then what will it be a month, I should like to know?" he laughed as he was swept along through the darkness, not knowing what to say or think.

"The crack! The crack! Quick, or we shall miss it!" cried the children in the same sentence, urging him heavily forward.

"What crack? Where are we going to? What does it all mean?" he asked breathlessly, trying to avoid treading on their toes and the toes of Smoke who flew beside them with tail held swiftly aloft as though to guide them.

They brought him up with a sudden bump just outside the door, and Nixie turned up a serious face to explain, while Jonah waited impatiently in front of them.

"Quick!" she whispered, "listen and I'll tell you. We're going to find the crack between Yesterday and To-morrow, and then—slip through it."

His heart leaped with excitement as he heard.

"Go on," he cried. "Tell me more!"

"You see, Yesterday really begins just after Midnight when To-day ends"; she said, "and Tomorrow begins there too."

"Of course."

"After Midnight, To-morrow jumps away again a whole day, and is as far off as ever. That's the nearest you can get to To-morrow."

"I see."

"And Yesterday, which has been a whole day away, suddenly jumps up close behind again. So that Yesterday and To-morrow," she went on, eager with excitement, "meet at Midnight for a single second before flying off to their new places. Daddy told us that long ago."

"Exactly. They must."

"But now the world is old and worn. There's a tiny little crack between Yesterday and To-morrow. They don't join as they once did, and, if we're *very* quick, we can find the crack and slip through—"

"Bless my Timber Limits!" he exclaimed; "what a glorious notion!"

"And, once inside there, there's no time, of course," she went on, more and more hurriedly. "*Anything* may happen, and *everything* come true."

"The very region I was thinking about just now!" thought Paul. "The very place! I've found it!"

"*Do* hurry up, oh *do!*" put in Jonah with loud whisper that echoed down the corridor, for his patience was at length exhausted by all this explanation. " You *are* so slow getting started."

"Ready!" cried Paul and Nixie in the same breath.

They were off! Down the dark and silent stairs on tiptoe, through the empty halls, past the hat-racks and the stuffed deer heads that grinned down upon them from the walls, along the stone passage to the kitchen region, where the row of red fire-buckets gleamed upon the shelves, and so, past the ghost pantry, to the back door. This they found open for Jonah had already run ahead and unlocked it. Another minute and they had crossed the yard by the stables, where the pump stood watching them like a figure with an outstretched arm, and soon were well out on to the lawn at the back of the house. The rain had ceased, but the wind caught them here with such tremendous blows and shouting that they could hardly hear themselves speak, and had to keep closely together in a bunch to make their way at all. It was pitch dark and the stars were hidden. Paul stumbled and floundered, treading incessantly on the toes of the more nimble children. Smoke ran like a black shadow, now in front, now behind.

"We're nearly there," Nixie cried encouragingly, as he made a false step and landed with a crash in the middle of some low laurel bushes. "But *do* be more careful, Uncle, please," she added, helping him out again.

"There's the clock striking!" Jonah called, a little in front of them. "We're only just in time!"

Paul recovered himself and pulled up beside them under the shadows of the big twin cedars that stood like immense sentries at the end of the lawn. He came rolling in, swaying like a ship in a heavy sea. And, as he did so, the sound of a church bell striking the hour came to their ears through the terrific uproar of the elements, blown this way and that by the wind.

It was midnight striking.

At the same instant he heard a peculiar sharp sound like whistling—the noise wind makes tearing through a narrow opening.

"The crack, the crack!" cried his guides together. That's the air rushing. It's coming. Look out!" They seized him by the hands.

"But I shall never get through," shouted Paul, thinking of his size for the first time.

"Yes you will," Nixie screamed back at him above the roar. "Between the sixth and seventh strokes, remember."

The fifth stroke had already sounded. The wind caught it and went shrieking into the sky.

Six! boomed the distant bell through the night. They held his hands in a vice.

There was a sound like an express train tearing through the air. A quick flash of brilliance followed, and a long slit seemed to open suddenly in the sky before them, and then flash past like lightning. Nixie tugged at one hand, and Jonah tugged at the other. Smoke scampered madly past his feet.

A wild rush of wind swept him along, whistling in his ears; there was a breathless and giddy sensation of dropping through empty space that seemed as though it could never end—and then Paul suddenly found himself sitting on a grassy bank beside a river, Nixie and Jonah on either side of him, and Smoke washing his face in front of them as though nothing in the whole world had ever happened to disturb his equanimity. And a bright, soft light, like the light of the sun, shone warmly over everything.

"Only just managed it," Nixie observed to Jonah. "He *is* rather wide, isn't he ?"

"Everybody's thin somewhere," was the reply.

"And the crack is very stretchy"—she added, —"luckily."

Paul drew a long breath and stretched himself.

"Well," he said, still a little breathless and dizzy, "such things were never done in my day."

"But this isn't your day any more," explained Nixie, her blue eyes popping with laughter and mischief, "it's your night. And, anyhow, as I told you, there's no time here at all. There's no hurry now."

CHAPTER XV

The imagination is not a state; it is the human existence itself. —W. B.

Paul, looking round, felt utterly at peace with himself and the world; at rest, he felt. That was his first sensation in the mass. He recovered in a moment from his breathless entrance, and a subtle pleasure began to steal through his veins. It seemed as if every yearning he had ever known was being ministered to by competent unseen Presences; and, obviously, the children and the cats—Mrs. Tompkyns had somehow managed to join Smoke—felt likewise, for their countenances beamed and blinked supreme contentment.

"Ah!" observed Jonah, sitting contentedly on the grass beside him. "This is the place." He heaved a happy little sigh, as though the statement were incontrovertible.

"It is," echoed Paul. And Nixie's eyes shone like blue flowers in a field of spring.

"The crack's smaller than it used to be though," he heard her murmuring to herself. "Every year it's harder to get through. I suppose something's happening to the world—or to people; some change going on—"

"Or we're getting older," Jonah put in with profounder wisdom than he knew.

Paul congratulated himself upon his successful entrance. He felt something of a dog! The bank on which he lay sloped down towards a river fledged with reeds and flowers; its waters, blue as the sky, flowed rippling by, and a soft wind, warm and scented, sighed over it from the heart of the summer. On the opposite shore, not fifty yards across, a grove of larches swayed their slender branches lazily in the sun, and a little farther down the banks he saw a line of willows drooping down to moisten their tongue—like leaves. The air hummed pleasantly with insects; birds flashed to and fro, singing as they flew; and, in the distance, across miles of blue meadowlands, hills rose in shadowy outline to the sky. He feasted on the beauty of it all, absorbing it through every sense.

"But where are we?" he asked at length, "because a moment ago we were in a storm somewhere?" He turned to Nixie who still lay talking to herself contentedly at his side. "And what really happens here?" he added with a blush. "I feel so extraordinarily happy."

They lay half-buried among the sweet-scented grasses. Jonah burrowed along the shore at some game of his own close by, and the cats made a busy pretence of hunting wild game in a dozen places at once, and then suddenly basking in the sun and washing each other's necks and backs as though wild-game hunting were a bore.

"Nothing 'xactly—*happens*," she answered, and her voice sounded curiously like wind in rushes—but everything—is."

It seemed to him as though he listened to some spirit of the ages, very wise with the wisdom of eternal youth, that spoke to him through the pretty little mouth of this rosy-faced child.

"It's like that river," she went on, pointing to the blue streak winding far away in a ribbon through the landscape, "which flows on for ever in a circle, and never comes to an end. Everything here goes on always, and then always begins again."

For the river, as Paul afterwards found out, ran on for miles and miles, in the curves of an immense circle, of which the sea itself was apparently nothing but a widening of certain portions.

"So here," continued the child, making a pattern with daisies on his sleeve as she talked, "you can go over anything you like again and again, and it need never come to an end at all. Only," she added, looking up gravely into his face, "you must really, *really* want it to start with."

"Without getting tired?" he asked, wonderingly.

"Of course; because *you* begin over and over again with it."

"Delightful!" he exclaimed, "that means a place of eternal youth, where emotions continually renew themselves."

"It's the place where you find lost things," she explained, with a little puzzled laugh at his foolish long words, "and where things that came to no proper sort of end—things that didn't come true, I mean, in the world, all happen and enjoy themselves—"

He sat up with a jerk, forgetting the carefully arranged daisies on his coat, and scattering them all over the grass.

"But this is too splendid!" he cried. "This is what I've always been looking for. It's what I was thinking about just now when I tried to write a poem and couldn't."

"*We* found it long ago," said the child, pointing to Jonah and Mrs. Tompkyns, Smoke having mysteriously disappeared for the moment. "We live here really most of the time. Daddy brought us here first."

"Things life promised, but never gave, here come to full fruition," Paul murmured to himself. "You mean," he added aloud, "this is where ideals that have gone astray among the years may be found again, and actually realised? A kingdom of heaven within the heart?" He was very excited, and forgot for the moment he was speaking to a child.

"I don't know about all that," she answered, with a puzzled look. "But it is life. We live-happily-ever-after here. That's what I mean."

"It all comes true here?"

"All, all, all. All broken things and all lost things come here and are happy again," she went on eagerly; "and if you look hard enough you can find 'xactly what you want and 'xactly what you lost. And once you've found it, nothing can break it or lose it again."

Paul stared, understanding that the voice speaking through her was greater than she knew.

"And some things are lost, *we* think," she added, "simply because they were wanted—wanted *very* much indeed, but never got."

"Yet these are certainly the words of a child," he reflected, wonder and delight equally mingled, "and of a child tumbling about among great spiritual things in a simple, intuitive fashion without knowing it."

"All the things that ought to happen, but never do happen," she went on, picking up the scattered daisies and making the pattern anew on a different part of his coat. "They all are found here."

"Wishes, dreams, ideals?" he asked, more to see what answer she would make than because he didn't understand.

"I suppose that's the same thing," she replied "But, now *please,* Uncle Paul, keep still a minute or I can't possibly finish this crown the daisies want me to make for them."

Paul stared into her eyes and saw through them to the blue of the sky and the blue of the winding river beyond; through to the hills on the horizon, a deeper blue still; and thence into the softer blue shadows that lay over the timeless land buried in the distances of his own heart, where things might indeed come true beyond all reach of misadventure or decay. For this, of course, was the real land of wonder and imagination, where everything might happen and nothing need grow old. The vision of the poet saw... far—far...

All this he realised through the blue eyes of the child at his side, who was playing with daisies and talking about the make-believe of children. His being swam out into the sunshine of great distances, of endless possibilities, all of which he might be able afterwards to interpret to others who did not see so far, or so clearly, as himself. He began to realise that his spirit, like the endless river at his feet, was without end or beginning. Thrills of new life poured into him from all sides.

"And when we go back," he heard the musical little voice saying beside him, "that church will be striking exactly where we left it—the sixth stroke, I mean."

"Of course; I see!" cried Paul, beginning to realise the full value of his discovery, "for there's no time here, is there? Nothing grows old."

"That's it," she laughed, clapping her hands, "and you can find all the lost and broken things you want, if you look hard and—really want them."

"I want a lot," he mused, still staring into the little wells of blue opposite; "the kind that are lost because they've never been 'got,' " he added with a smile, using her own word.

"For instance," Nixie continued, hanging the daisies now in a string from his beard, "all my broken things come here and live happily—if I broke them by accident; but if I broke them in a temper, they are still angry and frighten me, and sometimes even chase me out again. Only Jonah has more of these than I have, and they are all on the other side of the river, so we're quite safe here. Now watch," she added in a lower voice, "Look hard under the trees and you'll see what I mean perhaps. And wish hard, too."

Paul's eyes followed the direction of her finger across the river, and almost at once dim shapes began to move to and fro among the larches, starting into life where the shadows were deepest. At first he could distinguish no very definite forms, but gradually the outlines grew clearer as the forms approached the edges of the wood, coming out into the sunshine.

"The ghosts! The ghosts of broken things!" cried Jonah, running up the bank for protection. "Look! They're coming out. Some one's thinking about them, you see!"

Paul, as he gazed, thought he had never seen such an odd collection of shapes in his life. They stalked about awkwardly like huge insects with legs of unequal length, and with a lop-sided motion that made it impossible to tell in which direction they meant to go. They had brilliant little eyes that flashed this way and that, making a delicate network of rays all through the wood like the shafts of a hundred miniature search-lights. Their legs, too, were able to bend both forwards and backwards and even sideways, so that when they appeared to be coming towards him they really were going away; and the strange tumbling motion of their bodies, due to the unequal legs, gave them an appearance that was weirdly grotesque rather than terrifying.

It was, indeed, a curious and delightful assortment of goblins. There were dolls without heads, and heads without dolls; milk jugs without handles, china teapots without spouts, and spouts without china teapots; clocks without hands, or with cracked and wounded faces; bottles without necks; broken cups, mugs, plates, and dishes, all with gaping slits and cracks in their anatomy, with half their faces missing, or without heads at all; every sort of vase imaginable with every sort of handle unimaginable; tin soldiers without swords or helmets, china puppies without tails, broken cages, knives without handles; and a collection of basins of all sizes that would have been sufficient to equip an entire fleet of cross-channel steamers: altogether a formidable and pathetic army of broken creatures.

"What in the world are they trying to do?" he asked, after watching their antics for some minutes with amazement.

"Looking for the broken parts," explained Jonah, who was half amused, half alarmed. "They get out of shape like that because they pick up the first pieces they find."

"And *you* broke all these things?"

The boy nodded his head proudly. "I reckernise most of them," he said, "but they're nearly all accidents. I said 'sorry' for each one."

"That, you see," Nixie interrupted, "makes all the difference. If you break a thing on purpose in a temper, you murder it; but the accidents come down here and feel nothing. They hardly know who broke them. In the end they all find their pieces. It's the heaven of broken things, we call it. But now let's send them away."

"How?" asked Paul.

"By forgetting them," cried Jonah.

They turned their faces away and began to think of other things, and at once the figures began to fade and grow dim. The lights went out one by one. The grotesque shapes melted into the trees, and a minute later there was nothing to be seen but the slender larch stems and the play of sunlight and shadow beneath their branches.

"You see how it works, at any rate," Nixie said. "Anything you've lost or broken will come back if you think hard enough—nice things as well as nasty things—but they must be real, real things, and you must want them in a real, real way."

It was, indeed, he saw, the region where thoughts come true.

"Then do broken people come here too?" Paul asked gravely after a considerable pause, during which his thoughts went profoundly wandering.

"Yes; only we don't happen to know any. But all our dead animals are here, all the kittens that had to be drowned, and the puppies that died, and the collie the Burdons' motor killed, and Birthday, our old horse that had to be shot. They're all here, and all happy."

"Let's go and see them then," he cried, delighted with this idea of a heaven of broken animals.

In a moment they were on their feet and away over the springy turf, singing and laughing in the sunshine, picking flowers, jumping the little brooks that ran like crystal ribbons among the grass, Nixie and Jonah dancing by his side as though they had springs in their feet and wings on their shoulders. More and more the country spread before them like a great garden run wild, and Paul thought he had never seen such fields of flowers or smelt such perfumes in the wind.

"What's the matter now?" he exclaimed, as Jonah stopped and began to stare hard at an acre of lilies of the valley by the way.

"He's calling some things of his own," Nixie answered. "Stare and think—and they'll all come. But we needn't bother about him. Come along!" And he only had time to see the lilies open in an avenue to make way for a variety of furry, four-legged creatures, when the child pulled him by the hand and they were off again at full speed across the fields.

A sound of neighing made him turn round, and before he could move aside, a large grey horse with a flowing tail and a face full of gentle beneficence came trotting over the turf and stopped just behind him, nuzzling softly into his shoulder.

"Nice, silly-faced old thing," said Nixie, running up to speak to it, while a brown collie trotted quietly at her heels. A little further off, peeping up through a tangled growth of pinks and meadow-sweet, he saw the faces of innumerable kittens, watching him with large and inquisitive eyes, their ears just topping the flowers like leaves of fur. Such a family of animals Paul thought he had never even dreamed of.

"This is the heaven of the lost animals," Nixie cried from her seat on the back of the grey horse, having climbed up by means of a big stone. On her shoulder perched a small brown owl, blinking in the light like the instantaneous shutter of a photographic camera. It had fluffy feathers down to its ankles like trousers, and was very tame. "And they are always happy here and have plenty to eat and drink. They play with us far better here than outside, and are never frightened. Of course, too, they get no older."

Paul climbed up behind her on the horse's back.

"Now we're off!" he cried; and with Jonah and a dozen animals at their heels, they raced off across the open country, holding on as best they could to mane and tail, laughing, shouting, singing, while the wind whistled in their ears and the hot sun poured down upon their bare heads.

Then, suddenly, the horse stopped with a jerk that sent them sprawling forward upon his neck. He turned his head round to look at them with a comical expression in his big, brown eyes. Paul slid off behind, and Nixie saved herself by springing sideways into a bed of forget-me-nots. The owl fluttered away, blinking its eyes more rapidly than ever in a kind of surprised fury, shaking out its fluffy trousers, and Jonah arrived panting with his dogs and rabbits and puppies.

"Come," exclaimed Nixie breathlessly, "he's had enough by now. No animal wants people too long. Let's get something to eat."

"And I'll cook it," cried the boy, busying himself with sticks and twigs upon the ground. "We'll have stodgy-pudding and cake and jam and oyster-patties, and then more stodgy-pudding again to finish up with."

Paul glanced round him and saw that all the animals had disappeared—gone like thoughts forgotten. In their place he soon saw a column of blue smoke rising up among the fir trees close behind him, and the children flitting to and fro through it looking like miniature gypsies. The odour of the burning wood was incense in his nostrils.

"But can't I see something too—something of my own?" he asked in an aggrieved tone.

Nixie and Jonah looked up at him with surprise. "Of course you can," they exclaimed together. "Just stare into space as the cats do, and think, and wish, and wait. Anything you want will come—with practice. People you've lost, or people you've wanted to find, or anything that's never come true anywhere else."

They went on busily with their cooking again, and Paul, lying on his back in the grass some distance away, sent his thoughts roaming, searching, deeply calling, far into the region of unsatisfied dreams and desires within his heart....

For what seemed hours and hours they wandered together through the byways of this vast, enchanted garden, finding everything they wished to find, forgetting everything they wished to forget, amusing themselves to their heart's content; till, at last, they stood together on a big boulder in the river where the spray rose about them in a cloud and painted a rainbow above their heads.

"Get ready!   Quick!" cried Jonah. "The Crack's coming!"

"It's coming!" repeated Nixie, seizing Paul's hand and urging him to hold very tight.

He had no time to reply. There was a rushing sound of air tearing through a narrow opening. The sky grew dark, with a roaring in his ears and a sense of great things flying past him. Again came the sensation of dropping giddily through space, and the next minute he found himself standing with the two children upon the lawn, darkness about them, and the storm howling and crashing over their heads through the branches of the twin cedars.

"There's the clock still striking," Nixie cried. It's only been a few seconds altogether."

He heard the church clock strike the last six strokes of midnight.

For some minutes he realised little more than that he felt rather stiff and uncomfortable in his bedroom chair, and that he was chilly about the legs. Outside the wind still roared and whistled, making the windows rattle, while gusts of rain fell volleying against the panes as though trying to get in. A roll of distant thunder came faintly to his ear. He stretched himself and began to undress by the light of a single candle.

On the table lay a sheet of paper headed "How I climbed the Scaffolding of the Night," and he read down the page and then took his pen and wrote the heading of something else on another sheet "Adventure in the Land between Yesterday and To-morrow." With a mighty yawn he then blew out his candle and tumbled into bed.

And with him, for all the howling of the elements, came a strange sense of peace and happiness. Out of the depths rose gradually before his inner eye in a series of delightful pictures the scenes he had just left, and he understood that the pathway to that country of dreams fulfilled and emotions that never die, lay buried far within his own being.

"Between Yesterday and To-morrow" was to be the children's counterpart of that timeless, deathless region where the spirit may always go when hunted by the world, fretted by the passion of unsatisfied yearnings, plagued by the remorseless tribes of sorrow and disaster. There none could follow him, just as none—none but himself—could bring about its destruction. For he had found the mystical haven where all lost or broken things eternally reconstruct themselves.

The "Crack," of course, may be found by all who have the genuine yearning to recreate their world more sweetly, provided they possess at the start enough imagination to repay the trouble of training—also that *Wanderlust* of the spirit which seeks ever for a resting-place in the great beyond that reaches up to God.

Paul as yet had but discovered the entrance, led by little children who dreamed not how wondrous was the journey; but the rest would follow. For it is a region mapped gradually out of a thousand impulses, out of ten thousand dreams, out of the eternal desires of the soul. It is not discovered in a day, nor do the ways of entrance always remain the same. A thousand joys contribute to its fashioning, a thousand frustrated hopes describe its boundaries, and ten thousand griefs bring slowly, piece by piece, the material for its construction, while every new experience of the soul, successful or disastrous, adds something to its uncharted geography. Slowly it gath-

ers into existence, becoming with every sojourn more real and more satisfying, till at length from the pain of all possible disillusionment the way
opens to the heart of relief, to the peaceful place of hopes renewed, of purposes made fruitful and complete.

And from this deathless region, too, flow all the forces of the soul that
make for hope, enthusiasm, courage, and delight. The children might call it
"Between Yesterday and To-morrow," and find their little broken dreams
brought back to life; but Paul understood that its rewards might vary
immensely according to the courage and the need of the soul that sought it.

CHAPTER XVI

But one man loved the pilgrim soul in you.
—Yeats.

Thus, led delicately by the animals and the children, and guided to a certain extent, too, by the curious poesy of his own soul, Paul Rivers came gradually into his own. Once made free of their world, he would learn next that the process automatically made him free of his own. This simple expedient of having found an audience did wonders for him, for it not only loosened his tongue and his pen, but set all the deeper parts of him running into speech, and the natural love and poetry of the man began to produce a delightful, if somewhat extraordinary, harvest.

He understood—none better—that fantasy, unless rooted in reality, leads away from action and tends to weakness and insipidity; but that, grounded in the common facts of life, and content with idealising the actual, it might become an important factor for good, lending wings to the feet and lifting the soul over difficult places. His education advanced by leaps and bounds.

And in some respects he showed himself possessed of a wisdom that could only have belonged to him because at heart he was still a child, and the ordinary "knowledge of the world" had not come to spoil him in his life of solitude among the trees.

For instance, that "Between Yesterday and Tomorrow" bore some curious relation to reverie and dreams, he dimly discerned, yet, with this simple and profound wisdom of his, he refused to pry too closely into the nature of such relationship. He did not seek to reduce the delightful experience to the little hard pellet of an exact fact. For that, he felt, would be to lose it. Exact knowledge, he knew, was often merely a great treachery, and "fact" a dangerous weapon that deceived, and might even destroy, its owner. If he analysed too carefully, he might analyse the whole thing out of existence altogether, and such a contingency was not to be thought of for a single moment.

Moreover, the attitude of the children confirmed his own. They never referred to their adventures until he had given them form and substance in his reports as recording secretary of the society. No word passed their lips until they had heard them read out, and *then* they talked of nothing else. During the day they maintained a sublime ignorance of his "aventures of the night," as though nothing of the kind had ever happened; and this tended still further to relegate it all to a region untouched by time, beyond the reach of chance, beyond the destruction of mere talk, eternal and real in the great sense.

Meanwhile, as this hidden country he had discovered yielded to exploration, becoming more and more mapped out, and its springs of water tapped, Paul was conscious that the power from these vital sources began to modify his character, and to enlarge his outlook upon life. Imagination, released and singing, provides the greatest of all magics—belief in one's self. The rivers of feeling carve their own channels, which are ever the shortest way to the ocean of fulfilment. The effects spread gradually to the remotest corner of his being.

One rainy day he found himself alone in the schoolroom with Nixie, for it was Saturday afternoon, and Mlle. Fleury had carried off Jonah and Toby in their best clothes, and to their acute dismay, to have tea with the children—they were dull children—at the vicarage.

Dressed in blue serge, with a broad white collar over her shoulders and a band of gold about her waist that matched the colour of her hair, she darted about the room with her usual effect of brightness, so that he found himself continually thinking the sun had burst through the clouds. She was busily arranging cats and kittens in various positions in which they showed no inclination to remain, till the performance had somewhat the air of the old-fashioned game of "general post." Paul sat lazily at the ink-stained table, dividing his attentions between watching the child's fascinating movements and pecking idly into the soft wood with his little gold penknife.

"Aren't you *very* glad we found you out so soon, Uncle Paul?" she asked suddenly, looking up at him over a back of glossy and wriggling yellow fur. "Aren't you very glad *indeed,* I mean?"

He went on picking at the soft ditches between the ridges of dirty brown without answering for a moment.

"Yes," he said presently, in the slow manner of a man who weighs his words; "very glad indeed. It's increased my interest in life. It's made me happier, and healthier, and wealthier, and all the rest of it—and wiser too." He bent, frowning, over the ditches.

"It was all your own fault, you know, that we didn't get you sooner. Oh, years ago—ever so many."

"But I was in the backwoods, Nixie."

"That made no difference," she answered promptly. "If you had written to us, as mother often asked, we should have noticed at once what you were."

"How could that possibly be?" he objected, still without looking up.

"Of course!" was the overwhelming reply.

"Oh, come now " he said, staring at her solemnly over the table; "I admit your penetration is pretty keen, but I doubt *that.*"

She returned his gaze with an expression of grave, almost contemptuous surprise, tossing her hair back impatiently with a jerk from her face. She had finally established the kittens, Zezette and Sambo, in a sleepy heap just where she wanted them on the top of the squirrel's cage.

"But, Uncle," she exclaimed, "between yesserdayantomorrow you can meet people even after they've gone altogether. So America wouldn't have been difficult. How can you think such things?"

Not knowing exactly how it was he could think such things, Paul made no immediate reply.

"Anyhow," she resumed, "it didn't take long once you were here. We saw in a second in the drawinroom what you were—the day you arrived."

"But I acted so well! I'm sure now I behaved—"

"You behaved just like Jonah," she interrupted him with swift decision, "—only bigger!"

Paul laughed to himself. His inquisitor shot across the room to establish Pouf, another kitten, on the piano top. She moved lightly, with a dancing motion that flung her hair behind her through the air, again producing the effect of a sunlight gleam. Paul continued to destroy the table with his blunt penknife, chuckling inwardly at the figure he must have cut that summer afternoon in the "drawinroom" before these mercilessly observant eyes.

"You stood about shyly just like him and Toby—in lumps," she went on presently, "saying things in a sudden, jerky way—"

"In lumps!" cried Paul. "That's a nice way to talk to your Uncle!"

Nixie burst out laughing. "Oh, I don't mean that quite," she explained; "but you stood about as if you found it hard to balance, and were afraid to move off the mat. Just as Jonah does at a party when he's shy. I copied you exactly when I got upstairs."

"Did I indeed? Did you indeed, I mean?" said he, wondering whether he ought to feel offended or pleased at the picture.

"Yes, rather," declared the child emphatically, darting up with Pouf who had definitely rejected the top of the piano, and planting it on the table under his nose, where it immediately sat down, purring loudly and staring into his face. "I should think you did! You see, Pouf says so too; he's purring his agreement. Listen to him! That's fur language."

He listened as he was bid, gazing first into the green eyes of the kitten that opened so wide they seemed to have no lids at all, and then into the mischievous blue eyes of his other tormentor. He decided that on the whole he felt pleased.

"Then I wasted a lot of time," he observed presently, "about joining, I mean—coming into your world."

"H'mmmm, you did."

"Only, remember, you were all very young when I was in America, weren't you ?" he added by way of excuse.

Nixie nodded her head approvingly.

"And you, I expect," she replied thoughtfully, "were too hard then. I hadn't thought of that. You might never have squeezed through the Crack, mightn't you? You're much softer now," she decided after a second's reflection, "ever so much softer!"

"I *have* improved, I think," he admitted, blushing like a pleased schoolboy. "I am decidedly softer!"

He made a violent dig with his penknife, breaking down the hard barrier between two ditches, whereupon Pouf, thinking the resultant splinter was a plaything specially contrived for its happiness, opened its eyes wider than ever, and stretched out a paw that looked huge compared with the splinter and the penknife. Paul put the weapon away, and Pouf fixed its eyes intently on the pocket where it had vanished, leaving its paw absent-mindedly lying on the splinter which it had already wholly forgotten. It purred louder than ever, trying to give the impression that it was really a big cat.

Outside the rain fell softly. A blue-bottle buzzed noisily about the room, banging the ceiling and the walls as though it were exceedingly angry. Through the open window floated the smell of the English garden soaked in rain, odours of soused trees and lawns, and wet air—exquisitely fragrant.

A hush fell over the room; only the purring of the kittens broke it. Paul thought it was the most soothing sound in the whole world; something began to purr within himself. His head, and Nixie's head, and little Pouf's head—all lay very close together over that schoolroom table, each full of its own busy dreams. These queer, gentle talks with the child were very delightful to him, all his shyness and self-consciousness gone, and the spirit of true wonder, simple and profound, awake in his heart.

Together, for a long time, they listened in silence to these sounds of purring and breathing and the murmur of rain falling outside: deep, velvety breathing it was, almost inaudible. Everything in life, Paul caught himself reflecting, tragedy or comedy, goes on against a background of this deep, hidden, purring sound of life. Breathing is the first manifestation of life; it is the music of the world, the soft, continuous hum of existence. His thoughts travelled far....

"Yes, on the whole," he muttered at length inconsequently, "I think I may consider myself softer than before—kinder, gentler, more alive!"

But neither Nixie, nor Pouf, nor, for that matter, Sambo and Zezette either, paid the smallest attention to his remark; he was soon lost again in further reflections.

It was the child's voice that presently recalled him.

"Uncle Paul," she said very softly, her mind still busy with thoughts of her own, "do you know that sometimes I have heard the earth breathing too—akchilly breathing?"

Paul, coming back from a long journey, turned and gazed at the eager little face beside him in silence.

"The earth is alive, I'm sure," she went on with an air of great mystery. "It breathes and whispers, and even purrs; sometimes it cries. It's a great body, alive just like you and the other stars—"

"Nixie!"

"They are all bodies, though; heavenly bodies, Daddy called them. Only we, I suppose, are too small to see it that way perhaps."

Paul listened, stroking Pouf slowly. The child's voice was low and somewhat breathless with the excitement of what she was saying. She believed every word of it intensely. Only a very small part of what she was thinking found expression in her words. Her ideas beckoned her beyond; and mere words could not overtake them at her age.

"The earth," she went on, seeing that he did not laugh, "is somebody's big round body rolling down the sky. It simply must be. Daddy always said that a fly settling on our bodies didn't know we were alive, so we can't understand that the earth is alive either. Only I *know it.* Oh!" she cried out with sudden enthusiasm, "how I would love to hear its real out-loud voice. What a t'riffic roar it must be. I only wish my ears were further—"

"Sharper, you mean."

"But, all the same, I *have* heard it breathing," she added more quietly, lifting Pouf suddenly and wrapping its sleeping body round her neck like a boa, "just like this." She put her head on one side, so that her cheek was against the kitten's lips, and the faint stream of its breathing tickled her ear. "Only the breathing of the earth is much, ever so much, longer and deeper. It's whole months long."

Paul was listening now with his undivided attention. He was being admitted to the very heart of an imaginative child's world, and the knowledge of it charmed him inexpressibly. His eyes were almost as bright, his cheeks as pink with excitement, as her own. Only he must be very careful indeed. The least mistake on his part would close the door.

"Months, Nixie?"

"Oh, yes, a single breath is months long," she whispered, her eyes growing in size, and darkening with wonder and awe. "Pouf lies on me and breathes twice to my once, but I breathe millions of times—ever so many millions—as I lie on the earth's body. And it breathes in and out just as Pouf and I do. Winter is breathing in, and summer is breathing out, you see."

"So the equinoctial gales are the changes from one breath to the other?" he put in gravely.

"I hadn't thought about the—the gales," she said, putting her face closer and lowering her voice, "but I know that in the summer I often hear the earth breathing out—'specially on still warm nights when everything lies awake and listens for it."

"Then do 'Things' really listen as we do?" he asked gently.

"Not 'xactly as we do. We only listen in one place—our ears. They listen all over. But they're alive just the same, though so much quieter. Oh, Uncle Paul, everything is alive; everything, I know it!" She fixed a searching look on him. "You knew *that,* didn't you?"

There was a trace of real surprise and disappointment in her voice.

"Well," he answered truthfully, "I had often and often thought about it, and wondered sometimes—whether—"

But the child interrupted him almost imperiously. He realised sharply how the knowledge that the years bring—little, exact, precise knowledge—may kill the dreams of the naked soul, yet give nothing in their place but dust and ashes. And, by the same token, he recognised that his own heart was still untouched, unspoiled. The blood leaped and ran within him at the thought.

"The winds, too, are alive,"—she spoke with a solemn excitement that made her delicate face flush as though a white fire glowed suddenly beneath the skin and behind the charming eyes—"they run about, and sleep, and sing, and are full of voices. The wind has hundreds of voices—just like insects with such a lot of eyes." (Even her strange simile did not make him smile, so real was the belief and enthusiasm of her words.) "We (with scorn) have only one voice; but the wind can laugh and cry at the same time!"

"I've heard it," he put in, secretly thrilled.

"I know its angry voice as well as its pretended-angry voice, when it's very loud but means nothing in particular. Its baby-voice, when it comes through the keyhole at night, or down the chimney, or just outside the window in the early morning, and tells me all its little very-wonderful-indeed aventures, makes me so happy I want to cry and laugh at once."

She paused a moment for breath, dimly conscious, perhaps, that her description was somewhat confused. Her excitement somehow communicated itself to Pouf at the same time, for the kitten suddenly rose up with an arched back and indulged in a yawn that would have cracked the jaws of any self-respecting creature. After a prolonged stare at Paul, it proceeded inconsequently to wash itself with an air that plainly said, "You won't catch me napping again. I want to hear this too."

Paul, meanwhile, stared at the child beside him, thinking that the gold-dust on her hair must surely come from her tumbling journeys among the stars, and wondering if she understood how deeply she saw into the heart of things with those dreamy blue eyes of hers.

"Listen, Nixie, you fairy-child, and I'll tell you something," he said gently, "something you will like very much"; and, while she waited and held her breath, he whispered softly in her ear:

> Our birth is but a sleep and a forgetting:
> The soul that rises in us, our life's star
>> Hath had elsewhere its setting,
>> And cometh from afar:
>> Not in entire forgetfulness,
>> And not in utter nakedness,
> But trailing clouds of glory do we come
>> From God who is our home:

CHAPTER XVII

And snatches of thee everywhere
Make little heavens throughout a day.
                              ALICE MEYNELL.

"That's very pretty, I think," she said politely, staring at him, with a little smile, half puzzled. The music of the words had touched her, but she evidently did not grasp why he should have said it. She waited a minute to see if he had really finished, and then went on again with her own vein of thought.

"Then please tell me, Uncle," she asked gravely, with deep earnestness, "what is it people lose when they grow up?"

And he answered her with equal gravity, speaking seriously as though the little body at his side were habited by an old, discriminating soul.

"Simplicity, I think, principally—and vision," he said. "They get wise with so many little details called facts that they lose the great view."

The child watched his face, trying to understand. After a pause she came back to her own thinking—the sphere where she felt sure of herself.

"They never see things properly once they're grown up," she said sadly. "They all walk into a fog, *I* believe, that hides all the things *we* know, and stuffs up their eyes and ears. Daddy called it the cotton-wool of age, you know. Oh, Uncle, I do hope," she cried with the sudden passion of the child, "I *do* hope I shall never, never get into that horrid fog. *You* haven't, and I won't, won't, won't!" Her voice rose to a genuine cry. Then she added with a touch of child-wonder that followed quite naturally upon the outburst, "How did you ever stop yourself, I wonder!"

"I lived with the fairies in the backwoods," he answered, laughing softly. She stared at him with complete admiration in her blue eyes.

"Then I shall grow up 'xactly like you," she said, "so that I can always get out of the cage just as you do, even if my body is big."

"Every one's thin somewhere," Paul said, remembering her own explanation. "And the Crack into Yesterday and To-morrow is always close by when it's wanted. That's the real way of escape."

She clapped her hands and danced, shaking her hair out in a cloud and laughing with happiness. Paul took her in his arms and kissed her. With a gesture of exquisite dignity, such as animals show when they resent human interference, the child tumbled back into her chair by the table, an expression of polite boredom—though the faintest imaginable—in her eyes. Many a time had he seen the kittens behave exactly in the same way.

"But how do you know all these things, Nixie, and where do all your ideas come from?" he asked.

"They just come to me when I'm thinking of nothing in particular. They float into my head of their own accord like ships, little fairy ships, I suppose. And I think," she added dreamily after a moment's pause, "some of them are trees and flowers whispering to me." She put her face close to his own across the table, staring into his very brain with her shining eyes. "Don't you think so too, Uncle?"

"I think I do," he answered honestly.

"Though some of the things I hear," she went on, "I don't understand till a long time afterwards."

"What kind of things, for instance?"

She hesitated, answering slowly after a pause:

"Things like streams, and the dripping of rain, and the rustling of wet leaves, perhaps. At the time I only hear the noise they make, but afterwards, when I'm alone, doing nothing, it all falls into words and stories—all sorts of lovely things, but *very* hard to remember, of course."

She broke off and smiled up into his face with a charm that he could never have put into words.

"You'll grow up a poet, Nixie," he said.

"Shall I *really* ?   But I could never find the rhymes—simply never."

"Some never do," he answered; "and some—the majority, I think—never find the words even!"

"Oh, how dreadful!" she exclaimed, her face clouding with a pain she could fully understand. "Poets who can't talk at all. I should think they would burst."

"Some of them nearly do," he exclaimed, hiding a smile; "they get very queer indeed, these poor poets who cannot express themselves. I have known one or two."

"Have you? Oh, Uncle Paul!" Her tone expressed all the solemn sympathy the world could hold.

He nodded his head mysteriously.

The child suddenly sat up very erect. An idea of importance had come into her head.

"Then I wonder if Pouf and Smoke, and Zezette and Mrs. Tompkyns are like that," she cried, her face grave as a hanging judge—"poets who can't express themselves, and may burst and get queer! Because they understand all that sort of thing—scuttling leaves and dew falling, and tickling grasses and the dreams of beeties, and things we never hear at all. P'raps that's why they lie and listen and think for such ages and ages. I never thought of that before."

"It's quite likely," he replied with equal solemnity. Nixie sprang to her feet and flew round the room from chair to chair, hugging in turn each kitten, and asking it with a passionate earnestness that was very disturbing to its immediate comfort in life: "Tell me, Pouf, Smoke, Sambo, this instant! Are you all furry little poets who can't tell all your little furry poems? Are you, *are you,* ARE YOU?"

She kissed each one in turn. "Are you going to burst and get queer?" She shook them all till, mightily offended, they left their thrones and took cover sedately under tables and sofas well out of reach of this intimate and public cross-examination. And there they sat, looking straight before them, as though no one else existed in the entire world.

"I believe they are, Uncle."

A silence fell between them. Under the furniture, safe in their dark corners, the cats began to purr again. Paul got up and strolled to the open window that looked out across lawns and shrubberies to the fringe of oaks and elms that marked the distant hayfields. The rain still fell gently, silently—a fine, scented, melancholy rain; the rain of a minor key. Tinged with a hundred delicate odours from fields and trees—ghostly perfumes far more subtle than the perfumes of flowers—the air seemed to brush the surface of his soul, dropping its fragrance down into his heart like the close presence of remembered friends.

The evening mode invaded him softly, soothingly; and out of it, in some way he scarcely understood, crept something that brought a vague disquiet in its train. A little timid thought stole to the threshold of his heart and knocked gently upon the door of its very inmost chamber. And the sound of the knocking, faint and muffled though it was, woke echoes in this secret chamber that proclaimed in a tone of reproach, if not almost of warning, that it was still empty and unfurnished. A deep, infinite yearning, and a yearning that was *new*, stirred within him, then suddenly rose to the surface of his mind like a voice calling to him from far away out of mist and darkness.

"If only I had children of my own... !" it called; and the echo whispered afterwards "of my very own, made out of my very thoughts.... !"

He turned to Nixie who had followed, and now leaned beside him on the window-sill.

"So the language of wind and trees and water you translate afterwards into stories, do you?" he asked, taking up the conversation where they had left it. It was hardly a question; he was musing aloud as he gazed out into the mists that gathered with the dusk. "It's all silent enough now, at any rate there's not a breath of air moving. The trees are dreaming—dreaming perhaps of the Dance of the Winds, or of the love-making of the snow when their leaves are gone and the flakes settle softly on the bare twigs; or perhaps dreaming of the humming of the sap that brings their new clothes with such a rush of glory and wonder in the spring—"

Again the child looked up into his face with shining eyes. The magic of her little treasured beliefs had touched the depths of him, and she felt that they were in the same world together, without pretence and without the barriers of age. She was radiantly happy, and rather wonderful into the bargain, a fairy if ever there was one.

"They're just thinking," she said softly.

"So trees think too?"

She nodded her head, leaning her chin on her hands as she gazed with him into the misty air.

"I wonder what their thoughts are like," he said musingly, so that she could take it for a question or not as she chose.

"Like ours—in a way," she answered, as though speaking of something she knew beyond all question, "only not so small, not so sharp. Our thoughts prick, I think, but theirs stroke, all running quite smoothly into each other. Very big and wonderful indeed thoughts—big as wind, I mean, and wonderful as sky or distance. And the streams—the streams have long, winding thoughts that run down their whole length under water—"

"And the trees, you were saying," he said, seeing that her thought was wandering.

"Yes, the trees," she repeated, "oh! yes, the trees are different a little, I think. A wood, you see, may have one big huge thought all at once—"

"All at once!"

"I mean all at the same time, every tree thinking the same thought for miles. Because, if you lie in a wood, and don't think yourself, but just wait and wait and wait, you gradgilly get its great thought and know what it's thinking about exactly. You feel it all over instead of—of—"

"Instead of getting a single little sharp picture in your mind," Paul helped her, grasping the wonder of her mystical idea.

"I think that's what I mean," she went on. "And it's exactly the same with everything else—the sea, and the fields, and the sky—oh! and everything in the whole world." She made a sweeping gesture with her arm to indicate the universe.

"Oh, Nixie child!" he cried, with a sudden enthusiasm pouring over him from the strange region where she had unknowingly led him, "if only I could take you out to the big woods I know across the sea, where the trees stretch for hundreds of miles, and the moss is everywhere a foot thick, and the whole forest is such a conspiracy of wonder and beauty that it catches your heart away and makes you breathless with delight! Oh, my child, if only you could hear the thoughts and stories of woods like that—woods untouched since the beginning of the world!"

"Take me! Take me! Uncle Paul, oh! take me!" she cried as though it were possible to start next day. "These woods are such *little* woods, and I know all their stories." She danced round him with a wild and eager delight.

"Such stories, yes, such stories," Paul continued, his face shining almost as much as hers as he thought of his mighty and beloved forests.

"Please tell me, take me, tell me! " she cried. "All, all, all! Quick!"

"I can't. I never understood them properly; only the old Indians know them now," he said sadly, leaning out of the window again with her. "They are tales that few people in this part of the world could understand; in a language old as the wind, too, and nearly forgotten. You see, the trees are different there. They stand in thousands—pine, hemlock, spruce, and cedar—mighty, very tall, very straight, very dark, pouring day and night their great balsam perfumes into the air so that their stories and their thoughts are sweet as incense and very mysterious."

Nixie took the lapels of his coat in her hands and stared up into his face as though her eyes would pop out. She looked *through* his eyes. She saw these very woods he was speaking of standing in dim shadows behind him.

"No one ever comes to disturb their lives, and few of them have ever heard the ringing of the axe. Only giant moose and caribou steal silently beneath their shade, and Indians, dark and soft-footed as things of their own world, make camp-fires among their roots. They know nothing of men and cities and trains, and the wind that sings through their branches is a wind that has never tasted chimney-pots, and hot crowds, and pretty, fancy gardens. It is a wind that flies five hundred miles without taking breath, with nothing to stop its flight but feathery tree-tops, brushing the heavens, and clean mountain ridges thrusting great shoulders to the stars. Their thoughts and stories are difficult to understand, but *you* might understand them, I think, for the life of the elements is strong in your veins, you fairy daughter of wind and water. And some day, when you are stronger in body—not older though, mind, not older—I shall take you out there so that you may be able to learn their wonder and interpret it to all the world."

The words tore through him in such curious, impersonal fashion, that he hardly realised he was giving utterance to a longing that had once been his own, and that he was now seeking to realise vicariously in the person of this little poet-girl beside him. He stroked her hair as she nestled up to him, breathing hard, her eyes glistening like stars, speechless with the torrent of wonder with which her big uncle had enveloped her.

"Some day," she murmured presently, "some day, remember. You promise?"

"I promise."

"And—and will you write that all out for me, please?"

"All what ?"

"About the too-big woods and the too-old language and the winds that fly without stopping, and the stories—"

"Oh, oh!" he laughed; "that's another matter!"

"Yes, oh you must, Uncle! Make a story of it—an aventure. Write it out as a verywonerfulindeedaventure, and put you and me in it!" She forgot the touch of sadness and clapped her hands with delight. "And then read it out at a Meeting, don't you see?"

And in the end Paul promised that too, making a great fuss about it, but in his heart secretly pleased and happy.

"I'll try," he said, with portentous gravity.

The child stared up at him with the sure knowledge in her eyes that between them they held the key to all that was really worth knowing.

He stooped to kiss her hair, but before he could do so, with a laugh and a dancing step he scarcely heard, she was gone from his side and half-way down the passage, so that he kissed the empty air.

"Bless her mighty little heart!" he exclaimed, straightening himself up again. "Was there ever such a teacher in the world before?"

He became aware that the world held powers, gentle yet immense, that were urging him in directions hitherto undreamed of. With such a fairy guide he might find—he was already finding—not merely safety-valves of expression, but an outlet into the bargain for his creative imagination.

"And a little child shall lead them," he murmured in his beard, as he went slowly down the passage to his room to dress for dinner. Again he felt like singing.

CHAPTER XVIII

The tree which moves some to tears of joy is in the eyes of others only a green thing standing in the way.

—W. B.

Thus, gradually, the grey house under the hills changed into a palace; the garden stretched to include the stars; and Paul, the retired Wood Cruiser, walked in a world all new and brilliant. For to find the means of self-expression is to build the foundations of spiritual health, and an ideal companionship, unvexed by limitations of sense, holds potentialities that can change earth into heaven. His accumulated stores of imagination found wings, and he wrote a series of Aventures that delighted his audience while they healed his own soul.

"I wish they'd go on for ever and ever," observed Toby solemnly to her brother. "Perhaps they do really, only—"

"Of course they do," Jonah said decisively, "but Uncle Paul only tells bits of them to us—bits that you can understand."

Toby was too much in earnest to notice the masculine scorn.

"He does know a lot, doesn't he?" she said. "Do you think he sees up into heaven? They're not a bit like made-up aventures." She paused deeply puzzled; very grave indeed.

"He's a man, of course," replied Jonah. " Men know big things like that."

"The Aventures are true," Nixie put in gently. "That's why they're so big, and go on for ever and ever."

"It's jolly when he puts us in them too, isn't it?" said Jonah, forgetting the masculine pose in his interest. "He puts me in most," the boy added proudly.

"But *I* do the funniest things," declared Toby, slightly aggrieved. "It was me that rode on the moose over the tree-tops to the North Pole, and understood all it said—"

"That's nothing," cried her brother, making a huge blot across his copybook. "He had to get me to turn on the roarer boryalis."

"Nixie's always leader, anyhow," replied the child, losing herself for a moment in the delight of that tremendous blot. She often borrowed Nixie in this way to obliterate Jonah when her own strength was insufficient.

"Of course she is," was the manly verdict. "She knows all those things almost as well as Uncle Paul. Don't you, Nixie?"

But Nixie was too busy cleaning up his blot with bits of torn blotting-paper to reply, and the arrival of Mlle. Fleury put an end to the discussion for the moment.

And Paul himself, as the big child leading the littler children, or following their guidance when such guidance was clear, accepted his new duties with a happy heart. His friendship with them all grew delightfully, but especially, of course, his friendship with Nixie. This elemental child slipped into his life everywhere, into his play, as into his work; she assumed the right to look after him; with charming gravity she positively mothered him; and Paul, whose life hitherto had known little enough of such sympathy and care, simply loved it.

If her native poesy won his imagination, her practical interest in his welfare and comfort equally won his heart. The way she ferreted about in his room and study, so serious, so thoughtful, attending to so many little details that no one else ever thought of,—all this came into his life with a seductive charm as of something entirely new and strange to him. It was Nixie who always saw to it that his ink-pot was full and his quill pens trimmed; that flowers had no time to fade upon his table; and that matches for his pipes never failed in the glass match-stands. He used up matches, it seemed, almost by the handful.

"You're far worse than Daddy used to be," she reproved him. "I believe you eat them." And when he assured her that he did nothing of the sort, she only shook her head darkly, and said she couldn't understand then what he did with them all.

A hundred services of love and kindness she did for him that no one else would have thought of. On his mantelpiece she put mysterious little bottles of medicine.

"For nettle-stings and scratches," she explained. "Your poor hands are always covered with them both when you've been out with us." And it was she, too, who bound up his fingers when wounds were more serious, and saw to it that he had a clean rag each day till the sore was healed. She put the new red riband on his straw hat after it fell (himself with it) into the Gull Pond; and one service especially that earned her his eternal respect was to fasten his evening black tie for dinner. This she did every night for him. Such tasks were for magical fingers only. He had never yet compassed it himself. He would run to the nursery to say good-night, and Nixie, looking almost unreal and changeling in her white nightgown, with her yellow hair top-knotted quaintly for sleep, would deftly trim and arrange the strip of satin that he never could manage properly himself. It was a regular little ritual, Toby watching eagerly from the bed across the room.

"You ought to be ashamed of yourself, Uncle Paul," she said another time, holding up a mysterious garment, " I never saw such holes-never!" And then she darned the said socks with results that were picturesque if not always entirely satisfactory. And once she sewed the toes so tightly across with her darning that he could not get his foot into them. She allowed no one else to touch them, however. Little the child guessed that while she patched his clothes, she wove his life afresh at the same time.

And with all the children he took Dick's place more and more. His existence widened, filled up; he felt in touch with real things as of old in the woods; the children replaced the trees.

But it was Nixie in particular who crept close to his unsatisfied heart and tied him to her inner life with the gossamer threads of her sand-coloured hair. This elfin little being, with her imagination and tenderness, brought to him something he had never known before, never dreamed of even; a perfect companionship; a companionship utterly unclouded.

And the other children understood it; there was no jealousy; it was not felt by them as favouritism. Natural and right it seemed, and was.

"You must ask Nixie," Jonah would say in reply to any question concerning his uncle's welfare or habits. "She's his little mother, you know."

For, truth to tell, they were born, these two, in the same corner of the world of fantasy, bred under the same stars, and fathered by the same elemental forces. But for the trick of the years and the accident of blood, they seemed made for one another ideally, eternally.

Things he could speak of to no one else found in her a natural and easy listener. To grown-ups he had never been able to talk about his mystic longings; the very way they listened made such things instantly seem foolish. But Nixie understood in her child-way, not because she was sympathetic, but because she was *in and of* them. He was merely talking the language of her own world. He no longer felt ashamed to "think aloud." Most people were in pursuit of such stupid, clumsy things—fame, money, and other complicated and ugly things—but this child seemed to understand that he cared about Realities only; for, in her own simple way, this was what she cared about too.

To talk with her cleared his own mind, too, in a way it had never been cleared before. He came to understand himself better, and in so doing swept away a great deal of accumulated rubbish; for he found that when his thought was too confused to make clear to her, it was usually false, wrong—not real.

"I can't make that out," she would say, with a troubled face. "I suppose, I'm not old enough yet." And afterwards Paul would realise that it was himself who was at fault, not the child. Her instinct was unerring; whereas he, with those years of solitude behind him, sometimes lost himself in a region where imagination, self-devouring, ran the risk of becoming untrue, possibly morbid. Her wholesome little judgments brought sanity and laughter.

For, like other mystical temperaments, what he sought, presumably, was escape from himself, yet not—and herein he differed healthily from most of his kidney—so much from his Real Inner Self, as from its outer pettiness and limitations. True, he sought union with something larger and more perfect, and in so far was a mystic; but this larger "something," he dimly understood, was the star of his own soul not yet emancipated, and in so far he remained a man of action. His was the true, wholesome mysticism; hysteria was not—as with most—its chief ingredient. Moreover, this other, eternal part of him touched Eternity. To be identified with it meant to be identified with God, but never for one instant to lose his own individuality.

And to express himself through the creative imagination, to lose his own smallness by interpreting beauty, he had always felt must be a halfway house to the end in view. His inability, therefore, to find such means of expression had always meant something incalculably grave, something that hindered growth. But now this child Nixie, in some extraordinary yet utterly simple fashion, had come to show him the way. It was wonderful past finding out. He hardly knew himself how it had come about. Yet, there she was, ever by his side, pointing to ways that led him out into expression.

No woman could have done it. His two longings, he came to realise, were actually one: the desire to express his yearnings grew out of the desire to find God.

And so it was that the thought of her growing up was horrid to him. He could not bear to think of her as a "young woman" moving in a modern world where she would lose all touch with the elemental forces of vision and simplicity whence she drew half her grace and wonder. Already for him, in some mystical fashion of spiritual alchemy, she had become the eternal feminine, exquisitely focussed in the little child. With the advance of years this must inevitably pass from her, as she increased the distance from her source of inspiration.

"Nixie, you must promise never to grow up," he would say, laughing.

"Because Aventures stop then, don't they?" she asked.

"Partly that," he answered.

"And I should get tired, like mother; or stupid, like the head gardener," she added. "I know. But I don't think I ever shall, somehow. I think I am meant to be always like this."

The serious way she said this last phrase escaped him at the time. He remembered it afterwards, however.

It was so delightful, too, to read out his stories and aventures to her; they laughed over them, and her criticisms often improved them vastly. He even read her his first poem without shyness, and they discussed each verse and talked about "stealing Heaven's fire," and the poor "sparks" that never grew into flames. The "kiss of fire" she thought must be wonderful. She also asked what a "lyre" was. They made up other verses together too. But though they laughed and she asked odd questions, on the whole she grasped the sadness of the poem perfectly.

"Let's go and cry a bit somewhere," she remarked quietly, her eyes very wistful. "It helps it out awfully, you know."

He reminded her, however, of a sage remark of Toby's, to the effect that when men grew beards they lost the power to cry. Quick as a flash, then, she turned with one of her exquisite little bits of unconscious poetry.

"Lets go to the Gwyle then, and make the stream cry for us instead," she said gravely, with a profound sympathy, "because everybody's tears must get into the water some time—and so to the sea, mustn't they?"

And on their way, what with jumping ditches and flower-beds, they forgot all about the crying. On the edge of the woods, however, she raced up again to his side, her blue eyes full of a new wonder. "I know that wind of inspiration that your poetry said never blew for you," she cried. "I know where it blows. Quick! I'll show you!" The pace made him pant a bit; he almost regretted he had mentioned it. "I know where it blows, we'll catch it, and you shall see. Then you can always, always get it when you want it."

And a little farther on, after wading through deep bracken, they stopped, and Nixie took his hand. "Come on tiptoe now," she whispered mysteriously. "Don't crack the twigs with your feet." And, smiling at this counsel of perfection, he obeyed to the best of his ability, while she pretended not to notice the series of explosions that followed his tread.

It was a curve in the skirts of the wood where they found themselves; a small inlet where the tide of daylight flowed against the dark cliffs of the firs, and then fell back. The thick trees held it at bay so that only the spray of light penetrated beyond, as from advancing waves. "Thus far and no farther," very plainly said the pine trees, and the sunshine lay there collected in the little hollow with the delicious heat of all the summer. It was a corner hitherto undiscovered by Paul; he saw it with the pleasure of a discovery.

And there, set brightly against the sombre background, stood the slender figure of a silver birch tree, all sweet and shining, its branches sifting the sunshine and the wind; while behind it, standing forth somewhat from the main body of the wood, a pine, shaggy and formidable, grew close as though to guard it. The picture, with its striking contrast, needed no imagination to make it more appealing. It was patent to any eye.

"That"s *my* tree," said Nixie softly, with both arms linked about his elbow and her cheek laid against the sleeve of his coat. "My fav'rite tree. And that's where your winds of inspiration blow that you said you couldn't catch. So now you can always come and hear them, you see."

Paul entered instantly into the spirit of her dream. The way her child's imagination seized upon inanimate objects and incorporated them into the substance of her own life delighted him, for it was also his own way, and he understood it.

"Then that old pine," he answered, pointing to the other, "is my tree. See! It's come out of the wood to protect the little birch."

The child ran from his side and stood close to them. "Yes, and don't you see," she cried, her eyes popping with excitement, "this is me, and that's you!" She patted the two trunks, first the birch and then the pine. "It's us! I never thought of that before, never! It's you looking after me and taking care of me, and me dancing and laughing round you all the time!" She ran back to his side and hopped up to plant a kiss in his beard. He quite forgot to correct her a'venturous grammar.

"Of course," he cried, "so it is. Look! The branches touch too. Your little leaves run up among my old needles!"

Nixie clapped her hands and ran to and fro, laughing and talking, on errands of further discovery, while Paul sat down to watch the scene and think his own thoughts. It was just the picture to appeal strongly to him. At any time the beauty of the tree would have seized him, but with no one else could he have enjoyed it in the same way, or spoken of his enjoyment.

While Nixie flitted here and there in the sunshine, the little birch behind her bent down and then released itself with a graceful rush of branches as the pressure of the wind passed. Against the blue sky she tossed her leafy hands; then, with a passing shiver, stood still.

"I wonder," ran his thought, "why poets need invent Dryads when such an incomparable revelation lies plain in one of the commonest of trees like this?" And, at the same moment, he saw Nixie dart past between the fir trees and the birch, as though the very Dryad he was slighting had slipped out to chide him. Her hair spread in the sunshine like leaves. In the world of trees here, surely, was the very essence of what is feminine caught and imprisoned. Whatever of grace and wonder emanate from the face and figure of a young girl to enchant and bewitch here found expression in the silver stem and branches, in the running limbs so slender, in the twigs that bent with their cataracts of flying hair. Seen against the dark pinewood, this little birch tree laughed and danced; over that silver skin ran, positively, smiles; from the facets of those dainty leaves twinkled mischief and the joys of innocence. Here, in a word, was Nixie herself in the terms of tree-dom; and, as he watched, the wind swept out the branches towards him in a cluster of rustling leaves,—and at the same instant Nixie shot laughing to his side.

For a second he hardly knew whether it was the child or the silver birch that nestled down beside him and began to murmur in his ear.

"This is it, you see," she was saying ; "and there's your wind of inspiration blowing now."

"We shall have to alter the first verse then," he said gravely:

> "The winds of inspiration blow,
> Yet *never* pass me by."

"Of course, of course," she whispered, listening half to her uncle, half to the rustle in the branches. "And now," she added presently, "you can always come and write your poetry here, and it will be very-wonderfulindeed poetry, you see. And if you leave a bit of paper on the tree you'll find it in the morning covered with all sorts of things in very fine writing—oh, but *very very* fine writing, so small that no one can see it except you and me. One of the Little Winds we saw, you know, will twine round it and leave marks. And the big pine is you and the birch is me, isn't it?" she ended with sudden conviction.

The game, of course, was after her own heart. Up she sprang then suddenly again, picked a spray of leaves from a hanging branch, and brought it back to him.

"And here's a bit of me for a present, so that you can't ever forget," she said with a gravity that held no smile. And she fastened it with much tugging and arranging in his buttonhole. "A bit of my tree, and so of me."

"Then I might leave a bit of paper in the water too," he remarked slyly on their way home, "so as to get the thoughts of the stream."

"Easily," she said, "only it must be wrapped up in something. I'll get Jonah's sponge-bag and lend it you. Only you must promise faithfully to return it in case we go to the seaside in the summer."

"And perhaps some of those tears we were talking about will stick on it and leave their marks before they go on to the sea," he suggested.

"Oh, but they'd be too sad," she answered quickly. "They're much better lost in the sea, aren't they?"

ॐ

Thus the poetry in his soul that he could not utter, he lived.

Without any conscious effort of the imagination, the instant Nixie, or the thought of her, stood beside him—lo, he was in Fairyland. It was so real that it was positively bewildering.

And the rest of that quiet household, without knowing it, contributed to its reality. For, to begin with, the place was delightfully "out of the world"; and, after that, the gradations between the two regions seemed so easy and natural: the shadowy personality of his sister; the dainty little French governess flitting everywhere with her plaintive voice in the wake of the elusive children; then the children themselves—Jonah, the mischievous; Toby with her shining face of onion-skin; and, last of all, the host of tumbling animals, the mysterious cats, the kittens, all fluff and wonder; and the whole of it set amid the scenery of flowers, hills, and sea. It was impossible to tell exactly where the actual threshold lay, this shifting, fluid threshold dividing the two worlds; but there can he no question that Paul passed it day by day without the least difficulty, and that it was Nixie who knew all the quickest short-cuts.

And to all who—since childhood—have lived in Fairyland and tasted of its sweet innocence and loveliness, comes sooner or later the desire to transfer something of these qualities to the outer world. Paul felt this more and more as the days passed. The wish to beautify the lives of others grew in him with a sudden completeness that proved it to have been there latent all the time. Through the voices of Nixie, Jonah, and Toby, as it were, he heard the voices—those myriad, faint, unhappy voices—of the world's neglected children a-calling to him: "Tell us the Aventures too!"—"Take us with you through that Crack!"—"Show us the Wind, and let us climb with you the Scaffolding of Night."

And Paul, listening in his deep heart, began to understand that Nixie's education of himself was but a beginning: all unconsciously that elfin child was surely becoming also his inspiration. This first lesson in self-expression she had taught him was like the trickle that would lead to the bursting of the dam. The waters of his enthusiasms would presently pour out with the rush of genuine power behind them. What he had to say, do, and live—all forms of self-expression—were to find a larger field of usefulness than the mere gratification of his personal sense of beauty.

As yet, however, the thought only played dimly to and fro at the back of his mind, seeking a way of escape. The greater outlet could not come all at once. The germ of the desire lay there in secret development, but the thing he should do had not yet appeared.

So, for the time being, he continued to live in Fairyland and write Aventures.

It was really incalculable the effect of enchantment this little yellow-haired girl cast upon him—hard to believe, hard to realise. So true, so exquisite was it, however, that he almost came to forget her age, and that she was actually but a child. To him she seemed more and more an intimate companion of the soul who had existed always, and that both he and she were ageless. It was their souls that played, talked, caressed, not merely their minds or bodies. In her flower-like little figure dwelt assuredly an old and ripened soul; one, too, it seemed to him sometimes, that hardly belonged to this world at all.

There was that about their relationship which made it eternal—it always had been somewhere, it always would be—somewhere. No confinings of flesh, no limitations of mind and sense, no conditions of mere time and space, could lay their burden upon it for long. It belonged most sweetly to the real things which are conditionless.

Moreover, one of the chief effects of the world of Faery, experts say, is that Time is done away with; emotions are inexhaustible and last for ever, continually renewing themselves; the Fairies dance for years instead of only for a night; their minds and bodies grow not old; their desires, and the objects of their desires, pass not away.

"So, unquestionably," said Paul to himself from time to time as he reflected upon the situation, "I am bewitched. I must see what there is that I can do in the matter to protect myself from further depredations!"

Yet all he did immediately, so far as can be ascertained among the sources of this veracious history, was to collect the "Aventures" already written and journey with them one fine day to London, where he had an interview of some length with a publisher—Dick's publisher. The result, at any rate, was—the records prove it—that some time afterwards he received a letter in which it was plainly stated that "the success of such a book is hard to predict, but it has qualities, both literary and imaginative, which entitle it to a hearing"; and thus that in due course the said "Aventures of a Prisoner in Fairyland" appeared upon the bookstalls. For the publishers, being the foremost in the land, took the high view that seemed almost independent of mercenary calculations; and it is interesting to note that the years justified their judgment, and that the "Aventures" may now be found upon the table of every house in England where there dwells a true child, be that child seven or seventy.

And any profits that Paul collected from the sale went, not into his own pocket, but were put aside, as the sequel shall show, for a secret purpose that lay hidden at this particular stage of the story among the very roots of his heart and being.

The summer, meanwhile, passed quickly away, and August melted into

September, finding him still undecided about his return to America.

For the rest, there was no hurry. There was another six months in which to make up his mind. Meanwhile, also, he made frequent use of the "Crack," and the changes in his soul went rapidly forward.

CHAPTER XIX

There was a Being whom my spirit oft
Met on its visioned wanderings, far aloft,
In the clear golden prime of my youth's dawn,
Upon the fairy isles of sunny lawn,
Amid the enchanted mountains, and the caves
Of divine sleep, and on the air-like waves
Of wonder-level dream, whose tremulous floor
Paved her light steps;—on an imagined shore
Under the grey beak of some promontory
She met me, robed in such exceeding glory,
That I beheld her not.

Epipsychidion

One afternoon in late September he made his way alone across the hills.
Clouds blew thinly over a sky of watery blue, driven by an idle wind the
roses had left behind. It seemed a day strayed from out the summer that
now found itself, thrilled and a little confused, in the path of autumn—
and summer had sent forth this soft wind to bring it back to the fold.

The "Crack" was always near at hand on such a day, and Paul slipped in
without the least difficulty. He found himself in a valley of the Blue Mountains hitherto unknown, and, so wandering, came presently to a bend of
the river where the sand stretched smooth and inviting.

For a moment he stopped to watch the slanting waves and listen, when
to his sudden amazement he saw upon the shore, half concealed by the
reeds near the bank—a human figure. A second glance showed him that
it was the figure of a young girl, lying there in the sun, her bare feet just
beyond reach of the waves, and her yellow hair strewn about the face so
as to screen it almost entirely from view. A white dress covered her body;
she was slim, he saw, as a child. She was asleep.

Paul stood and stared.

"Shall I wake her?" was his first thought. But his second thought was
truer: "Can I help waking her?" And then a third came to him, subtle and
inexplicable, yet scarcely shaping itself in actual language: "Is she after all
a stranger?"

Flying memories, half-formed, half-caught, ran curiously through his
brain. What was it in the turn of the slender neck, in the lines of the little mouth, just visible where he stood, that seemed familiar? Did he not
detect upon that graceful figure lying motionless in repose some indefinable signature that recalled his outer life? Or was it merely that fancy
played tricks, and that he reconstructed a composite picture from the gal-
leries of memory, with the myriad expression and fugitive magic of dream
or picture—ideal figures he had conjured with in the past and set alive in

some inner frame of his deepest thoughts? He was conscious of a delicious bewilderment. A singular emotion stirred in his heart. Yet the face and figure he sought utterly evaded him.

Then, the first sharp instinct to turn aside passed. He accepted the adventure. Stooping down for a stone, he flung it with a noisy splash into the river. The girl opened her eyes, threw her hair back in a cloud, and sat up.

At once a wave of invincible shyness descended upon Paul, rendering words or action impossible; he felt ridiculously embarrassed, and sought hurriedly in his mind for ways of escape. But, before any feasible plan for undoing what was already done suggested itself, he became aware of a very singular thing—the face of the girl was covered! He could not see it clearly. Something, veil-like and misty, hung before it so that his eyes could not focus properly upon the features. The recognition he had half anticipated, therefore, did not come.

And this helped to restore his composure. It was, in any case, futile to pretend he did not see her. For one thing, he realised that she was staring at him just as hard as he was staring at her. The very next instant she rose and came across the hot sand towards him, her hair flying loose, and both hands outstretched by way of greeting. Again, the half-recognition that refused to complete itself swept confusingly over him.

But this spontaneous and unexpected action had an immediate effect upon him of another kind. His embarrassment vanished. What she did seemed altogether right and natural, and the beauty of the girl drove all minor emotions from his mind. His whole being rose in a wave of unaffected delight, and almost before he was aware of it, he had stepped forward and caught both her hands in his own.

This strange golden happiness at first troubled his speech.

"But surely I know you!" he cried. "If only I could see your face—!"I

"You ought to know me," she replied at once with a laugh as of old acquaintance, "for you have called for me often enough, I'm sure!" Her voice was soft; curiously familiar accents rang in it; yet, as with the face, he knew not whose it was.

She looked up at him, and though he could not make out the features, he discerned the expression they wore—an expression of peace and confidence. The girl trusted him delightfully.

"Then what hides you from me?" he insisted.

She answered him so low that he hardly caught the words. Certainly, at the moment he did not understand them, for happiness still confused him. "The body," she murmured; "the veil of the body."

She returned the firm and equal pressure of his hands, and allowed him to draw her close. Their faces approached, and he looked searchingly down upon her, trying to pierce the veil in vain. The hot sunshine fell in a blaze upon their uncovered heads. The next moment the girl raised her lips to his, and almost before he knew it they had kissed.

Yet that kiss seemed the most natural thing in the world; at a stroke it killed the last vestige of shyness. Youth ran in his veins like fire.

"Now, tell me exactly who you are, please," he cried, standing back a little for an inspection, but still holding her hands. They swung out at arm's length like children.

"I think first you should tell me who you are," she laughed. "I want to be a mystery a little longer. It's so much more interesting!"

Leaning backwards with her hair tumbling down her neck, she looked at him out of eyes that he half imagined, half knew. Laughter and gentleness played over her like sunlight. Standing there, framed against the reeds of the river bank, with the blue waters behind and the wind and sky about her head, Paul thought that never till this moment had he understood the whole magic of a woman's beauty. Yet at the same time he somehow divined that she was as much child as woman, and that something of eternal youthfulness mingled exquisitely with her suggestion of maturity.

"Of course," he laughed in return, like a boy in mid-mischief, "that's your privilege, isn't it? My name, then, is—"

But there he stuck fast. It seemed so foolish to give the name he owned in that other tinsel world; it was merely a disguise like a frock-coat or evening dress, or the absurd uniform he had once assumed to deceive the children with. He almost felt ashamed of the name he was known by in that world!

"Well?" she asked slyly, "and have you forgotten it quite?"

"I'm the *Man who saw the Wind,* for one thing," he said at length; "and, after that, well—I suppose I'm the man who's been looking for you without knowing it all his life! Now do you know me?" he concluded triumphantly.

"You foolish creature! Of course I know you!"

She came closer; the sunshine and the odour of the flowers seemed to come with her. "It's *you* who couldn't find *me!* I've been waiting for you to claim me ever since—either of us can remember."

A queer, faint rush of memory rose upon him from the depths—and was gone. For an instant it seemed that her face half cleared.

"Then, in the name of beauty," he cried, starting forward, "why can't I see your face and eyes? Why do I only see you partly—?"

She hesitated an instant and drew back; she lowered her eyes—he felt that—and the voice dropped very low again as she answered:

"Because, as yet, you only know me—partly."

"As through a glass, darkly, you mean?" he said, half grave, half laughing.

The girl took both his hands and pressed them silently for a moment.

"When you know me as I know you," she whispered softly, "then—we shall know one another—see one another—face to face. But even now, in these few minutes, you have come to know me better than you ever did before. And that is something, isn't it?"

She moved quite close, passing her hands down his bronzed cheeks and shaking his head playfully as one might do to a loved child.

"You take my breath away!" gasped the delighted man, too bewildered in his new happiness to let the strangeness of her words perplex him long. "But, tell me again," he added, slowly releasing himself, "how it is that you know me so well? Tell me again and again!"

She replied demurely, standing before him like a teacher before a backward pupil. "Because I have always watched, studied, and loved you—from within yourself. It was not my fault that you failed to know me when I spoke. Perhaps, even now, you would not have found me unless—in certain ways—through the children—you had begun to come into your own—"

Paul interrupted her, taking her in his arms, while she made no effort to escape, but only laughed. "And I'll take good care I never lose you again after this!" he cried.

"You know, I wasn't really asleep just now on the sand," she told him a little later. "I heard you coming all the time; only I wanted to see if you would pass me by as you always did before."

"It's very odd and very wonderful," he said, "but I never noticed you till to-day."

"And very natural," she added under her breath, so low that he did not hear.

And Paul, moving beside her, murmured in his beard, "If she's not my Ideal, set mysteriously somehow into the framework of one I already love—I swear I don't know who she is!"

They made their way along the sandy shores of the river, the waves breaking at their feet, the wind singing among the reeds; never had the sunlight seemed so brilliant, the day so wonderful and kind. All nature helped them; playing their great game as if it was the only game worth playing in the whole world—the game loved from one eternity to another.

"So the children have told you about me, have they?" he whispered into the ear that came just level with his lips.

"And all you love, as well. Your dreams and thoughts more than anything else—especially your thoughts. You must be very careful with those; they mould me; they make me what I am. If you didn't think nicely of me—verynicelyindeed—"

"But I shall always think nicely, beautifully, of you," he broke in eagerly, not noticing the familiar touch of language.

"You have so far, at any rate," she replied, "for the yearning and desire of your imagination have created me afresh." And he discerned the smile upon her veiled face as one may see the sun only through troubled glass, yet know its warmth and brilliance.

"Then it is because you are part and parcel of my inner self that you seem so real and intimate and—true?" he asked passionately.

"Of course. I am in your very blood; I beat in your heart; I understand your every passion and emotion, because I am present at their birth. The most fleeting of your dreams finds its reflection in me; your spirit's faintest aspiration runs through me like a trumpet call; and, now that you have found me, we need never, we *can* never, separate!"

The passion of her words broke over his heart like a wave. He felt himself trembling.

"But it is all so swift and wonderful that it makes me almost afraid—afraid it cannot last," he objected, knowing all the time that his words were but a common device to make his pleasure the more real.

"If only, oh, if only I could carry you away with me into that outer world—!"

She laughed deliciously in his face. "It is from that very 'outer world' that you have carried me *in here*," she told him softly, "for I am always with you." And with the words came that fugitive trick of voice and gesture that made him certain he knew her—then was gone again. "In the house with your sister and the children," she continued; "when you write your Aventures and your verses; in your daily round of duties, small and great; and when you lie down at night—ah! especially then—I curl up beside you in your heart, and fly with you through all your funny dreamland, and wake your dear eyes with a kiss so soft you never know it. In your early morning rambles, as in your reveries of the dusk, I never leave you—because I cannot. All day long I am beside you, though you little realise my presence. I share half your pleasures and all your pains. And in return you hand over to me half that soul whose unuttered prayers have thus created me afresh for your salvation."

"But it must be my own voice speaking," he cried inwardly, satisfied and happy beyond belief. "It is the words of my own thoughts that I hear!"

"Because I am your own thoughts speaking," she replied instantly, as though he had uttered aloud. "I lie, you see, behind your inmost thoughts!"

They walked through sunny meadows, picking their way among islands of wild flowers. There was no sound but the murmur of wind and river, and the singing of birds. Fleecy clouds, here and there in the blue, hung cool and white, watching them. The whole world, Paul felt, listened without shyness.

"And so it is that you love me without shyness," she went on, marvellously linking in with his thought; "I am intimate with you as your own soul, and our relations are pure with the purity that was before man. There can be no secrets between us, or possibility of secrets, for your most hidden dreams are also mine. So mingled with your ultimate being am I, in fact, that sometimes you dare not recognise me as separate, and all that appears on the surface of your dear mind must first filter through myself. Why!" she cried, with a sudden rush of mischievous laughter, "I even know what you are made of; why your queer heart has never been able to satisfy itself—to 'grow-up,' as you call it; and all about this endless desire you have to find God, which is really nothing but the search to find your true inner Self."

"Tell me! tell me!" he cried.

"Besides the sun," she went on with a strange swiftness of words, "there's the wind and the rain in you; yes, and moon and stars as well. That's why the fire and restlessness of the imagination for ever tear you. No mere form of expression can ever satisfy *that,* but only increase it; for it means your desire to know reality, to know beauty, to know your own soul; to know— God! Your blood has kinship with those tides that flow through all space, even to the gates of the stars; dawns and sunsets, moonrise and meteors haunt your thoughts with their magic lights; wild flowers of the fields and hillside nod beside you while you sleep; and the winds, laughing and sighing, lift your dreams upon vast wings and flash with them beyond the edges of the universe!"

"Stop," he cried with passion, "you are telling all my secrets."

"I am telling them only to myself," she laughed, "and therefore to you. For I know all the fevers of your soul. The wilderness calls you and the great woods. You are haunted by the faces of the world's forgotten places. Your imagination plays with the lightning about the mountain tops, and seeks primeval forests and the shores of desolate seas...."

Paul listened spellbound while she put some of the most intangible of his fancies into the language of poetry. Yet she spoke with the quiet simplicity of true things. The man felt his soul shake with delight to hear her. Again and again, while she spoke, the feeling came to him that in another moment her face must clear and he would know her; yet the actual second of recognition never appeared. The girl's true identity continued to evade him. The enticing uncertainty added enormously to her charm. It evoked in him even the sense of worship.

"And this shall be the earnest of our ideal companionship," she whispered, holding up a spray of leaves which she proceeded to fasten into the buttonhole of his coat; "the symbol by which you shall always know me— the sign of my presence in your heart."

The top of her head, as she bent over the task, was on a level with his lips, and when he stooped to kiss it the perfumes of the earth—flowers, trees, wind, water—rose about her like a cloud. Her hair was hot with sunshine, all silken with the air of summer. They were one being, growing out of the earth that he loved—the old, magical, beautiful earth that fed so great a part of his secret life from perennial springs.

As she drew away again from his caress he glanced down and saw that what she had pinned into his coat was a little cluster of leaves from the branch of a silver birch tree.

"Then I, too, shall give you a sign," he said, "that shall mean the same as yours." And he picked a twig of pine needles from a tree beside them and twined it through a coil of her hair. Then, seizing her hands, he swung her round in a dance till they fell upon the river bank at last, tired out, and slept the sleep of children.

And after that, for a whole day it seemed, they wandered through this summer landscape, following the river to its source in the mountains, and then descending on the farther side to the shores of a blue-rimmed sea.

"There are the ships," she cried, pointing to the shining expanse of water, "and, see, there is *our* ship coming for us."

And as she stood there, laughing with excitement like a child, a barque with painted figure-head and brown sails yielding to the wind, came towards them over the waves, the bales of fruit upon her decks scenting the air, the smell of rope and tar and salty wood enticing them to distance and adventure. Through the cordage the very sound of the wind called to them to be off.

"So at last we start upon our long, long voyage together," she said mysteriously, blushing with pleasure, and leading him down towards the ship.

"And where are we to sail to?" he asked; for the flap of the sails and the waves beating against the sides made resistance impossible. The sea-smells were in his nostrils. He glanced down at the veiled face beside him.

"First to the Islands of the Night," she whispered so low that not even the wind could carry it away; "for there we shall be alone."

"And then—?"

"And then to the Islands of Delight," she murmured more softly still; "for there we shall find the lost children of the world—our children, and so be happy with them ever after, like the people in the fairy tales."

With something like a shock he realised that some one else was walking beside him, talking of things that were real in a very different sense. He had been out walking longer than he knew, and had reached the house again. The autumnal mist already drew its gauze curtains about the old building. The smoke rose in straight lines from the chimneys, melting into dusk. That other place of sunshine and flowers had faded—sea, ship, islands, had all sunk beneath the depths within him. And this other person had been saying things for some minutes...

"I don't believe you've been listening to a single word, Paul. You stand there with your eyes fixed on vacancy, and only nod your head and grunt."

"I assure you, Margaret, dear," he stammered coming to the surface as from a long swim under water, "I rarely miss anything you say. Only the Crack came so very suddenly. You were saying that Dick's niece was coming to us—Joan—er—Thingumybob, and—"

"So you heard some of it," she laughed quietly relenting. "And I hope the Crack you speak about is in your head, not in mine."

"It's everywhere," he said with his grave humour.

"That's the trouble, you see; one never knows—" Then, seeing that she was looking anxiously at the walls of the house and at the roof, he dropped his teasing and came back to solid earth again. "And how soon do you expect her?" he asked in his most practical voice. "When does she arrive upon the scene?"

"Why, Paul, I've already told you twice! You really are getting more absent-minded every day. Joan comes to-morrow, or the day after—she's to telegraph which—and stays here for as long as she can manage—a fortnight or so, I expect. She works herself to death, I believe, in town with those poor children, and I want her to get a real rest before she goes back."

"Waifs, aren't they?" he asked, picking up the thread of the discourse like a thing heard in a dream, "lost children of the slums?"

"Yes. You'll see them for yourself probably, as she has some of them down usually for a day in the country. One can be of use in that way—and it's so nice to help. Dick, you know, was absorbed in the scheme. You will help, won't you, when the time comes?"

He promised; and they went in together to tea.

CHAPTER XX

"This is him," cried Jonah breathlessly, pointing with a hand that wore ink like a funeral glove. "I've got him this time. Look!" And he waved a half-sheet of paper in his uncle's face.

"I've made one too—oh, a beauty!" echoed Toby; "and I haven't made half such a mess as you." Three of her fingers were in mourning. A crape-like line running from the nose to the corner of the mouth, lent her a certain distinction. She, too, waved a bit of paper in the air.

"Mine's the real Jack-of-the-Inkpot though, isn't he, Uncle Paul?" exclaimed the boy, leaving the schoolroom table, and running up to show it.

"They're all real—as real as your awful fingers," decreed Paul.

He had been explaining how to make the figure of the Ink Sprite that leaves blots wherever he goes, blackens penholders and fingers, and leaves his crawly marks across even the neatest page of writing. Two blots and a line—then fold the paper. Open it again and the ink has run into the semblance of an outlandish figure with countless legs and arms, and a fantastic head; something between a spider, a centipede, and a sprite.

"It's Jack-of-the-Inkpot," he told them. "Half the time he does his dirty work invisibly, and if he touches blotting paper—he vanishes altogether."

Jonah skipped about the room, waving his hideous creation in the air. Toby, in her efforts to make a still better one, almost climbed into the inkstand. Nixie sat on the window-sill, dangling her legs and looking on.

"Very little ink does it," explained Paul, frightened at the results of his instruction. "You needn't pour it on! He works with the smallest possible material, remember!" His own fingers were no longer as spotless as they might have been.

"Look!" shouted Jonah, standing on a chair and ignoring the rebuke. "There he goes—just like a black spider flying!" He let his half-sheet drop through the air, ink running down its side as it fell, while Toby watched with the envy of despair.

Paul pounced upon the wriggling figure just in time to prevent further funeral trappings. He turned it face downwards upon the blotting paper.

"Oh, oh!" cried the children in the same breath; it's drank him up!"

"Drunk him up," corrected Paul, relieved by the success of his manoeuvre. "His feet touched the blotting-paper, you see."

A pause followed.

"You promised to tell us his song, please," observed Nixie from her perch on the window-sill.

"This is it, then," he answered, looking round at the smudged and solemn faces, instantly grown still. "To judge by appearances you know this Sprite better than I do!

I dance on your paper,
I hide in your pen,
I make in your ink-stand
My black little den;
And when you're not looking
I hop on your nose,
And leave on your forehead
The marks of my toes.

When you're trying to finish
Your 'i' with a dot,
I slip down your finger
And make it a blot;
And when you're so busy
To cross a big 'T,'
I make on the paper
A little Black Sea,

I drink blotting-paper,
Eat penwiper-pie,
You never can catch me,
You never need try!
I hop *any* distance,
I use *any* ink!
I'm on to your fingers
Before you can wink."

Paul's back was to the door. He was in the act of making up a new verse, and declaiming it, when he was aware that a change had come suddenly over the room. It was manifest from the faces of the children. Their attention had wandered; they were looking past him—beyond him.

And when he turned to discover the cause of the distraction he looked straight into the grey eyes of a woman—grave-faced, with an expression of strength and sweetness. As he did so the opening words of verse four slipped out in spite of themselves:—

"I'm the blackest of goblins,
I revel in smears—"

He smothered the accusing statement with a cough that was too late to disguise it, while the grey eyes looked steadily into his with a twinkle their owner made no attempt to conceal. The same instant the children rushed past him to welcome her.

"It's Cousin Joan!" they cried with one voice, and dragged her into the room.

"And this is Uncle Paul from America—" began Nixie.

"And he's crammed full of sprites and things, and sees the wind and gets through our Crack, and—and climbs up the rigging of the Night—   " cried Jonah, striving to say everything at once before his sisters.

"And writes the aventures of our Secret S'iety," Toby managed to interpolate by speaking very fast indeed.

"He's Recording Secre'ry, you see," explained Nixie in a tone of gentle authority that brought order into the scene. "Cousin Joan, you know," she added, turning gravely to her uncle, "is Visiting I'spector."

"Whose visits, however, are somewhat rare, I fear," said the new arrival, with a smile. Her voice was quiet and very pleasant. "I hope, Mr. Rivers, you are able to keep the Society in better order than I ever could."

The introduction seemed adequate. They shook hands. Paul somehow forgot the signs of mourning he wore in common with the rest.

"Cousin Joan has a *real* Society in London, of course," Nixie explained gravely, "a Society that picks up *real* lost children."

"A-filleted with ours, though," cried Jonah proudly.

" 'ffiliated, he means," explained Nixie, while everybody laughed, and the boy looked uncertain whether to be proud, hurt, or puzzled, but in the end laughing louder than the rest.

When Paul was alone a few minutes later, the children having been carried off shouting to receive the presents their "Cousin" always brought them on her rare visits from London, he was conscious first of a curious sense of disappointment. That strong-faced woman, grave of expression, with the low voice and the rather sad grey eyes, he divined was the cause; though, for the moment, he could not trace the feeling to any definite detail. In his mind he still saw her standing in the doorway—a woman no longer in her first youth, yet comely with a delicate, strong beauty that bore the indefinable touch of high living. It was peculiar to his intuitive temperament to note the spirit before he became aware of physical details; and this woman had left something of her personality behind her. She had spoken little, and that little ordinary; had done nothing in act or gesture that was striking. He did not even remember how she was dressed, beyond that she looked neat, soft, effective. Yet, there it was; something was in the room with him that had not been there before she came.

At first he felt vaguely that his sense of disappointment had to do with herself. Not that he had expected anything dazzling, or indeed had given her consciously any thought at all. The male creature, of course, hearing the name of a girl he is about to meet, instinctively conjures up a picture to suit her name. He cannot help himself. And Joan Nicholson, apart from any deliberate process of thought or desire on his part, hardly suited the picture that had thus spontaneously formed in his mind. The woman seemed too big for the picture. He had seen her, perhaps, hitherto, only through his sister's eyes. It puzzled him. About her, mysteriously as an invisible garment, was the atmosphere of things bigger, grander, finer than he had expected; nobler than he quite understood.

Ah, now, at last, he was getting at it. The vague sense of disappointment was not with her; it was *with himself*. Tested by some new standard her mere presence had subtly introduced into the room—into his intuitive mind—he had become suddenly dissatisfied with himself. His play with the children, he remembered feeling, had seemed all at once insignificant, unreal, almost unworthy—compared to another larger order of things her presence had suggested, if not actually revealed.

Thus, in a flash of vision, the truth came to him. It was with himself and not with her that he was disappointed. He recalled scraps of the conversation. It was, after all, nothing Joan Nicholson had said; it was something Nixie had said. Nixie, his little blue-eyed guide and teacher, had been up to her wizard tricks again, all unconsciously.

"Cousin Joan has a *real* Society in London, you know—*a Society that picks up real lost children*."

That was the sentence that had done it. He felt certain. Combined with the spiritual presentment of the woman, this apparently stray remark had dropped down into his heart with almost startling effect—like the grain of powder a chemist adds to his test tube that suddenly changes the colour and nature of its contents. As yet he could not determine quite what the change meant; he felt only that it was there—disappointment, dissatisfaction with himself.

"Cousin Joan has a *real* Society." She was in earnest.

"*Real* lost children"—perhaps potential Nixies, Jonahs, Tobys, all waiting to be "picked up."

The thoughts ran to and fro in him like some one with a little torch, lighting up corners and recesses of his soul he had so far never visited. For thus it sometimes is with the chemistry of growth. The changes are prepared subconsciously for a long while, and then comes some trivial little incident—a chance remark, a casual action—and a match is set to the bonfire. It flames out with a sudden rush. The character develops with a leap; the soul has become wiser, advanced, possessed of longer, clearer sight.

Paul was certainly aware of a new standard by which he must judge himself; and, for all the apparent slightness of its cause, a little reflection will persuade of its truth. Real, inner crises of a soul are often produced by causes even more negligible.

The desire, always latent in him, to be of some use in the world, and to find the things he sought by losing himself in some Cause bigger than personal ends, had been definitely touched. It now rose to the surface and claimed deliberate attention.

What in the world did it matter—thus he reflected while dressing for dinner—whether his own personal sense of beauty found expression or not? Of what account was it to the world at large, the world, for instance, that included those "lost children" who needed to be "picked up"? To what use did he put it, except to his own gratification, and the passing pleasure of the children he played with? Were there no bigger uses, then, for his imagination, uses nobler and less personal?...

The thoughts chased one another through his mind in some confusion.

He felt more and more dissatisfied with himself. He must set his house in order. He really must get to work at something *real!*

Other thoughts, too, played with him while he struggled with his studs and tie. For he noticed suddenly with surprise that he was taking more trouble with his appearance than usual. That black tie always bothered him when he could not get the help of Nixie's fingers, and usually he appeared at the table with the results of carelessness and despair plainly visible in its outlandish shape. But to-night he tied and re-tied, determined to get it right. He meant to look his best.

Yet this process of beautifying himself was instinctive, not deliberate. It was unconscious; he did not realise what he had been about until he was half-way downstairs. And then came another of those swift, subtle flashes by which the soul reveals herself—to herself. This "dressing-up," what was it for? For whom? Certainly, he did not care a button what Joan Nicholson thought of his personal appearance. That was positive. Then, for whom, and for what, was it? Was it for some one else? Had the arrival of this "woman" upon the scene somehow brought the truth into sudden relief?...

A delightful, fairy thought sped across his mind with wings of gold, waving through the dusk of his soul a spray of leaves from a silver birch-tree that he knew, and disappearing into those depths of consciousness where feelings never clothe themselves in precise language. A line of poetry swam up and took its place mysteriously—

> My heart has thoughts, which, though thine eyes hold mine,
> Flit to the silent world and other summers,
> With wings that dip beyond the silver seas.

Could it be, then, that he had given his heart so utterly, so exquisitely, into the keening of a little child ?...

At any rate, before he reached the drawing-room, he understood that what he had been so busy dressing up was not anything half so trumpery as his mere external body and appearance. It was his interior person. That black tie, properly made for once, was an outward and visible sign of an inward and spiritual grace; only, having forgotten, or possibly never heard the phrase, he could not make use of it!

"It's that little, sandy-haired witch after all!" he thought to himself. "Joan's coming—a woman's coming—has made me realise it. I must behave my best, and look my best. It's my soul dressing up for Nixie, I do declare!"

CHAPTER XXI

Persons with real force of purpose carry about with them something that charges unconsciously the atmosphere of others. Paul "felt" this woman. The first impact of her presence, as has been seen, came almost as a shock. The "shocks," however, did not continue—as such. Her influence worked in him underground, as it were.

She slipped easily and naturally into the quiet routine of the little household in the Grey House under the hill, till it seemed as if she had been there always. Margaret had insisted at once that there could be no "Missing" and "Mistering"; Dick's niece must be Joan, and her brother Paul; and the more familiar terms of address were adopted without effort on both sides.

The children helped, too. They were all in the same Society, and before a week had passed she had heard all the "aventures," and entered into the discovery of new ones, even contributing some herself with a zest that delighted Paul, and made him feel wholly at his ease with her. It was all real to her; she could not otherwise have shown an interest; for sham had no part in her nature, and her love for these fatherless children was as great as his own, and similar in kind.

"You have given their 'Society' a new lease of life," she told him; "you are an enormous addition to it."

"Enormous—yes!" he laughed.

"Enormously useful at the same time," she laughed in return, "because you not only increase their imagination; you train it, and show them how to use it."

"To say nothing of the indirect benefits I receive myself," he added.

And, after a pause, she said: "For myself, too, it's the best kind of holiday I could possibly have. To come down here into all this, straight from my waifs in London, is like coming into that Crack-land you have shown them. I wish—I wish I could introduce it all to my big sad world of unwashed urchins. They have so few chances." A sudden flash of enthusiasm ran over her face like sunlight. "Perhaps, when they come down here next week for a day's outing, we might try!—if you will help me, that is?" She looked up. Something in the simple words touched him; her singleness of aim stirred the depths in him.

He promised eagerly.

"When it's out," she added presently, "I'm going to give copies of your book of aventures to some of them. A good many will understand—"

"You shall have as many as you can use," he put in quickly, with a thrill of pleasure he hardly understood. "I'm only too delighted to think they could be of any use—any *real* use, I mean."

There was something in the simple earnestness of this woman, in the devotion of her life to an unselfish Cause, that increased daily his dissatis-faction with himself. She never said a word that suggested self-sacrifice. A call had come to her, turning her entire life into an instrument for help-ing others—others who might never realise enough to say, "Thank you"—and she had accepted it. Now she lived it, that was all. The Scheme that had provided the call, too, was Dick's. It was all conceived originally in that big practical, imaginative heart of the one intimate friendship he had known. Moreover, it concerned children, lost children. The appeal to the deepest in himself was thus reinforced in several ways. More and more, beside this quiet, determined woman, with her singleness of aim and her practical idealism, his own life seemed trivial, cheap, selfish. She had found a medium of expression, selfexpression, compared to which his own mind was insignificant.

From the "Man who splashed on the Deck" to Joan Nicholson was a far cry; as far almost as from the amoeba to the dog—yet both the man and the woman knew the relief of Outlet. And, now, he too was learning in his own time and place the same truth. Nixie had brought him far. Joan, per-haps, was to bring him farther still.

Yet there was nothing about her that was very unusual. There are scores and scores of unmarried women like her sprinkled all along the quiet ways of life, noble, unselfish, unrecognised, often, no doubt, utterly unappreci-ated, turning the whole current of their lives into work for others—the best they can find. The ordinary man who, for the mother of his children seeks first of all physical beauty, or perhaps some worldly standard of attractiveness, passes them by. Their great force, thus apparently neglect-ed by Nature for her more obvious purposes, runs along through more hid-den channels, achieving great things with but little glory or reward. To Paul, who knew nothing of modern types, and whose knowledge of women was abstract rather than concrete, she appeared, of course, simply normal. For all women he conceived as noble and unselfish, capable natu-rally of sacrifice and devotion. To him they were all saints, more or less, and Joan Nicholson came upon the scene of his life merely as an ordinar-ily presentable specimen of the great species he had always dreamt about.

But it was the first time he had come into close contact with a living example of the type he had always believed in. Here was a woman whose interests were all outside herself. The fact thrilled and electrified him, just as the peculiar nature of her work made a powerful and intimate appeal to his heart.

As the days passed, and they came to know one another better, she told him frankly about the small beginnings of her work, and then how Dick's idea had caught her up and carried her away to where she now was.

"There was so much to be done, and so much help needed, that at first," she admitted, "my own little efforts seemed absurd; and then he showed me that if everybody talked like that nothing would ever be accomplished. So I got up and tried. It was something definite and practical. I let my big-ger dreams go—"

"Well done," he interrupted, wondering for a moment what those "bigger dreams" could have been.

"—and chose the certainty. And I have never regretted it, though sometimes, of course, I am still tempted—"

"That was fine of you," he said. He realised vaguely that she would gladly, perhaps, have spoken to him of those "other dreams," but it was not quite clear to him that his sympathy could be of any avail, and he did not know how to offer it either. To ask direct questions of such a woman savoured to his delicate mind of impertinence.

"There was nothing 'fine' about it," she laughed, after an imperceptible pause; "it was natural, that's all. I couldn't help myself really. Human suffering has always called to me very searchingly. *Au fond,* you see, it was almost selfishness."

He suddenly felt unaccountably small with this slip of a woman at his side, tired, overworked, giving all her best years so gladly away, and even in her "holidays" thinking of her work more than of herself. He noticed, too, the passing flames that lit fires in her eyes and illumined her entire face sometimes when she spoke of her London waifs. Pity and admiration ran together in his thoughts, the latter easily predominating.

"But you must make the most of your holiday," he said presently; "you will use up your forces too soon—"

"Perhaps," she laughed, "perhaps. Only I get restless with the feeling that I'm wanted elsewhere. There's so little time to do anything. The years pass so quickly—after thirty; and if you always wait till you're 'quite fit,' you wait for ever, and nothing gets done."

Paul turned and looked steadily at her for a moment. A sudden beauty, like a white and shining fire, leaped into her face, flashed about the eyes and mouth, and was gone. Paul never forgot that look to the end of his days.

"By Jove," he said, "you *are* in earnest!"

"Not more than others," she said simply; "not as much as many, even, I'm afraid. A good soldier goes on fighting whether he's 'fit' or not, doesn't he?"

"He ought to," said Paul—humbly, for some reason he could hardly explain.

They had many similar talks. She told him a great deal about her rescue work in London, and he, for his part, became more and more interested. From a distance, meanwhile, his sister observed them curiously, —though nothing that was in Margaret's thoughts ever for a single instant found its way either into his mind or Joan's. It was natural, of course, that Margaret, the reader of modern novels, should have formed certain conclusions, and perhaps it would have been the obvious and natural thing for Joan and Paul to have fallen in love and been happy ever afterwards with children of their own. It would also, no doubt, have been "artistic," and the way things are made to happen in novels.

But in real life things are not cut always so neatly to measure, and whether real life is artistic or not as a whole cannot be judged until the true, far end is known. For the perspective is wanting; the scale is on a vaster loom; and of the threads that weave into the pattern and out again, neither end nor beginning are open to inspection.

The novels Margaret delighted in, with their hotch-potch of duchesses and valets, Ministers of State and footmen, libertines and snobs, while doubtless portraying certain phases of modern life with accuracy, could in no way prepare her for the Pattern that was being woven beneath her eyes by the few and simple characters in this entirely veracious history. And it may be assumed, therefore, that Joan had come into the scenery of Paul's life with no such commonplace motive—since the high Gods held the threads and wove them to their own satisfaction—as merely to marry off the hero.

And if Paul did not fall in love with Joan Nicholson, as he might, or ought, to have done, he at least did the next best thing to it. He fell head over ears in love with her work. And since love seeks ever to imitate and to possess, he cast about in his heart for means by which he might accomplish these ends. Already he possessed her secret. Now he had only to imitate her methods.

He was finding his way to a bigger and better means of self-expression than he had yet dreamed of; while Nixie, the *dea ex machina,* for ever flitted on ahead and showed the way.

It remained a fairy-tale of the most delightful kind. *That,* at least, he realised clearly.

CHAPTER XXII

Among the branches of the ilex tree, whose thick foliage rose like a giant swarm of bees at the end of the lawn, there were three dark spots visible that might have puzzled the most expert botanist until he came close enough to examine them in detail. The fact that the birds avoided the tree at this particular hour of the evening, when they might otherwise have loved to perch and sing, hidden among the dense shiny leaves, would very likely have furnished a clue, and have suggested to him—if he were a really intelligent man of science—that these dark spots were of human origin.

In the order in which they rose from the ground towards the top they were, in fact, Toby, Joan Nicholson, Paul, Nixie and, highest of all, Jonah. Paul felt safer in the big fork, Joan in the wide seat with the back. In the upper branches Jonah perched, singing and chattering. Toby hummed to herself happily nearer the ground, and Nixie, her legs swinging dizzily over a serpentine branch immediately above Paul's head, was really the safest of the lot, though she looked ready to drop at any moment.

They were all at rest, these wingless human birds, in the tree where Paul had long ago made seats and staircases and bell-ropes.

"I wish the wind would come," said Nixie. "It would make us all swing about."

"And Jonah would lose his balance and bring the lot of us down like ripe fruit," said Paul.

"On the top of Toby at the bottom," added Joan.

"But my house is well built," Paul objected, "or it would never have held such a lot of visitors as it did yesterday."

"Look out! I'm slipping!" cried Jonah suddenly overhead. "No! I'm all right again now," he added a second later, having thoroughly alarmed the lodgers on the lower floors, and sent down a shower of bark and twigs.

"It's certainly more solid than your 'Scaffolding of Night,'" Joan observed mischievously as soon as the shower was past; "though, perhaps, not quite as beautiful." And presently she added, "I think I never saw boys enjoy themselves so much in my life. They'll remember it as long as they live."

"It was your idea," he said.

"But you carried it out for me!"

They were resting after prolonged labours that had been, at the same time, a prolonged delight. At three o'clock that afternoon, after twenty-four hours of sunshine among woods and fields, the party of twenty urchins had been seen safely off the premises into the London train. Two large brakes had carried them to the station, and the gardens of the grey house under the hill were dropping back again into their wonted peace and quiet.

There is nothing unusual—happily—in the sight of poor town-children enjoying an afternoon in the country; but there was something about this particular outing that singled it out from the majority of its kind. Paul had entered heart and soul into it, and the combination of woods, fields, and running water had made possible certain details that are not usually feasible.

Margaret had given Paul and her cousin *carte blanche*. They had planned the whole affair as generals plan a battle. The children had proved able lieutenants; and the weather had furnished the sun by day and the moon by night, to show that it thoroughly approved. For it was Paul's idea that the entire company of boys should camp out, cook their meals over wood fires in the open, bathe in the pools he had contrived long ago by damming up the stream, and that not a single minute of the twenty-four hours should they be indoors or under cover.

With a big barn close at hand in case of necessity, and with four tents large enough to hold five apiece, erected at the far end of the Gwyle woods, where the stream ran wide and full, he had no difficulty in providing for all contingencies. Each boy had brought a little parcel with his things for the night; and blankets, bedding of hay and pillows of selected pine branches—oh, he knew all the tricks for making comfortable sleeping-quarters in the woods!—were ready and waiting when the party of urchins came upon the scene.

And every astonished ragamuffin had a number pinned on to his coat the moment he arrived, and the same number was to be found at the head of his place in the tent. Each tent, moreover, was under the care of a particular boy who was responsible for order; while, midway in the camp, by the ashes of the fire where they had roasted potatoes and told stories till the moonlight shamed them into sleep, Paul himself lay all night in his sleeping-bag, the happiest of the lot, sentinel and guardian of the troop.

The place for the main fire, where meals were cooked, had been carefully chosen beforehand, and wood collected by the busy hands of Nixie & Co. The boys sat round it in a large ring; and Paul in the middle, stirring the stew he had learned to make most deliciously in his backwoods life, ladled it out into the tin plates of each in turn, while Joan saw to the bread and cake, and watched the huge kettle of boiling water for tea that swung slowly from the iron tripod near by.

And that circle of happy urchin faces, seen through the blue smoke against the background of crowding tree stems, flushed with the hours of sunshine, the mystery of happiness in all their eyes, remained a picture in Paul's memory to the end of his life. The boys, certainly, were not all good, but they were at least all merry. They forgot for the time the heat of airless brick lanes and the clatter of noisy traffic. The perfumes of the wood banished the odour of ill-ventilated rooms. Dark shadows of the streets gave place to veils of a very different kind, as the rising moon dropped upon their faces the tracery of pine branches. And, instead of the roar of a city that for them meant hardship, often cruelty, they heard the singing of birds, the rustle of trees, and the murmur of the stream at their very feet.

And Paul, as he paced to and fro softly between the sleeping crew, the tents all ghostly among the trees, had long, long thoughts that went with him into his sleeping-bag later and mingled with dreams that were more inspired than he knew, and destined to bear a great harvest in due course....

The branches of big forest trees shifted noiselessly forwards from the scenery that lay ever in the background of his mind, and pressed his eye-lids gently into sleep. With feathery dark fingers they brushed the surface of his thoughts, leaving the perfume of their own large dreams about his pillow. The shadowy figures that haunt all ancient woods peered at him from behind a million stems and, while they peered, beckoned; whisper-ing to his soul the secrets of the wilderness, and renewing in him the sources of strength, simplicity, and joy they had erstwhile taught him.

All that afternoon he had spent with the romping boys, organising their play, seeing to it that they enjoyed utter freedom, yet did no mischief. Joan seconded him everywhere, and Nixie flitted constantly between the camp and the source of supplies in the kitchen. And, to see their play, came as a revelation to him in many ways. While the majority were content to shout and tumble headlong with excess of animal spirits let loose, here and there he watched one or two apart, all aghast at the beauty they saw at close quarters for the first time; dreaming; apparently stunned; drinking it all in with eyes and ears and lips; feeling the moss and branches as others feel jewels and costly lace; and on some of the little faces an expression of grave wonder, and of joy too deep for laughter.

"This ain't always 'ere, is it, Guv'nor?" one had asked. And another, whom Paul watched fingering a common fern for a long time, looked up presently and inquired if it was real— because it isn't 'arf as pretty as what *we* use!" He was the son of a scene-shifter at an East End theatre.

And a detail that made peculiarly keen appeal to his heart, a detail not witnessed by Joan or the children, was the morning ablutions in the stream, when the occupants of each tent in turn, went into the water soon after sunrise, their pinched bodies streaked by the shadow and sunlight of the dawn, their laughter and splashing filling the wood with unwonted sounds. Soap, towels, and water in plenty! Water perfumed from the hills! Faces flushed and almost rosy after the sleep in the open, and the inex-haustible draughts of air to fan them dry again!

And then the eager circle for breakfast, hatless, eyes all fixed upon the great stew-pot where he mixed the jorum of porridge! And the noise—for noise, it must be confessed, there was—as they smothered it in their tin plates with quarts of milk hot from the cow, and busily swallowed it.

"You took them straight into the Crack, you know," Joan said from her seat below.

"Everything came true," Nixie's voice was heard overhead among the branches.

Jonah clattered down past them and scampered across the lawn with Toby at his heels, for their bedtime was close at hand. The other three lay there, half hidden, a little longer, while the shadows crept down from the hills and gathered underneath. They could no longer see each other properly. For a time there was silence, stirred only by the faint rustle of the ilex leaves. Each was thinking long, deep thoughts.

"Next week," said Joan quietly, as though to herself, "the other lot will come. Your sister's as good as gold about it all."

Then, after a pause, Nixie's voice dropped down to them again:

"And had some of them really never seen a wood before?" she asked. "Fancy that! When I grow up I shall have a big wood made specially for them—the 'Wood for Lost Children' I shall call it. And you'll see about the tents and cooking, won't you, Uncle Paul? Or, perhaps," she added, "by that time I shall know how to make a real proper stew and porridge, and be able to tell them stories round the fire as you did. Don't you think so?"

"I think you know most of it already," he answered gently. "It seems to me somehow that you have always known all the important things like that."

"Oh, do you really? How splendid if I really did!" There was a slight break in her voice—ever so slight. "I should so dreadfully like to help—if I could. It's so slow getting old enough to do anything."

Paul turned his head up to her. It was too dim to see her body lying along the bough, but he could just make out her eyes peering down between the dark of the leaves, a yellow mist where her hair was, and all the rest hidden. Very eerie, very suggestive it was, to hear this little voice amid the dusk of the branches, putting his own thoughts into words. Were those tears that glistened in the round pools of blue, or was it the reflection of sunset and the coming stars that filtered past her through the thinning tree-top? Again he thought of that silver birch standing under the protection of the shaggy pine.

"Sing us something, Nixie," rose the voice of Joan from below.

"What shall I sing?"

"That thing about the two trees Uncle Paul made up."

"But he hasn't given me the tune yet!"

"The tune's still lost," murmured the deep voice from the shadows of the big fork. "I must go into the Crack and find it. That's where I found the words, at least—" The sound of his voice melted away.

"Of course," Joan was heard to say faintly, "all lost things are in there, aren't they?"

And then something queer happened that was never explained. Perhaps they all slipped through the Crack together; or perhaps Nixie's funny little singing voice floated down to them through such a filter of listening leaves that both words and tune were changed on the way into something sweeter than they actually were in themselves.

> Who told the Silver Birch tree
> The stories that we made?
> And how can she remember
> The very games we played?

Who told her heart of silver
    That, almost from her birth,
The roots of that old Pine tree
    Had sought hers under earth?

For always when the wind blows
    Her hair about the wood,
It blows across my eyes too
    Her pictured solitude.

And then Aventures gather
    On little hidden feet,
And mystery and laughter
    The magic things repeat.

For, O my Silver Birch tree,
    Full half the "things" we do,
We did—or e'er you sweetened
    The starlight and the dew!

They stood there, all in order,
    Ready and waiting even,
Before the sunlight kissed you,
    Or you, the winds of heaven.

Who told you, then, O Birch Tree,
    The 'Ventures that we play?
And how can you remember
    The wonder—and the Way?

CHAPTER XXIII

PANTHEA.	Look, sister, where a troop of spirits gather
	Like flocks of cloud in spring's delightful weather,
	Thronging in the blue air!
IONE	And see! More come.
	Like fountain-vapours when the winds are dumb,
	That climb up the ravines in scattered lines.
	And hark! Is it the music of the pines?
	Is it the lake? Is it the waterfall?
PANTHEA.	'Tis something sadder, sweeter far than all.

Prometheus Unbound.

"It's all very well for you two to play at being trees," the voice of Joan was heard to object, "but I should like to know what part I—"

"Hush! Hush! I hear them coming," Nixie said quickly with a new excitement.

She had apparently floated up higher into the ilex to the place vacated by Jonah. Her voice had a ring of the sky in it.

"Come up to where I am, and we can *all* see. They're rising already—"

"Who—what's rising?" called Joan from below; "I'm not!"

"There's something up, I expect," said Paul quickly. "I'll help you." He knew by the child's voice there was aventure afoot. "Give me your hand, Joan. And put your feet where I tell you. We're all in the Crack, remember, so everything's possible."

"Undoubtedly something's up, but it's not *me*, I'm afraid," she laughed.

"Hush! Hush! Hush!" Nixie's voice reached them from the higher branches. "Talk in whispers, please, or you'll frighten them. And be quick. They're rising everywhere. Any minute now they may be off and you'll miss them—"

Joan and Paul obeyed; though in his record of the aventure he never described the details of their ascent. A few minutes later they were perched beside the child near the rounded top of the ilex.

"It's fearfully rickety," Joan said breathlessly.

"But there's no danger," whispered Nixie,"because this is an evergreen tree, and it doesn't go with the others."

"How—'Go with the others?'" asked the two in the same breath.

"Trees," answered the child. "They're emigrating. Look! Listen!"

"Migrating," suggested Paul.

"Of course," Nixie said, poking her head higher to see into the sky. "Trees go away south in the autumn just like birds—the real trees; their insides, I mean—"

"Their spirits," Paul explained in his lowest whisper to Joan.

"That's why they lose their leaves. And in the spring they come back with all their new blossoms and things. If they find nicer places in the south, they stay, that's all. They—die. Listen—you can hear them going!"

High up in that still autumn sky there ran a sweet and curious sound, difficult to describe. Joan thought it was like the rustle of countless leaves falling: the tiny tapping noise made by a dying leaf as it settles on the ground—multiplied enormously; but to Paul it seemed that sudden, dreamlike whirr of a host of birds when they wheel sharply in mid-air—heard at a distance. There was no question about the distance at any rate.

"Are they just the trees of our woods, then?" asked Joan in a whisper that held delight and awe, "or—?"

The child laughed under her breath. "Oh, no," was the reply, "all the South of England below a certain line meets here. This is one of the great starting-places. It's just like swallows collecting on the wires. Some big tree, higher than the rest, gives a sign one night—and then all the other woods flock in by thousands. Uncle Paul knew *that!*" There was a touch in her voice of something between scorn and surprise.

"Did you, Uncle Paul?" Joan asked.

He fidgeted in his precarious perch. "I write the Record of it all, so I ought to," he answered evasively.

And high up in the autumn sky, now darkening, ran on that curious sweet sound. Across the heavens, silvery in the coming moonlight, they saw long feathery clouds drawn thinly from north to south, known commonly as mares' tails.

"Those are the tracks they follow," whispered Nixie. "Look! Now you can see them—some of them!"

Her voice was so thrilled that it startled them. But for the fact that they were in the Crack where nothing can be ever "lost," both Paul and Joan might have lost their hold and their seats—to say nothing of their lives—and crashed downwards through the branches of that astonished ilex tree. Instead, they turned their eyes upwards and stared.

They looked out over the world of tree-tops. On all sides rose Something in a silent tempest, almost too delicate for words—something that touched the air with a Presence, swift and wonderful—then was gone. With it went the faint music as of myriad wheeling birds, too small for sight. And through the sky ran a vast fluttering of green. They saw the coming stars, as it were, through immense transparencies of green, stained here and there with the washed splendours of wet and dying leaves—the greens, yellows, aye, and the reds too, of autumn. For a few passing seconds the night was positively robed with the spirit-hues of the dying year, rising rapidly in the sheets of their dim glory.

"They're off!" murmured Nixie. "It's the first flight. We *are* lucky!"

Far overhead the pathways of fleecy cloud were tinged with pale yellow as when the moon looks sometimes mistily upon the earth—tinged, then suddenly white and silvery as before.

They collect—Paul drew upon the child's account for his Record—far
over-seas upon some lonely strand or headland, and then swarm inland,
sometimes following their companions, the birds, sometimes leading them.
In countless thousands they go, yet for all their numbers never causing
more than a passing tremble of the air. Their armies add, perhaps, a shadow to the night, a new tint to the clouds that veil the moon; or, if owing to
stress of autumn weather, they start with the daylight, then the sunset
gains a strange new wonder that puzzles the heart with its beauty, and
makes unimaginative people write foolish letters to the newspapers. Their
speed makes it difficult to catch even the slightest indication of their flight;
the sky is touched with glory, there is a reflection in the river or the sea—
and they are gone! Or, perhaps, from the evergreens that stay behind, often
fringing the coast, the wind bears a message of farewell, wondrous sweet;
or some late birds, delaying their own departure, wake in the branches and
sing in little bursts of passion the joy of their own approaching escape.

And when they return, each tree in the order of its leaving, and according to its times and needs, they bring with them all the essential glory of
southern climes, and the magic of spring is due as much to the tales and
memories they have collected to talk about, as to the clear brilliance of the
new dresses with which they come to clothe their old bodies at home.

The Record of the Aventure, as Paul wrote it faithfully from the child's
description, makes curious and instructive reading, and the loneliness of
the stalwart evergreens who remain behind to face the winter brought a
pathos into the tale that all lovers of trees will readily appreciate, and may
be read by them in the published account.

Yet to Paul and Joan, to each according to temperament and cast of mind,
the little Aventure brought thoughts of a more practical bearing. To him,
especially, in the escape of the tree-spirits—of their "insides," as Nixie
intuitively phrased it—he divined an allegory of the temporary escape of
the little army of city waifs. Those boys, old in face as they were cramped
in body, had enjoyed, too, a migration that clothed them for a time, outwardly and inwardly, with some passing beauty which they could take
back to London with them just as the trees come back with the freshness
of the spring.

And this thought led necessarily to others. The little migration of their
bodies from town was important enough; but what of their minds and
souls? What chance of escape was there for these?

The conclusions are obvious enough; they need no elaboration. He had
already learned from Joan of their sufferings. His heart burned within him.
It was all mixed up in his queer poetic mind with the swift vision of the
Tree Spirits, and with the picture of Joan, Nixie, and the other children
perched like big berries in that astonished ilex tree. In due season both
berries and dreams must ripen. He was beginning to see the way.

"They're gone already," Nixie interrupted his long reverie in a whisper;
"and to-night there'll be great rains to wash away all the signs. To-morrow
morning, you'll see, half the trees will be bare."

And high in the heavens, incredibly high and faint it seemed, ran the curious sweet sound, driven farther and farther into the reaches of the night, till at last it died away altogether.

"Gone," murmured Joan, "gone!" The beauty of it touched her voice with sadness. "I wish we could go like that—as beautifully, as quietly, as easily!"

"Perhaps we do," Paul thought to himself.

"I think we do," Nixie said aloud. "Daddy did, I'm sure. I shall, too, I think—and then come back in the spring, p'rhaps."

CHAPTER XXIV

See where the child of heaven, with winged feet,
Runs down the slanted sunlight of the dawn.
Prometheus Unbound.

Very often in life, when the way seems all prepared for joy, there comes instead an unexpected time of sadness that makes all the preparation seem useless and of no purpose. Those coloured threads, whose ends and beginnings are not seen, weave this unexpected twist in the pattern, and one knows the bitterness that asks secretly, What can be the use of efforts thus rendered apparently null and void at a single stroke? forgetting the roots of faith that are thereby strengthened, and shutting the eyes to the glory of the whole pattern, which it is always the endeavour of the imagination to body forth.

And so it seemed to Paul a few weeks later when he returned to England from America, where he had been to settle up his affairs. For he had decided to sever his connection with the Lumber Company, and to devote his life henceforward to battling against the wrongs and sufferings of childhood. The call had come to him with no uncertain voice. Nixie had unintentionally sown the seeds; Joan had deliberately watered them; his own liberated imagination girded its loins to go forth as a labourer to the harvest.

Then, coming back with the joy of this approaching labour in his heart, the veil of great sadness descended upon his newly-opening life and set him in the midst of a dreadful void, a blank of pain and loneliness that nothing seemed able to fill. Nixie went from him. The Hand that gilds the stars, and touched her hair with the yellow of the sands, drew her also away. Just when her gentle companionship had justified itself for him as something ideally charming that should last always, a breath of wintry wind passed down upon that grey house under the hill, and, lo, she was gone—gone like the spirit of her little birch tree from the cruelties of December.

He was in time to say good-bye—nothing more; in time to see the awful shadow fall silently upon the wasted little face, and to feel the cold of eternal winter creep into the thin hand that lay to the last within his own. Not a single word did he utter as he sat there beside the bed, choked to the brim with feelings that never yet have known the words to clothe them. That cold entered his own heart too, and numbed it.

Nixie it was that spoke, though she, too, said little enough. The lips moved feebly. He lowered his head to catch the last breath.

"I shall come back," he heard faintly, "just as the trees do in the spring!"

The voice was in his ear. It sank down inside him, entering his very soul.

For a moment it sang there—then ceased for ever. With eyes dry and burning, he buried his head in the tangle of yellow hair upon the pillow, and when a moment later he raised them again to speak the words of comfort to his weeping sister, Nixie was no longer there to hear him or to see.

"I shall come back in the spring just as the trees do."

And so she died, leaving Paul behind in that sea of loneliness whose waves drown year by year their thousands and tens of thousands—the vast army that know not Faith. Her blue eyes, so swiftly fading, were on his to the last. It seemed to him that for a moment he had seen God. And perhaps he had; for Nixie assuredly was close to divine things, and he most certainly was pure.

ș❦

Sad things are best faced squarely, very squarely indeed; dealt with; and then—deliberately forgotten. In this way their strength, and the beauty that invariably lies within like a hidden kernel, may be appropriated and their bitterness destroyed. But such platitudes are easily said or written, and at first, when Nixie left him, Paul felt as though the world lay for ever broken at his feet.

What this elfin child had done for him must appear to some exaggerated, to many, incredible; for the relationship between them had somehow been touched with the splendour and tenderness of a world unknown to the majority. The delicate intimacy between their souls, as between souls of a like age, is difficult to realise outside the region of fantasy. Yet it had existed: in her with a simple, childlike joy that asked no questions; in him, with an attempt at analysis that only made it closer and more dear. What Paul had been to her was a secret she had taken away with her; what she had been to him, however, was to remain a most precious memory, and at the same time a source of strength and happiness that was to prove eternal.

Not, however, in the manner that actually came about—and, at first, not realised by him in any manner whatsoever.

For, at first, he found himself alone, horribly alone. What her little mystical heart of poetry had taught him is hard to name. Expression, of course, in its simpler form, and the joy of a sympathetic audience; but more than that. In all fine women lies hidden "the child"—the simple vision that pierces—and perhaps in Nixie he had divined, and ideally reconstructed for himself, the "fine woman"! Who can say? A dream so rich and tender can never be caught in a mere net of words. The truth lay buried in the depths of his being, to strengthen and to bless; and some few others may divine its presence there as well as himself perhaps. The only thing he understood clearly at the moment was that he had been robbed of an intimate little friend who had crept into every corner of his heart, and that—he was most terribly alone.

CHAPTER XXV

Donnez vos yeux, donnez vos mains,
Donnez vos mains magiciennes;
Pour me guider par les chemins
Donnez vos yeux, donnez vos mains,
Vos mains d'Infante dans les miennes.

From *Les Unes et les Autres*

There is nothing to be gained by dwelling upon sadness; the details of
Paul's suffering may be left to the imagination. It was characteristic of him
that he sought instinctively, and without cant, for the Reality that lay
behind his pain; and Reality—though seas of grief may first be plunged
through to find it—is always Joy. For love is joy, and joy is strength, and
both are aspects of the great central Reality of the life of the soul. The child
was so woven into the strands of his inmost being that her going seemed,
as it were, to draw out with her these very strands—drew them out away
from himself towards—towards what? He hardly knew how to name it.
The word "God" rarely passed his lips: towards "Reality," then; towards the
deep things he had sought all his life.

Part of himself, however, the child had taken away with her. He passed
more and more away from the things of the world, though these had never
yet held him with any security in their mesh. Nixie had gone ahead, that
was all. Before long, as years measure time at least, he would follow her.
She might even come back, "like the trees in the spring," to tell him of the
way.

His great longing, unexpressed, had always been to know something of
the Beyond—to see into the heart of things; not by the uninspired methods of an unsavoury spiritualism, or the artificial forcing-house of an audacious Magic; but by some inner, as yet undetermined, way in his own
heart. For he had always clung to the secret belief that there must be some
interior way of finding "Reality," some process, simple, piercing, profound,
that would have authority for himself, if not for all the world. In the heart
of all true mystics some such Faith is ingrained. They are born with it. It
is ineradicable—lived, but rarely spoken.

And the root of this belief it was that Nixie had unknowingly watered
and fed. Her going seemed suddenly to have coaxed it almost into flower.
His need of the great, satisfying Companion that knows no shadow of
turning was incalculably quickened thereby. Love and Nature were the
veils that screened the Beyond so thinly that he could almost see through
them; and to both these mysteries the child had led him better than she
knew.

The energy of his mystical yearnings suddenly increased a hundredfold.

Whether these remain within to poison, or go out to bless, depends, of course, upon the nature of the heart that feels them. Paul, fortunately for himself, had found ways of expression; he was always provided now with the safety of an outlet. And, for the immediate moment, the path was clear enough, and very simple. He was to comfort the mother that mourned her; himself that mourned her; the puzzled little brother and sister, and even the army of more or less disconsolate four-footed friends that missed her presence vaguely, and haunted the door of her room with the strange instinct that there must still be caresses for them within, and that for the moment she was merely hiding.

It was Smoke, the furry black fellow, however, always her favourite and his own, participant in all their old Aventures, who brought him a strange comfort by secret ways that no man understands. For Smoke asked no questions. He knew; and though he missed her in all their games, and meals, and undertakings of every kind, in house or garden, he showed no obvious symptoms of grief as a dog might have shown. And sometimes he was positively uncanny: he behaved almost as though he still saw her.

The others, however,—! With most of them out of sight was out of mind. The kittens, now growing up, purred and played as of old in the school-room, and the Chow puppies, China and Japan, more like yellow puddings than ever, tore about the house, tumbling and thudding, as though they had never known their little two-legged elfin playmate. The household dropped back into the old routine; Margaret, sadder, less alive than before, pressed down by her new grief into the semblance of a vision; and the children, hushed and pale, but gradually yielding to the stress of bursting life which at that age has no long acquaintance with grief.

It was winter, and the woods and gardens were so altered that the usual corners of play and mischief were unrecognisable. "Out-ov-doors" was dead, the sunshine unreal, the darkness hovering close even on the clear-est day. The haunts that Paul and Nixie knew were too much changed, mercifully for him, who often sought them none the less, to remind him keenly. The little silver birch tree that danced in summer before the skirts of the fir wood was bare and shivering in the winds. Behind it, however, unchanged and shaggy, still stood the dark sheltering pine, steady among the blasts.

And Paul, meanwhile, beyond the smaller sphere of his immediate duties in the grey house under the hill, took up with all the enthusiasm he could spare from sorrow the work among the lost waifs. As has been seen, he found the complete organisation ready to hand. And, to his great satisfac-tion, he found, as he became familiar with the detail, that it was work suit-ed to the best that was in him. He was the right man in the right place.

Moreover, it was Dick's scheme, and to lose himself in it was to get into touch again delightfully with the great friendship of his youth. Nixie, too, who had meant when she grew up to provide a Wood for Lost Children, seemed ever pushing him forward from behind. Thus his zeal never less-ened, and he lost himself in others to some purpose.

The test of time, of course, proved this. At the moment, however, it can only be known by the trick of "looking at the last chapter"—which is unlawful, as well as logically impossible. And, before he got so far, he had first learned another profound truth: that only he who carries in his heart a great sorrow, borne alone, can know the mystery of interior Vision, inspiring and truly marvellous, which comes from a blessing so singularly disguised as pain.

CHAPTER XXVI

I feel, I see
Those eyes which burn through smiles that fade in tears,
Like stars half quenched in mists of silver dew.
Prometheus Unbound.

The readjustment of self—the renewal—that follows upon great
bereavement having thus been faced courageously, Paul threw himself
into his work with energy. Every Friday night he came down to the house
under the hill, and every Monday morning he returned to London. But the
details of the work, beyond the fact that their fulfilment blessed both himself and those for whom he laboured, are not essential to the story of what
followed. For the history of Paul's education is more than anything else a
history of Aventures of the inner life. Outwardly, his existence was quiet
and uneventful.

Almost immediately with the disappearance of his little friend, for
instance, he discovered that the region through the Crack—the land
betweenyesserdayandtomorrow—became more real, more extraordinarily
real, than ever before. The entrances now seemed everywhere and always
close; it was the ways of exit that were difficult to find. He lived in it. Even
in London he moved among those fields of flowers, and the winter gloom
that depressed the majority only enhanced the bright sunshine that lay
about his path. His thoughts were continually following the windings of
the river to the far horizon; and the horizon, too, was wider, more enticing and mysterious, more suggestive than ever of that blue sea beyond
where he had sailed with that other Companion.

The land became mapped out and known with an intimacy that must
seem little short of marvellous to those who have never even dreamed of
the existence of so fair a country. For, the truth was, his Companion, who
was now his guide and leader, had suddenly revealed herself.

It came about a few days after the funeral—when the emptiness and
hush of sorrow that lay over the house found its exact spiritual
correspondence in the silence and sense of desolation that filled his own
heart. He was in his bedroom, battling with that loneliness in loneliness
which at the first had threatened to overwhelm him. He had just left his
sister's side, having soothed her with what comfort he could into the sleep
of weariness and exhaustion. By the open window, as so often before, he
stood, staring into the damp winter night. Smoke moved restlessly to and
fro behind him, sometimes sitting down to wash, sometimes jumping on
the bed and sofa as though to search for something it could never find.
Mrs. Tompkyns, who had scratched at the door a few minutes before, for
the first time in her life, and for reasons known to none but herself and

her black companion, lay at last curled up before the fire.

The room was filled with a soft presence, once silvery and fragrant, but now draped with the newly woven shadows that rendered it invisible. The invasion was irresistible. His heart ached. He knew quite well that his own soul, too, was being measured for its garment of shadow—garment that, unlike ordinary clothes, fits better and closer with every year. He was in that dangerous mood when such measurements are made only too easily, and the lassitude of grief accepts the trying-on with a kind of soft, almost pleasurable, acquiescence—when, sharply and suddenly, a sound was audible outside the window that instantly galvanised him into a state of resistance. The night, hitherto still as the grave, sighed in response to a rising wind. And through his being at the same moment ran the answering little Wind of Inspiration some one had taught him to find always when he sought it.

And the sound brought comfort. It was as though an invisible hand had reached down inside him and touched the source of joy!

Paul turned quickly. Mrs. Tompkyns was awake on the mat. Smoke rubbed against his legs. On the table, where he had spread them a few minutes before, were the black tie, the mended socks, the unused bottle for nettle stings and scratches, and beside them the faded spray of birch leaves, now withered and shrivelled. And, as he looked, the wind entered the room behind him, and he saw that the brown branch turned half over towards him. It rattled faintly as it moved. He was just in time to rescue it from Smoke, who saw in the sound and movement an invitation to play. He pinned it out of reach upon the wall over the mantelpiece.

And it was just as he finished, that this sound of wind sighing through the dripping and leafless trees outside was followed by another sound—one that he recognised.... There was a rush and a leap, a swift, whistling roar—and the next second he found himself among the sunny fields of flowers that he knew, and heard the water lapping at his feet... through the Crack!

"Everybody's thin *somewhere*," was what he almost expected to hear; but what he did hear was another sentence, followed by merry and delicious laughter: "Everybody can be happy somewhere!"

And close in front of him, rising, it seemed, out of the reeds and waves and yellow sands, stood—that veiled Companion whom he knew to be a part of himself.

She was turned away from him so that he could not see her face, yet he instantly divined a movement of her whole body towards him. Something within himself rushed out to meet her halfway. His life stirred mightily. The thrill of discovery came close. The next second his arms were about her and she was looking straight into his eyes.

But her own eyes were no longer veiled; her laughing face was clear as the day; the figure that he held so close was Nixie, child and woman. If ever it can be possible for two beings to melt into one, it was possible then. Each possessed the other; each slipped into the other.

"Face to face at last!" he heard himself cry. "Bless your little fairy heart! Why in the world didn't I guess you sooner?"

A flame of happiness sped through him, and grief ran away utterly. The sense of loss that had numbed his soul vanished. And when she only answered him by the old mischievous laughter, he asked again: "But how did you disguise yourself so well—your voice, and everything—? Even if your face *was* veiled I ought to have recognised you! It's too wonderful!"

"It was you who disguised me!" she replied, standing up close in front of him, and playing with his waistcoat buttons as of old. "Your thoughts about me got twisted—sometimes. You thought too much. You should have *felt* only."

"They never shall again," he exclaimed.

"They never can. We are face to face now."

Paul turned to look again more closely. He saw her with extraordinary detail and vividness. It was indeed Nixie, but Nixie exactly as he had always wanted her, without quite knowing it himself; at least, without acknowledging it. No gulf of age was there to separate them now. She was the perfect Companion, for he had made her so. He smoothed her hair as they turned to walk by the river, and he caught the old childish perfume of it as it spread untidily over his shoulder, her eyes like dropped stars shining through it.

"Isn't it awfully jolly?" she whispered: "we can have twice as many aventures now, and you can go on writing them for Jonah and Toby just the same as before, only faster."

He felt her hand steal into his; his heart became most strangely merged with hers. He had known a similar experience in Canadian forests, when the beauty of Nature had sometimes caught him up till he scarcely felt himself distinct enough from it to realise that he was separate. He now knew himself as close to her as that. It was exquisite and yet so simple that a little child might have felt it—without perplexity. Perhaps it was precisely what children always *did* feel towards what they loved, animate or inanimate.

"But how is it you can come so close?" he asked, though he fancied that he thought, rather than spoke, the question.

"Because, in the important sense, you are still a child," he caught the answer, "and always have been, and always will be."

The whole world belonged to him. In the midst of the sea of sorrow he had discovered the little island of happiness.

"We never can lose each other—now!" he said.

"As long as you think about me," she answered. "Please always think hard, veryhardindeed thoughts. Through the Crack you can find everything that's lost—."

"And we're through the Crack now."

"Rather!"

 è▲

CHAPTER XXVII

....Straightway I was 'ware,
So weeping, how a mystic Shape did move
Behind me, and drew me backward by the hair;
And a voice said in mastery, while I strove,
"Guess now who holds thee ?"—"Death," I said. But there
The silver answer rang—"Not Death, but Love."

                                                        E. B. B.

....It was only when the sky grew dark and the shadow of clouds fell over that sunny landscape that he realised he was still standing half dressed beside a dying fire, and that through the open window behind him the cold night air brought discomfort that made him shiver. He drew the curtains, lit a candle, spoke a soft word or two to the curled-up forms of Mrs. Tompkyns and Smoke, who were far too busy in their own Crack-land to trouble about replying, and so finally got into bed.

He felt happier, strangely comforted. The wings of memory and phantasy, withdrawing softly, left a soothed feeling in his heart. In that region of creative imagination known as the "Crack" he always found peace and at least a measure of joy. Until sleep should come to captain his forces, he deliberately turned the current of his thoughts to the work he was about to take up in London. Nixie, Joan, Dick—all helped him. His will erected an iron barrier against the insidious attacks of sadness—the disease which strikes at the roots of effort. He would dream his dreams, but also, he would do his work....

The shadows thickened about the house, crowding from the heart of winter. The fire died down. The room lay still. It was between one and two o'clock in the morning, when silence in the country is a real silence, and the darkness weighs. Chasing Smoke and Mrs. Tompkyns down the winding corridors of dream—Paul slept.

A faint sound in the room a little later made him stir in his sleep and smile. His lips moved, as though in that land of dreams where he wandered some one spoke to him and he answered. Then the sound was repeated, and he woke with a start, sat up in bed, and stared hard into the darkness.

The fire was quite out; nothing was visible but the dim frame of the window on his right where he had forgotten to draw the curtains. A glimmer of light revealed the sash. Thinking it must be the winter dawn, he was about to lie down again and resume his slumbers, when the sound that had first wakened him again made itself audible.

A slight shiver ran down his spine, for the sound seemed to bring over some of the wonder of his dreams into that dark and empty room. Then, with a tiny revelation of certainty, the knowledge came that he was wide awake, and that the sound was close in front of him. Moreover, he knew at once that it was neither Smoke nor Mrs. Tompkyns. It was a sound, deliberately produced, with conscious intelligence behind it. And it shot through him with the sweetness of music. It was like a breath of wind that rustled through a swinging branch—of a birch tree; as though such a branch waved to and fro softly above his head.

His first idea was that some one was in the room, and had taken down the spray of withered leaves from the wall; and he strained his eyes in the direction of the mantelpiece, trying to pierce the darkness. In vain, of course. All he could distinguish was that something moved gently to and fro like a spot of light—almost like a fire-fly, yet white—about the room.

From some deep region of sleep where he had just been, the atmosphere of dream was still, perhaps, about him. Yet this was no dream. There *was* somebody in the room with him, somebody alive, somebody who wished to claim his attention—who had already spoken to him before he woke. He knew it unmistakably; he even remembered what had been said to him while yet asleep! "How *can* you go on sleeping when I am here, trying to get at you?"

It was just as if the words still trembled on the air. Confusedly, scarcely aware what he did, yet already thrilling with happiness, his lips formed an answer:

"Who are you? What is it you want?"

There was a pause of intense silence, during which his heart hammered in his temples. Then a very faint whisper gathered through the darkness: "I promised...."

The point of light wavered a little in the air, then came low and seemed to settle on the end of the bed. Into the clear and silent spaces of his lonely soul there swam with it the presence of some one who had never died, and who could never die.

"Is that *you*—?" The name seemed incredible, for this was no Aventure through the Crack, yet he uttered it after an imperceptible moment of hesitation—"*Nixie?*"

Even then he could not believe an answer would be forthcoming. The light, however, moved slightly, and again came the faint tones of a voice, a singing voice:

"Of course it is!" There was a curious suggestion of huge distance about it, as though it travelled like an echo across vast spaces. "I'm here, close beside you; closer than ever before."

He heard the words with what can only be described as a spiritual sensation—the peace and gratitude that follow the passion of strong prayer, of prayer that believes it will be heard and answered.

"You know *now*—don't you?" continued the tiny singing voice, "because I've told you."

"Yes," he answered, also very low, "I know now." For at first he could think of nothing else to say. A huge excitement moved in him. Those invisible links of pure aspiration by which the soul knits herself inwardly to God seemed suddenly tightened in the depths of his being. He understood that this was a true thing, and possible.

"You've come back—like the trees in the spring," he whispered stammeringly, after another pause, gazing as steadily as he could at the point of clear light so close in front of him.

"The real part of me," she explained; "the real part of me has come back."

"The real part," he echoed in his bewilderment. He began to understand.

But even then it all seemed too utterly strange and wonderful to he true; and a subtle confirmation of the child's presence that followed immediately only added at first to his increasing amazement. For both Smoke and Mrs. Tompkyns, he became aware, had jumped up softly upon the foot of the bed, and were sitting there, purring loudly with pleasure, close beneath the fleck of light. And their action made him seek the further confirmation of his own senses. He leaned forwards, hesitating in his bewilderment between the desire to find the matches and the desire to touch the speaker with his hands.

But even in that darkness his intention was divined instantly. The light slid away like a wee torch carried on wings.

"No, Uncle Paul," whispered the voice farther off, "not the matches. Light makes it more difficult for me." He sank back against the pillows, frightened at the reality of it all. The old familiar name, too, "Uncle Paul," was almost more than he could bear.

"Nixie—!" he stammered, and then found it impossible to finish the sentence.

Then she laughed. He heard her silvery laughter in the room, exactly as he had heard it a hundred times before, spontaneous, mischievous, and absolutely natural. She was amused at his perplexity, at his want of faith; at the absurd difficulty he found in believing. He lay quite still, breathing hard, wondering what would come next; still trying to persuade himself it was all a dream, yet growing gradually convinced in spite of himself that it was not.

"And don't come too near me," he heard her voice across the room. "Never try and touch me, I mean. *Think of me at your centre.* That's the real way to get near."

Very slowly then, after that, he began to accept the Supreme Aventure. He talked. He asked questions, though never the obvious and detailed sort of questions it might have been expected he would ask. For it was now borne in upon him, as she said, that only her *real* part had come back, and that only *his* real part, therefore, was in touch with her. It was, so to speak, a colloquy of souls in which physical and material things had no interest. His very first question brought the truth of this home to him with singular directness. He asked her what the tiny light was that he saw moving to and fro like a little torch.

"But I didn't know there was a light," she answered. "Where I am it is all light! I see you perfectly. Only—you look so young, Uncle Paul! just like a boy! About my own age, I mean."

And it is impossible to describe the delight, the mystical rapture that came to him as he heard her. The words, "Where I am it is all light," brought with them a sudden sense of reality that was too convincing for him to doubt any longer. From her simple description he recognised a place that he knew. But, at the same time, he understood that it was no *place* in the ordinary sense of the word, but rather a *state* and a *condition*. He himself in his deepest dreams had been there too. That light had some-times in brief moments of aspiration shone for him. And the curious sense of immense distance that came so curiously with her tiny voice came because there was really no distance at all. She was no longer conditioned by space or time. Those were limitations of life in the body, temporary scales of measurement adopted by the soul when dealing with temporary things. Whereas Nixie was free.

A sense of happiness deep as the sea, of peace, bliss, and perfect rest that could never know hurry or alarm, surged through him in a tide. He thought, with a thrill of anticipation, of the time when his own eyes would be opened, and he should see as clearly as she did. But instantly the rebuke came.

"Oh! You must not think about that," she said with a laugh; "you have a lot to do first, a lot more aventures to go through!"

As she spoke the light slid nearer again and settled upon the foot of the bed. His thoughts were evidently the same as spoken words to her. She knew all that passed in his mind, the very feelings of his heart as well. This was indeed companionship and intimacy. He remembered how she had told him all about it in the Crack weeks ago, before he realised who she was, and before he knew her face to face. And at the same moment he noticed another curious detail of her presence, namely, that the little torch—for so he now called it to himself—in passing before the mirror produced no reflection in the glass. Yet, if his eyes could perceive it, there ought to have been a refraction from the mirror as well—a reflection! Did he then only perceive it with his interior vision? Was his spiritual sight already partially opened?

"That's your 'terpretation of me—inside yourself," he caught her swift whisper in reply, for again she *heard* his thought; and he almost laughed out aloud with pleasure to notice the long word decapitated as her habit always was on earth. "In your thoughts I'm a sort of light, you see."

The explanation was delightful. He understood perfectly. The thought of Nixie had always come to him, even in earthly life, in the terms of bright-ness. And his love marvelled to notice, too, that she still had the old pierc-ing vision into the heart of things, and the characteristically graphic way of expressing her meaning.

The purring of the cats made itself audible. They were both "kneading" the bed-clothes by his feet, as happy as though being stroked.

"No, they don't see," she explained the moment the thought entered his mind; "they only feel that I'm here. Lots of animals are like that. It's the way dogs know 'sti'ctively if a person's good or bad."

Oh, how the animals after this would knit him to her presence! No wonder he had already found comfort with them that no human being could give.... The thought of his sister flashed next into his brain—the difficulty of helping her—

"I tried to get at her before I came here to you," he heard, "but her room was all dark. It was like trying to get inside a cloud. She's cold and shadowy—and ever such a long way off. It's diff'cult to explain."

"I think I understand," he whispered.

"You can get closer than I can."

"I'll try."

"Of course. You must."

It was Nixie's happiness that seemed so wonderful and splendid to him. Her voice almost sang; and laughter slipped in between the shortest sentences even. Brightness, music, and pure joy were about her like an atmosphere. He was breathing a rarefied air, cool, scented, and exhilarating. He had already known it when playing with the children and enjoying their very-wonderful-indeed aventures; only now it was raised to a still higher power. In its very essence he knew it.

"Toby and Jonah are with me the moment they sleep," she continued, ever following his least thought. "The instant their bodies fold up they shoot across here to me. Toby comes easiest. She's a girl, you see. And Daddy's here too—"

"Dick?" he cried, memory and affection surging through him with a sudden passion.

"Of course. You've thought about him so much. He says you've always been close to each other—"

The voice broke off suddenly, and the torch of light moved to and fro as though agitated. Paul heard no sound, and saw no sign, but again, into the clear and silent spaces of his soul, now opened so marvellously, so blessedly to receive, there swam the consciousness of another Presence...

There was a long pause, while memory annihilated all the intervening years at a single stroke....

His mind was growing slightly confused with it all. His mortal intelligence wearied and faltered a little with the effort to understand how time and distance could be thus destroyed. He was not yet free as these others were free.

"How is it, then, that you can stay?" he asked presently, when the light held steady again. By "you" he meant "both of you." Yet he did not say it. This was what seemed so wonderful in their perfect communion; words really were not necessary. Afterwards, indeed, he sometimes wondered whether he actually spoke at all.

"I was going on—at first," came the soft answer, "when I heard something calling me, and found I couldn't. I had something to do here."

"What?" he ventured under his breath,

"*You!*" She laughed in his face, so to speak. "You, of course. Part of you is in me, so I couldn't go on without you. But when you are ready, and have done your work, we'll go on together. Daddy is waiting, too. Oh, it's simply splendid—a very-splendid-indeed aventure, you see!" Again she laughed through that darkened room till it seemed filled with white light, and the light flooded his very soul as he heard her.

"You *will* wait, Nixie?" he asked.

"I *must* wait. Both of us must wait. We are all together, you see."

And, after another long pause, he asked another question:

"This work, then, that keeps me here?"

"Your London boys, of course. There's no one in the whole world who can do it so well. You've been picked out for it; that's what really brought you home from America!" And she burst out into such a peal of laughter that Paul laughed with her. He simply couldn't help himself. He felt like singing at the same time. It was all so happy and reasonable and perfect.

"You've got the money and the time and the 'thusiasm," she went on; "and over here there are thousands and millions of children all watching you and clapping their hands and dancing for joy. I've told them all the Aventures you wrote, but they think this is the best of all—the London-Boys-Aventure!"

He felt his heart swell within him. It seemed that the child's hair was again about his eyes, her slender arms clasping his neck, and her blue eyes peering into his as when she begged him of old in the nursery or school-room for an aventure, a story.

"So you'll never give it up, will you, Uncle Paul?" she sang, in that tiny soft voice through the darkness.

"Never," he said.

"Promise?"

"Promise," he replied.

The thought of those "thousands and millions" of children watching his work from the other side of death was one that would come back to strengthen him in the future hours of discouragement that he was sure to know.

And much more she told him besides. They talked, it seemed, for ever—yet said so little. Into mere moments—such was the swift and concentrated nature of their intimacy—they compressed hours of earthly conversation; for his thoughts were heard and answered as soon as born within him, and a whole train of ideas that the lips ordinarily stammer over in difficult detail crowded easily into a single expression—a thought, a desire, a question half uttered, and then a reply that comprehended all. There was no labour or weariness, no sense of effort.

Moreover, when at length he heard her faint whisper, "Now I must go," it conveyed no sense of departure or loss. She did not leave him. It was more as though he closed a much-loved book and replaced it in his pocket. The pictures evoked do not leave the mind because the cover is closed; they remain, on the contrary, to be absorbed by the heart; Nixie's silvery presence was *in him;* he would always feel her now, even when his thoughts seemed busy with outer activities.

The little torch flickered and was gone; but as Paul gazed into the darkness of the room he knew that the light had merely slipped down deep into himself to burn as an unfailing beacon at the centre of his soul. And then it was that he realised other curious details for the first time. Some of the more ordinary faculties of his mind, it seemed, had been in suspension during the amazing experience, while others had been exalted as in trance. For it now came to him that he had actually *seen* her—with a clearness that he had never known before. That torch lit up her little form as a lantern lights up a person holding it in darkness. Just as he had felt all the sweet and essential points of her personality, so also he had been vividly aware of her figure in the terms of sight—eyes, hair, sunburned little hands, and twinkling feet. Her very breath and perfume even!

If the working of his ordinary senses had been in abeyance so that he hardly knew the hunger for common sight and touch, he now realised that it was because they had been replaced by these higher senses with their keener, closer satisfaction. And this intimate knowledge of her was as superior to the ordinary methods as flying is to crawling—or, better still, as a draught of water in the throat is to dipping the fingers in the cup.

For who, indeed, shall define the standard of reality? And who, when the senses are such sorry reporters, shall declare with authority that one thing is false and could not happen, and another is true and actually did happen?

Experiences of the transcendental order are, perhaps, beyond the power of precise words to describe, for they are not common enough to have become incorporated into the language of a race. And words are clumsy and inadequate symbols at best. The deepest thoughts, as the deepest experiences, ever evade them. It is difficult to convey the sense of fierce reality the presence of Nixie brought to him. It flooded and covered him; spread through and over him like light; entered into his essential being to cherish and to feed, just as the body assimilates earthly nourishment. He absorbed her. She nourished while she blessed him.

She had told him the secret: *to think centrally.* He now began to understand how much nearer he could be to others by thinking strongly of them than by walking at their side. Physical touch is distant compared to the subtle intimacy of the desiring mind. The mystical conception of union with God came home to him as something practically possible.

Yet when he got up a few minutes later to write down the conversation as he remembered it, the mere lighting of the candle, the noise of the match, the dipping of his pen in the ink—all contrived somehow to bring him down to a lower order of things that dimmed most strangely the memory of what had just passed. Most of what he had heard escaped him. He could not frame it into words. All he could recapture is what has been here set down so briefly and baldly.

It then seemed to him—the thought laboured to and fro in his mind as he got back into bed and sleep came over him—that it was only the Higher Self in him that had been in communication with the child. The eternal part of him had talked with the eternal part of her. In the body, however, this was commonly submerged. Her presence had temporarily evoked it. It now had returned to its Throne at the core of his being.

All that he remembered of the colloquy was the little portion that, as it were, had filtered through into his normal self. The rest, the main part, however, was not lost. He had absorbed it. If he could not recall the actual words and language, he understood—it was his last thought before sleep caught him—that its *results* would remain for ever.

And those who have known similar experiences will understand without more words. The rest will never understand. Perhaps, after all, the best and purest form of memory is—*results*.

CHAPTER XXVIII

.... Ne son giá morto; e ben ch' albergo cangi,
resto in te vivo, ch' or mi Verdi e piangi,
se l' un nell' altro amante si trasforma.

And one of the clearest impressions that remained next morning when he woke was that he had actually *seen* her. The reality of it increased with the daylight instead of faded. While he dressed he sang to himself, until it occurred to him that his signs of joy might be misunderstood by any of the household who heard; and then he stopped singing and moved about the room, smiling and contented.

Something of the radiance of that little white torch still seemed in the air. The heavy gloom of the chill December morning could not smother it. Something of it remained too about him all day like a halo; looking out of his eyes; communicable, as it were, from the very surface of his skin to all with whom he came in contact. His sister, especially, and the children felt the comfort of his presence. They followed him about from room to room; they clung close; they were instinctively aware that peace and strength emanated from him, though little guessing the real source of his serene and tranquil atmosphere.

For, of course, he told no one of what had happened. During the day, indeed, it lay in him submerged and unassertive, like the presence of some great glowing secret, feeding the sources of energy for all his little outward duties and activities, yet never claiming individual attention itself. Only with the fall of night, when the doings of the day were instinctively laid aside like a garment no longer required, did it again swim up upon him out of the depths, and speak.

"Now!" he heard the tiny singing voice, "we can be alone. Your body's tired. I can get closer to you."

"I've felt you by me all day, though," he said, as though it were the most natural thing in the world.

"Of course," came the answering whisper, soft as moonlight, "because I never left you for a single moment. I was in everything you did—in your very words. Once or twice, I even got into mother too, *through you,* and made her feel better. Wasn't that splendid?"

Paul longed to give the child one of his old hugs—to feel her little warm and sunny body pressed against his own. Instead, her laughter echoed suddenly all about the room.

"That's impossible now!" he heard. "I'm ever so much closer this way. You'll soon get used to it, you know!"

This spontaneous laughter was the music to which all their talks were set. He laughed too, and blew the candles out.

"I tried very hard to say the true things," he murmured, referring to her remark about comforting his sister.

"I know you did. That's how I got into her—through you. You must go on and on trying. In the end we'll get her all soft and happy again. She'll feel me without knowing it."

Suddenly it struck him that, although the room was dark, he did not see the light of the little torch as before. He missed it. He was just going to ask why it was absent when the child caught his thought and replied of her own accord:

"Because it's spread all over now, instead of being just a point. You are in it, I mean. There's light everywhere about you, and I see you much clearer than last time."

The explanation described exactly what he felt himself.

"Let them in, please," Nixie suddenly interrupted his thoughts again. "They're both coming up the stairs. It was very naughty of you to forget them, you know."

After a moment of puzzled hesitation he understood what she meant, and was out of bed and across the floor. He did not wait to light a candle, but opened the door and stood there waiting in the darkness. Almost at once two soft, furry things brushed past his feet as Smoke, followed by Mrs. Tompkyns, marched into the room, uttering that curious sharp sound of pleasure which is something between a purr and a cry. They disappeared among the shadows beyond the fireplace, and Paul sprang back into bed again pleased that they were there, yet annoyed with himself for having forgotten them.

"But it was my fault *really*," she laughed. "I've been with them out in the garden, and they've only just got in through the pantry window. My presence excites them awfully. Oh, it's all right," she added quickly, in reply to his further thought; "Barker's very late to-night doing the silver. But he'll shut the window before he goes."

It was his turn to laugh. She had caught his thought about the window almost before it reached the surface of his mind. Moreover, he found that both Mrs. Tompkyns and Smoke had very cold wet soles under their padded little feet.

In this way, most strangely, sweetly, naturally, even the trivial details of their daily life as they had always known it together, intermingled with the talk that was often very earnest, mystical, and pregnant with meanings. It was in every sense a continuation of their former relationship, touched on her side with a greater knowledge—almost as though she had suddenly developed to the point she might have reached in time upon the earth; on his side, with a delicate sense of accepting guidance from some one with greater privileges than himself, who had come back on purpose to help and inspire him.

For more and more it seemed to partake of the nature of genuine inspiration. Speech came direct and swift as thought, without hesitation or stammering as in the flesh. She told him many things, often quaintly enough expressed, but that yet seemed to hold the kernel of deep truths. There had never been the least break in their companionship, it seemed.

"I knew all this before," she said, after a singular exchange of questions and answers about the nature of communion with invisible sources of mood and feeling, "only I suppose my brain had not got big enough, or whatever it was, to tell it. Like your poets you used to tell me about who couldn't find their rhymes, perhaps."

And her laughter flowed about him in a rippling flood that instantly woke his own. They always laughed. They felt so happy. It was a communion between old souls that surely had bathed deeply in the experiences of life before they had become imprisoned in the particular bodies known as Paul Rivers and Margaret Christina Messenger.

He became convinced, too, more and more that she really did not speak at all—that no actual sound set the waves of air in motion but that she put her words into him in the form of thoughts, and that he it was, in order to grasp them clearly, who clothed them with the symbols of sound and language. It was essentially of the nature of inspiration. She *blew* the ideas into his heart and mind.

And many things that he asked her were undoubtedly little more than his own thoughts, half-formed and vague, lying in the depths of him.

"Then, over there, where you now are, is it—more real? Are you, as it were, one stage nearer to the great Reality? What's it like—?"

"It's through the real 'Crack,' I think," she answered. "Everything is here that I imagined—but *really* imagined—on earth. And people who imagined nothing, or wanted only the world, find very little here."

"Then is the change very great—?"

"It doesn't seem to me like a change at all. I've been here before for visits. Now I've come to stay, that's all!"

"You yourself have not changed?"

She roared with laughter, till he felt that his question was really absurd. "Of course not! How can I change? I'm always Nixie, wherever I am!"

"But you feel different—?" he insisted.

"I feel better," she answered, still laughing. "I feel awfully jolly."

Then after a long pause he asked another question. It was really a question he was always asking in one form or another, only he had never yet put it so directly perhaps. He whispered it from a grave and solemn heart:

"Are you nearer to—God, do you think?"

It was a word he rarely used. In his conversations with the child on earth he had never once used it. She waited a long time before replying. Instinctively, very subtly, it came to him that she did not know exactly what he meant.

"I'm *in* and *with* Everything there is—Everywhere," she said softly. "And I couldn't possibly be nearer to anything than I am."

More than that she could not explain, and Paul never asked similar questions again. He understood that they were really unanswerable.

And it was the same with other thoughts, thoughts referring to the fundamental conditions of temporal existence, that is. Nothing, for instance, made time and space seem less real than the way she answered questions involving one or other. Out of curiosity he had gone to the trouble of reading up other records of spirit communion—the literature (saving the mark) of Spiritualism brims over with them—and he had asked her some question with regard to the detailed geography there given.

"But there's no *place* at all where I am," the child laughed. "I am just *here*. There was no place really in our Aventures, was there? Place is only with you on earth!"

And another time, talking of the "future" when he should come to join herself and Dick at the close of his earthly pilgrimage, she said between bursts of the merriest laughter he had ever known: "But that's now! already! You come; you join us; we *are* all together—always!"

And when he insisted that he could not possibly be in two places at once, and reminded her that she had already told him she was "waiting" for his arrival, the only reply he could get was this jolly laughter, and the assurance that he was "awfully muddled and c'fused " and would "never understand it *that* way!"

The main thing these "silent" conversations taught him seemed to be that Death brings no revolutionary change as regards character; the soul does not leap into a state much better or much worse than it knew before; the opportunities for discipline and development continue gradually just as they did in the body, only under different conditions; and there is no abrupt change into perfection on the one hand, or into desolation on the other. He gathered, too, that these "conditions" depended very largely upon the kind of life—especially the kind of thought—that the personality had indulged on earth. The things that Nixie "imagined" and yearned for, she found.

His communion with her became, as time passed, more frequent and more real, and soon ceased to confine itself only to the quiet night hours. She was with him all day long, whenever he needed her. She guided him in a thousand unimportant details of his life, as well as in the bigger interests of his work in London with his waifs. And in murky London she was just as close to him as in the perfumed stillness of the Dorsetshire garden, or in the retirement of his own chamber....

And one singular feature of their alliance was that it continued even in sleep. For, sometimes, he would wake in the morning after what had been apparently a dreamless night, yet later in the day there would steal over him the memory of a long talk he had enjoyed with the child during the hours of so-called unconsciousness. Dreams, forgotten in the morning, often, of course, return in this fashion during the day. There is nothing new or unusual in it. Only with him it became so frequent that he now rose to the day's work with a delightful sense of anticipation: "Perhaps later in the day I shall remember! Perhaps we have been together all night!"

And in this connection he came to notice two things: first, that after these nights together, at first forgotten, he woke wonderfully refreshed, blessed, peaceful in mind and body; and secondly, that what recalled the conversation later was always contact with some object or other that had been associated with the child. Thus—the picturesquely-mended socks, the medicine bottle for scratches, or the spray of birch leaves, now preserved between the pages of his Blake, never failed in this latter respect.

It was curious, too, how the alliance persisted and fortified itself during the repose of the body; as though, during sleep, the eternal portion of himself with which the child communed, enjoyed a greater measure of freedom. It recalled the closing lines of a sonnet he had always admired, though his own experience was true in a literal sense hardly contained, probably, in the heart of the poetess:

> But when sleep comes to close each difficult day,
>   When night gives pause to the long watch I keep,
>   And all my bonds I needs must loose apart,
>
> Must doff my will as raiment laid away
>   *With the first dream that comes with the first sleep*
>   *I run, I run, I am gathered to thy heart.*

He filled a book with these talks as the years passed, though to give them in more detail could serve little purpose but to satisfy a possible curiosity. They had value and authority for himself, but for the majority might seem to contain little sense, or even coherence. They expressed, of course, his own personal interpretation of life and the universe. And this was quite possibly poetic, queer, fantastic—for others. Yet it was his own. He had learned his own values in his own way, and was now engaged in sorting them out with Nixie's fairy help to guide him.

And all souls that find themselves probably do likewise. The strength and blessing they shed about them as a result is beneficial, but the close details of the process by which they have "arrived" can only seem to the world at large unintelligible, possibly even ridiculous; and this late interior blossoming of Uncle Paul, though it actually happened, must seem to many a tissue of dreams knit together with a strange fantastic nonsense.

CHAPTER XXIX

Donnez vos yeux, donnez vos mains,
Donnez vos mains surnaturelles:
Pour me conduire aux lendemains
Donnez vos yeux, donnez vos mains,
Vos mains comme deux roses frêles.

And thus, as the region where he met and held communion with the freed child seemed to draw deeper and deeper into his interior being, the reality and value of the experience increased.

That there was some kind of definite external link, however, was equally true; for the cats, as well as certain other of the animals, most certainly were aware sometimes of her presence. They showed it in many and curious ways. But it was distinctly a shock to Paul to learn one day from his sister that queer stories were afoot concerning himself; that some of the simple country folk declared they had seen "Mr Rivers walking with a young lady that was jest like Miss Nixie, only taller," who disappeared, however, the moment the observer approached. And the way the household felt her presence was, perhaps, not less remarkable, for more than one of the servants gave notice because the house had become "haunted," and there had been seen a "smallish white figure, all shiny and dancing," in his bedroom, or going down the corridor towards his study.

Perhaps the glamour of his vivid creative thought had cast its effect upon these untrained imaginations, so that his vision was temporarily communicated to them too. Or, perhaps, they had actually seen what they described. But, whatever the explanation may be, the effect upon himself was to increase, if that were possible, the reality of the whole occurrence...

And when the spring came round again with its charged memories of perfume, and sight, and the singing of its happy winds; when the tree-spirits returned to their garden haunts, all flaming with the beauty of new dresses gathered over-seas; when the silver birch tree combed out her glittering hair to the sun and shook her leaves in the very face of that old pine tree—then Paul felt in himself, too, the rejuvenation that was going forward in all the world around him. He tasted in his heart all the regenerative forces that were bursting into form and energy with the spring, and knew that the pain and desolation he had felt temporarily in the winter were only spiritual growing-pains and the passing distress of a soul forging its way outwards through development to the best possible Expression it could achieve.

For Nixie came back, too, gay and glorious like the rest of the world—sometimes dressed in blossoms of lilac or laburnum, sometimes with skirts of daisies and feet resting upon the Little Winds, sometimes with the soft hood of darkness over her head, the cloak of night about her shoulders, the stars caught all shivering in her hair, and dusk in the deeps of her eyes....

His life became "inner" in the best sense—a Life within a Life; not given over to useless dreaming, but ever drawing from the inner one the sustenance that provided the driving force for the outer one: the mystic as man of action!

The Wind of Inspiration blew for him now always, and steadily; but it was no longer the little wind that stirred the measure of his personal emotion into stammering verse, but the big, eternal wind that "blew the stars to flame," and at the same time impelled him irresistibly along the path of High A'venture to the loss of Self in work for others...

"Then why is it we are in the body—and spend so much time there?" he asked in one of those intimate and mysterious conversations he held with the child to the very end of his life. "Why need the soul descend to such clumsy confinings?"

For their talk was very close now about "real things," and neither found any difficulty in the words of question or answer.

"To get experience that can only be got through the pains of limitation," the answer sang within him, as he lay there upon the lawn beneath the cedars, absorbing the spring beauty. "Everything is doing the same thing everywhere—from Smoke, Mrs. Tompkyns and Madmerzelle, right up to you, me, Daddy, and the waifs! They all have a bit of Reality in them working upwards to God. Even stones and plants and trees are learning experiences they could learn only in those particular forms—"

"I know it! Of course, I know it!" Paul interrupted, with a rush of joy in his heart he could not restrain; "but go on and tell me more, for I love to hear your little voice say it all."

"It's only, perhaps, that the stones are learning patience and endurance; the flowers sweetness; the trees strength and comfort; and the rivers joy. Later they change about, so that in the end each 'Bit of Reality' has gathered all possible experiences in nature before it passes on into men and women.

"Think, Uncle Paul, of the joy of a stone, who after centuries of patience and endurance, cramped and pressed down, knows suddenly the freedom of wind and sea! Of the restlessness of flame that, after ages of leaping unsatisfied to the sky, learns the repose of a tree, moved only by the outside forces of wind and rain! And think of the delight of all these when they pass still further upwards and reach the stage of consciousness in animals and men—and in time enter the region of development where I— where you and I, and all we knew and loved, continue together, ever climbing, fighting, learning—"

It was curious. Afterwards he could never remember the way she ended the sentence. For the life of him he could not write it down. Definite recollection failed him, together with the loss of the actual words. Only the general sense remained in such a way as to open to his inner eye a huge vista of spiritual endeavour and advance that left him breathless and dizzy when he contemplated it, but at the same time charged most splendidly with courage and with hope.

"Then the pains of limitation," he remembered asking, "the anguish of impossible yearnings that vainly seek expression—these are symptoms of growth that in the end may produce something higher and nobler?"

"Must!" he heard the answer amid a burst of happy laughter, as though from where she stood it were possible to look back upon earthly pangs and see them in the terms of joy; "just like any other suffering! Like the stress of heat and pressure that turns common clay into gems—"

He interrupted her swiftly, high hopes crowding through his spirit like the rush of an army.

"Then the life in us all—the 'Bits of Reality' in you and me—have passed through all possible forms in their huge upward journey to reach our present stage—?" He stammered amid a multitude of golden memories, half captured.

"Of course. Uncle Paul, of course!" he caught deep, deep within him the silvery faint reply. "And your love and sympathy with trees, winds, hills, with all Nature, even with animals"—again her laughter ran out to him like a song—"is because you passed long ago through them all, and *half remember.* You still *feel with* them, and your imagination for ever strives to reconstruct the various beauty known in each stage. You remember in the depths of you the longings of every particular degree—even of the time when your soul was less advanced, and groping upwards as your London waifs grope even now. This is why your sympathy with them, too, is deep and true. You *half remember.*"

"And Death," he whispered, trembling with the joy of infinite spiritual desire.

The answer sank down into him with the Little Wind that stirred the cedars overhead, or else rose singing up from the uttermost depths of his listening heart—to the end of his days he never could tell which.

"What you call Death is only slipping through the Crack to a great deal more memory, and a great deal more power of seeing and telling—towards the greatest Expression that ever can be known. It is, I promise you faithfully, Uncle Paul, nothing but a verywonderfulindeed Aventure, after all!"

THE END

Stark House Press

FANTASY/SUPERNATURAL

ALGERNON BLACKWOOD
1-933586-15-x
**Pan's Garden/
Incredible Adventures** $19.95
0-9749438-7-8
**Julius LeVallon/
The Bright Messenger** $19.95
1-933586-04-4
**The Lost Valley/
The Wolves of God** $19.95

STORM CONSTANTINE
0-9667848-0-4
**The Oracle Lips:
A Collection** $45
0-9667848-1-2
Calenture $17.95
0-9667848-3-9
Sign for the Sacred $24.95
0-9667848-4-7
**The Thorn Boy & Other Dreams
of Dark Desire** $19.95

MYSTERY/SUSPENSE

BENJAMIN APPEL
1-933586-01-x
The Brain Guy/Plunder $19.95

MALCOLM BRALY
1-933586-03-6
**Shake Him Till He Rattles/
It's Cold Out There** $19.95

GIL BREWER
1-933586-11-7
**Wild to Possess/
A Taste for Sin** $19.95

A. S. FLEISCHMAN
1-933586-12-5
**Look Behind You, Lady/
The Venetian Blonde**
19.95

ELISABETH SANXAY HOLDING
0-9667848-7-1
Lady Killer/Miasma $19.95
0-9667848-9-8
The Death Wish/Net of Cobwebs
$19.95
0-9749438-5-1
**The Strange Crime in
Bermuda/Too Many Bottles** $19.95

DAY KEENE
0-9749438-8-6
**Framed in Guilt/
My Flesh is Sweet** $19.95

STEPHEN MARLOWE
1-933586-02-8
**Violence is My Business/
Turn Left for Murder** $19.95

MARGARET MILLAR
1-933586-09-5
**An Air That Kills/
Do Evil in Return** $19.95

E. PHILLIPS OPPENHEIM
0-9749438-0-0
**Secrets & Sovereigns:
The Uncollected Stories of
E. Phillips Oppenheim** $19.95

VIN PACKER
0-9749438-3-5
**Something in the Shadows/
Intimate Victims** $19.95
0-9749438-6-x
**The Damnation of Adam
Blessing/Alone at Night** $19.95
1-933586-05-2
**Whisper His Sins/
The Evil Friendship** $19.95

PETER RABE
0-9667848-8-x
The Box/Journey Into Terror
$19.95
0-9749438-4-3
**Murder Me for Nickels/
Benny Muscles In** $19.95
1-933586-00-1
**Blood on the Desert/
A House in Naples** $19.95
1-933586-11-7
**My Lovely Executioner/
Agreement to Kill** $19.95

ROBERT J. RANDISI
0-9749438-9-4
**The Ham Reporter/The
Disappearance of Penny** $19.95

DOUGLAS SANDERSON
0-9749438-2-7
**Pure Sweet Hell/
Catch a Fallen Starlet** $19.95
1-933586-06-0
**The Deadly Dames/A Dum-Dum
for the President** $19.95

HARRY WHITTINGTON
1-933586-08-7
**A Night for Screaming/Any
Woman He Wanted** $19.95

RUSSELL JAMES
1-933586-17-6
Underground/Collected Stories
$19.95 *(Coming soon!)*

DAN J. MARLOWE/
FLETCHER FLORA/CHARLES RUNYON
1-933586-14-1
**The Vengeance Man/
Park Avenue Tramp/
The Prettiest Girl I Ever Killed:
A Trio of Gold Medals** $23.95
(Coming soon!)

FILM

KEVIN McCARTHY
& ED GORMAN (ED)
1-933586-07-9
**Invasion of the Body Snatchers:
A Tribute** $17.95

If you are interested in purchasing any of the above books, please send the cover price plus $3.00 U.S. for the 1st book and $1.00 U.S. for each additional book to:

STARK HOUSE PRESS
2200 O Street, Eureka, CA 95501
(707) 444-8768
www.starkhousepress.com

Order 3 or more books and take a 10% discount. We accept PayPal payments.